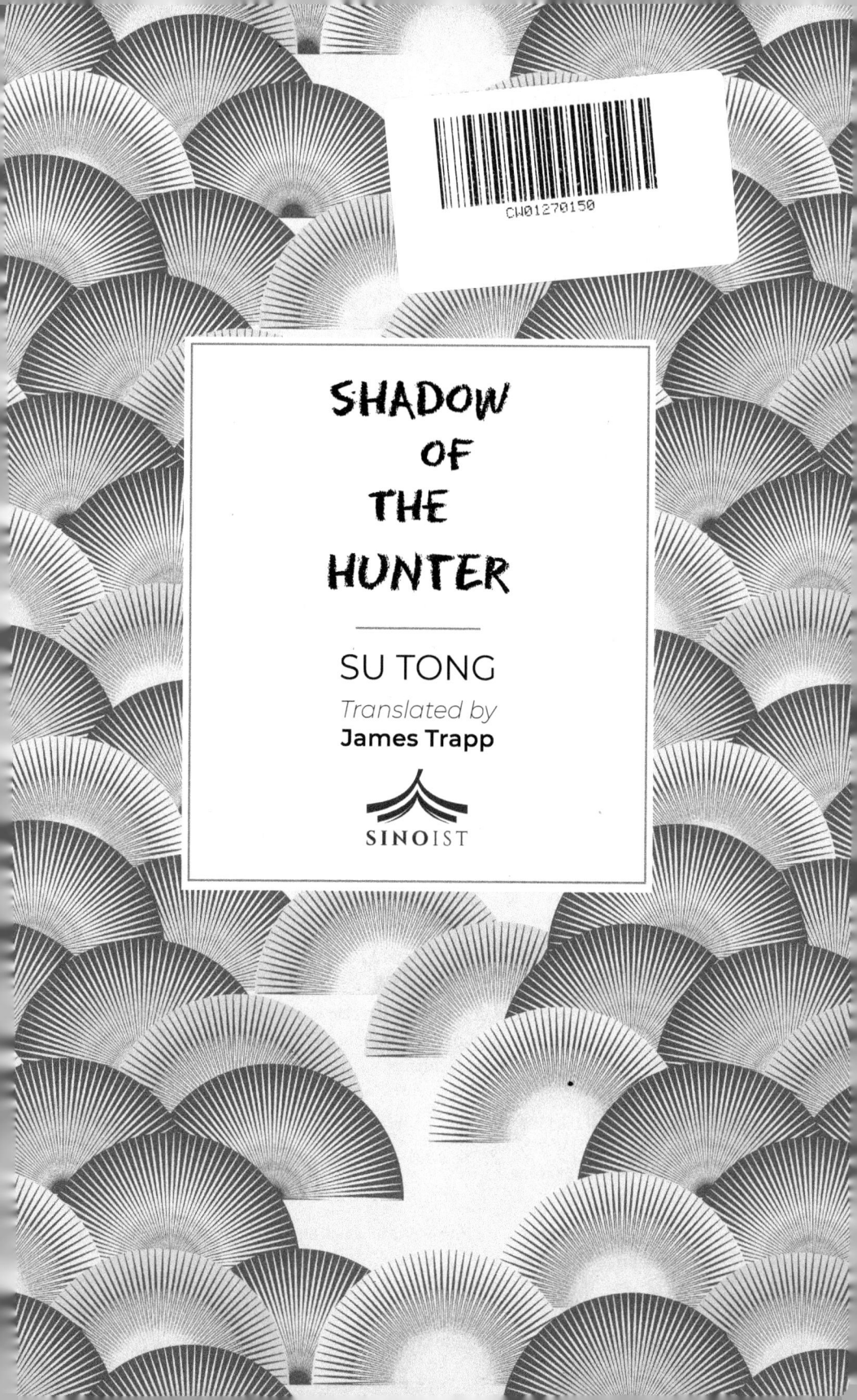

ACA Publishing Ltd
University House
11-13 Lower Grosvenor Place
London SW1W 0EX, UK
Tel: +44 (0)20 3289 3885
E-mail: info@alaincharlesasia.com
Web: www.sinoistbooks.com

Beijing Office
Tel: +86 (0)10 8472 1250

Author: Su Tong
Translator: James Trapp
Editor: Martin Savery
Translation Proofreading: Professor Haiwang Yuan

Published by ACA Publishing Ltd in association with the People's Literature Publishing House

Original Chinese Text © 黄雀记 (*Huang Que Ji*) 2013, by People's Literature Publishing House Co Ltd, Beijing, China

English Translation © 2020, by ACA Publishing Ltd, London, UK

ALL RIGHTS RESERVED. NO PART OF THIS PUBLICATION MAY BE REPRODUCED IN MATERIAL FORM, BY ANY MEANS, WHETHER GRAPHIC, ELECTRONIC, MECHANICAL OR OTHER, INCLUDING PHOTOCOPYING OR INFORMATION STORAGE, IN WHOLE OR IN PART, AND MAY NOT BE USED TO PREPARE OTHER PUBLICATIONS WITHOUT WRITTEN PERMISSION FROM THE PUBLISHER.

This novel is entirely a work of fiction. The names, characters and incidents portrayed in it are the work of the author's imagination. Any resemblance to actual persons, living or dead, events or localities is entirely coincidental.

Hardback ISBN: 978-1-83890-505-7
Paperback ISBN: 978-1-910760-87-1
eBook ISBN: 978-1-910760-88-8

A catalogue record for *Shadow of the Hunter* is available from the National Bibliographic Service of the British Library.

SHADOW OF THE HUNTER

SU TONG

Translated by
JAMES TRAPP

SINOIST BOOKS

PART ONE
BAORUN'S SPRING

ONE
PHOTOGRAPHS

E<small>VERY YEAR</small> when the flowers began to open in the warmth of Spring, Grandfather would go and have his photograph taken.

After seventy years, he had come to take a mathematical view of death, and he was more than happy with his own extended lifespan. The arithmetic was quite simple. In his fifty-third year he was eating *tang yuan* in a snack bar when he was scalded by the hot pork fat inside one of the dumplings, and that triggered a heart attack. At the hospital where he was sent, he actually died, but was resuscitated. Based on this, he calculated that he had already lived an extra 17 years. There was another event that might have precipitated his death, and this one was premeditated. When he was just forty-five, he suddenly tired of life and, one day that Spring, he went to lie down across the railway tracks. He had put himself in position but the train was late and as he lay there, a wolf-dog reared by the pointsman came by. Grandfather was afraid of dogs, and although he was quite prepared to be run over by a train, he really did not want to be bitten by a dog. He leapt up from the tracks and ran away. Come Summer, Grandfather still wanted to die, and this time he chose drowning. He jumped from a secluded spot on the city walls of the West Gate into the moat below. He fully expected this one leap to take him straight into death's welcoming embrace. But, to his astonishment, when he opened his eyes, he found himself lying on the ground at the bottom of the walls, surrounded by a noisy group of middle school students asking inquisitively why he had jumped. When Grandfather looked up into the children's innocent and unaffected gaze, he couldn't decide whether to reprimand them for interfering in something that wasn't their business, or whether he should be thanking them. The sudden baptism in the moat seemed rather to have cleansed and refreshed Grandfather, apart from some slight discomfort in the palm of his right hand. When he looked, he saw that at some point, he didn't know when, he had caught hold of some maple leaves and, in grasping them too tightly, had driven them slightly into the skin of his palm. He sat up, carefully picked the leaves from his hand, mumbled to the children "It's hard to explain", scrambled to his feet, and made his soggy way off.

When he was some distance away, Grandfather heard the children all vigorously discussing what was up with him. One shrill voice could be heard saying what he said about being "hard to explain" is nonsense; this guy seems to be tired of life. Don't you think he's going to go and find somewhere else to kill himself? Grandfather looked up at the towering city walls, and down at the moat beneath them; then he looked up again at the heavens, and abruptly turned back towards where the children were. Although his steps were a little slow and clumsy, the look in his eye was of a life renewed, as clear and far-reaching as a summer sky. He faced the children and said, brusquely but resignedly, that since the wolf-dog had stopped him from killing himself, and now they, too, had done the same, he was going to make the best of it and keep on living; and that he would treat each day of his life as a bonus.

Then he left and disappeared from sight around a corner of the city walls, an impenetrable mystery to the children he left behind, leaving them trying to guess at his motives. Those children were simply classmates on a Spring outing who now, after this chance rescue of an attempted suicide, in itself a noble and admirable deed, found themselves deeply troubled by the man's apparent indifference to life and death. All this considerably affected their sense of achievement. They had no knowledge of my grandfather from Red Toon Street, nor of why one minute he should want to die and the next to go on living. They did not know that he was a man of his word and that from that time on he relinquished all thoughts of suicide. And if we now resume the above-mentioned method of calculation, treating each further day lived as a bonus, then Grandfather, in living a further 25 years, gained an astonishing 9,125 days: a total which he naturally found extremely gratifying.

There were a lot of old people living on Red Toon Street, most of whom were afraid of dying; and those who were afraid of dying tended to die first. One unusually hot summer, death lurked under cover of the heat wave and, cruising along Red Toon Street, in one gulp swallowed seven of these fearful oldies. Braving the searing heat, Grandfather visited each household, one by one, to offer his condolences. There he discovered that preparations for the funerary rites in each of the seven families were disorganised and half-hearted; a fact that filled him with sorrow and regret on several levels. The most egregious case was that of the family of the dock worker, Master Qiao, where his children could not find a proper photograph of their father, and what they had ended up using on the funerary hanging made everyone who saw it uncomfortable. It was, in fact, the duplicated photograph, cut out of Master Qiao's dock-worker's ID card, and it showed him as he was many years ago, a much younger man bearing a striking resemblance to his two sons. So everybody who saw the hanging was startled to find themselves looking, not at Master Qiao, but at someone who resembled either his elder or younger son, depending on your point of view. Grandfather considered this carefully for a long time and decided that his real feelings were not suitable to be shared with the family. It was only when he had left the house that he heaved a deep sigh and said to the neighbours that Master Qiao's life had been too shortchanged by the photograph, and that whatever else one might economise on in life, that photograph was a step too far, and much too open to misinterpretation.

Grandfather's opinion was that a man can't organise his own funerary rites after he is dead, so it behoves him to do it while he is still alive. So every year when the flowers began to open in the warmth of Spring, my grandfather would go to the Hongyan Photographic Studio to have his picture taken. This had been going on for many years, so his neighbours were all well aware of his little eccentricity, and quizzed him over it. He always replied that they all knew he had a large air bubble in his brain, and if it burst, it burst, and that would be the end of him. At that point he was not sure his dependents could be relied on to his bidding, so he was taking the opportunity, whilst he was still alive, to arrange his own memorial portrait.

Portrait day was a festival day for Grandfather, and on festival days, he paid particular attention to his appearance. First he would go to the barber to have his hair cut and his face shaved, and a specially requested expert would be brought in to clean his ears and pluck his nose hairs. He used to make the journey from Red Toon Street to the centre of town on foot but now he was older he took the bus as well. It was around noon that he would appear at the Hongyan Photographic Studio, leaning on his dragon-headed walking stick, his coat and hat just so, his demeanour serious; his grey wool Sun Yat-sen suit smelled of mothballs, his leather shoes were polished till they gleamed, and he emanated a distinctly funereal aura.

Although the photographer, Master Yao, always recognised Grandfather, he could never remember his name and referred to him behind his back as the old gentleman who came to have his portrait done every year. Grandfather was always a little embarrassed when he saw Master Yao, almost as if he was ashamed of his own longevity:

"As you can see Master Yao, I'm not dead yet, and have managed another year, so I'm back to bother you again", he would say apologetically. "Just take this one more photograph, and it will be the last. The air bubble in my brain has been getting bigger and bigger recently, and it is sure to burst soon. I am certain I won't be bothering you again next year."

Grandfather's little obsession didn't bother Master Yao in the slightest, but it did bother his own family, especially his daughter-in-law, Su Baozhen. The way Su Baozhen saw it, every photograph Grandfather had taken dug a deeper pit for his family, and the more his memorial portraits piled up, the more she felt his sons and grandsons were sinking deeper and deeper into a quagmire of unfilial and uncharitable feelings.

In her sensitive and susceptible imaginings, Grandfather's footsteps towards the photographer's studio reverberated with the sombre words: I'm worried, I'm worried, I'm worried. And these words were treacherously translated to the neighbours as: my sons are no good, my daughters-in-law are no good, my grandsons are no good; none of them are any good and I'm worried about what they may do.

So every year when the flowers began to open in the warmth of Spring, Su Baozhen adopted a certain combative attitude and sought to recruit her husband and son to her side but her husband remained rather indifferent toward Grandfather and her son simply ignored her. It was not a particularly harmonious household at the best of times and, come Spring, it constantly broke out into open warfare. The gun smoke of that war came from Grandfather's photographs, and it gave off a weird suffocating reek. Although the family covered three generations, they only numbered four people, and no matter how the battle lines were drawn up, the combat was always short-lived and any sparks that flared up inevitably fell on the head of Baorun. He could be sitting there quietly eating only to be struck on the back of his head with a chopstick as Su Baozhen vented her anger at the attitude of neutrality he adopted and cursed him for being about as useful as a single chopstick:

"All you know how to do is eat! And what are you grinning at? Do you think your grandfather is only making me lose face? He's making our whole family lose face!"

Su Baozhen would push Baorun out of the door, ordering him to hunt down Grandfather:

"You're beefy enough after all that eating you've done so you'd better put it to use! Hurry up and drag that old idiot back here."

When his mother was angry, Baorun didn't dare disobey, so he would go out onto the street and tug at Grandfather, trying to hold him back. One time, he even followed him onto the bus.

"Gramps," Baorun said, "don't go and have your picture taken! What's the use of so many portraits? If you're buying pork, of course you want it to be fresh, but all memorial portraits do is hang on the wall gathering dust, and isn't one as good as another?"

Grandfather said, driving Baorun away with his dragon-headed stick:

"Why does it bother you all so much that I have my picture taken every year? Go home and tell your mother that I pay for my portrait with my own money and it's got nothing to do with you lot!"

Baorun couldn't help feeling there was something wrong with Grandfather's reasoning, and said:

"You're talking nonsense, Gramps! Of course it concerns us! Are you going to be looking at it when you're dead? We can hang whichever one we like on the wall, and if it's the wrong one, are you going to clamber out of your urn and change it?"

Happily, Baorun's bluntness helped Grandfather come to recognise the real sorrow of the dead; that he could indeed not clamber out of his urn, and would have to rely on the filial piety of his family as to whether they actually hung up any photograph, and which one they chose. Grandfather had no faith at all in the filial feelings of his descendants, and after considerable thought, came up with a plan. He went to a picture-framer to buy a suitable black frame for the most recent photograph, which he took home and hung up in a prime spot in the living room. Anticipating his family's opposition, and worried about the framed photograph's future fate, he bought a bottle of universal glue, so he could harness the power of science to ensure the permanence of the frame's place on the wall. He climbed on a chair to perform this task under the watchful eye of Baorun, who evinced neither approval nor disapproval of the tactic. To ensure the boy's tacit support, Grandfather explained to him the necessity for his actions:

"This year's portrait is excellent, and I'm completely satisfied with it; besides, the air bubble in my head is getting bigger and bigger, so whenever I actually kick the bucket, if the portrait is already up on the wall, then you lot won't have to worry about picking the wrong one."

Unfortunately, the universal glue wasn't as universal as it claimed; it needed a very long time at an appropriate temperature to dry properly, and Baorun's father was later easily able to prise the picture off the wall with a fruit knife. Baorun's mother, Su Baozhen, was so angry at this whole business that she shook with anger from head to toe. Her accumulated rancour towards him was already deep enough, and her taunts now took on a particular venom:

"How can your head have an air bubble in it, when all that's in there is garbage? Who do you think you are? Chairman Mao? Do you think you're going to live on in people's hearts forever? I'm telling you, let alone while you're still alive, even when you're dead, your portrait isn't sure to go up on that wall: the living room is the face of the family, and if an oldie doesn't merit being commemorated, why should he have his picture there? Much better to free up the space and put up a picture of a pretty girl."

Grandfather wailed at this. He picked the framed portrait up off the floor and, clutching it to his breast, took it into his own room:

"So, my portrait isn't fit to hang in the living room, eh? I'll put it in my room then, where it won't pollute your eyes. Is that alright for you?"

He slammed the door and then announced loudly from behind it:

"I'm going to look at my portrait myself, and from now on, none of you are allowed in my room!"

So every year when the flowers began to open in the warmth of Spring, Baorun would make the trip to the Hongyan Photographic Studio to collect Grandfather's photographs. Grandfather had always been old, and each extra year of age was just a repetition of the previous year's. Baorun never looked at Grandfather's photos, except once; and that once ended in disaster. On that occasion, he was cycling back from the studio and, halfway back, he stopped to go into a household goods shop to buy a packet of sugar for his mother. As he carelessly pulled the money out of his pocket, he also pulled out the envelope of photographs from the studio, and the contents spilled out onto the ground. It was not Grandfather. The studio owner had committed the gravest of errors. There, innocently looking up from the dirty floor of the household goods store, were the two-inch, black and white photographs of a young girl: a big-eyed, round-faced, thin-lipped girl, with her hair in a ponytail. She wasn't smiling, but there was a slight upturn at each corner of her mouth. She gave every appearance of already knowing the fate of her photograph, and her look of angry reproach seemed to be directed at the whole world, Baorun included.

Baorun was inclined to forgive the photographer's mistake, as he was entranced by the happy coincidence, by which, through one small accident, his ageing grandfather was transformed into a teen-age beauty. He was unsure, however, whether this would turn out to be a good omen or an evil one. As Baorun squatted down to pick up the photographs, at first he found the situation amusing, but then a feeling of nameless unease crept over him. He made his way back to the Hongyan Studio, and as he stood outside, he fished out the envelope of photographs and had another look at them. The sunlight on the corner of the street illuminated the face of the unknown girl, reduced to a small square by the artifice of the dark-room, suffusing it with a gold-tinged aura. He didn't find her particularly beautiful, but the camera lens had imbued her angry and reproachful look with an air of mystery, and it was that thread of anger that made Baorun feel an indefinable closeness to her. He couldn't bring himself to hand her back over, to relinquish that little cameo of wrath. On the spur of the moment, he took one of the three photographs in the envelope, and slipped it into his wallet.

Not all mistakes are rectifiable, and Baorun was unable to get back Grandfather's photographs. It was to be a Spring of accidents, beginning with this mistake over the photographs, and ending in confusion and opacity. Baorun had secretly gained photographs of an unknown young girl, but the Hongyan Studio had lost, forever, Grandfather's most recent portrait.

Paper can't resist fire. Grandfather blamed Baorun at first, but then calmed down, and having separated primary and secondary responsibilities, went himself to the Hongyan Studio to see what the photographer had to say for himself. In order to pacify this eccentric old man, the studio offered him free photographs for the rest of his life, considering this to be fair recompense. But Grandfather burst into bitter tears and said to Master Yao:

"What is 'the rest of my life' worth? I may only live a few more days, so you'd better take the chance while you can, and take a whole load now."

Master Yao took three more pictures for him. When the flash went off for the third time, there was a weird noise, and Grandfather suddenly shouted out:

"It's burst!"

Master Yao didn't hear what he said, and only saw the old man holding his head in his hands and trembling with pain as he sat on the stool.

"It's burst!" Grandfather's eyes filled with tears as he stared, terrified, at Master Yao. "It's burst! The air bubble in my head has burst! Did you see that blue-green smoke? That was my soul escaping, and I'm going to die! My head is empty, completely empty!"

TWO
SOUL

THE NEWS that Grandfather had lost his soul swept through Red Toon Street.

Whenever we met him in the street, we found ourselves unconsciously looking at his head. If our heads can be thought of as rich, fertile fields, Grandfather's was a stretch of pillaged wilderness and a scene of desolation. His white hair was dishevelled like wild grass blanketed by frost and snow. The back of his head was now bald, revealing an unusually shaped zigzag scar, that was said to have been inflicted by a Red Guard with a poker. Perhaps this scar, that had remained hidden for so many years, was the very spot from which Grandfather's soul had escaped. When we looked at his neck, where there was originally a dark red groove, a reminder of a cord that used to hang there, the skin had loosened with age, and now rippled down in pendulous wattles and loops of flesh. This made some people suspect that Grandfather's soul had not actually escaped, but had disintegrated and trickled down into these coils of loose flesh.

No one has ever seen a man's soul. Grandfather said his soul had escaped, but how could it be proved that he had a soul in the first place, or that he had now lost it? And where would it have gone? Most of the residents of Red Toon Street were not very well educated, and they were accustomed to thinking of the soul as a plume of smoke. Those of them who tended the coal-burning stoves along the street now felt their hearts lurch slightly whenever they saw the blue-green smoke coming out of them, as they made the association - smoke, soul, Grandfather's head - and were quite sure that his soul was in that spiralling smoke. Certain intellectual parties, equipped with a little religious knowledge and a sprinkling of cultural awareness, persisted in believing that the soul was, in fact, a ray of light, and not smoke at all. A sacred ray of light was usually possessed only by great men and heroes, categories to which Grandfather certainly did not belong. None of them, however, were so cruel as to express this opinion to Grandfather's face, and tell him that he had no soul, and was just a walking corpse. Most confused by all this were the street children; they were fascinated by the idea of souls, and because they knew nothing about them, their imaginations took full flight, trying to find comparisons to help them in the world of birds, beasts and insects, and amongst ghouls and ghosts. One day, the grandson of Old Barber Yan gave grandfather a crude sketch of a multi-coloured horned death's head; the young lad told him:

"Don't be sad, Grandpa! This is your soul; I found it for you."

Grandfather could not be angry with the cute little lad and his horned death's head representing his soul, which was actually quite impressive. By contrast, Wang Deji's little boy, Xiao Guai was really annoying: he picked up a dead bat with a pair of chopsticks and followed Grandfather around with it, saying:

"Gramps! Gramps! This is your soul. I climbed up the Ruiguang Pagoda to find it for you. It wasn't easy and you owe me two *yuan* for it; and that's cheap for such hard work!"

An old man who loses his soul can't help but also lose his self-respect. Amongst the many elderly inhabitants of Red Toon Street, Granny Shaoxing was the most sympathetic to what Grandfather was going through. She came running over to tell him that losing one's soul wasn't such a terrible thing. When she was a young girl growing up in the countryside, the same thing had happened to her, and it had come about in the most peculiar fashion. She was sitting quietly in the reed-walled latrine behind her house, relieving herself, when she felt something licking the soles of her feet. When she looked, she saw it was a red-eyed wild dog, with an equally red tongue. In her fright and surprise, she tumbled into the latrine pit, and when she clambered out, she had lost her soul. She said that after she had lost her soul in this manner, she could neither piss nor shit in that latrine any more, and had to run over to a pine tree half a kilometre away, to do it. Otherwise, she would just hold it in. A shaman from a neighbouring village came over to reprimand her parents, saying:

"You must have offended your ancestors, and the wild dog that stole your daughter's soul has come as a warning to you. For many years you have not been burning incense at your family graves, and your ancestors have had neither food to eat nor clothes to wear, so they have left their tombs and their wanderings have taken them to the base of that pine tree. If you continue to neglect them, then it will not just be your daughter who has lost her soul, but none of you will be able to relieve yourselves if you're not in sight of that pine tree."

When Granny Shaoxing's parents heard the shaman's diagnosis, they gathered together all their children and domestic animals, and hurried over to the family graves, where they killed some chickens and sacrificed some sheep to beg for their daughter's soul back. They prayed for a day and a night non-stop, and the next morning, she was cured, and was quite happy to use the latrine again.

Grandfather was intrigued by Granny Shaoxing's story, but he felt that his own experience was even more peculiar.

"You're a woman, Granny Shaoxing, so our souls are not the same, and it's different too, when we lose them; I still know how to relieve myself alright, but I forgot where I lived. I tried to go home the other day, and I went straight to the Ruiguang Pagoda. Now, is that weird or not? I thought I lived at the top of the pagoda; I struggled up there and couldn't find my room anywhere. I went to ask someone, but there were only tourists around, who didn't know me, and all they did was swear at me and call me a lunatic!"

"If you lose your soul, you lose your soul", Granny Shaoxing replied.

"What's the difference? For me, it was the pine tree, and for you it's the Ruiguang Pagoda. I lost my soul first, so you should listen to my advice: the way I see it, when someone loses their soul, sooner or later, they're going to have problems with relieving themselves, and if you decide you have to go to the Ruiguang Pagoda to do it, how can that be good? It's such a long way! If that's how it turns out, you're in real trouble. Now you're old, you won't be able to hold it in long enough to get there. Listen to me, Baorun's grandfather, and take all your descendants to go and pray for your soul to come back. Buy lots of offerings and go to your family graves, and beg for your soul back!"

Grandfather clutched his knees, looking rather embarrassed:

"You don't understand the problem, Granny Shaoxing; my family history isn't like yours, and my family graves were bulldozed long ago to make way for a plastics factory. Where can I go to beg for my soul?"

Granny Shaoxing gave a cry of alarm:

"Aiya! How could anyone let their family graves be bulldozed? You can do without anything else, but not your family graves. Without their graves, ancestors become lonely souls and wandering ghosts, so how can they help you get your soul back?"

Grandfather found himself with nowhere to turn, and sank into the depths of a vast and nameless dread, followed by grief, and then a kind of humble acceptance in which he said to himself:

"Well, if there's no help for it and I've lost my soul, then there's no help for it. In any case, I've already profited from several extra lives, so if death comes calling, I'll just go with it."

"You mustn't say that, Baorun's Grandfather!" Granny Shaoxing stared at him, and lifted her hand to cover his mouth. "How stupid are you? If you can't beg to get your soul back, you can't come back as a man in your next life. You'd count yourself lucky to come back as an ox or a horse, but it might just as easily be as a mosquito. Then you could be squashed by a single swat of someone's hand, and be on to your next life in a matter of seconds. How pitiful would that be? If you're not careful, you might be a dung beetle. Wouldn't you be disgusted at yourself, living in a dung heap, stinking to high heaven?"

When she saw Grandfather's face go ashen, Granny Shaoxing began to feel uneasy, and she softened her tone and tried to suggest some different ways of looking at it.

"You've had some tough breaks in your life; it's not your fault your family graves were bulldozed, it's the fault of those conscienceless Red Guards. Your ancestors' wandering spirits have been displaced and you don't know where they've gone, so you must pray to them all over the place. Do you have photographs of them, or ancestor portraits? Gather them all together, pray hard to them for several days and perhaps they'll hear you."

Grandfather hesitated and was about to speak but stopped himself. He almost looked as though he was going to weep.

"I used to have lots of photos of my father, and some portraits of my grandfather, but I burned them." Grandfather lowered his head, not daring to look Granny Shaoxing in the eye. "My father was a traitor to China, and my grandfather was a warlord. I didn't dare court disaster by keeping those things around, so I burned them."

Granny Shaoxing could see that Grandfather had given up any hope of getting his soul back; she rolled her eyes, as if to say there was nothing more she could do, folded her arms and went out of the door, saying:

"Even lousy ancestors are still ancestors, but if you haven't got any graves, and have burned all the photographs, of course you're going to lose your soul. And there's no point blaming anyone else; as I see it, you brought it on yourself."

Granny Shaoxing was Grandfather's last hope, and he didn't want to let her get away so he brazenly hurried over to the door and shouted after her, begging her to come up with one final idea.

"I've got some of my ancestors' bones; are they any use? I sneaked back to the grave site and found two bones. I didn't want anyone to know, so I hid them in a flashlight. Then I buried it."

Granny Shaoxing looked at him in amazement:

"Bones are much more real than photographs! Bones are excellent! It doesn't matter if there are only a couple of them. Where did you bury the flashlight? Hurry up and go and dig it up!"

Grandfather just stood there, rooted to the spot, blinking his eyes and desperately trying to remember. But ever since the air bubble in his head burst, his memory had been shot and, try as he might, he couldn't remember where he had buried the flashlight. Under Granny Shaoxing's questioning gaze, Grandfather's broke out in a sweat, and he began to wail and moan. He cudgelled his brains:

"The flashlight! Where did I bury the flashlight? Oh misery! I can't remember a thing!"

THREE

THE FLASHLIGHT

IN APRIL, Grandfather was in excellent health but, come May, he was totally deranged. There are thousands of unhappy ways of going mad, but Grandfather's way was both desolate and obscure. In my opinion, although his madness was perhaps not the most unusual in the whole world, but within our own little world of Red Toon Street, his story became the stuff of legend.

Grandfather said he had buried the flashlight under these holly trees.

As everybody knows, there aren't any red toon trees on Red Toon Street, and the only greenery is the holly trees. Outside the gates of the factory, in the empty lots along the street, lining the walls of the buildings, everywhere can be seen holly trees of all sizes. But which was the one where the flashlight was buried? On this vital question Grandfather, unfortunately, had no idea.

At first, Grandfather confined his target search area to the gates of Master Meng's residence, imploring his son to go and dig there. His son refused to undertake this absurd task, and passed it on to the grandson. Baorun didn't want to do it either, for fear of losing face. Grandfather had no option but to shoulder his spade, and go and do it himself.

When Master Meng heard the noise, he came out and asked if

Grandfather was digging for earthworms. To which, Grandfather replied simply:

"Why would I be digging for earthworms at my age? I'm digging for a flashlight."

"What flashlight? And what's it doing buried in my gateway?" Master Meng asked in amazement.

"It's a long story! Some years ago, I collected a couple of bones from my family graves and stored them inside a flashlight. I didn't have anywhere special to bury them at the time, and I may have put them under this holly tree."

Master Meng hopped up and down in indignation:

"You're a wicked old man, Baorun's Grandfather! What do you mean by burying your ancestors' bones in front of my gates? If you weren't so old, I'd punch you all the way back home."

Grandfather had no choice but to shoulder his spade, but he wasn't happy to go, and twisted to look back at the hole he had dug. Brazenly playing on the respect he felt due to his advancing years, he pleaded:

"Do the right thing, Master Meng, and let me dig a little more. I've lost my soul and my memory. Who knows if a few more spadesful might not bring them back."

"You come here conducting your archaeological excavations in front of my gate, but why on earth should your ancestors' bones be buried here? What right do you think you have to come here and pile shit like this on my head?" Master Meng asked.

Shamefacedly clutching his spade, Grandfather mumbled:

"No right, no right at all."

He retreated a few steps and then, summoning up his courage under cover of a violent bout of coughing, suddenly launched a new line of historical enquiry at Master Meng:

"I'm not digging at random, Master Meng; have you forgotten on whose family lands your house is built? This place used to be my family's beancurd factory. If I was going to bury something, surely I'd bury it on my own family land, wouldn't I?"

Master Meng looked at him blankly:

"Are you speaking Chinese, Baorun's Grandfather, or some foreign language? I don't understand what you mean."

"Of course you don't understand; you're too young to remember. Go and ask your old mother, she'll set you straight", Grandfather said with a smarmy smile.

Master Meng thought Grandfather had lost his marbles, and held three fingers up in front of his face:

"How many fingers can you see, you old fool?"

"Three!"

Not satisfied, Master Meng leaned in closer to look at the pupils of Grandfather's eyes, but saw that they were bright with comprehension. He shoved open a window that looked out on the street and called out:

"Come here, Mother. Whose land is my house built on? Did it used to be the site of Baorun's Grandfather's family beancurd factory?"

There was a clacking sound from behind the window, and the shrill, cracked voice of an old woman suddenly made itself heard:

"Who's digging up ancient history? We're in the new society now. It doesn't matter what anyone else says about who used to own the house or the land, Chairman Mao has decided it."

"Chairman Mao died a long time ago, Mother!" Master Meng reminded her.

The old woman fell silent for a moment, and then swiftly recovered her ground:

"Chairman Mao may be dead, but there's still a government, isn't there? So what are you afraid of? The government owns all the land and buildings, and they decide who gets what!"

Grandfather had learned a profound lesson from this experience when he moved on to dig under the holly trees in front of Wang Deji's house. What remained of his sense of self-preservation told him that if the other residents of Red Toon Street were to tolerate his investigations, he had to use his native wit to curry favour with them. So when Wang Deji came rushing out to snatch away Grandfather's spade, Grandfather grabbed his hand, and traced the word 'gold' on the back of it with the tip of his finger. Wang Deji didn't bother to try to read what Grandfather was writing, and snatched back his hand, saying:

"What do you think you're doing, using my hand as a blackboard? I heard you've lost your soul, Baorun's Grandfather, but have you lost your tongue as well?"

So Grandfather gave up, and whispered in his ear that he didn't want word to get around that it was no ordinary flashlight he had buried, but a flashlight filled with gold. This had the desired effect on Wang Deji, who scratched his forehead, blinked, and said:

"Where do you get all this energy at your age? So you're digging for gold, are you?"

His eyes glistened with acquisitiveness, and he went on, in a low voice:

"A flashlight full of gold, eh? That must be at least a *jin* (equivalent to a weight of 500 grams)! Is it a gold bar, or an old-style ingot? Or is it gold rings and suchlike?"

Grandfather nodded his head and replied coolly:

"It's a bit of everything… a bit of everything!"

So all the members of the Wang family, young and old alike, trooped out to watch Grandfather dig for gold. Wang Deji's daughter, Qiuhong, was a quick-witted, worldly-wise young girl, who stood there knitting, as she asked Grandfather, pointedly:

"This is my family's land, Grandad, so we get half of any gold you find, don't we? Don't try and cheat us!"

Wang Deji was an impetuous kind of fellow, and when he felt Grandfather was being too slow with his digging, he brought a spade of his own out of the house and said:

"You're an old man, Grandfather. Have a rest and let me do some of the digging. Take no notice of my daughter. I'm not greedy; if we find any gold, we'll split it 60-40: you get 60, I get 40, OK?"

Only Xiaoguai, amongst Wang Deji's family members, remained sceptical. He said:

"You've lost your soul, Grandad, and I think you must have lost your wits as well. Why would you bury something as valuable as gold at our house and not at your own?"

Grandfather put down the spade in his hand and explained patiently:

"The way I've lost my soul is a bit odd: I can't remember anything about the last few decades, but I'm quite clear about what happened when I was young. Your house used to be the coal yard of my family's coal business. There was lots of space and no one ever came here so I could well have buried the gold here."

The route traced by Grandfather's search for the flashlight seemed random and chaotic but there was, in fact, a hidden logic to it, as he unintentionally laid out a map of his ancestors' property for the inhabitants of Red Toon Street. This drew ever-expanding ripples of discussion on the street, as it became apparent that Grandfather's family had owned all the land along the 200 metres from Master Meng's house to the stone loading platform. This was, effectively, half the street, along which there were not only more than 70 residents, but also a tool works, a cement warehouse, an ironmonger, a charcoal merchant, a pharmacy, a sweet shop and a grocery store: the heart of Red Toon Street, in fact. As people got on with their own lives, they had gradually forgotten the history of the place and Grandfather's sudden appearance with his spade had reminded them:

"Your houses are built on my ancestral land, and everything you eat, drink and shit, your jobs and your work, are all on my land!"

As Grandfather marched hither and yon over the street with his spade on his shoulder, he spread the creeping grey moss of history wherever he went. No matter how carefully he trod, to a greater or lesser degree he caused the residents offence. Opinions were divided over the state of Grandfather's sanity but no one could deny his spade set a trend in Red Toon Street, and no one could deny that he was the pioneer and instigator of the gold fever that swept through the street that May.

But what was actually hidden inside Grandfather's flashlight? The speculations of the inhabitants of Red Toon Street, whether based on logical reasoning or romantic imagination, basically fell into two camps: the bones school of thought, and the gold school of thought. It goes without saying that with the opening up of the country and the economic revival, the majority of members of both camps shared the dream of becoming rich overnight. Some of them privately made the calculation that no matter what the truth of Grandfather's words, there was no need for risk or financial outlay, as a simple stroke of the spade or pick-axe would decide whether they struck ill luck with bones, or struck it lucky with gold. The first to undertake their own excavations were Wang Deji and his family, and for the next two mornings the neighbours saw the holly trees in front of their door lying by the wall, surrounded by mud, and even the cement floor seemed to have been ploughed up during the night. This raised a few eyebrows, for didn't Wang Deji belong to the bones school of thought? And hadn't he cursed Baorun's Grandfather as a liar? So what was he doing joining in the excavations? Someone hit the nail on the head when they said with a sneer that Wang Deji was just the kind of man to say one thing and do another. He wasn't in the bone camp, he was in both camps!

The gold craze swept along the south end of Red Toon Street, carrying all before it, then gradually rolled on to the north end, before spreading to Lotus Alley on the opposite bank of the river. Men emerged every night to go digging and the quiet of the night was shattered by the sound of picks and shovels driving into the earth. May nights hold many secrets, and this secret was more a source of amusement than anything malign; a kind of half-secret. Groups of men carrying spades gathered in the moonlight, some smiling openly, others looking rather sheepish, and set about their digging. Enemies by day became comrades-in-arms by night, or co-conspirators at least. Each had their own style of excavating: those of the gold party dug deep but carefully, whilst those of the bone persuasion were rather more slipshod and half-hearted. Nevertheless, as the saying goes, the more people bring firewood, the higher the flames rise, and soon the only strip of green on Red Toon street was stripped bare and amongst the fallen holly trees you could clearly distinguish a path, formed of excavated mud and concrete, giving off an acrid freshly-dug smell. Along this road within a road, travelled the gold-laden dreams of the inhabitants of Red Toon Street.

This was all a real nightmare for the residents' committee responsible for the cleanliness of the street, and three of its female representatives burst in on Baorun's family, conducting a punitive expedition against the main offender. Grandfather was on his knees, fixing a strip of wood onto the handle of his shovel to reinforce it where it had worked loose.

"Has Baorun been causing trouble outside again?" he asked the representatives.

Seeing Grandfather's blank and guileless expression, two of the women burst into tears, and the third, who was of a particularly angry temperament, sent his spade flying across the room with a kick, rolled up her sleeves, and said forthrightly:

"Grandad, I really want to belt you round the ear, just to make me feel better!"

At noon that day, when Baorun came home from cookery school, he felt that there was something of a festive air pervading the street. A group of children were gathered around the door to his house, batting around an empty cigarette packet with every evidence of great enjoyment. He noticed that the door was ajar, and Wang Deji's son, Xiaoguai, was standing by the crack in the door, poking his head inside to have a look. Baorun went over and took him by the ear. Even so, Xiaoguai gave every evidence of enjoyment as he passed on the news:

"Baorun, Baorun, your grandpa has been taken away; he's been taken away in the big white car from Jingting Hospital!"

Baorun was stunned, and let go of Xiaoguai's ear.

"Who? Who took my Grandpa away?"

"Two men in big white gowns, someone from the residents' committee, and your mum and dad."

Baorun pushed open the door to the empty house and, on the floor of the living room, he saw one of Grandfather's Liberation plimsolls, and noticed that three of the four chairs in the room had been knocked over, and that a teapot had been broken into two pieces. He took these as evidence of Grandfather's struggles. He saw also a ribbon of steam coming from the kitchen, and when he went over to investigate, he discovered a kettle of hot water on the stove, which had almost boiled dry. The door to Grandfather's room was dangling open, clearly having been forced, and when he went in, he almost trod on a pickaxe handle. Heaven knows where Grandfather had found the pick, but he had turned his room into an excavation site. Baorun was bewildered by this evidence of Grandfather's activities: there were no holly trees in the room, so why had he been digging there? As he examined the floor and the corners of the room, Baorun could see chalk marks in the form of question marks, exclamation marks, and a few mysterious circles and triangles. The room was full of the thick foetid smell of humidity, and the big grey-green bricks were all missing from the floor, as they had been carefully removed and neatly stacked along the walls; there were three clammy pits distributed around the room in three of its corners, looking like three dried-up quagmires.

"He's gone mad!" Baorun thought to himself. "Grandfather has really gone mad!"

Grandfather's dreams were rotting away in those quagmires, dissipating in the putrid smell that issued from them. Somehow or other, the fine black-framed photograph that had once hung neatly on the wall, had fallen into one of these pits. He looked distinctly disgruntled at this change in location; his gaze was largely obscured by smears of mud, but what could still be distinguished showed the wan expression of a man in distress. He seemed to be looking up at Baorun imploringly, pleading for help:

"Save me, Baorun! Come and save me!"

Baorun fished the frame out of the pit, hung it back on the wall again, and wiped the mud off Grandfather's face with a rag. But that was all he did. Grandfather was his parents' concern, not his, and he had no idea what to do about him anyway. He missed him, but it was going to be too bothersome to help him, and Baorun didn't like bother. He sat on Grandfather's bed, looking round the darkened room, vaguely remembering the pale, wrinkled soles of Grandfather's feet, the creases of which resembled nothing more than a landscape painting, with precipitous mountains and crags, and gently flowing rivers and streams. When he was little, Baorun had shared a bed with Grandfather, and had always drifted off to sleep looking at the landscapes on his feet. When he thought of Grandfather now, the soles of his feet were what first came to mind, something that he found both rather troubling and rather comic.

FOUR

THE ANCESTORS AND THE SERPENT

ONE SUNDAY MORNING, Baorun dreamed he saw the unknown girl.

She was standing in front of the Hongyan Photographic Studio, a parasol in her hand, her lips pouting as she looked angrily up at the sky. It was sunny and cloudless, but she seemed to regard it as an enemy. Even in his dream, Baorun remembered he had hidden her photograph, and when he walked furtively past her, glancing sidelong at her, he heard her say:

"Drop dead!"

Even in his dream, Baorun was not going to take that from anyone, so he turned back and asked;

"Who the fuck are you telling to drop dead?"

The girl suddenly opened the pale green parasol at him, so that its ferrule poked him in the shoulder. She flourished it at him, and said:

"You! You can just drop dead!"

The dream impinged on reality to the extent that he felt a sharp pain in his shoulder, which slowly travelled down his body into his abdomen; at which point, he woke up.

Strange noises drifted up from Grandfather's room downstairs: the sound of an iron hammer persistently beating on wood – thunk, thunk,

thunk. It had the sound of demolition work, and sure enough, the noise of hammer on wood did not last long before there was a sharp crack. An old, but stubborn, wooden tenon snapped, and the attic space echoed furtively with further 'cracks'. Crack, crack, crack. The blows of the hammer became more decisive, and their rhythm picked up, as Grandfather's ornately carved bed collapsed. Eighty-eight wooden tenons hastily took leave of each other after a hundred years of association; maybe that association between mortice and tenon had palled a little, so the partings were curt, all one-hundred-and-seventy-six of them, and sounded like thunderclaps – kerchack! Goodbye! This is it! But each joint had the same regret, that the original owner of the bed had died long ago, without farewells, and its current young owner was fast asleep up in the attic, indifferent to its fate. The tenons missed their old master, and hurried to leave some words of reluctant parting, some sharp and shrill, some deep and sonorous. There were many sighs of regret, some tinged with resentment, and some with deep emotion. It was such a venerable bed, and its regrets were so ancient that only the spiders in the bed curtains could understand them. But the spiders could do nothing about them, so they passed them on to the multitude of moths that lived in the intricate carvings. And the moths, sacrificing themselves to such a noble cause, flew up to Baorun's attic. The shame was, however, that nature had rendered moths mute, and it was all they could do to rouse Baorun from his slumbers. They flew up and settled on his face and shoulders, but Baorun didn't understand their intentions, and he killed three of them with a swat of his hand:

"What is it? Who is it? Go away and let me sleep!"

It was Sunday morning, and Baorun's parents were clearing out Grandfather's room.

"Come quickly, Baorun! There's a snake!" His mother's shrill voice finally put an end to any intention Baorun had to keep sleeping. He ran down the stairs to where his parents were running round in panic. He saw the snake, for there was indeed a snake, and a large one at that. It was coiled round one of the bedposts of Grandfather's bed, almost two feet long, with black and brown markings. Its head was raised up high, and its glistening eyes were looking round, helplessly, so it had the appearance of a question mark, querying the reason for all this unexpected commotion.

Baorun's father was holding Grandfather's spade in his hand and his mother was standing behind him. They had been like this, in a stand-off with the snake, for a long time already. Baorun made to take the spade from his father, but his father wouldn't let go, saying:

"This is clearly a house snake which has been disturbed from its lair by the demolition of the bed. You can't hit a house snake; it's forbidden!"

"What's a house snake?" Baorun asked. "Do they bite people?"

"They don't bite people from their own household. I've heard people say they are the reincarnation of ancestors, watching over later generations."

"That's interesting! Grandfather goes, and it comes out of its lair! Wasn't grandfather looking for the spirit of an ancestor? I should catch it and take it to the Jingting Hospital."

"What kind of nonsense is that?!" Baorun's mother cried out from one side. "Your grandfather was looking for the bones of two of your ancestors, not for a snake! You've got sharp eyes; hurry up and find the snake's lair, so you can put it back in and stop up the hole. Then it can't come out again and bite anyone."

Baorun made a thorough search in every corner of the room but he couldn't find the snake's lair. He turned his head to look at the creature, and it seemed to him as though the snake was nodding at him, trying to tell him that it belonged to Grandfather.

"Better to take it to Grandfather!" Baorun said. "I'll do it. After all, it is an ancestor, and Grandfather was looking for ancestors. What does it matter whether it is a snake or a couple of bones?"

His mother stamped her foot and said, angrily:

"I don't want to hear any more of your nonsense! A snake is a snake, and snakes want to bite people. If you can't find its lair, then hurry up and throw it out of the house. Even if it is one of the family ancestors, I don't want it. You only have to look at your Grandfather to know what ancestors are like. I don't have any faith in ancestors like that!"

At his mother's insistence, Baorun put on a glove and went to grab hold of the snake. But his father stopped him:

"You need to be polite to it, and treat it carefully", he said. "For Heaven's sake, don't just grab it! Ask it nicely to leave. That should do the trick."

Baorun had no idea how to ask a snake to leave and, after thinking it over for a little while, he fetched a red plastic bucket from the kitchen. He took hold of one end of the bedpost, waved it a few times at the plastic bucket, and addressed the snake:

"Ancestor, can we have a little talk about this? Is it alright if I ask you to come down into this bucket?"

The spirit of the ancestor was overcome by the astuteness of one of its descendants, and the stiffened body of the snake suddenly relaxed and it fell softly into the bucket with a muffled sound like a sigh. Baorun's mother hastily put a saucepan lid over the plastic bucket and ordered Baorun:

"Quick now, take it outside! I don't want the bucket but bring me back the saucepan lid."

Baorun took the bucket outside and put it down beside a concrete waste-bin. Baorun couldn't help feeling there was something a little blasphemous about this cavalier treatment of the spirit of an ancestor but that feeling was mixed with a faint frisson of indefinable excitement.

"I'm sorry, Ancestor!" he said, apologetically.

He lifted the lid off the bucket and waved to the snake inside:

"Goodbye, Ancestor; go and find Grandfather! Goodbye, Ancestor!"

After about five minutes, they all went over to the door to look for the house snake. There were people coming and going along the street and the red plastic bucket was lying on its side beside the waste-bin. There was no sign of the snake. Baorun heard his father sigh and his mother saying, regretfully:

"I'd only just bought that red bucket! Why didn't you stop to think, and go a few steps further over to the courtyard? Besides, you should have used the blue bucket."

Baorun could make out the faint trace of a glistening, white, sinuous trail, winding out of Red Toon Street. It was the snake's trail: a trail replete with the sighs of the ancestors, and carrying the resentments of times gone by. It was guided by a pale green shadow, and lost itself at the end of the street. When Baorun strained to look, he saw that the shadow was, in fact, a pale green parasol. On this bright, warm Spring Sunday morning, who could it be coming out onto the street, carrying a pale green parasol?

FIVE
GRANDFATHER'S HAIR

THE NEXT DAY, Bao Sanda's flatbed tricycle turned up.

Bao Sanda was leaning back in the saddle, feet up on the handlebars, picking his teeth. There was an earpiece in one ear, attached to a transistor radio nestling in his lap. Surprised, perhaps, by a news item on the radio, he gave a sudden start, his mouth opened wide, and he blindly jabbed his toothpick into the roof of his mouth, causing him considerable confusion.

Baorun didn't know why Bao Sanda was there. He had gone out to the public lavatory to relieve himself and when he came back, about 10 minutes later, he found Bao Sanda's tricycle in front of the doorway of the house. He pulled the toothpick out of Bao's mouth and dropped it to the ground.

"Why do you have to clean your teeth in front of our house? Are you having a laugh, parking your tricycle across our door, so I can't get back in?"

Grudgingly, Bao Sanda snatched the earpiece out of his ear, and pushed the tricycle aside, to clear the way for Baorun.

"Do you think I'm in front of your door for fun? I'm making a pickup; someone ordered me to collect your grandfather's old bed."

"What kind of joke do you think you're playing? Who ordered you to collect Grandfather's bed?"

Bao Sanda took another toothpick out of his pocket and gestured behind him:

"It's Boss Deng, the owner of the antiques shop there. You know Boss Deng, don't you? He used to have the coal briquette shop on the corner but now he's a millionaire – nouveau riche, that's what the papers call people like him."

"Why should I give a stuff if he's rich or not? You're taking the piss if you're telling me he can take my granddad's bed just because he's a millionaire!"

"Don't ask me about it, ask your mum and dad!" Bao Sanda pursed his lips towards the house. "They're the ones who sold the bed; sold it to Boss Deng. He specialises in old-style rosewood beds, and I heard he paid a lot of money for your granddad's."

Grandfather's old room had already been turned into a fresh pile of rubble, which seemed to be giving off eddies of warm air. The massive ornately carved rosewood bed had collapsed in pieces onto the floor, heaped up there like some bizarre wooded skeleton. Some pieces were piled on the floor and others leaned up against the wall, all thinking their own weighty thoughts, and carrying their own regrets. Sunlight filtered in through the window from the street outside and fell on Baorun's father and mother. Baorun looked at them standing there amidst the dust and rubbish, holding one of the bedposts. His father's face was beaded with sweat, and there were streaks of black on his forehead and cheeks; his movements were rather sluggish and he had a vaguely apologetic expression, directed either at the bed itself or at the last vestiges of himself that Grandfather had left there. Baorun's mother was wearing her blue overalls from the chemicals factory, and her dishevelled hair was liberally dotted with dust balls. Her face, which carried a permanently disgruntled expression, was now looking furious as she totted up all the things that Grandfather had squirrelled away over many years: grain coupons, sugar coupons, handfuls of ten and twenty-cent banknotes, all expired and wrinkled, now dusted off and laid out in rows on the table, proof of Grandfather's transgressions.

When Baorun came in through the door, his father was being scolded for his grandfather's transgressions. His mother spoke out furiously:

"Look at that! Just look at that! What kind of a man was your father? When anyone else searched the house, or tried to seize his money, he didn't even dare to break wind; but while no one was looking, he was stealing from his own family! It's no wonder we were always short of food and had no money! We had a thief in our midst!"

Baorun's father was kneeling on the floor amidst the bits of bed, looking anxiously at a red rash on his wrist.

"Alright, alright! Where can this rash have suddenly appeared from? It's itching like hell! I bet it's the ancestors protesting about us selling the bed!"

Baorun's mother went over to look at Father's wrist, beginning to look a little worried. She put one of her feet up on a chair and compared the rash on her ankle with the one on Father's wrist. The inspection didn't take long and resulted in her expression becoming even more contemptuous:

"Those have got nothing to do with the ancestors! You're getting all worked up over nothing! Those are flea bites from the fleas the old lunatic seemed to keep as pets. I've got the same on my ankle."

Baorun's mother fetched a small pot of soothing ointment, applied some to Father's wrist and then put some on her own ankle. Then she picked up one of the bed posts herself, and took them outside, saying:

"That Bao Sanda has been waiting for ages outside, so you two had better hurry up and get to work. Even when we've moved everything, it's still going to take an age to clean up. This room is a health hazard; it's full of the old fool's germs!"

Baorun's father always deferred to Mother's instructions and ordered Baorun to carry the ancestral bed, bit by bit, out into the street. Big imposing objects seem frail and inconsequential once they are dismantled. The timbers where the Ancestors had laid their heads had their own particular scent: a little sour, a little acrid, with a rancid tinge. Picking up a decorated bed post was like taking hold of a lofty and dignified male ancestor, and carrying a carved bed rail was like carrying a refined and gentle female ancestor. In Baorun's hands, the wood at one moment felt hard and heavy, and the next, soft and pliant. The spirits of the ancestors scattered hither and yon from the cracks in the wood. They displayed different levels of magnanimity: some seemed forgiving to later generations, setting out quietly on their journey, whilst others were more petty, and showed no leniency to their unworthy descendants. One bed post showed particular animosity, not only digging especially hard into Father's shoulder as he carried it, but also banging Baorun on the head as it passed him. Another departing ancestral spirit bared its icy fangs, which were hidden amongst the carvings of birds, flowers, fish and insects, waiting for the chance to punish its unfilial family. Baorun found himself pecked hard in the thigh by a magpie amongst the carvings on a bed rail he was carrying. And that was not all; later on, when he was carrying a panel carved with peaches and peach blossom out of the house, one of the fruits slyly and unexpectedly bit him on the ear.

Baorun didn't think he had done anything to deserve being bitten by the ancestors. Their bite was icy cold; it stung at first, then went numb and finally gradually began to itch. He stopped to scratch, berating his parents:

"So just what do you think you are doing? Grandpa says he's going to be better soon. He'll want to come home, and now you've sold his bed, where's he going to sleep?"

"Do you still believe what he says? He is so mad now, do you really think he's going to get better?" Baorun's mother said. "Didn't you hear what the doctor at the hospital said? Grandfather's illness is totally unique. The only way to look after him, unless you can turn back time, is for him to make the Jingting Hospital his home from now on."

Baorun looked to see what his father thought about this, but his father was looking very embarrassed and awkward. He raised his hand, palm facing Baorun, and smiled broadly:

"What are you grinning at?"

"I sold Grandpa's bed for five hundred yuan!"

Baorun considered this:

"That's chickenfeed. Boss Deng is a dealer; he'll sell it on for at least a thousand!"

Baorun's father seemed to approve of these words, in a rather disengaged way; then he turned, his eyes shining, and waved two fingers in front of Baorun, saying:

"Selling that bed, and clearing the room, is going to bring us another two hundred yuan. Another two hundred yuan every single month!"

Baorun didn't understand, and asked:

"Who? Who's going to give you two hundred yuan every month?"

"Master Ma! He's taking the plunge into the business world and wants to rent Grandpa's room. He's going to knock through the wall and open a shop. He's going to pay two hundred yuan a month rent."

Baorun stared at him, wide-eyed in amazement, and then suddenly flared up:

"Has poverty driven you mad? Why not sell Granddad himself? Isn't his illness unique in the whole world? His brain must be worth dissecting! You could probably sell it for ten thousand yuan."

This annoyed his mother:

"Who do you think you are mocking? You may not think 200 is very much, or even 500, for that matter, but how much money have you ever earned? Do you think we're compromising ourselves for the sake of money? Are we chasing cash so we can take it to the grave with us? Is that what you think? Don't you understand we're doing this for you?"

When she saw Baorun just standing there staring at her, she really lost her temper, and jabbed her finger at his chest.

"I saw right through you long ago! If you don't go bad sometime, then we should offer thanks to the gods of Heaven and Earth. You've got no prospects, so you need money. With money you can buy a good job and a good wife. Do you understand what trouble we're going to for you?"

Baorun did, in fact, understand that; but understanding was not the same as approval. As he carried the bed out, bit by bit, he berated his parents:

"What do you think you mean by prospects? In another twenty years, the world's going to come to an end, and nobody's prospects will be worth a fart. Prospects or no prospects, money or no money, we'll all come to the same end. We'll all be buried alive and no one will escape."

When the last piece of bed was carried out, all traces of the ancestors disappeared too, and Grandfather's bedroom became a whole new world in the blink of an eye. The sunlight summoned the dust in the room; dust so old it wavered unsteadily, and moved only very slowly, making several vague attempts to coalesce, before it finally succeeded in forming a grubby rainbow that slanted lazily across the room. It lent Grandfather's room an obscure elegance. Baorun noticed that Grandfather's photograph was still hanging on the wall, its glass covered in a layer of dust. Grandfather was hiding beneath the dust, smiling gently. It was the smile of the seventy-year-old Grandfather, which underwent an unfathomable, almost magical transformation. If you stood to the left of the photograph, the smile had a sinister, malevolent quality; but if you stood to the right, it was purer and more innocently mischievous than a child's. If you stood right in front of the photograph, the treacherous smile disappeared completely, and you saw Grandfather as he usually was: a shrunken, desiccated face, sharp as a knife; a pair of deeply worried eyes; a distrustful expression, and a pair of thin lips compressed into Grandfather's golden rule: be careful, and then be more careful.

There was a damp patch on the wall where the portrait hung and the damp had spread into the corner. In the spot which had originally been covered by the wardrobe, there was an oval hole. This hole seemed to be emitting strange rippling waves, which cascaded down in alarming fashion. When Baorun tried to cover the hole with his hand, he felt a shaft of piercing cold air, which made him shiver uncontrollably. Was this hole, hidden in the darkness, the house snake's lair? And was the house snake's lair, in fact, where the spirits of the ancestors lived? Baorun looked up at Grandfather's photograph and, in that instant, he suddenly understood Grandfather's worries and fears. The hole was waiting there for Grandfather, waiting for him to tumble into it. And that was what his soul had already done. In that instant, he heard Grandfather's piteous cries and wailing:

"Someone has thrown my soul in there! Quickly! Help me pull it out!"

Baorun had no idea how to rescue Grandfather's soul from there. He crouched beside the hole, staring thoughtfully into it for a long time. Taking advantage of his parents still being outside talking to Bao Sanda, he surreptitiously took the photograph of the unknown girl out of his pocket.

The photograph was warm, still carrying his body heat. The girl's expression was angry; even all this time later, that unknown anger still moved him. He loved that anger but, at the same time, was wary of it. He blushed furiously as he gripped the photograph in his fingers. He couldn't detach himself from that tiny face and those even tinier lips. She had triggered his anger but also unleashed his, as yet unformed, love and he couldn't part with her. But Grandfather spoke to him from the wall:

"That's her! She's the one who threw away my soul. Make her go in and get it back!"

Baorun listened and, gritting his teeth, he tore the photograph into pieces and stuffed the pieces into the hole. Thus the unknown girl was handed over to the even more unknown ancestors. The world inside the hole extended long and deep, and he heard the innocent young girl plunge into its abyss. As she fell through the darkness, clutching her pale green parasol, she collided with the ancient spirits of the ancestors who were assembled there. The sound of her weeping echoed mournfully and she wailed as she fell until, in the end, she settled her debt to Grandfather. Baorun felt at peace, but beside that, he also felt a twinge of guilt. He seized some handy pieces of glass and plaster, and used them to block up the hole completely. The ancestors' way out was blocked and their secret was stoppered up, just as were all the echoes that emanated from the darkness.

It was a busy and tiring afternoon. Baorun ran dazedly up to his attic and sat on his bed, lost in thought. Bao Sanda's flat-bed tricycle had long since departed and his parents were busy downstairs. After a while, some wisps of black material drifted up into the attic from below. It was stuff that Baorun's mother had swept out of Grandfather's room and fluttered round him like black butterflies. At first he paid no attention to them until he felt a violent itching on his neck. He reached back and grasped a knotted-up tuft of hair. It was the length of his little finger, soft and snowy white. He recognised it as Grandfather's hair, a tuft of hair without a soul. Then he found another tuft that had latched onto his breast, like a hand holding on for dear life. When he plucked it up to examine it, he saw that it was half black, half white and had lost its lustre but it still had solidity and substance. It was, of course, Grandfather's hair too, but Baorun had no way of knowing if it was his sixty-year-old or fifty-year-old hair. Perhaps it was even younger! Could it even be his forty-year-old hair?

SIX
THE JINGTING HOSPITAL

The Jingting Hospital was out in the suburbs, far from the bustle of the city itself, but quite close to a number of the main public cemeteries. To get there from Red Toon Street, you had to pass through half the city and a fair amount of farmland. In principle, there was a bus-stop close to the hospital, but it took five changes to get there, making it a very tiresome journey. It was a little easier to go by bicycle but it was a long way and the trip took more than an hour. So, for the people who lived in the north of the city, a trip to the Jingting Hospital wasn't exactly a full-scale journey but had to be prepared for like one.

The first time Baorun went to the Jingting Hospital was at the time of the Qingming Festival, and he went in old Driver Jin's truck. Old Jin and his family were going to sweep the family graves and they gave Baorun's family a lift on their way. The purposes of the two households' journeys were different as they climbed aboard the East Wind brand truck and they were in different moods. The Jin family, on their way to sweep the graves, were happy and relaxed, almost as though they were going on a Spring holiday. For the womenfolk it was a welcome break in their busy routine, and they were sitting in the back of the truck putting the finishing touches to the offering money they were making out of tinfoil. Su Baozhen was reluctantly helping them make some fake ingots when she was suddenly overcome with grief and some of the tears she could no longer hold back splashed down onto one of the ingots. Mother Jin was astonished:

"What's this, Baorun's Mother? We are going to sweep our ancestors' graves but we're not sad; and you're going to visit a sick relative, and you're in pieces. Why are you so sad?"

Su Baozhen wiped away her tears and replied, resentfully:

"I'm not sad; these are tears of anger! If you want to know the truth, I don't have any filial feelings, and I have no wish to go and visit the old lunatic who's done us so much harm. We're only going to pay the bill because if we don't, they'll send him home."

When she saw that the Jin women didn't understand what she was talking about, she took a bundle of envelopes made of kraft paper, from her cloth bag. They were all official letters from the Jingting Hospital.

"Look at these: they're all demanding money!"

Waving the letters at the other women, she went on:

"A hundred yuan for fifteen holly trees; another hundred for eight yellow poplars, and they want two hundred for a single osmanthus tree. That old fool is still digging away, and he's dug me into a five hundred yuan hole."

The letters were passed round everyone to read and they all reacted with outrage and indignation. Mother Jin said she thought the hospital was guilty of extortion; the osmanthus tree, in particular, was twice what it should be. She said that, since an osmanthus tree was only scented for six months a year, there was no way it should be that expensive."

Su Baozhen nodded vigorously in agreement:

"I think they're trying to rob us, too. I've tried phoning them several times to kick up a fuss but what's the use! They tell me the Jingting Hospital is a model unit for the government's greenification policy, and that all their trees are model specimens that people come specially to photograph. That's why they're more expensive than ordinary trees."

"Pah! What model unit? What model specimens? It's all lies!" Mother Jin said. "I know how to handle them. Just ignore their bills and give them half what they ask for each type of tree."

While the rest of the people on the truck were discussing the price of trees, Baorun's father stayed silent. He sat by the air vent, his hair blowing around like a flock of birds, avoiding his wife's eyes, nursing an expression of private grief and remorse. Old Jin's family were full of questions for him, and bombarded him with enquiries:

"Didn't he say that the flashlight was buried in Red Toon Street?"

"Didn't he say it was buried under a holly tree?"

"Why has he been digging at the Jingting Hospital?"

"Why should he want to dig under yellow poplars and osmanthus trees?"

Baorun's father gave a bitter laugh:

"What flashlight are you talking about? All my family's old property is gone, so what is there to dig for? You shouldn't believe a word my father says. He really has lost his soul, and he's just filled with rubbish now. Nothing he says to you has any more value than a fart."

Seeing his distress, Mother Jin told the children to be quiet and tried a different angle:

"The hospital has some responsibility, too, for letting Grandfather dig up trees all over the place. People who are mentally ill can't control their behaviour, so why aren't the people at the hospital controlling him?"

"There's something you don't know", Baorun's father replied. "My father's illness is the only case like it in the whole world. The hospital has called in all kinds of important specialists, and none of them know what drugs to treat this illness with, or which department should be treating him. When it comes down to it, doctors are only interested in cases they can cure, and no one wants to take responsibility for my father. So there's no one who can control him!"

"Are you saying that even such a famous mental hospital as this can't treat your father?" Mother Jin exclaimed. "Then what are you doing sending him there? Change hospitals as soon as you can!"

At this point, her young son Ah Si piped up:

"You'd do better sending him to prison because there, at least, he'll get board and lodging for free. And there aren't any trees in prison, so the old man won't be able to dig them up, even if he wants to."

Some of the other people on the truck laughed behind their hands, and Mother Jin was about to slap him, when Su Baozhen stopped her, saying:

"Ah Si wasn't joking about this. If the prison was willing to take him, I'd send him there, and I'd like to see anyone try to stop me."

The others in the truck automatically looked at Baorun's father, who grimaced, avoided their gaze and glanced at his wife. Then, staring out at the passing landscape, he said:

"This has been a lesson to me. I had too much trust in the hospital. It's no good leaving the old man there by himself; from now on, someone has to take proper responsibility for him."

When the truck reached the Jingting Hospital, the two families split up: those going to sweep graves went to sweep graves and those going to the hospital went to the hospital. Baorun always remembered very clearly that a light drizzle was falling from the ash-grey sky when he followed his parents into the Jingting Hospital, just as a young girl was coming out of the gates, opening a pale green umbrella. They brushed shoulders as they passed and a corner of the umbrella dipped like a swooping bird, and pecked him on the forehead. Before Baorun could say anything, the girl rebuked him sharply:

"Hey, why don't you look where you're going!"

Irritated, Baorun shoved at the umbrella, and said:

"You're one to talk! It's your umbrella that hit me in the face! So what were you doing with *your* fucking eyes?"

The girl moved the handle of her umbrella to reveal her face which wore a fierce expression, the combative nature of which was tempered by a touch of curiosity. She looked Baorun up and down, and a smile twitched at the corners of her mouth:

"Hey, which section are you from? You'd better get back to your ward quickly, it's time for your medication!"

Baorun didn't know how to respond to this quiet but mischievous teasing, so he just stepped angrily to one side and watched the girl with the pale green umbrella pass swiftly through the wrought-iron gates of the hospital. As she went, he murmured automatically:

"You just wait!"

He remembered his dream. The real girl was different from the imaginary one. The girl with the umbrella was fourteen or fifteen years old, with her hair in a simple ponytail. She had a thin, delicate face, and jet-black, almond-shaped eyes; her skin was a little dark, her lips compressed; and her eyebrows were raised. All of this served to emphasise her haughty expression, which verged on contempt. She was much prettier than the girl in the photograph and her anger was more solid, in the same way that the pale green umbrella was more practical, more animated, its colours more vivid and its shape more defined. Baorun hesitated a moment but couldn't help following her. He grimaced at her and called out in a loud voice:

"Hey, did you ever lose a photograph at the Hongyan Photographic Studio?"

The umbrella stopped, and the girl underneath it turned back to look, with an expression of disgust. Baorun thought she was going to abuse him again but this time she was almost civil, apart from showing her contempt for the photographic studio.

"The Hongyan Photographic Studio? Who uses the Hongyan Photographic Studio?" She twirled the umbrella. "Only country bumpkins like you have their pictures taken there!"

Baorun's parents made their way to the hospital office to try to negotiate some kind of settlement but they ran into a brick wall. The hospital said that they were a public institution, not some vegetable stall in the local market, and that the compensation for damage to public property was not something to be haggled over. They also warned Su Baozhen to mind what she said:

"Hey sister, are you seriously suggesting that we are trying to pull a fast one on you? This hospital has not taken advantage of your relative, though it is a matter deserving of close consideration by us all whether he needs to stay in this hospital or not. He is no danger to other people, only to trees. If you are not willing to compensate us for those trees, then we will order him to be taken home today."

The discussion went on for a long time, with the hospital not giving an inch until, finally, with gritted teeth, Su Baozhen agreed to pay in full.

"Pay up!" She said to her husband. "Give them whatever they want! But even if it beggars us, the old fool is not coming home. If you want him to, then I won't. If you sign his release papers, then I will commit myself on the spot!"

Su Baozhen was so full of anger and resentment that she refused to see Grandfather or to stay in the hospital any longer, preferring to go and wait on the side of the road until the Jin family truck came back from the cemetery. Baorun saw his parents part company at the bottom of the office staircase, both of them looking as though they had been stricken by calamity. His mother had the pained look of a victim and his father looked like a repentant sinner.

Baorun followed his father over to the men's section to visit Grandfather. This was the first time he had been into the inner workings of the Jingting Hospital. It's reputation as a model of greenification was not undeserved, and wherever one looked there was a sea of flowers and vegetation: cherry trees, peach and apricot, all in glorious bloom and, on the ground, the dark green of bamboo, flowering crab-apple, climbing roses and rose bushes. The security measures at the men's section were far less stringent than Baorun had expected; the guard on the gate asked a few questions, and when they had filled in their names on a visitors' list, father and son were allowed on their way. Baorun was almost disappointed, and asked:

"Can we just go in now?"

The security guard laughed:

"What more do you expect? Going in is easy enough, it's getting out you have to worry about. Just make sure you hold onto your exit permit!"

Baorun looked around him as he went in through the second set of iron gates, and felt even more disappointed. He couldn't stop himself from complaining out loud:

"Is this place a mental hospital or a sanatorium? It's so quiet! I thought the Jingting Hospital would be all lively and noisy!"

Baorun's father looked at him angrily:

"Did you just come here to have a good time? Well, that's easily fixed. If you come here every day to keep Grandpa company, then you'll certainly see fun enough."

As soon as they reached the second floor, they saw Grandfather. He was sitting at the top of the stairs, waving to his relatives. He had clearly been misinformed by someone and had already packed up all his things; he was sitting on the top step, clutching a bulging string bag and looking like a lost child waiting to be taken home. A hulking male attendant was standing behind Grandfather, sucking on a cigarette. He was wearing a white tunic, long black rubber boots and a pair of black vinyl gloves. Baorun thought the gloves looked very smart as they rested on Grandfather's shoulders like a pair of big, black bats.

It was quite some time since they had seen Grandfather and he looked even thinner than before. His expression was both aggrieved and, at the same time, apprehensive.

"I've been waiting for ages!" Grandfather said. "What's the matter with you, making me wait so long?"

Baorun's father stopped at the top of the stairs, and surveyed Grandfather coldly:

"Well, Dad, you've excelled yourself yet again. I've paid out five hundred yuan because of you today!"

Grandfather pretended not to hear and stretched out his hands to his son to help him up. But Baorun's father just looked at his hands and said:

"Why aren't you digging today? There are still lots of trees here, so go and dig them up! I don't care how many you dig up, I've got the money!"

It was hard to tell whether Grandfather's expression was guilty or embarrassed. When he tried to stand up, he was held down by the attendant standing behind him, who asked Baorun's father:

"Is he really being discharged today? The old man has been sitting here since first thing this morning, saying his son is going to take him home today, and he wanted to get away as early as possible. I don't look after the patients, I'm a lavatory attendant, and there are eight lavatories I haven't cleaned yet."

"Then go and clean your lavatories", Baorun's father said. "We're not going home yet; we've paid every cent I owe."

The light in Grandfather's eyes went out. He struggled against the grip of the attendant as incoherent curses bubbled out of him, though it was unclear whether they were directed at his son, at the hospital, or at the attendant. As he struggled, he threw his string-bag at his son, but it was too heavy for him, and Baorun easily intercepted it and clutched it to his chest. Grandfather's mouth gaped open and he began to wail. Tears and mucus mixed with dribbles of saliva flowed in a mournful, sluggish tide down his chin. Baorun had never seen his Grandfather weep like this before, as the old man's involuntary wails combined with bitter curses:

"If you're not going to let me go home, then I'm going to dig, dig, dig! I want to dig! I'm going to keep digging!"

Baorun made his way along the passageway, carrying Grandfather's luggage, and finally discovered where all the action was in the Jingting Hospital. There were patients roaming the corridor and a bald-headed man was leaning against the wall, eyes closed and brows knitted, as though contemplating some impenetrable problem. As Baorun went past him, his eyes suddenly snapped open, and he grabbed hold of Baorun with one hand:

"Are you from the Party Committee? Secretary Zhang has wronged me, and the Party Committee must look into it!"

Baorun shook himself free from the bald man:

"What Party Committee? You must be joking if you think I'm going to do anything to help you out! Who would help me out then?"

The corridor led Baorun past the lavatories where he almost bumped into another eccentric patient. The man was naked from the waist down, with his trousers down around his knees. His buttocks were sticking out and he walked crablike along the corridor, his legs pressed together to hold onto his trousers. Baorun slowed his pace to keep a prudent distance from the man but he could hear him muttering that he had to save paper, water and electricity. Baorun didn't dare look at his pale, withered buttocks, nor did he dare laugh. He averted his eyes and held his breath as he walked on, saying to himself:

"Well, I was looking for action, and I've certainly found it here!"

There were two chairs at the door to Grandfather's ward, Ward No 9, and on one of them was sitting a delicately featured young man with hair as long as a girl's, pulled back in a pigtail. He greeted Baorun in English:

"Hello!"

Then he turned less friendly and blocked Baorun's way with his hands and feet. Abruptly and pointedly, he asked:

"What is love?"

Not understanding what he wanted, Baorun replied:

"I don't give a toss about love. This is Granddad's ward, and I'm his grandson."

"I don't care whose grandson you are! If you don't answer, you can't come in. What is love? Please give me your answer!"

Baorun poked his head into the dormitory to look around and replied:

"What is love? Tell me. I've never been in love, so I don't know."

The young man's expression seemed unfathomable:

"I can't tell you the answer. It's the password, so think hard."

Instinctively, Baorun replied:

"What is love? Love is bullshit!"

Fortunately, Baorun's instincts proved sound, and he got the password half-right. The young man corrected him tolerantly:

"It's not bullshit; it's stinking bullshit."

With a howl of laughter, he moved his chair, freeing the way for Baorun to go into Grandfather's dormitory.

There was an indescribable odour to Ward No 9, an acrid smell overlaid with Lysol. Grandfather's bed was already neatly tidied, with a rolled-up mattress topped by a black-coloured pillow. Baorun unrolled the mattress, revealing a dark-red stain, somewhat in the shape of a bird. He inspected it closely, sniffed it, and determined that it was old blood, someone else's blood, and nothing to do with Grandfather. After a while, he heard the sound of angry footsteps, the chair blocking the doorway was kicked aside, and the young man guarding the door leapt hurriedly to his feet. He had no time to ask for his password before the doorway echoed to his father's angry voice:

"Stop your racket, Dad! I give up! I'll stay with you today; I'll stay with you till you die!"

SEVEN
GRANDFATHER, FATHER AND SON

AMID THE CROWDED hustle and bustle of Red Toon Street, Baorun's family was one of the simplest households: although it encompassed three generations, there were only four people and now those four people were divided into two camps. One camp had gone to the Jingting Hospital and the other stayed on Red Toon Street.

The news of Baorun's father's sacrifice appeased the criticism of their neighbours on Red Toon Street. Although the daughter-in-law had treated the old man badly, and the grandson had shown himself deficient in fulfilling his obligations, at least the son was showing proper filial piety. Baorun often bumped into gossipy neighbours, who were particularly attentive to him because of their interest in his family affairs. Superstitious old people were eager to know whether or not the Jingting Hospital was helping Grandfather get his soul back, and still more neighbours stopped him to praise his father's dutiful behaviour, and then took the opportunity to probe his own attitude to his grandfather. Baorun was very impatient with the latter, saying:

"My father's looking after his father, my mother's looking after my father, and I'm not looking after anyone. So stop asking me. I've got nothing to do with anything!"

Baorun's father never knew whether it was his filial behaviour that moved the hospital authorities or whether they had been persuaded by his arguments but, whatever the case, they treated him with leniency and consideration. He was accorded the extraordinary rank of patient's guardian. He brought a folding deck-chair into Ward No 9 from which he could conduct a permanent, close-range surveillance of Grandfather, day and night. But after he had been sleeping in this deckchair for six months or so, he was beginning to suffer serious consequences. He developed problems with his spine and began to walk along, hunched over. He wasn't worried about his spine or his posture, but he was worried that his surroundings were beginning to have a detrimental effect on his own mental health. On one of his occasional visits home, he hesitantly told his wife about an odd occurrence. He said that recently he had become possessed, and developed an unusual interest in digging; whenever he saw a hole in the ground of any size, he had to stop beside it, and the only thing he wanted to do was find a tool of some kind and start digging. Su Baozhen was stunned:

"You want to start digging now? Are you looking for the flashlight too?"

Baorun's father said defensively:

"I'm not looking for the flashlight, I just can't resist the urge to dig to see what's there underground."

Su Baozhen went pale and challenged her husband, in a shrill voice:

"And what, exactly, do you think you are going to find?"

Baorun's father thought about this for a moment, and replied:

"There are lots of noises underground, and they're really interesting."

And despite his wife's alarm, he launched into an enthusiastic description of the subterranean noises he had heard. He said that all the holes amongst the trees at the Jingting Hospital were wailing holes; that the new holes that had been dug there all gave off the cries of new-born babies, loud and clear, morning and night. The old holes sounded like the grief-stricken mutterings of old people, mutterings followed by weeping; then, after a while, this turned to hacking coughs, as though they were trying to clear their throats but couldn't. The holes behind the office building, however, buzzed like beehives, sounding like an eternal gaggle of old women gossiping, quarrelling one minute, then laughing, then whispering, then falling silent, all as though they were all spinning thread. Yes, just as though they were all spinning.

"Do you remember how my mother used to spin all the time? That's the sound I heard; my mother spinning underground, spinning, day after day."

Su Baozhen grew more and more scared as she listened. In her terror, she put a hand over her husband's mouth to keep him quiet, and with her other hand she snatched up an ear-cleaning scoop:

"How terrible! You've got a demon lodged in your ear!"

She took hold of her husband's ear, and began to probe it forcefully, saying, through gritted teeth:

"I've got to dig it out! Don't worry about how much it hurts, we've got to get that demon out. You must know the ear leads into the brain. If it goes on like this, you'll lose your soul too!"

No one can be sure whether losing one's soul is a hereditary condition, but Baorun's father was clearly not a well man, mentally or physically, while he was at the Jingting Hospital. Thoughts of excavations whirled around inside his head, and the heavy responsibility of watching over his father wore down his body. One night, he got up in the middle of the night to relieve himself when his latent heart condition suddenly flared up and he collapsed onto the filthy concrete floor of the lavatory. A young inmate discovered him there and, not knowing enough to call for help, proceeded to drag him out of the lavatory and along the long corridor to the top of the staircase. Exhausted, the young patient saw the slide beside the staircase which was used for moving goods. Using what there were of his wits, he tipped Baorun's father onto it, so he slid headlong down to the bottom like a sack of grain. This tumultuous descent ended with Baorun's father suffering several fractures to his arms and legs. But some good came of it, as the rumbling and tumbling shook him out of his faint and, by good luck, he fell straight into the director of the hospital, Director Qiao, who was doing his nightly rounds. Director Qiao knew the basics of treatment for a heart attack and immediately arranged for an ambulance to take Baorun's father to the People's Hospital. It was just in time and Baorun's father's life was saved.

Su Baozhen went to the Jingting Hospital to express her deep thanks to Director Qiao and to offer him a silk brocade banner. As for the other benefactor, she showed her gratitude in somewhat more mundane form, by giving the young patient two apples. But after that, her attitude altered, and she was transformed from someone repaying a kindness, to someone exacting revenge. She rushed over to Ward No. 9 and wept and wailed at Grandfather for a good long time. She berated him directly for his longevity:

"An old fool like you doesn't contribute anything to the nation; you don't bring any favours to your son or grandson; so what do you think you are doing living so long? You're just a burden on your family, and how are you going to bear it when they die before you?"

Grandfather understood what she was saying, and said defiantly:

"I don't want to die. Before, I did, so why didn't you let me go then? Now I've lost my soul, so I can't die, but you want me to. How can I die without my soul? I'm determined not to die, so even if you do, I won't!"

Baorun's father came home from the hospital, like a wounded soldier coming back from the war. His arms were bandaged and his legs were still in plaster. He sat in the doorway, leaning on a metal crutch, but it was hard to tell whether he was deep in thought or just enjoying the sunshine. His appearance had changed greatly; his eyes protruded like a goldfish and, no matter what he was looking at, his gaze was tinged both with ferocity and sorrow. When the neighbours exchanged pleasantries with him and the conversation turned to his impressions of his six months at the Jingting Hospital, he just mocked himself, saying:

"It was all a big waste of time! My dad's soul hasn't come back and I almost lost mine there!"

When the neighbours asked about Grandfather, Baorun's father replied:

"Dad's much better; in fact he's in better health than me. I'm as helpless as a clay bodhisattva crossing a river, and all I can do is let Baorun look after him."

And when the neighbours came to think about it, they realised they hadn't seen Baorun for quite some time.

The baton of responsibility for the care of Grandfather had passed to Baorun.

They were a family. The son looked after the Grandfather's affairs and when his strength failed, the grandson had to stand up and be counted. It was a family matter and, in the end, he could not shirk his responsibilities.

EIGHT
APRIL

THE BEST TIME of Baorun's adolescence was squandered in the Jingting Hospital.

He was always mature for his years and he had already grown to his full height some years ago, and his whole body was sturdy and well-built. His thighs were thick and his back broad, so that he bulged out of his clothes, and the cloth looked as though it might split at any moment. The moustache around his mouth grew thicker and thicker and, since he didn't tend to it or trim it, it began to resemble a black straw mat covering his upper lip, which others thought looked sloppy, but he considered rather fetching. Some time even before this, his cheeks had been covered in acne, which he used to squeeze with his fingers. This had left behind a load of dark red scars, which immediately suggested an excess of hormonal secretions.

Facially, he resembled his mother and, at a cursory glance, he had a delicate air to him, but his eyes held a particular expression, the origins of which it was hard to discern. Stemming from his prolonged supervision of his grandfather, his eyes became like two searchlights, scanning the scene far and wide, gleaming brightly, but with an icy light. No matter who he was surveying, his gaze was always challenging, not to say threatening, as though to say:

"Behave yourself; you just behave yourself!"

When this look fell on boys, they found it provocative and incendiary, so that they couldn't help but point provocatively at Baorun:

"What are you looking at? You're a pretty sight yourself! Let's go over there if you want a fight!"

Baorun was unaware his look was so offensive to others and so was always baffled by this response. He wasn't a fighter himself, so he always tried to explain it away, saying:

"What do you mean, looking at you? Prove it! I don't know you, and you're not a girl, so why should I want to look at you?"

In fact, girls were particularly sensitive to Baorun's gaze and many of them would gather in the street to discuss amongst themselves why he was so unappealing to them, and it always came down to his eyes. His gaze was suspicious of everything, negative about everything, and confused about everything. It made anyone who came under it feel as though they had put on the wrong clothes that day, that the way they were walking was all wrong, that their whole demeanour was wrong. Under Baorun's gaze, even the prettiest girls were reduced to equality with the plainest, even the ugliest; they all felt as though they had committed some unpardonable fault. The girls competed to describe this gaze: some said it was that of a secret agent, others that it was that of a judge; some said it was that of a pervert, others that it was that of a wolf. Wang Deji's daughter, Qiuhong, had the most original description of all of them; she said Baorun's gaze was like a coiled rope.

"He's always staring at me. I don't want him to stare at me. When he does, my scalp crawls and I have to run away", Qiuhong said. "I'm always afraid when he's walking behind me. I'm afraid I'll hear a swishing noise, and a coil of rope will come flying towards me. He knows how to tie people up, you know! I'm afraid he's going to tie me up with the rope, and start taking liberties with me."

The other girls didn't agree with this, and rather felt that Qiuhong was showing excessive self-regard. Annoying as Baorun was, he wouldn't go as far as tying someone up; and even if he did, he wouldn't do it to such an ill-favoured girl as her. But Qiuhong swore blind it was true:

"I'm not lying! He's addicted to tying people up! Do you know how he treats his grandfather? He ties him up with rope; trusses him up so he can't move. If you don't believe me, go and ask Liu Sheng's mother. I went to the butcher's yesterday and I heard her describe it with my own ears."

Qiuhong was telling no more than the truth. Shao Lanying was the first to reveal Baorun's weirdly intimate relationship with rope to the neighbours. That Spring, Shao Lanying's household had met with ill fortune, and as the peach blossom came out, her daughter, Liu Juan, became hopelessly lovesick, and there was nothing for it but to consult the Jingting Hospital. So, Liu Sheng's family were just as familiar with the place as Baorun's, and anything Shao Lanying reported could be totally relied on.

Shao Lanying had chanced upon Baorun and his grandfather in the hospital gardens. Grandfather was ambling round a flowerbed, and Baorun was sitting on a long bench eating steamed bread. He was also twirling a length of rope. The rope attracted Shao Lanying's attention: it was seven or eight metres long, and sometimes it lay loose, but at others it tautened. At first, she thought Baorun was walking a dog, but when her eyes followed the length of rope, what she saw was not a dog, but a person. The end of the rope was attached to the pitiful figure of Grandfather.

Grandfather certainly recognised Shao Lanying as someone he knew, but he just couldn't remember her name. He had a blue Sun Yat-sen jacket draped over his shoulders. Smiling at her as warmly as the morning sun, he said:

"What are you doing here, Aunty Li? Which member of your family has lost their soul?"

Shao Lanying replied:

"My name isn't Li; I'm Aunty Shao, and no one in my family has lost their soul. It's just that my daughter is having a little problem and can't sleep properly. It's nothing serious, and I've just come to get a prescription for some sleeping pills."

But Grandfather saw through this deception:

"You can get a prescription for sleeping pills from the Union Clinic; there's no need for you to come running out here. There's no shame in losing your soul; the way the world is going now, it's happening to lots of people. But once your soul is lost, it's not easy to get it back."

Shao Lanying hurriedly changed the subject:

"Isn't it inconvenient for you to have a rope tied round your waist, Grandpa? Why don't you get Baorun to take it off?"

"He won't do that. He won't let me go outside, if it's not tied on. If I want to go outside, I have to have the rope. That's the rule."

Shao Lanying exclaimed in disapproval:

"Aiya! How dreadful for you! You shouldn't have to obey rules like that at your age!"

In the normal course of events, Shao Lanying's family and Baorun's minded their own business and never had anything to do with each other but now, through none of their own doing, a bridge had been built between them at the Jingting Hospital as the two unfortunate families were thrown together by what must be considered fate. Shao Lanying took a banana out of her bag and went over to the flowerbed:

"Here's a banana for you, Grandpa."

Grandfather thanked her, his eyes fixed on the banana, but he didn't reach out to take it. Taken aback, Shao Lanying looked closer and jumped back in alarm when she saw that, under Grandfather's blue Sun Yat-sen jacket, the rope was knotted so tightly around his body that there was no way he could reach out his hand to take the banana. She was outraged and couldn't stop herself remonstrating with Baorun, as an adult to a child:

"Your Grandfather has always loved you and treated you as his favourite in the past, so how can you tie him up like this and lead him round like an animal? Untie the rope immediately! Your Grandfather is sick, not mad! And he's certainly not a dog!"

According to Shao Lanying, Baorun just sat on the bench, eating his steamed bread, completely unperturbed. He looked her up and down, gave a tug on the rope and said:

"Prisoners don't dig up trees; he does. Dogs don't dig up trees; he does. What have you got to say to that? If I let him go, he'll start digging again, and each tree costs us a hundred yuan. Are you going to pay for them?"

APRIL

. . .

From one Spring to the next, on the mornings when the weather was clement, you could always see Baorun and his Grandfather in the garden of the Jingting Hospital. It would be fair enough to say they were taking walks there since, despite the necessity of the rope, the pinioned old man still looked as though he was out for a walk.

It was the doctors' opinion that walking was good for Grandfather's circulatory system, but his strange condition continued to baffle them and, other than the walks, they could come up with no proper course of treatment. The Jingting Hospital sat in about 9,000 sqm of grounds which became Grandfather's little world on these walks: not huge, but not too small. The Spring Grandfather was a dangerous Grandfather, and Baorun was very careful on his walks, as though he was walking a dozing wild horse. There was a delightful soft moistness about this season, with birdsong and the fragrance of flowers all about: cedars, acacias and ancient pines along with all manner of other trees grew in abundance. And if the morning dew from these trees dripped onto Grandfather's head, that was when Baorun had to be on his guard. The Spring Grandfather could transcend time and space and, if he looked up, he could see the spirits of the ancestors clinging wretchedly to the trunks of the trees, hanging from the branches; their clothes were ragged, and they had no home to go to. At the sight of them, Grandfather wept piteously as he stood under the trees and said, remorsefully:

"It's all my fault; I have failed my ancestors! I couldn't even keep hold of a simple flashlight, and because of me, you have nowhere to go!"

Because of this, Baorun never let Grandfather stand under a tree for any length of time. But Spring was a season beset with perils, and although Baorun could circumvent its trees, he could not stop the Spring winds. If the fresh warm southeasterly winds happened to blow on Grandfather's face, Baorun had to redouble his care. Not only did these winds bring the salty tang of the distant ocean, they also ferried the friendly spirits of other ancestors:

"Hurry up! Hurry up! Stop suffering here! Go and find your soul and come back to us here!"

Grandfather cracked the code of the Spring winds to discover that these spirits were mostly those of garrulous female ancestors, full of understanding and indulgence. So he stood in the Spring winds weeping and wailing, as he explained his plight to this sympathetic audience. At the same time, he also lamented his grandson's lack of filial feeling:

"Baorun won't let me dig! He won't let me dig! I can't find your remains. I can't get my soul back. How can I come back to you like this?"

Spring Grandfather was also the stupidest Grandfather, and Baorun had to keep an extra close eye on him to save him from himself. He continued to tie him up every day. It was reasonable and legitimate to tie Grandfather up; tying him up also met the majority of people's needs. Because of this both the hospital authorities and the relatives of other patients were understanding of Baorun's actions. With Grandfather tied up, the Jingting Hospital's precious trees and rare flowers were left in peace and quiet, and the gardeners could relax, knowing there was no one wantonly digging up trees in their green preserve. Nor did they have to mount any rescue missions for their precious trees and flowers. With Grandfather tied up, the labourers could relax, knowing that the spades in their toolshed were not going to disappear one by one, nor were the secluded nooks and crannies of the gardens going to be filled up with all manner of rubble and rubbish. With Grandfather tied up, Baorun's father could relax, and with Grandfather's actions under control, Baorun's mother's purse was safe.

Spring Grandfather was often in tears. But those grubby tears had no power to move Baorun, and even though he cried a whole vat of them, they didn't buy him a single shovel's worth of excavation. Baorun's task was simple: control Grandfather's actions; manage Grandfather's actions; and absolutely no digging.

Absolutely no digging
Absolutely no digging

Spring Grandfather was a bound Grandfather. His face was a little swollen and there was a strange flush to his cheeks. The expression in his eyes was always apprehensive because of his pinioned arms, and his gait was stiff and comically awkward, like a goose. Spring Grandfather's gaze was downcast, scanning the lay of the land on both sides, using the trees as coordinates, across a radius of six or seven metres. The Spring ground was soft and springy, so it was the very best season for digging, and he was afraid someone else might make off with his ancestors' bones. One flashlight. Two ancestors' remains. Every little hump in the ground attracted his attention and he was suspicious of every little depression. Spring Grandfather was under Baorun's close supervision so, no matter how keen he was, he was doomed to achieve nothing.

In the face of Grandfather's mania, Spring Baorun was no ordinary Baorun. He dedicated himself to experimenting on Grandfather's body, researching and innovating to reach the pinnacle of the art of rope bondage. Spring was Baorun's most productive season, and at his best he produced six different types of knot in one day to use on Grandfather. So Spring Grandfather, more than anything, was like a shop window for Baorun's latest creations.

Using Grandfather as a model, Baorun displayed his talents to the world. Just think of it! In the fullness of the April Spring, the other patients were suffering from seasonal spikes in the various dementias, and were tied to their beds, either with leather straps or with chains. They bellowed like beasts in an abattoir, deprived of any dignity. Grandfather alone had freedom of movement around the Jingting Hospital, constrained only by more humanitarian ropes, causing no injury, no bloodshed and no suffering. Often, some of the hospital attendants would cluster round Grandfather, gawping at his bonds. The first thing they looked at was the rope itself, which was formed from two different fibres - one green, one white - woven together; it was a finger-width thick, and of the kind you could buy in any household goods store, with nothing at all unusual about it. What merited attention was the composition of the knot. It was both inventive and practical, and so fine in line and composition it was almost unworldly. To tie someone up so beautifully and so scientifically, that was what was so amazing, the attendants opined in praise of Baorun.

"Seeing how docile you are, we would never have thought you were so talented. Grandfather is really beautifully tied up today. What knot did you use?"

Baorun did not like blowing his own trumpet, and said that Grandfather could tell them himself. Sullenly, Grandfather replied:

"It's called a 'civilised knot'; that's my grandson's name for it, not mine."

The attendants were amazed:

"Why's it called that?"

Baorun didn't want to answer, so he said to Grandfather:

"Show it to them."

Grandfather feigned reluctance, then took hold of the rope, feeling down it until his hand was in the vicinity of his flies, where he made an unbuttoning gesture:

"You see? Even though I'm tied up, I can still piss."

The attendants were as amazed as if they had discovered a new continent:

"Even tied up so tightly, you can still piss? No wonder it's called the 'civilised knot'!"

From April on we heard more and more about Baorun's consummate skill with knots. We heard that he had mastered more than twenty sorts of pinioning ligature, many of which he had named himself. Knots such as the 'people's knot' or the 'legal knot', the 'banana knot' or the 'pineapple knot'. There was also the 'plum blossom knot' and the 'peach blossom knot'. The inspiration for the 'legal knot' came from the 'five flower' knot used to pinion criminals condemned to death, its various strands many and complicated, its structure thick and impressive. All in all, it was a tricky knot to construct. Baorun experimented with it several times, but Grandfather was never cooperative; indeed, every time he saw the diamond shapes of the knot develop, he began to scream. In the end, Baorun realised that those shapes were reminding Grandfather of the year when his own father was executed by firing squad. In these circumstances, his resistance seemed quite reasonable, so Baorun allowed him a temporary reprieve. But at the same time, he also promised Grandfather:

"If you don't like the 'legal knot' I won't force you, but I'm warning you that, if you go back to your old crazy ways, the 'legal knot' is the one and only knot I will use on you, and I'll use it every day."

. . .

Baorun became a celebrity in the Jingting Hospital, and his fame spread to every ward. Often there would be family members of the patients rushing up, looking for Baorun, saying that such and such a patient was having a bad turn, and they needed Baorun to step in and tie him down. At first, Baorun was reluctant and would tell them:

"Go find an attendant if someone needs tying down. What are you doing bothering me?"

The relatives would reply:

"The attendants are too ham-fisted. When they tie someone up, it's like trussing a pig; they're not nearly as good as you. Everyone says when you tie someone up it doesn't leave any marks."

Baorun was not swayed by this faint praise, and replied:

"Do you think I'm just some kind of bailing machine? So just stop bullshitting me. I can't tie up anyone. When I tie my grandpa up, he is cooperative, and I can do a proper job; but if I try to tie someone else up who isn't cooperating, then I can't."

The relatives wouldn't give up, and offered cigarettes and ingratiating smiles; some of them went as far as to slip money into his pocket. Out of the kindness of his heart, Grandfather would act as their go-between, telling Baorun:

"Go on, hurry up and do it; look how much they trust you; you've got a specialist skill. You should use it to 'serve the people', and not be so cocky!"

In the end Baorun had to give in to the relatives' pleas, and he went to the wards of several patients unknown to him. He was nervous of using unfamiliar rope and usually took his own. When it came down to it, he wasn't a master electrician or plumber going on a house call, and the patients weren't his grandpa; Baorun found himself facing some fierce resistance from the patients themselves. Sleeping pills and tranquillisers had no effect on many of them, and going to tie them up turned into a real battle – a battle which Baorun had to win. Some of the patients were big strong men who would strike out with hands and feet; some of them were less robust and resorted to spitting and biting, and the use of medicine bottles and chamber pots to resist Baorun. There were also some who were particularly sneaky, adopting a woman's approach and grabbing at his testicles. Every time Baorun went to help out, he went into battle. The most perilous situation was trying to tie down a patient nicknamed 'Piggy'. Before Piggy was taken ill, he had worked in a fruit and vegetable warehouse, and was expert at trussing things up. He was also stronger than Baorun, and almost turned the tables on him. Indeed, if it hadn't been for the timely assistance of a number of attendants, Baorun might have found himself neatly packaged up by Piggy.

With his bare hands, Baorun subdued more and more anonymous patients. Tying up someone he didn't know had a greater novelty than tying up Grandfather, and was definitely more stimulating. Watching the rope gnawing through their clothes and biting into their flesh, he felt like a dragon sliding through the undergrowth and coiling silently in a thicket; he could feel when the bodies moved from full-bodied resistance to vain struggles, becoming weaker and emptier, until finally they yielded up to the rope. In Baorun's sport with the rope, each of his fingers became probing spearpoints. His rope had its own rules, its own principles. His rope could satisfy every twist and turn you could imagine. His rope was like a new layer of skin, protecting or confining every body that came its way, however fat or skinny. His rope was a free agent, full of ingenuity, which could wrap its coils around any shape of human and, at a whim, take up any form it chose. With just a single coil of rope, Baorun became a master craftsman. He had complete faith in his own skill with the rope, and every time he finished tying someone up, he got the people who had commissioned him personally to inspect the quality of the knots:

"See this 'pineapple knot'? What do you think of that!"

There was no doubt about it that Baorun's knots were of the highest quality, leaving no room for criticism. The clients all exclaimed in astonishment at their almost mystical ornateness, praising the bonds, saying:

"It really does look just like a pineapple! It's so well tied! Who would have thought someone so young could be so skilful!"

Nonetheless, Baorun remained a bit dubious about all these good works. Every time Baorun emerged from some other patient's ward, he was exhausted; exhausted and full of regret. He felt like an executioner working without pay, arbitrarily slaughtering the innocent since, other than the grateful expressions of the patients' relatives, he received no reward.

"Just this once. Just this once", he would tell himself each time. But in his heart he knew that this bondage was such a marvellous art, so inexpressibly wonderful, that he was, perhaps, under its spell.

NINE

THE ARRIVAL OF LIU SHENG

ONE DAY, the famous Liu Sheng from Red Toon Street came to the hospital.

Cigarette in his mouth, he was leaning against the doorway of Ward No 9, looking blankly at Baorun. Baorun pretended he hadn't noticed him, until Liu Sheng couldn't hold his pose any longer, and he threw him a cigarette.

"I'm Liu Sheng. Haven't you heard of me?"

They lived on the same street but, in the normal course of events, had nothing to do with each other. Liu Sheng had no particular reason to recognise Baorun, but Baorun certainly knew who Liu Sheng was. Liu Sheng was a prominent celebrity and everyone knew him. Liu Sheng's parents worked for the local butchers, his father, Master Liu, in the shop on the east side of the street, and his mother, Shao Lanying, in the shop on the west side. Together they had, for a long time, held the destiny of the dinner tables of the inhabitants of Red Toon Street in their hands. Father and mother doted on their son and, in order to secure a good living for his son, Master Liu had taken early retirement, and handed his cleaver over to his son. Thus, the Liu family strengthened their hold on the dinner tables of the street and, young as he was, it was clear Liu Sheng was going to be in command for a long time. If you ate meat, there was no avoiding the Liu family, and everybody on Red Toon Street knew it. Fresh pork and piping hot offal bestowed power and subverted relations, so the Liu family's importance on the street went without saying. When it came to comparisons, Liu Sheng's family certainly ranked as the most respected on the street, so it was a shame that Liu Sheng had a love-struck elder sister, Liu Juan. Every Spring, when the peach blossom came out, she would go down to the peach grove under the northern city walls, on a secret mission. This secret mission may have entertained the youth of the northern sector of the city, but it also tarnished the reputation of her family.

Baorun once went to see her in the peach grove with Black Balls and his gang. She was wearing a plain white sweater and sitting on a stone bench. On her knees was a plastic bowl for the money she was hoping to earn for herself. The youths gathered noisily round her, and one of them threw some coins into the bowl with a clatter. She smiled sweetly, and pulled up her sweater, exposing two rather meagre breasts, by way of thanks. One of the youths asked:

"What are you raising money for, Liu Juan?"

"To go to Beijing. I'm going to find my boyfriend, Xiao Yang. He's playing violin in an orchestra there."

The youths started clamouring:

"How does Xiao Yang play the violin? Why don't you show us how to play!"

Liu Juan didn't understand the double-entendre, and put one hand under her chin, and the other in the posture of drawing a bow across strings:

"This is how you play the violin; it's the only way to play it."

One of the youths said:

"Your family's got pots of money. Why don't you just take some? Why do you have to come out here begging?"

Liu Juan looked miserable:

"The family money is all locked in one of my mother's drawers. My younger brother's got a key and he can take what he likes. I'm not allowed a single cent because they're afraid I'll just go and buy a train ticket. Do any of you know how much a ticket to Beijing costs?"

None of the youths had ever been to Beijing and couldn't answer. There was only Black Balls, who had been to Nanjing, and he walked over to count the coins in the plastic bowl:

"That won't even get you to Nanjing, let alone Beijing!"

He laughed nastily and suddenly reached out to tug at Liu Juan's sweater:

"A ticket to Beijing is really expensive. You can't keep yourself covered up like this; you've got to show it all, you've got to show it all. That's the only way you'll earn enough money."

No one had expected anything like this from Black Balls and it drew an angry yelp from Liu Juan:

"Stop pawing me! Look, don't touch!"

Her cry attracted the attention of passers-by and, seized by guilt, the youths scattered in all directions, fleeing the scene of the crime. Baorun hastily threw a coin into Liu Juan's plastic bowl and, as she lifted her sweater, he glimpsed five deep red marks on the snowy white flesh to the left of her breasts. They resembled a five-petalled flower. As the youths looked down on the peach grove from on top of the city walls, they debated the likely origin of these marks. Some of them thought it was a birth mark, and others that it was a bite. Baorun thought Black Balls had the most likely explanation. He said that they were burns from Shao Lanying's cigarette, meted out as punishment: one burn for each time Liu Juan went out trying to raise money. She had been out five times, and so had been burned five times to make this flower pattern.

Liu Sheng's arrival reminded Baorun of Liu Juan, and when he thought of Liu Juan, he couldn't help seeing, in his mind's eye, the dark red flower beside her breasts. He couldn't stop himself blushing, and the best he could do was put his hands to his cheeks, and ask coldly:

"What are you looking for me for?"

"What do you think?" Liu Sheng gestured behind him with his thumb. "To tie someone up. I want you to tie my sister up."

Baorun shook his head:

"I won't do it. I won't tie her up."

"Why not?" Liu Sheng's eyes widened. "You do it for everyone else, so why not me? Are you deliberately trying to make me lose face?"

"I don't go over to the women's wards", Baorun said, excavating one of his nostrils with a finger. "I've never tied up women."

Liu Sheng looked as though he was about to press him on the need to tie his sister up, but then he seemed to grasp the undesirability of airing his family's dirty linen in public. Abruptly, he lapsed into obscenity:

"Fuck it! She's not a proper woman. Come over there with me, and tie her up as you please, just don't treat her like a woman!"

Baorun shook off Liu Sheng's insistent grasp, changed benches and said, unmoved:

"I'm not a bailing machine. If you want your sister tied up, ask a female attendant to do it. I'll tie up anyone else, but not a woman. It wouldn't be good for my reputation."

As the two of them remained deadlocked, Liu Sheng's expression became uglier. He stuck a finger under Baorun's nose, and spluttered angrily:

"Are you an agent of the Women's League? Why else are you acting like an old woman? Should I order you up a wedding sedan? We live on the same street, and we've seen each other often enough. I've always treated you with respect, so why are you deliberately insulting me? Go on, give me one good reason!"

Seeing that Liu Sheng was spoiling for a fight, Baorun decided to compromise a little, to stop him kicking up a fuss in Ward No 9. He pulled his rope out from under his bed and took Liu Sheng out into the corridor.

"Tying someone up isn't very difficult. If I teach you a knot, I guarantee you'll master it in a few seconds. Then you can go back and tie her up yourself."

He gave Liu Sheng the rope, then, using his own body as a dummy, taught him how to tie one of the easiest knots, the 'plum blossom' knot.

"As far as your sister is concerned, one plum blossom knot should be enough: it won't hurt her flesh, but she won't be able to move, and she won't be able to bring shame on your family."

But, as easy as the 'plum blossom' knot was, Liu Sheng just couldn't get the hang of it. After a few turns of the rope he got all muddled and, instead of getting angry with his own ineptness, he flared up at Baorun for making it so difficult. Throwing the rope round Baorun's neck, he exclaimed:

"I don't care whether it's a plum blossom or a peach blossom, I can't get the hang of it. Would it kill you to come and help me tie her up?"

When Liu Sheng tried to manhandle him, Baorun was having none of it. He shook off the rope, and gave Liu Sheng his marching orders:

"Get out of here and stop disturbing other people. I offend people every day, lots of them, and I'm not worried if you make one more!"

But Liu Sheng was in no mood to give up. He looked sidelong at Baorun, saying:

"Can't we come to some arrangement? Do you want cash or payment in kind? Just say the word and I'll send a basket of pig's liver round to your house. How about it?"

"No deal. I don't want your money or your liver. In any case, my family doesn't eat liver."

"How about a basket of pig's trotters? Fresh from the Allied Butchers – you can't even get them for ready cash."

Liu Sheng seemed suddenly to remember something and his tone became more confident:

"You may not want them but your mother certainly will. A few days ago, she queued up for some trotters, but they were sold out, and she stood in the shop doorway making all sorts of wild accusations, and damning the way society was going."

Baorun began to soften a little. His whole family liked pig's trotters, and they were his favourite. But he still couldn't help feeling that selling himself for a basket of trotters was too demeaning. "Would it kill me to go without pig's trotters?" he asked, in mocking imitation of Liu Sheng.

He went back into the ward, then turned to look at the other lad:

"Or, you could bring her over here. If you bring her over here, I'll tie her up."

This time it was Liu Sheng's turn to hesitate. He looked about him, assessing the surroundings of the male section of the hospital, just as the patient from Bed 17 came out of the lavatory, trousers around his ankles, muttering:

"We must save paper, we must save electricity, we must save water!"

Liu Sheng stared at Bed 17's exposed nether regions and an expression of revulsion, stemming from some unknown train of thought, came over his face:

"No, it won't do! If I bring her over here, my mother will really chew me out."

Thus vetoing Baorun's suggestion, Liu Sheng dropped the rope and headed off, muttering resentfully:

"Let her go where she likes; I'm not going to stand guard over her. Let her take her clothes off! Let her play the stripper! I couldn't give a shit!"

Of course he was just letting off steam and wasn't really ready to give up. When he reached the top of the stairs, he suddenly thought of something, and his eyes lit up. He picked up the rope and, slapping it thoughtfully against the stair-rail, said:

"Come over here, Baorun; there's something I want to ask you."

There was a sly look in Liu Sheng's eyes which intrigued Baorun, so he went over to him. Liu Sheng took him by the shoulder and, with his other hand to his mouth, whispered:

"Aren't you a bit bored here, Baorun? Wouldn't you like a little sister?"

The question was carefully phrased with just a hint of titillation. Baorun wasn't sure quite what Liu Sheng was up to:

"What little sister? Where from?"

"A little sister I know you like!" Liu Sheng winked at him and tipped his head to one side. "Come with me, and I'll show her to you."

"Who is it? Who do I like?"

"Don't play dumb with me, I've got my sources. You know the old gardener's granddaughter, don't you? She was feeding the rabbits when you saw her, and you asked if she wanted to go to the cinema with you. You did ask her to go to the cinema, didn't you? Go on, admit it!"

Baorun's averted eyes showed that there was at least some truth to this. He grimaced, but couldn't stop himself asking:

"Who told you?"

"It doesn't matter who told me. Do you admit it?"

Baorun admitted it, at least partially:

"The girl likes to pretend she's got lots of admirers! What kind of fairy princess does she think she is? I wasn't trying to pick her up, I just had a spare ticket, and it would have been a shame to waste it. I bumped into her, and asked her on the off-chance."

"A spare ticket, eh? Why didn't you give it to me?" Liu Sheng scoffed, then he suddenly clapped Baorun on the shoulder. "But that's enough of that; we're brothers, us two. Let's get to the point: do you want to go out with her or not?"

At first, Baorun shook his head, but when he saw the look in Liu Sheng's eyes, he quickly changed his mind and mumbled:

"I dunno, I don't mind really."

With Baorun so clumsily trying to hide his real feelings like this, Liu Sheng took heart. Stifling a smile, he looked at Baorun and aimed a playful punch at his crotch. Baorun dodged it, and at a stroke, it seemed that they had come to an understanding. Liu Sheng took Baorun by the ear and gave it a pinch:

"Come with me and I'll fix it for you. The two of you will go to the pictures together; I'll set it up."

Baorun was not comfortable with Liu Sheng's display of friendship, and he shook himself free, his eyes still suspicious:

"What's your connection with her? Why should she do what you say?"

"My connection? I'm her boss, aren't I!"

This time Liu Sheng grasped Baorun by the shoulders and pushed him ahead of him, asserting:

"I'd be finished on the street if I tricked you. Of course, I'm her boss and she'll listen to me. If you don't believe me, go home and ask!"

Baorun still only half-believed him and this showed in the way he dragged his feet. He'd only gone a few paces with Liu Sheng when he was struck by a serious doubt:

"Hang on a minute! You wanted to go out with her yourself, didn't you! Have you? Have you been out with her?"

"I'm not interested in her and I've never been out with her. Don't get the wrong idea. She wants to earn some money and she's been helping my older sister. I've already given her quite a lot of cash." Seeing Baorun undecided, he went on: "You don't really understand girls, do you? How can you be their boss if you don't spend some money, make an investment?"

Baorun didn't really understand what Liu Sheng was talking about, but his excitement was growing, and he snapped up this last piece of bait that Liu Sheng threw to him, as eagerly and helplessly as a hungry fish. Outside was bright sunshine, with a gentle Spring breeze; the magnolia flowers were out beside the road and their fine, delicate petals attracted the attention of Baorun, who had never been interested in flowers before. If he had to compliment her, hadn't he better be a bit 'flowery'? Perhaps he could compare her face to the magnolias? A brown butterfly, its wings edged with gold, fluttered amongst the flowers and swooped over his head. Baorun had never showed any interest in butterflies before, but now he suddenly discovered their beauty. The butterfly reminded him of her neck: that Spring, she had started wearing a purple plastic pendant in the shape of a butterfly around her neck. He was like a hooked fish being dragged across the water on the end of Liu Sheng's fishing-rod. His chest felt tight, and his head swam. Liu Sheng had brought his rope along, and its green and white coils swayed on his arm: a tempting white loop over a vicious green snare; a green snare over a white loop of nothingness. April was April; a season full of snares, snares formed from your desires. A Fairy Princess! A Fairy Princess! How did this all begin? When did he start thinking of her? His body had the stirrings of comprehension, but his head was completely at a loss. It was all down to the Spring, this weird, wonderful, totally extraordinary Spring.

On the lawn outside the women's section, there was a rabbit cage made of bluish wire mesh. Inside were two rabbits - one white, one grey – as delicate as finely-carved statues. They stood in a pile of cabbage leaves, shaded by a straw hat placed on top of the cage. Liu Sheng had been straight with him: it was the Fairy Princess's rabbit cage. And Baorun was quite sure that if he could see the Fairy Princess's rabbit cage, soon he would see the Fairy Princess herself.

"Just wait; she'll be down in a moment", Liu Sheng said.

Baorun squatted down and poked his index finger into the cage. The two rabbits came over to sniff at it, but they didn't like the smell, and they went back to nibbling their cabbage leaves. A sharp cry came from the direction of the staircase:

"Whose dirty hand is that? Leave my rabbits alone!"

Baorun hurriedly withdrew his finger and looked up to see the Fairy Princess come flying out of the doorway to the building, the purple plastic butterfly swinging from her neck. Oh, that lucky butterfly! It looked as though it were about to take wing. Baorun stepped to one side, to make way for the Fairy Princess, expecting her to go on scolding him. But instead, she picked up the rabbit cage and went straight over to Liu Sheng.

"I've sung your sister five lullabies, Boss, and she's gone to sleep."

The Fairy Princess smiled at Liu Sheng, and patted his jacket pocket meaningfully.

"Aren't you going to pay me today, Boss? I need the money!"

TEN
THE GARDENER'S GRANDDAUGHTER

THE OLD GARDENER was the chief architect of the Jingting Hospital's greenification project. He came from a remote mountain area, was hard of hearing, and had a strange accent. When he spoke quickly it sounded like a foreign language and people found him very hard to understand. He was quite retiring and didn't find it easy talking to strangers, tending to rely on smiles and nods when it came to the social niceties. But the trees, shrubs, plants and flowers of the hospital were used to his voice and, under its instruction, developed into a veritable national marvel. Over the years, the environment of the Jingting Hospital had undergone many changes, but no director ever had the heart to do anything to the old gardener's lodgings. Thus the gardener and his family continued to live peacefully in the galvanised iron shack under the walls of the hospital grounds. Because of its location and appearance, people wandering in the grounds often mistook this residence for a public lavatory, a fact that gives one a fair idea of its general state. The old gardener asked the hospital's publicity officer to paint a notice on the wall saying: "Defecation and urination strictly forbidden". However, the publicity officer was a man of refined sensitivities and felt that this bald prohibition lacked the civilised touch, so he took a brush and changed the sign to the more pleasing: **Plant Nursery, closed to the public**.

The old gardener's household was late coming together. It seems that he had some problem with his genitalia, and it was said that when he was a boy growing up in the countryside, he was bitten in the testicles by a wild dog. He spent half his life as a bachelor and only then did he marry a widow. She too could not have children but this did not drive a wedge between the couple. Being unable to reproduce does not mean that one is devoid of all love and compassion, and one year, the couple made a trip back to the gardener's old home in the countryside, and brought back a skinny little girl. They said she was their granddaughter. But they didn't have any children, so how could they have a granddaughter? People were loth to delve too deeply into the mystery of the girl's parentage, so they contented themselves with asking the girl's name. The old gardener hummed and hawed and then said:

"Little girls in the countryside don't really bother with things like that, so she was just called 'little girl'."

When the girl heard this, she punched the old man with her little fist:

"That's what you say!" she said angrily, and then continued defiantly: "My name is Fairy Princess! That's what I'm called, Fairy Princess!"

She said she was Fairy Princess and from then on, that's what everyone called her.

She grew up at the knees of the old gardener and his wife, almost as if she was one of the plants in the 'Plant Nursery', the only difference being that the trees, flowers and grasses had friends, and she had none. Children were in short supply in the specialised environment of the Jingting Hospital grounds and, more often than not, her only companion was her own shadow. When she wanted to have fun, she remembered quite vividly the games the country children used to play. She would draw a large hopscotch grid on the ground, squat down beside it, and impatiently stare at any passers-by, inviting them to join in the game with her. Because of her youth, she wasn't able to distinguish between the mental condition of grown-ups, and also because she treated everyone the same, it was inevitable that she would sometimes end up with a wandering patient as her play-fellow.

Most people like children, and that includes loonies. Some of the patients, when they saw Fairy Princess, felt in their pockets for sweets to give her, and if they didn't have any candy, they would give her one of their pills, to save face. Most of these pills were sedatives, pretty to look at with a pink or sky-blue sugar coating. Fairy Princess would put the pills in her mouth and suck off the sugar coating; as soon as the bitter taste of the medicine began to break through, she would neatly spit them out, and so suffer no significant effects from the medication. Once, Fairy Princess was careless and actually swallowed one of the pills. She kept on playing until the drug began to take effect, when she abandoned her playmate and gave herself over to sleep, lying down in one of the squares of the hopscotch grid, like an exhausted little dog. When her grandmother in the galvanised iron shack realised she hadn't heard any noise from her for quite a while, she went out to have a look. She saw a bespectacled patient, who at first sight seemed quite refined and respectable, but on closer inspection was grinning with teeth bared. He was hopping back and forth over Fairy Princess's prostrate body, shouting triumphantly as he did so. The grandmother broke out in a cold sweat. She picked up a bamboo pole and rushed over to beat off the attacker. Then she took Fairy Princess back into the shack.

She was too ill-educated to be able to explain the dangers a mentally-ill person posed to a young child, on top of which her head was full of superstitions; instead, she tried to scare Fairy Princess by telling her that the patients were all demons in human form, and that if she ate their sweets, and asked them to play with her, they would steal her soul. Clapping her hands and stamping her feet, she said:

"You mustn't play hopscotch with those people anymore, my little Fairy Princess. If you do, you'll lose your soul!"

Fairy Princess remembered the time she had lost that afternoon, and how the bespectacled man had danced back and forth over her body as she sank into the ground with a strange throbbing in her ears. How she had tried to push his leg away, but couldn't even raise her hands or keep her eyes open. All she could feel was her body sinking; sinking into the throbbing noise, and sinking into the land of dreams. She believed this was a sign that her soul was going to be stolen away, and she took fright. Still she was unwilling to admit her mistake, and she wailed at her grandmother:

"It's all your fault! Why do we have to live with demons? Why can't I go to kindergarten?"

"It's not that we choose to live with demons, or that we don't want to send you to kindergarten. It's your granddad's fault: he doesn't have any special skills, and all he knows how to do is look after trees and flowers. We're countryfolk, and there's nowhere else we can go apart from the Jingting Hospital."

The old gardener also felt a twinge of guilt over this affair, but he couldn't see any way of finding his granddaughter more suitable playmates. So he went to the market and bought some rabbits as companions for her. This tactic proved very effective. Fairy Princess liked the rabbits and they quickly became firm friends, meaning she no longer went out looking for people to play with. Each of the rabbits she looked after had its own name, so the first white rabbit she had was called Little White, the grey one Little Grey. Later, when she went to school, and gained some education, she felt this way of naming them was too unsophisticated, and she gave them foreign names like Mary, Lucy, Jack and William.

She grew up like a bramble thicket in the gloomy undergrowth, covered in sharp thorns from head to toe. The drugged sleep brought on by one small red pill had undermined her faith in humanity. As the only world she appreciated was to be found in a rabbit cage, and the only living creatures she valued were the rabbits, she became extraordinarily isolated and reclusive. No one came along to challenge her view of humanity, and as she got older even the innocent around her suffered from it. There was no one inside or outside the hospital who made a good impression on her, and that included the old people who had brought her up. She was arrogant and rude to everyone and, since no one understood what made her so angry, generally people left her alone.

Everyone recognised that she had a pretty face, especially when she was feeding the rabbits, with her head tilted to one side and her lips pursed like a rabbit nibbling a cabbage leaf. She retained her girlish appearance, pretty and charming. In Spring, when others were tending sheep out in the fields, she was looking after her rabbits. Baorun had seen her several times as she was hurrying with her rabbits over to a fresh patch of underbrush. She would keep watch over the cage, a book open on her knees, but not reading it. She just sat there biting her fingernails, or just staring into space. More often, she could be seen just carrying the cage to and fro around the hospital grounds, head held high and a haughty expression in her eyes. She looked like a female knight-errant guarding her precious burden as she made her way through a world of blood-sucking demons. She had a finely-featured face, the shape of a melon seed, and sparkling, jet-black, almond-shaped eyes; her features were compact and perfectly symmetrical. Her aggressiveness seemed to stem from her childlike nature and because her anger was of unknown origin, it seemed all the more unusual and all the more cutting. Her harsh gaze followed people, seeming to say: "Go away, go away! Get away from me!" There was something weirdly poetic about the figure this young girl cut and, although Baorun could not define what it was he liked about it, he knew he liked her; and because he liked her, he often thought about writing her a letter. But, because he had little education, he only ever got as far as the first line: "Dear Comrade Fairy Princess". Think as he might, he had no idea what to write next.

Once, Baorun saw her at the water boiler, fetching water, and he summoned the courage to call out a greeting to her retreating form: "Hi!"

She turned round:

"Who are you talking to? Who's Hi?"

Baorun took an involuntary step backwards:

"I was talking to you. We've met before. I've got a spare cinema ticket; do you want to go to the movies?"

At first she smiled broadly, then she turned her head away, as if to consider the situation. When she looked back, she said, now with an offended look:

"I expect you've met lots of people, your mother more often than anyone else. Why don't you invite her!"

Her rudeness was already part of her character, or habitual at any rate. Baorun didn't know how Liu Sheng had made himself into this girl's boss, and it had become something of a burning question. One to which Baorun had no answer. One day Liu Sheng came running up to the building of the men's section and shouted loudly at Baorun to come downstairs:

"I've kept my promise; I've fixed up the cinema business."

Fairy Princess had agreed to go to the cinema with him, but there were a few conditions: he had to meet her at the bus stop, three hundred metres west of the Jingting Hospital; they had to go to the Workers' Cultural Palace; they had to see a foreign romance and when the film was over, he had to take her roller-skating.

Baorun was not keen on these conditions, and muttered:

"We're going to see a film, not getting married. What's all this nonsense about?"

Liu Sheng raised his eyebrows:

"What are you calling nonsense? She's giving you a chance. She wants you to take her out and have some fun. The more fun, the better your chances, eh?"

"What chances?" Baorun asked innocently.

Liu Sheng laughed disbelievingly, and patted Baorun on the shoulder:

"Are you playing dumb with me? What chances do you want? You can make any chances you choose!"

Baorun still had one lingering reservation: the money for the roller-skating. He had been to the Worker's Cultural Palace roller-skating rink before. So, he knew that to prevent people from stealing their skates, the Worker's Palace had stringent rules requiring the payment of a hefty deposit for hiring skates. Baorun was strapped for cash, so he asked Liu Sheng:

"Do you know how much the deposit on the skates is now?"

Liu Sheng understood:

"You haven't got the money, then? Not having the balls, is a big problem, but not having the money is nothing. I'll lend it to you."

Baorun blushed in embarrassment:

"Who said I don't have the money. The money's nothing. Recently my mother has had lots of cash in her little box. If she won't give it to me, I'll take it for myself."

. . .

The weather was bad that day, the sky overcast and a light rain was falling on the suburban streets. Baorun saw Fairy Princess standing at the bus stop with a handkerchief tied on her head as a makeshift rain hat. She was wearing a white blouse with a pattern of red flowers, and a denim miniskirt. She had a huge satchel on her back, and from a distance, she looked like a schoolgirl waiting for the bus to school. Even though her clothes were quite ordinary, she looked very beautiful. It was the first time Baorun had seen her outside the hospital, and suddenly overcome by shyness, he rode his bicycle round in circles a few times on the street, before heading over to the bus stop.

"Are you going to the Workers' Cultural Palace?" he asked. "Hop aboard!"

He always remembered the haughty look she gave him.

She didn't bother to conceal her contempt for the rickety old bicycle:

"Turn up at the Worker's Cultural Palace on a wreck like that? I'd be an international laughing stock! And my arse would get shaken to bits!" She stared at Baorun as though he was cheating her somehow, and kept on berating him. "Don't you have a motorbike? And a white crash-helmet?"

Baorun was completely taken aback:

"What motorbike? What white helmet?"

"Aren't you Dr Luo's son? Well, aren't you? Where's your motorbike? Have you got a helmet or not? I want to wear the white one!"

So that was the reason for all the weird conditions. Baorun realised that Liu Sheng had played a trick on her, and even if she hadn't been taken in by it, she still had the wrong person. He was both angry and ashamed, and said, huffily, that no he wasn't Dr Luo's son, he was Dr Luo's father.

"And no, I don't have a motorbike, just this push-bike. Do you want to go to the Worker's Cultural Palace, or not? I'll count to three, and if you're not coming, you're not coming. One, two...are you listening? You'd better listen....I'll get to three in a second!"

She hesitated, gnawing on a fingernail. Then her eyes lit up as she came up with a suggestion:

"How stupid you are! If you haven't got a motorbike, you can borrow one. Run back to the hospital, there are lots of motorbikes there. There are several in the women's section: the younger brother of the patient in Bed 9 has one, and so does the husband of Bed 36. The doctors' motorbikes are the best, and Dr Luo's one is the prettiest and trendiest. It's a white Yamaha, imported. It's parked in the grounds. Do you know Dr Luo? Go and find him so you can borrow it."

"If that's what you want, Dr Luo can take you!"

Baorun gave a few furious pushes on the bike's pedals, and rode away from the bus stop. He'd gone some way when suddenly he heard a strange whooshing noise behind him. When he turned to look, he saw that Fairy Princess was running after him. She was actually running after him! She was running really fast and excitedly, puffing and blowing; the contents of her satchel were clattering around inside it, and her delicate little face was spattered with raindrops, looking as though it was surrounded by a halo of indignant anger. Her expression as she ran, was that of someone chasing a hated enemy. Non-plussed by this pursuit, Baorun slowed down, expecting to hear her telling him to wait for her. But she didn't say a word, so he had no choice but to stop:

"What do you want now?"

Before he had finished speaking, there was the same clattering noise from the big satchel as it came flying round straight at his head.

Not knowing what was inside the satchel, Baorun ducked just in time, but his left shoulder was still caught by a numbing blow. There was a clunk, which was echoed by the sound of the bicycle falling to the road. He'd never been attacked with a satchel before, and didn't know how dangerous they were, so he simply didn't know what to do. A Coca-Cola bottle full of water came flying out of the satchel. He picked it up off the ground and threw it at her. Fairy Princess had very quick reactions, and leaped to one side, dodging his return blow. With another jump, she cleared the bicycle, which then formed a natural defensive barrier for her. She stood on her side of this barrier, hands on hips, and glared at Baorun:

"Well then? Do you dare hit me? Who said you could have my bottle? Give it back!"

She understood the importance of taking the initiative, and there was an exaggeratedly vengeful expression on her face. The violent exertion had made the curves of her small, but well-formed breasts reveal themselves from under her shirt, and those curves were burning red with righteous anger. That anger seemed to have its effect on Baorun who, with unexpected obedience, returned the bottle to the satchel. But Fairy Princess was in no mood to relent:

"Come on, you cheat! Come and hit me!" She waved her finger under his nose. "I'm telling you, the person who'd dare hit me hasn't been born yet!"

There were tears gathering in the corners of her eyes, small tears but bright as crystal. Baorun was rooted to the spot. He saw the changing emotions flit across her face as the tears diluted her anger, partly aggrieved, partly resentful; her damp face took on a new, fresher appearance, with even, remarkably, a trace of sensuality. He said:

"What are you so worked up about? You hit me, I didn't hit you!"

"Not for want of trying! You are just too stupid and it serves you right!"

At this point, the first signs of a degree of balance began to show in the affair. Baorun got back on his bicycle, saying:

"OK, so it served me right. Now I'm going to settle up with Liu Sheng!"

As far as Baorun was concerned, the public carriageway had lost its identity as a road, and was a desolate spot, isolated from the rest of the world. He had been duped by Liu Sheng. Maybe the girl had been duped too. Baorun rode very slowly, trying to come up with a plan, whether to go back to the hospital, or to go to the cinema, or perhaps to go back to Red Toon Street to settle things with Liu Sheng. He had no idea; he didn't want to go to any of those places. What was going to be a great day, had crumbled away to nothing, and now he didn't know what to do with it.

He looked at the road and thought it looked more desolate than ever. The colours of Spring were hidden under dust, and even a couple of bouts of rain hadn't cleaned them off; if anything, they looked even filthier. At the nine-kilometre marker on the road, there was an old elm tree, which the crows visited every Spring. They roosted in its branches and announced the beauties of the season with harsh, ear-splitting cries. But Spring wasn't always that beautiful. Baorun remembered the first time he had hitched a lift out to the hospital to visit Grandfather. It had also been in April. As he made his way home, he had passed the nine-kilometre marker, around which he saw a crowd of people gathered, making a real racket. There was a man lying dead under the old elm tree. He always remembered the cut length of hempen rope, about a metre long, lying like a snake on the man's blue and white hospital trousers. The head of the snake pointed towards the ground, and its tail draped across the man's lower abdomen. His two feet pointed towards the road, dark grey and covered in mud, and from a distance they resembled nothing more than a couple of wild mushrooms.

Baorun's heart felt empty, and he seemed to have forgotten the young girl left on the roadside behind him. He had given up on the whole affair, when events took a turn for the better. First, he heard the clattering noise from the satchel again, and then the sound of Fairy Princess's breathing behind him. This time, he didn't turn to look, but just spat out his warning:

"If you want to kick off again, I won't be so nice this time!"

She remained as silent as before, and all he could hear was the sound of rapid breathing behind the bicycle. The back of the bike suddenly shook, and its handlebars wobbled; he realised she had climbed on board. He laughed coldly:

"So you want a ride do you? Who gave you permission to get on? Get off!"

She ignored this, and poked him hard in the back with a finger:

"I've let you off lightly, and you're still showing off? I'm saving your face just by riding your bike!"

He wasn't mollified by this, and was in no mood to accept her charity:

"Get off! Get off!" Angrily, he steadied the handlebars, and went on, tight-lipped. "I don't want any face from you! Go and ride Dr Luo's motorbike!"

"You're only making matters worse for yourself!" the voice behind him said. "Now you have to pay a forfeit, OK? And the forfeit is to take me to the Workers' Cultural Palace."

"You're joking! What forfeit?"

"What forfeit? You've been stringing me along, and you think I'm just going to take it? Anyone who messes me around has to pay the price!"

Baorun wasn't entirely clear about the difference between a forfeit and a favour, but his self-respect made him loth to accept either. He was hesitating over what to do next, when the sky suddenly darkened, threatening heavy rain. He looked up:

"It's going to rain, and Heaven seems to be on your side, so fine, yes, let's say I tricked you and be done with it."

Thus, for the first time in his life, Baorun had a girl on the back of his bicycle, and it was Fairy Princess. Sensing the change in atmospheric pressure, and perhaps the turmoil of the boy's emotions, a swarm of dragonflies flew across the road towards the bicycle, their wings brushing the two youths' heads.

"Dragonflies!" she exclaimed, pleasantly surprised.

"Yes, dragonflies!" he said, imitating her in a sing-song voice.

The imitation got an immediate response from her, and she gave him a shove.

"Funny boy! You think it's funny imitating a girl, do you? Sissy! You're disgusting!"

He didn't reply. Sometimes Baorun's silence was a product of his patience and tolerance, but sometimes it was a sign of secret pleasure. As the wind blew in off the fields, damp and heavy, he found himself surrounded by a clear but faint scent of flowers. He wasn't sure whether it was jasmine or gardenia. Several times he thought of asking her: "Is that your perfume? What perfume is it?" But in the end, he was too embarrassed. Separated as they were by only a couple of centimetres, or even a single centimetre, he could feel rays of warmth emanating from her, particularly from her shoulders, and when they accidentally touched, the warmth was transmitted directly to his back. A secret passageway straight to his core was opened up, and the tender warmth flowed along it like a river, occupying his entire being.

He greatly regretted so recklessly squandering this hard-won opportunity to talk to Fairy Princess, especially given the length of the journey. In fact, the conversation didn't start too badly. He asked:

"What's so special about a motorbike? Why are you so keen to ride one?"

He wasn't sure whether to laugh or not when she replied:

"You get to wear a helmet on a motorbike. I like wearing helmets and white ones are really smart."

He asked her how she knew Dr Liu, and she replied:

"I work for him; I take milk to his elder sister."

"How much do you earn for one bottle of milk?"

She didn't want to tell him, and changed the subject:

"I take milk to lots of the patients; I want to earn enough to buy a tape recorder."

"Why do you want a tape recorder?"

"To learn to sing." Then she added cuttingly: "Don't try and pretend you don't want one, too; you just can't afford one."

He wanted to say to her:

"Don't you patronise me. Soon we're going to rent out a room in our house, and we're going to become nouveaux riches. Forget your tape recorder, we're going to have a television."

But he found he couldn't boast about any supposed wealth to this girl, and he swallowed his words. Instead, he said:

"Alright, let's leave it that I'm too poor to afford a tape-recorder."

He knew that one of the fundamentals between boys and girls was that you had to follow the girl's logic. But there was one dumb question that he couldn't get out of his head, and it sat there flaming like a beacon. Several times he tried to put it out, but he couldn't, and finally he burst out:

"Why do you do what Liu Sheng tells you? If he tells you to go to the cinema with someone, do you just go with them?"

"He tricked me. He said you were Dr Luo's son. I've seen Dr Luo's son riding his motorbike; he's got a white helmet and black leather trousers. He looks really cool."

She may have noticed Baorun suddenly stiffen, because she hesitated a moment, then went on:

"You may not be Dr Luo's son, but you seem well-behaved enough, so that's alright. At least you're not a lout."

Baorun wasn't very happy with this character assessment, and he couldn't stop himself exclaiming:

"What do you know about it? Do you think louts have it tattooed on their foreheads? If Liu Sheng told you to go and eat shit, would you go and eat shit?"

There was dead silence for a second, then the sudden sound of a slap, as Fairy Princess hit him across the ear from behind. His face went bright red. It was too late for any explanation, and besides, he didn't even know how to explain his jealousy. Fairy Princess jumped down from the bike and spat at his back.

"Anyone who went to the pictures with you would be eating shit!"

Shouldering her satchel, she set off at a run towards the Jingting Hospital. But she hadn't yet vented enough of her anger, so she stopped and, pointing at her forehead, shouted towards Baorun:

"You should get back to the hospital as soon as you can, and get them to do a lobotomy on you. Your head's full of germs and it needs opening up so they can disinfect it and scrub it out with wire wool!"

Baorun knew he'd made a mistake, and regretted it. He really wanted to apologise but the words wouldn't come out. Other people were used to saying sorry but Baorun hadn't acquired the habit. He went after her on the bicycle and rode in a circle round her. But the words "I'm sorry" still wouldn't come out, so he rode round her again, took the two cinema tickets out of his pocket and tore one off to give to her:

"Here's your ticket. You can go or not, it's up to you."

She brushed it aside:

"Idiot! Do you think I can't afford my own cinema ticket? Fuck off!"

Baorun was left foolishly clutching the ticket, not knowing what to do next. Suddenly he realised that Fairy Princess was standing next to the nine-kilometre road marker, and a half-dried up branch of the old elm tree, which had been broken off by the wind at some point, was hanging directly over her head. A strange thought came into his head, and he folded the ticket several times, then rolled it up and put it onto the broken branch.

"Take it or not, it's your decision!" he said. "But I tell you, you shouldn't stand here. A man was hanged from this tree."

He sped off alone on the bicycle, going faster and faster, just wanting to get off that road as soon as possible. His first date, and he'd let it slip through his fingers like this. An opportunity? What opportunity? There was no opportunity left. He felt so ashamed. He went back in through the north gate of the city and stopped the bicycle under the walls inside. He caught his breath, anger still burning in his heart. It was raining heavily now. Patter! Patter! The air around the walls was permeated with the slightly acrid smell of wet dust. He had lost his purpose. Should he still go to the cinema? That was the question. He only watched two types of movie: war movies or spy movies. This Mexican film was a war movie, and it didn't have any spies; it only had two foreign actors talking about love and emotion. It would suit Fairy Princess just fine but Baorun had no interest in it at all. Patter! Patter! Patter! The rainwater was splashing down from the city walls now, falling on him as cold as shards of ice. The spot where he was standing, which would have been fine to shelter two lovers, was not good enough for him. He got back on his bicycle and looked blankly around him. Because of the rain, and because he didn't know where to go, he rode round in circles a few times at the crossroads, before heading off towards the Workers' Cultural Palace.

On rainy days, a smell of damp and mould filled the cinema; the floor was sticky and the audience sparse. A few white faces flickered through the darkness, mainly in the form of couples, but Baorun felt very much alone and isolated. Once in his allocated seat, he flipped down the seat next to him, and casually leaned his hand on it. There were some sunflower seed shells sticking out of the seat cover, and he pulled them out, one by one. The seat flipped back up by itself, as if offended by these actions and Baorun, offended in turn by its rebellion, stretched out a foot and pushed it back down so he was effectively occupying both seats.

He watched the Mexicans. The Mexican girl on the screen was dressed to the nines and heavily made-up; she was wild and bold, big-breasted with a slender waist. Her whole body radiated glamour and an alluring ripeness. The louche and elegant Mexican soldier had a dashing moustache, so dashing it had a touch of the bandit about it. The two of them were quarrelling by the waterside, and at first Baorun couldn't understand what they were arguing about, but he gradually worked it out. The couple were involved in a pure and innocent love affair, which didn't ring too true given the ages of the actors. Baorun had no problem with that, but he did find that this love story between two Mexicans was too far removed from his own experience, and so was generally baffled by the details of their affair. Yes, definitely baffled. In this state of dissatisfaction, Baorun began to doze off, surrounded by a faint scent of gardenia that wafted through the darkness. He didn't know how long he had been dozing, but he was suddenly startled awake. The film was reaching its climax on the flickering silver screen, and the Mexican woman was attacking the passionate soldier with a rock. This was provoking some tongue-clicking in the auditorium as the audience stirred. Some of them sympathised with the man:

"Aiya! That's not good! He's bleeding!"

Others attacked the woman:

"How dreadful! Why is she so vicious? It would be awful to be married to a woman like that!"

A single girl's voice was laughing and cheering the Mexican woman on:

"Good hit! Well done!"

He immediately recognised the voice as it exulted in someone else's misfortune. At some point, he didn't know when, Fairy Princess had slipped into the cinema and sat down in an isolated seat five or six rows away from Baorun. Baorun couldn't see her face clearly, only her hair as the light from the projector played on it, and her ponytail flickered like a silver flame. Baorun stood up, blocking other people's view of the screen, and a woman in the row behind remonstrated with him:

"Hey you! Don't you know how to watch a movie?"

Someone pushed him so he had to sit back down, muttering:

"Who wants to watch anyway? No, I don't know how!"

When the cinema emptied at the end of the film, it was still raining heavily. Baorun made a dash for a spot beside the door, which was the most favourable place for his purpose. This was his chance to regain his lost opportunity, and he didn't want to lose her again. As the audience came out, they temporarily had nowhere to go because of the rain, so they crowded into the vestibule to take shelter. He was shoved to and fro as he blocked the passageway, but he didn't care. In the confusion, he and Fairy Princess chanced to come face to face, him like someone who has seen the light at the end of the tunnel, her like someone trapped by an enemy on a narrow track. Baorun had a plastic rain cape in his hand, and when Fairy Princess's eye fell on it, he waved it at her, as if to say:

"I've got a rain cape! Are you coming?"

Fairy Princess looked away scornfully:

"Fuck off! Who cares about your rain cape?"

It has to be admitted that movies have an educational effect on their audience, even incomprehensible Mexican love stories. In this case it was also a stimulant, plunging Baorun into a joyful, albeit illusory, state of mind. An opportunity! Baorun recognised his last opportunity, and when he saw Fairy Princess put her satchel over her head, and run off in the direction of the roller-skating rink, the hot blood coursed through his veins. He opened out the plastic rain cape and set off in pursuit. He held up the cape, so it covered the two of them. Then Fairy Princess cried out in surprise:

"What do you think you're doing? What do you think is going on here? Who wants to share a smelly cape with you?"

"It's a big cape", he said hopefully. "Big enough for both of us. But if you're uncomfortable, I'll get out. I don't mind a bit of rain."

She took hold of one corner of the cape, and elbowed him away, as he expected. He held out against her for as long as he could, then just as he was about to extricate himself from under the cape, he heard her say:

"Alright, alright! It's raining really hard. You can stay inside."

They walked fifty or sixty metres along the road under the cape. It wasn't very far, but it hadn't been easy getting there, and Baorun didn't know how to show how much he appreciated it. Their proximity had come about rather suddenly and, perversely, seemed to have formed a kind of taboo between them; they didn't talk but just concentrated on where they were putting their feet. The further they walked, the more they kept in step with each other. The pattering of the rain on the blue plastic, created a silent world for them under the cape. A world half-enclosed, subtle and full of hidden meanings, suffused with an unidentifiable odour. Because their heads were so close together, Baorun didn't dare look at her; he even held his breath, listening to the faint noise of her own breathing, and the squelching of her chewing gum. There was a waft of invisible warmth, but Baorun's body gave a shiver, and he said:

"It's a bit cold. Are you cold?"

This was the only topic of conversation he could think of under the blue plastic canopy, but sadly it didn't work. Fairy Princess just considered this as an attempt to get fresh with her, and carefully shifted a few centimetres further away. She looked him up and down:

"A bit cold? What do you mean, a bit cold?"

There was already a crowd of people sheltering from the rain outside the doors of the roller-skating rink. Most of them looked like high school students, and one seemed to recognise Fairy Princess. When he saw the two of them emerging from under the blue rain cape, he didn't know whether to mock them or envy them. He put two fingers in his mouth and gave a piercing whistle. One of the girls said:

"Oooooh, how romantic!"

Fairy Princess blushed, squeezed the rainwater out of her ponytail, and hurried, head down, into the rink, shouting:

"Get out of the way! Get out of the way!"

The crowd opened up a path for her, leaving Baorun behind. Baorun stood on the threshold, shaking the rain off the cape, then unhurriedly folding it up.

"Has the price gone up?" he asked a boy next to him. "How much is the deposit on the skates now?"

They were the skates that the Fairy Princess had chosen for herself. Size 37 and acid green. She scrambled over to a bench, and sat down to change her shoes, in a bit of a fluster. Baorun held her street shoes for her. The shoes were open towards him, nice and warm, with traces of sweat on the white insoles. So, her feet sweated too. Then, her ankle attracted his attention as he noticed that it was decorated with a ballpoint pen drawing of a garland of flowers, with a dove on top.

"Is that the dove of peace?" Baorun asked.

She covered her ankle with her hand.

"It's just a bit of fun. Don't look at it."

She looked up, smiling, although the smile seemed a little forced. He had never seen her with such a warm expression before; it showed a rarely seen gentleness, with just a touch of the coquette. Baorun could tell she really loved roller-skating, and that it was the roller skates, not him, that had won her over.

There wasn't much evidence of workers at the roller-skating rink in the Workers' Cultural Palace, and for a long time it had been the most important meeting place for the cool young people of the area. Baorun was only 18, but he found himself feeling old and past-it in comparison to the others there. He was wearing khaki green army trousers, while the others wore blue jeans; he was wearing a big, dark-coloured overcoat, while the others sported bright-coloured, tight-fitting jackets. And it wasn't just the clothes; he found that he didn't fit in with their expressions and general behaviour either. They were happy, and he was uptight; they were carefree while he was sullen and reserved; they were bright and cheerful, and he was gloomy. He didn't know whether these young folk were all lovers, but he did know that he himself was a long way from any such state, and he didn't fit in here; he was a gate-crasher, just there to make up the numbers, and that was all there was to it.

Baorun could skate just well enough to be able to give Fairy Princess some instruction, but compared to the jumps of the other young lads, his own performance was distinctly flat. He cautiously tried a few moves of his own, so that Fairy Princess wouldn't notice his shortcomings, but mainly contented himself with acting like an instructor, leaning on the railing, and watching her, shouting instructions:

"Keep your balance! Keep your balance!"

Fairy Princess's gaily-coloured, green skates were very eye-catching, her cheeks were flushed, and her eyes sparkling with the half-nervous, half-excited look of an explorer. Her skating veered from the crude and impetuous to the hesitant and tentative. Baorun shouted at her:

"Watch your posture! You're hunched over like a prawn!"

She stopped, and grabbed hold of the rail, breathing hard.

"You're the one who looks like a prawn! Anyway, how do I know how good you actually are?" she shot back at him, her eyes sliding away from him. She wasn't very good at hiding her own thoughts, and her gaze settled on a young lad in a white hooded baseball jacket, with an expression of admiration verging on adoration.

He was a tall, slender lad, with a pair of beautiful but empty eyes. Most of the time he stood in a corner of the rink, watching. He only entered the rink himself when an expert skater appeared, and then his own skill was astonishing. Baorun recognised that this lad was king of the rink, but what he didn't notice, until too late, was the interaction between him and Fairy Princess. When did it begin? Who made the first move? Baorun remembered bending down to tighten his skates, and when he straightened up, he saw that the lad was holding Fairy Princess's hand. They began skating in sweeping S-curves, taking up more and more of the rink, and speeding up, the young lad leading Fairy Princess, until they looked like a pair of speedboats whizzing across the rink. The other skaters on the rink gave way to them, one by one. Either the lad was a good coach or the girl was a quick learner, and Baorun couldn't believe his eyes at the speed with which Fairy Princess had improved. Boldly, she spread her arms, like a bird, flashing its wings, and on one wing dangled a cheap imitation turquoise bracelet which flashed out dazzling loops of blue-green light as it was swept across the rink. In celebration of her new life on the roller-skating rink, Fairy Princess was emitting strange whoops of triumph: Ooo! Wa! Ooo! Wa!

Baorun was embarrassed. He felt as though everyone was watching him and waiting for his reaction. As a young man from Red Toon Street, he had never pretended to be a gentleman. If a boy offended him, or a girl two-timed him, he always gave as good as he got. But he wasn't in Red Toon Street now, and it wouldn't do to use force. He'd have to give a verbal warning first. Irascibly, Baorun edged his way sideways onto the rink, blocking the path of their figure-of-eights, and yelled:

"What do you think you are up to? Stop! Just stop, will you!"

His blockade proved useless, and his shout was just ignored. Displaying his skill at high speed manoeuvres, the young lad led the Fairy Princess round and past Baorun. The two youths were briefly face-to-face, and Baorun immediately recognised the other as coming from a prosperous family from the city: rich, but no balls. He had the beginnings of a moustache on his upper lip, and there were beads of sweat on the sides of his nose. His eyes were guileless, and his expression switched between bashfulness and pride. A naïve young man like him, naturally couldn't understand the rules of life on Red Toon Street, or what it meant to provoke another man. Baorun felt a little put-out, and an involuntary flash of envy coloured his forehead. He went impetuously after them, and slapped the other lad on the head.

"Where have you popped up from? Your pubes haven't even finished growing, so what do you think you're doing trying to pick up girls?"

This time, the warning had some effect, and as realisation dawned, the young lad let go of Fairy Princess's hand, and tactfully stood to one side. Baorun knew that he was asking for trouble and, sure enough, trouble arrived. There was a hush around the rink, and everyone was looking over at them. Fairy Princess's face, running with sweat, was suffused with red as she came charging over and shoved Baorun. When he didn't move, she ducked her head and butted him.

"Idiot! What do you think you are doing?" she sounded hysterical, rather than just angry. "You're really showing me up, so just fuck off! I don't even know who you are!"

Baorun felt like the host at a banquet being deserted by his guests before he could even raise the first glass. Sullenly, he took off his roller skates, and went and sat down in a corner outside the rink. He pretended to have lost interest, leaned back against the wall, closed his eyes, and feigned sleep. After a while, he realised reluctantly that Fairy Princess was completely ignoring him, and his pretence of sleeping had had absolutely no effect. He got back up, and carried his skates back over to the railing, where he stood silently watching Fairy Princess and the young lad skating round the rink. Suddenly reduced to the status of a spectator, he tried to keep his poise, and even applauded them. But even this display of sangfroid didn't attract Fairy Princess's attention. She and the young lad were holding hands again, and she seemed deliberately to flash him a look, as they skated past him looking like a regular couple; like an arrow, in fact, piercing Baorun's heart. He knew he had been stupid, and the fact that a hard-won moment of happiness had been transformed, in an instant, into burning shame, was not her fault, but entirely his. Baorun went to the lavatory, and then over to the water dispenser, where he drank several cups of water. These two activities distracted him, and his mood began to lift a little. He decided to give up, and put an end to this day of mistakes. He banged his skates on the rail, and shouted to Fairy Princess:

"The deposit. Don't forget to bring me back the deposit!"

Even if Fairy Princess heard him, she didn't take any notice. Baorun took the Coca-Cola bottle out of her satchel, and sent it flying with a kick. The plastic bottle skittered into the middle of the rink, interrupting pretty much all of the skaters, and those of them that had been directly affected by the sudden halt, stared accusingly at Baorun as he yelled: "Are you fucking deaf? The deposit! Eighty yuan! Remember to give it back." Fairy Princess glared at him from the middle of the rink, and after a couple of seconds, she pointed at him, shouting shrilly at the crowd:

"Take no notice of him! Just ignore him! He's an escaped patient from the Jingting Hospital, and he's sick in the head!"

Baorun gave a wry laugh, but didn't reply. This time he had to take the dignified option, and he left with his head held high.

ELEVEN

RECLAIMING THE DEBT

HE HAD THOUGHT she would come, but after two days there was still no sign of her.

She still had the deposit for the roller skates. He didn't know why she hadn't brought back the money, but if she didn't come, then he had an excuse to go and find her. An excuse that cost eighty yuan; maybe a lot, maybe too little, but still not enough to make it a good excuse. Fairy Princess and eighty yuan. These two things combined became a sticky problem, which put him on edge. He kept turning it over in his head until, in the end, he came up with the most self-centred solution: it all depended on her attitude; if she was nice to him, then the eighty yuan didn't matter, but if she was horrid to him, then he wanted it all back, every last cent.

He decided on a new route for Grandfather's walk, and led him to the strategic location of the Plant Nursery. He walked over to a camphor tree and tied the end of Grandfather's rope to its trunk, saying:

"You be good, and walk around here for a bit. I'm going over to the old gardener's house to see to something."

A thicket of tall castor oil plants and several sunflowers partly concealed the old gardener's shack and, perhaps deliberately effaced by Fairy Princess, all that remained of the warning sign was the word

'Public'. This gave the shack a rather mischievous air, so that it looked less like the home of an old gardener, and more like that of a fairy princess. Directly behind the shack was the perimeter wall of the Jingting Hospital, on top of which were the remnants of some barbed wire. The dawn redwoods, false acacias and gingko trees all around had grown very tall, so the roof of the galvanised iron shack looked lower and lower as time went by. The felt-covered roof had a basket of turnip shreds air-dried on it and a multi-coloured plastic windmill, sticking out at an angle from under the eaves, rotated in the wind. A patched and mended piece of calico served as a door curtain, hiding from view the householders and their jumbled odds and ends of furniture inside. There was a half-open plywood door, from behind which came the sound of an old woman constantly clearing her throat and spitting.

Fairy Princess's window was bathed in Spring sunshine. It was a somewhat unusual window, being shaped like the window on a train; one small and meanly-proportioned pane was filled with clear glass, and another was opaque with frosted glass. There was still a New Year paper-cut stuck on it at the top. An apricot-yellow sun hat hung at one side, presenting a regular semi-circular outline; there were books piled on the window sill along with a ballpoint pen, a hairband and a comb. A piled-up string of parti-coloured beads flashed with dazzling but phony light, and there was also a large IV bottle in which were stuck several pink roses with a white insole poking incongruously out from among their leaves. This small window illustrated two key facts about the young girl's life: one, she was in the prime of her life, and two, she was very disorganised.

Baorun remembered that white insole, that discarded insole which reminded him of how he too had been discarded. He was just like that insole: both of them had been trampled underfoot by her; used as she pleased and then discarded as she pleased. Anger exploded in his brain, and he swore obscenely. He jumped up onto a large overturned water butt, and shouted at the window:

"You come the fuck out of there, Fairy Princess!"

The faint sound of music from inside the room stopped completely. There was the pitter-patter of someone beyond the window running in plastic sandals, the calico door curtain was swept aside, and it was Fairy Princess's grandmother who emerged. Her white hair was disordered, she had a miserable expression on her face, and there was a herbal plaster on her temple, as she squinted to see where the noise outside was coming from. Grandfather's fame in the Jingting Hospital was such that the old woman recognised him immediately, even though he was standing quite some distance away under the camphor tree. Was he digging up his soul?

Why had he come here? She spread her hands out in front of her, and made a flapping motion, as though shooing away chicks:

"Go away! Go away! Don't come here looking for your soul. This is a plant nursery; you won't find your soul here."

Grandfather stood beside the tree, indignantly defending himself:

"I haven't been digging; I haven't done any digging for a long time. How can I be digging up your seed beds when I'm trussed up like this?"

Standing on the water butt, Baorun whistled to attract the old woman's attention:

"Hey, over here! Forget about Grandfather. I'm looking for Fairy Princess. Tell her to come out."

The old woman weighed Baorun up, taking in the angry expression on his face.

"She's not here, and even if she was, she wouldn't see a little hoodlum like you. Look at you stamping around on my water butt. Get down immediately! If you break it, you'll have to pay for it!"

Baorun got down off the butt and, without waiting to be invited, went over to Fairy Princess's window.

"Who are you calling a hoodlum? You can't go around slandering people as you please, old woman. If you do, you'll have to answer to the law."

Before he could stick his head in through the window, the old woman came after him brandishing a long bamboo broom.

"Are you trying to tell me you don't think you're a hoodlum? What do you think you're doing, sticking your head in through our girl's window? You're not a little hoodlum, you're a proper gangster!"

There was the sound of stifled laughter on the other side of the window, indicating that someone inside was finding all this rather amusing. Baorun was incensed at this, and determined to get to the bottom of it. With one leg straddling the window sill, he called out:

"Get yourself out here, Fairy Princess!"

He thought he saw her shadow on the wall but, unluckily for him, the old woman didn't let him find out for sure. She hurled herself at his other leg and held onto it, dragging him down from the window sill.

"Damn you! I know your granddad's sick in the head, but what about your mum and dad? They must be the same, not to have brought you up properly. How dreadful not to have any manners at your age!"

Baorun shook off the old woman and angrily withdrew from the window. He was not happy about being made to pull back like this. He turned back and shouted at the window:

"You owe me eighty yuan. Bring it to Ward 9 in the men's section tomorrow. If you don't, I'll start charging you one yuan interest every day!"

Fairy Princess's grandma was initially taken aback; she blinked, then after a few seconds of confusion, she regained her cool. With an angry shout, she lifted her broom and brandished it at Baorun's legs, cursing him as she did so:

"What eighty yuan? What interest? Are you trying to extort money out of us? You've got to find someone who has got money before you can do that, so what are you doing coming here? Everyone knows we haven't got two cents to rub together! Are you blind as well as stupid?"

The old woman went after him with every ounce of her strength. Even though he dodged and weaved, Baorun still received a good few fierce blows on the legs from the bamboo broom. He had always expected he would have to retreat empty-handed, but what he hadn't anticipated, despite knowing his actions in pursuit of his rights had been inappropriate, was sinking to such depths of ignominy. He made a panicky departure from the shack, as though fleeing the scene of a crime. After he'd gone some distance, he became aware of Grandfather crying out to him:

"Where are you going, Baorun? I'm still tied to the tree!"

He went back to the camphor tree and released a terrified Grandfather, muttering breathlessly as he did so:

"I'll give them a break this time, but next time will be a different story!"

The bamboo broom had left its mark on Baorun's nearly-new trousers. The most difficult to shift were some sticky little black pellets, which stuck there and wouldn't come off. At first, he didn't realise what they were but later, when he inspected them more closely, he saw that they were rabbit droppings.

His final ultimatum had absolutely no effect on Fairy Princess, and Baorun saw neither hide nor hair of her over the next few days.

He did, however, see Liu Sheng. He saw him from Grandfather's ward, as he rode his bicycle towards the women's section. To Baorun's eyes, Liu Sheng was both a sinner and a saviour; he hurled himself down the stairs but stopped when he reached the bottom. What was he going to say to him when he saw him? The affair was over: he had already pardoned Liu Sheng and he didn't yet know what he was going to do about Fairy Princess. He was a young man who liked to preserve face, and to discuss Fairy Princess with Liu Sheng would be humiliating; to have discussed the eighty yuan with him would have been petty and vulgar. The best thing he could do was keep it all to himself.

He was unsettled by all this, and his treatment of his grandfather became a lot rougher as a result. Over the next few days, when he took Grandfather out for his walk, he used the legal knot to tie him up. It was a very uncomfortable knot and it put Grandfather in a very contrary mood. Not only did he resist, he also cried out:

"I don't want the legal knot, I want the democratic knot!"

Grandfather's spirit of resistance disturbed his fellow patients on Ward 9, and they clustered round to look. They all thought the legal knot was a terrifying thing: it was used on prisoners condemned to death, and to tie his old and decrepit grandfather up with it was most unfair. Each of them made suggestions to Baorun according to their particular tastes and proclivities: some of them favoured the plum blossom knot, others proposed the pineapple knot. Still others, who thought the democratic knot was a really easy knot to tie, went over to Baorun's rope and had a go at tying Grandfather up with it themselves. It was only with some difficulty that Baorun fought them off, and then took out his anger on Grandfather, ending up by tying him down to the iron bedframe. He kicked a spittoon over to Grandfather's feet, saying:

"If you need to piss, you can piss in there. You're on your own today, I've got some shopping to do."

"What are you going to waste your money on?" Grandfather asked.

Baorun stood up straight, thought for a moment, then said:

"I'm going to buy a knife!"

As he rode over to the hospital gates, ahead of him he saw the grey ribbon of the main road stretched out desolately across the open country; there was not a car or a pedestrian in sight, only a discarded plastic bag being blown, tumbling fitfully, down the road. He suddenly felt more at a loss than that plastic bag. What kind of knife was he going to buy? Where was he going to buy it? What was he going to do with it once he had it? He really hadn't given it any thought. All he wanted to do was let off some steam. But where? That was the question. He didn't have any close friends, nor any particular hobbies and he had nowhere particular to go. He stopped beside the public information noticeboard for a while, then went on, pushing his bike and walking angrily through the Jingting Hospital grounds. He had a vague vision of a pair of green roller skates, skating along in S-shaped curves, teasing him, not to say taunting him. As he passed through a small thicket of trees, the air filled with a penetrating smell of pesticides, and he saw the old gardener. He had a spray tank on his back and was busy treating some fruit trees.

Baorun stopped his bike under a peach tree and shouted over to the old gardener. He folded his arms, and looked sidelong at the old man, weighing him up censoriously. When the old man heard the unexpected greeting, he immediately recognised Baorun, and asked:

"How come you're alone today? Where's your grandfather?"

Baorun shook his head, as much as to say he wasn't interested in talking about family matters. But the old gardener went on:

"Has your grandfather done something wrong and therefore is not allowed out today?"

Baorun snorted:

"My grandfather's offence is only a small one, there are others who have done much worse."

The old gardener didn't understand what he was obliquely referring to, and grinned, baring his yellow teeth. He offered his belated thanks to Baorun:

"Thank you, young man! Because of you and your amazing rope, your grandfather has been very quiet this year, and my trees and plants have been left in peace too. This time last year, your grandfather was digging things up all over the place, and I was rushed off my feet."

The old man's cordial greeting was taken by Baorun as evidence of a guilty conscience, and he seized the opportunity to tackle the thorny subject:

"What are you chattering about?" he asked reproachfully. "I can't make out a word you're saying. Are you trying to sweet-talk me?"

The old gardener looked at Baorun in surprise:

"You say you can't understand what I'm saying, young man. Well, I don't understand what you're going on about. What do you mean 'sweet-talk'?"

"You must know that your granddaughter owes me money. If you want your thanks to be worth more than a fart in the wind, then tell her to come and see me, and give me my money. Then it'll be me thanking you, OK?"

The old man had perhaps heard about Baorun's attempt to recover his money, and he looked at him, blinking. He took advantage of the other's outrage to find out exactly what was going on. What was going on quickly became apparent, and the old gardener showed his own hand.

"My Fairy Princess isn't very worldly. She has got her own way ever since she was little, and you'd be better off not bickering with her."

The old man fished in his trouser pocket and took out an envelope, which he opened carefully. He counted out six yuan and gave it to Baorun, saying:

"Here's six yuan. That's two yuan short; I'll be sure to give the rest to you next time."

Baorun stood rooted to the spot in amazement for at least two seconds:

"You're kidding me! You're fucking kidding me!", he kept repeating. Then he suddenly knocked the envelope out of the old man's hand, and howled:

"It's not eight yuan, it's eighty yuan! She's been lying to you!"

It was the old gardener's turn to be astounded. He couldn't seem to believe the discrepancy between the debt each party thought was owed. He stared straight at Baorun, considering for a long time, until his fear turned to outrage. A trace of disbelief still remained in his eyes, however.

"Young man, in life one must be upright in one's behaviour and conscientious in one's speech. It's me who has raised Fairy Princess, so do you think I don't know what she's like? She's never even had eight yuan to her name, and if you tried to lend her eighty, she wouldn't even dare take forty!"

Baorun's face turned bright red. Because he wanted both to get himself out of this tricky situation, and to show Fairy Princess up in her true colours, he allowed an element of personal attack to creep into his indignant assertions:

"Do you think your granddaughter really is a fairy princess? Some fairy princess! She's contemptible! She's a cheat and a swindler! What are you looking at me like that for? I never lie! Go and ask at the Workers' Cultural Palace whether the deposit on a pair of roller skates is eight yuan or eighty!"

The old gardener looked at him stonily, but there was anger flaring in his eyes:

"What do you mean 'cheat'? What do you mean 'swindler'? You should wash your mouth out, young man! I don't know anything about skates, roller or not, and I'm not going to the Workers' Cultural Palace. If I go anywhere, it'll be to the police station. I don't know what's going on between you two, or whether its eight yuan or eighty, and the only way I'm going to find out which of you is a cheat and a swindler is to go to the police station and let them sort it out!"

They were both convinced they were in the right, and the difference between them left them brimming with hostility. Thus this unlikely negotiation ended unsuccessfully, and broke up.

The old gardener, spray tank on his back, headed into the depths of the plantation as though he wanted to hide away from this shameless scoundrel. Baorun followed him in, not sure whether he wanted to continue his self-defence or keep chasing his debt. It didn't seem there was any way he was going to get his eighty yuan out of the old gardener. The old man's work clothes were salt-stained with sweat; he must have been wearing the same straw hat for at least ten years, and on its brim there was a slogan that had been popular some time ago: serve the people. When he turned to switch on the pesticide, a hole was revealed in the crotch of his trousers, through which could dimly be seen his calico underpants. His Liberation plimsolls must have been manufactured in the 1970s, and each of them had a hole in the uppers, through which a yellowish big toe protruded.

The thicket filled with the piercing acid smell of the pesticide, and a host of nameless insects fled, with a whirring noise, from the leaves and branches. Baorun held his nose with one hand, and flapped away the insects with the other. Several times he wanted to try to dispel the charged atmosphere between the two of them, but he didn't know where to begin. In the end, glancing sidelong at the treetops, he issued a vaguely-targeted threat:

"Alright, alright! You just wait!"

Aware that Baorun was tailing him, the old gardener shot him a volley of disgusted warning glances:

"What are you following me for, young man? Are you so used to tying people up, you want to tie me up as well?"

"Tie you up?" Baorun snapped back. "What would be the point of that?"

The old gardener didn't reply, but lifted his spray gun and squirted it in Baorun's direction. He took a pace forward and squirted again. The series of squirts was accompanied by meaningful glances, so it was quite clearly a warning: you've got a rope but I've got pesticide. It's poisonous, so you'd better keep a bit further away from me."

Baorun laughed coldly and, looking up at the cloud of pesticide, went over to stand under an old cypress. A bulbul came flying out of the tree, and as he watched its disappearing form, he suddenly realised that there was absolutely no point in getting mixed up with the old gardener. He stood up:

"I don't know why I'm wasting my breath on you!"

He launched a kick at the trunk of the cypress, and said:

"Go home and tell your granddaughter that we'll just wait and see who's right!"

TWELVE
HOME

NIGHT HADN'T FALLEN, but the door of Baorun's home was aglow with neon light.

Or rather, night hadn't fallen, but the outside of Master Ma's shop was aglow with neon light. This was Red Toon Street's very first up-to-date fashion shop preparing for its grand opening on May Day; decorations on the shop front were all in place, and now the lighting was being tested.

Dazzling multi-coloured lights illuminated almost half of Red Toon Street, attracting many of the local residents. An impatient relative or friend had got in early by sending a big basket of flowers, and the basket was now sitting on the threshold, encircled by thick red ribbons which read "Good Luck for the Opening. Happiness and Prosperity", in particularly eye-catching slogans. Passers-by got off their bicycles to congratulate Master Ma, and some people even interrupted their meals to hurry, bowls in hand, to stand gawping in front of the shop. The boutique's frontage was not huge, but it was the largest possible display of dazzling contemporary luxury, and might be considered a paragon of its kind. The wallpaper was gold, the floor tiles were painted silver, the screens were multi-coloured glass, the display stands were stainless steel, and the lamps were artificial crystal, hanging in clusters and emitting competing rays of dazzling light. The large quantities of clothing ordered from wholesalers in Fujian, Guangdong and Zhejiang were still in transit, and the blonde-haired, green-eyed plastic mannequins were standing amongst the flowers, waiting bare-breasted to enter the fray to realise their proprietor's dreams. As local residents emerged from the shop, their opinions were mixed. Master Ma had used his wealth so easily to rewrite the story of Red Toon Street; poverty-stricken, run-down Red Toon Street, fuddy-duddy, reactionary Red Toon Street had been thrust into the modern mainstream by Master Ma's hard work, and by Master Ma's money. Many residents whole-heartedly acclaimed Master Ma's handling of the business: How much money must you have spent, Master Ma? In just a few days, you've turned that old lunatic's room into a little Hong Kong! Others expressed their own regrets to Master Ma, saying: I was too timid, it would have been better if I'd had the courage to take the plunge and go into business like you; if I'd made a go of it, I would be opening a karaoke bar next door to you, and inviting all the neighbours to come and sing, free of charge.

Others, like Wang Deji, were less charitable in their attitude. He strolled up, hands clasped behind his back, to see what all the fuss was about. He didn't say a word of congratulation, but just looked on enviously. There was nothing to be done about that, and Master Ma didn't chase him away; but he hadn't expected Wang Deji to stay there, stuck to the wall like a house lizard, ears flapping to catch everything that was said. Master Ma gave him a bit of a nudge:

"What are you listening for, Master Wang? I'm opening a clothes shop here; it's not the Echo Wall at the Temple Of Heaven."

This stirred Wang Deji up a bit, and, pointing at the gold wallpaper, he asked, unexpectedly:

"Is the old idiot dead? Did he die at the Jingting Hospital?"

"Go and ask next door!" Master Ma replied irritably. "I'm just about to open a new business here, so would it be too much to ask for you to offer some good wishes of some kind?"

No matter whether Grandfather was dead or alive, in the hands of Master Ma, his old room had lost all connection with him. As for his current condition, there were two schools of thought on Red Toon

Street. One held that Grandfather was confined to his bed, with death imminent, and that he would never return to Red Toon Street. This version came from Baorun's mother, and became the most popular account as it spread rapidly among the neighbours to left and right. But there was another version, more of a rumour, in fact, which held that the old fool had already dug up his ancestors' bones, and recovered his soul. Every day at the Jingting Hospital, he was agitating to go home, but his relatives were preventing him from doing so. The younger generation was short of money, so had converted his old room into cash.

Baorun remained on guard at the Jingting Hospital, and was unaware of the rapid pace of change at home. On the day his father came to take over from him so he could go home, he didn't dare get off his bike when he arrived at the front door. It was as though Grandfather's room had been swallowed up by some strange monster, and disappeared from sight. The window looking out on the street and its associated wall had changed and expanded into a glistening glass sliding door, which opened onto what would be a veritable forest of clothes. A dark and decaying world had been meticulously whitewashed and given a complete makeover: it was someone else's world now. Holding his bike, Baorun stood in the doorway of his home in a daze. He thought of the fuss Grandfather had made about going home on National Day last year, and how he had promised to bring him home next Spring Festival. When Spring Festival came, Grandfather had made repeated forays down to the main gate of the Jingting Hospital, and Baorun had kept promising that they would see how he was in the Spring: if his behaviour had improved, then he would take him home on May Day. The truth of it was that, come Spring, Grandfather's behaviour was really not too bad, but the fates were against him, and once again Baorun's promises proved to be just empty words. By the time May Day approached, Grandfather's room had already been transformed into someone else's fashion boutique.

Baorun did not know the particulars of the agreement between his parents and Master Ma, so he was surprised to find that even the front door had been divided in two, with half now belonging to the boutique. Only one leaf of the black lacquered double door remained, and the area behind that had become a peculiar kind of alleyway, very dark and very narrow. Baorun carried his bike carefully along this corridor, feeling very dejected, then loudly called out his mother's name:

"Congratulations, Su Baozhen! Next year this will be a 10,000 a year household!"

The noise of a pan lid being dropped on the floor came from the kitchen, and his mother replied from beside the gas stove:

"Who are you making fun of? We're getting old and we don't have money to burn. If we're earning a little money by renting out that room, who do you think it's for? If we do manage to earn that kind of money, who do you think it's for? You had it easy growing up, young lad!"

Baorun had nothing against the way his parents had decided to make some money, but now he was confronted by the reality of it, he found the going a bit too muddy, and the whole thing rather lowly and rather sad. Now the house had been split up, it was much more cramped and unfamiliar, and the stuffy atmosphere of meanness and poverty in the room had thickened. He was beginning to detest this house: to detest the seventy-year-old furniture, the damp and discoloured walls, the dimness of the light from the 15-watt lamps, even the blue-rimmed bowl on the table. As his mother put the evening meal on the table, he looked askance at it and said:

"Even now you're rich, you're still using that lousy old bowl? Still eating stir-fried cabbage? Give me some money and I'll go and get us some spiced beef!"

His mother was not at all pleased to see him. He had taken money from her money box, and that was not something that could just be glossed over. After dinner, she asked him about the loss of the eighty yuan. Feeling guilty about the affair, he tried to make light of it:

"Let's just call it a loan, OK? It's only eighty yuan, isn't it! To look at you, you'd think the sky had fallen in!"

His mother pursued her questioning:

"You've taken up with a girl, haven't you? And you wasted the money on a date, didn't you?"

Baorun just snorted in reply, but this kind of attitude only served to make his mother more suspicious, and her interrogation became more and more intense, and more and more incisive.

"Have you been struck dumb? Where did you actually go with that much money? Gambling? Whores?"

Baorun was immediately incensed, and shouted:

"I've been looking after Grandpa every day, where could I go gambling or whoring? You've got money now, haven't you? I went for a shit and there was no paper, so I used the 80 yuan instead!"

Infuriated, his mother snatched up a scrubbing brush, and rushed at him. She rapped him smartly on the head, saying:

"I've had just about enough of you, you wretched child. You didn't grow up eating rice, you must have grown up eating shit to talk like that. You've squandered eighty yuan, God alone knows how, and you sound like you're really pissed off."

He seldom went home these days, but now he had, as usual, it turned into an annoying night. He could hear his mother in her room downstairs, cursing and reviling him but, after a while, she changed her aim and directed her scorn at how useless his father was, not even able to educate his own son; she also bemoaned the bad bloodline coming from Grandfather, setting such a poor model for future generations, and how the current three generations of menfolk were all useless, one way or another. His mother's recriminations reflected her personality, and no matter whether they were angry or sorrowful, they always had a slow tempo and a tendency to the chaotic. When she reviewed her life, she was adamant as usual that its tragedy stemmed from the time she married into this family. She had chosen both the wrong family and the wrong man, and given birth to the wrong son. When one thing went wrong, her whole life went wrong, and no matter how she strove to make things different, she was doomed to this bitter fate.

Baorun had long ago got used to his mother's all-encompassing criticism.

"You must be joking, Mother!" was his only response.

Before he went to bed, he took a pair of trousers out of his wardrobe and hung them on a chair, ready for the next day. The dirty trousers he had been wearing, he threw downstairs, but he didn't throw them hard enough and they landed at the top of the stairs. When he went to pick them up, he noticed that the legs still smelled faintly of rabbit droppings.

He felt in the pockets, and from deep inside one he pulled out two crumpled ticket stubs, one red, one blue, tightly rolled together. He carefully opened them out: Workers' Cultural Palace, Roller-Skating Rink, 4th April. These tiny characters brought back to him the damp memory of that rainy day, and as they gradually unfurled, they seemed to wink at him in the dim lamplight, perhaps just wishing him good night, or perhaps reminding him: keep us! Keep us as a souvenir.

He did indeed keep those two ticket stubs, stuffing them under his pillow.

The household's pillows were very soft and comfortable. His quilt had retained a gentle fragrance from the sunshine, and it calmed him down, and made him sleepy. The sound of his mother's grief and recrimination still floating intermittently up to the attic, underwent a change, and gradually became a lullaby, gently lulling him to sleep.

A cloud entered the attic through the small window onto the street and drifted up into the nooks and crannies of the rafters, just out of reach. Baorun recognised the cloud. Its face was the fresh, clean, pure face of a young girl smiling mischievously with a touch of arrogance. He knew that cloud's name. The air was filled with a pale blue vapour and the smell of cape jasmine. As the cloud descended, it unexpectedly displayed a pair of feet, wearing green roller skates. He stretched his arms out inquisitively but he couldn't grasp hold of the cloud. Even though he was dreaming, he seemed to know quite clearly that the cloud was the unattainable spirit of that young girl. He got out of bed to light the lamp and closed the little window, shutting the cloud outside; but the dream remained with him. In the second half of the night the dream welded itself to reality in the form of a large roller-skating rink. The rink floated, suspended in mid-air, shimmering slightly, looking like a large oval flying carpet. A crowd of unfamiliar boys stood round the edge of the carpet, like a circle of lamp posts. The lights from the lamps were very bright, and he could see Fairy Princess's green roller skates flashing out green rays as she leaped and bounded on the enormous carpet. All the others had no trouble climbing up onto the carpet, but not him. The ranks of the boys on the carpet continued to swell, surrounding Fairy Princess like stars around the moon, and following her sweeping arcs across the carpet, cheering as they went. The arcs of Fairy Princess. Arcs of happiness. He could hear Fairy Princess's exaggerated laughter and he could also faintly make out the sound of the fibres of the carpet rupturing. He wanted to jump, jump, jump – jump up and grab the carpet to pull it back down to earth, but he couldn't move his hands. He couldn't reach the carpet. He couldn't reach Fairy Princess.

As his hands grasped vainly for the edge of the carpet, they filled with anger, which coursed down to his fingertips. At first it constrained him and then it began to tantalise him. It dragged his hands down and down. A pleasant tingling settled itself in his groin, and he came uncontrollably. Such a profound dream, such an angry dream: it was inevitable that it would end in an explosion like this, with a noise like a cork popping: pffft! An eruption! He came back to his senses in the darkness, and couldn't help feeling both angry and humiliated; also a little scared. He tried to analyse what had happened with his body, and the more he did, the more puzzled he became. He had heard other boys talk about wet dreams, and they were always to do with sex; but his was different. His was to do with humiliation, and with anger, and even with sweeping arcs across the rink. And why did his body make that popping sound? It was the sound of failure, the sound of a bubble bursting. This wet dream had posed his body a riddle, a riddle to do with his soul, and he was determined to solve it through his experiences with Grandfather. Grandfather had lost his soul; it had flown out of the scar on the back of his head, which was the most common route for an escaping soul to take. But it wasn't the same for him. He suspected his soul had sunk from his head right down into his genitals. That 'pffft' noise. That was the sound of his soul shattering; he'd heard it. His soul wasn't like other people's; his was white, with a faint fishy smell. It was cunning and could change its form, morphing from liquid to solid and from solid to nothingness; it could flow, it could fly, and it could escape through his genitals. He was not the same as Grandfather. His soul had been stolen by the night. His soul had been stolen by her!

He was very tired when he got up the next day, since losing your soul during the night always leaves its mark the following morning. He went over to the attic's little window and looked down on the scene outside, seeing once again, after a long separation, Red Toon Street, stretched out in the grey morning light. A light rain was falling, and the road surface was slick with water, and glinting with circular points of light like clam shells. Pedestrians were hurrying across the road, long bodies on short legs, hurrying as urgently as if they were on fire. Only one woman, wearing a rain cape, was moving more slowly. She was using the cape to shelter the stick of incense in her hand, and calling out a name as she walked along the street:

"Xiao Mei! Xiao Mei! Come back!"

It was a mournful sound that made the hairs on the back of his neck stand up. He leaned out of the window to follow her progress, and realised it was Old Chen the accountant's wife. Her daughter, Xiao Mei, was one of the most beautiful girls on Red Toon Street, so Baorun was naturally intrigued to find out what was going on with her. He ran over to the top of the stairs and shouted down to his mother:

"What's up with Xiao Mei?"

Baorun's mother was still simmering with anger, and didn't want to talk to him:

"Don't talk to me. I don't bandy words with shit-eating little boys!"

Nonetheless, her curiosity piqued, she hurried outside to listen to what was being said on the street. When she'd caught up with the news, she went back in to tell her son:

"They're saying Xiao Mei has lost her soul. She can't speak, she can only cry. Old Chen's wife has been out trying to call back her soul for several mornings already, but it hasn't come back."

Another lost soul?

"But she's still at middle school! How can she have lost her soul?" Baorun exclaimed.

"Last year it was old people losing their souls", his mother said. "This year it's youngsters! Who can tell what that's all about! Old Chen's wife says Xiao Mei ate a rotten peach by mistake. She had the runs, and when she stood up from the chamber pot, she'd lost her soul. But that's bullshit. Which of us hasn't had the runs sometime. How can you lose your soul because you ate a rotten peach? How can you lose your soul because you've got the runs? I'm sure she's lying because she doesn't want to wash her family's dirty linen in public. Master Ma's mother says Xiao Mei's got a lover, but no one knows who it is who's knocked her up."

"So, who can it be?" Baorun persisted. "Who's knocked her up?"

"Only the devil knows." His mother broke off for a moment, and suddenly became more guarded, tapping her fingers on the staircase. "Why are you so interested anyway? Xiao Mei is underage, and it doesn't matter who it is, he's going to be shot!"

A mother is a mother after all, and when he went downstairs, he saw his breakfast already laid out on the kitchen table. He sat down and looked dazedly at the flatbreads, fried dough-sticks and soya milk. His head had been taken over by two girls, one on the left, one on the right. On the left was Xiao Mei, sitting on a chamber pot, and on the right was the Fairy Princess, standing on the roller-skating rink.

"Eat up!" his mother said. "It's all made of grain, which is man's food, and if you eat that kind of food, you have to act like a man."

He said he wasn't hungry, but his mother replied:

"Hungry or not, you've got to eat and go to school on a full stomach."

He started, as though waking from a dream, as he remembered that the reason his father had swapped places with him at the hospital was so that he could go back to classes at the cookery school. He pushed the breakfast away impatiently:

"Eat up and go and face the firing squad, is that it? I'm not eating it."

"Is that how a man should talk?" his mother said. "Is the school really like a firing squad? Not eating won't save you, you'll just get to school earlier. We've already fixed it with Headmaster Wang. You're to go to his office today, and he'll bring you up-to-date with what's going on at the school."

His long-neglected book bag was at the top of the stairs, and his snowy-white chef's hat and apron were hanging on the back of his chair. His mother had got them all ready the day before. According to his parents' plans for him, he would go back to the cookery school for a few days, pass his practical exams, and get his chef's certificate. His father said it was his future career, and his mother said it was his meal ticket. He studied his blue book bag thoughtfully, reached into it, and pulled out a recipe book with coloured illustrations. It was grease-stained and tatty, with an illustration of a dish of 'Squirrel Mandarin Fish' (a famous Jiangsu fish dish) on the front cover. Squirrel Mandarin Fish. At the school, he had been obsessed with the production of this famous dish but this morning, just the sight of the golden-hued, sticky-sauced dish made him want to vomit. He reached out and hurled the recipe book into the attic.

Taking advantage of the fact that his mother was busy in the kitchen filling a thermos flask with boiled water, he ran through the room, seized his bicycle and pushed it out into the street. Unfortunately for him, the bicycle seemed to have decided to take his mother's side, and deliberately obstructed him. He had already got on the machine when he discovered that one of the tyres was flat, and in the time it took him to go back for a pump, a matter of a couple of minutes, he was discovered. First his mother noticed that his chef's hat was still on the kitchen table, and then she saw his book bag at the bottom of the stairs. She picked the things up and chased outside after him with them, shouting:

"You really have lost your soul, haven't you! What are you doing going off to school without your book bag and your chef's hat?"

Baorun hurriedly pumped the tyre back up:

"We'll talk about school later", he said. "I'm not going there today, I'm going back to the Jingting Hospital."

"Don't you dare!" His mother flushed angrily, and laid hold of the bicycle, gritting her teeth. "I fixed it all up with Headmaster Wang. Two bottles of quality wine, and two cartons of good cigarettes – it wasn't cheap. I don't care how many times I have to tell you, you just have to muddle your way through a few days at the school, and then you'll get your chef's licence."

"Who cares about a chef's licence? It's not like it's a pilot's licence! I'm not lying to you; there's a demonstration session for the nurses today, and Hospital Director Qiao wants me to lead it. It's in Number 1 Section in the morning, and Number 2 Section in the afternoon, and they can't do without me."

His mother was astonished:

"What do you mean they can't do without you? What are you

demonstrating? What does Director Qiao actually want you to demonstrate?"

Baorun rolled up his sleeves and replied:

"What do you think I could demonstrate? Tying people up, of course!"

Suddenly everything became clear to Baorun's mother, and tears sprang to her eyes as she stamped her foot and said:

"It's all your granddad's fault! You should never have gone to the Jingting Hospital! You've lost your soul! Lost it! Lost it! Tomorrow I'm going to do the same as Xiao Mei's mother; I'm going to go out on the street to call for it!"

Mother and son stood on the street struggling over the bicycle. In the end his mother wasn't strong enough and Baorun prised open her hands. She stood there staring after the bicycle as it disappeared rapidly from view. When the neighbours came out to see what the fuss was about, they saw that Baorun had already made off, and Su Baozhen was sitting, stunned, on the front doorstep, slapping herself in the pit of her stomach to try and relieve her fury. They asked:

"What's up with Baorun?"

She raised her eyes to the heavens and, pointing upwards, said:

"He's lost his soul! It's not fair! There are only four of us in the family and we've already lost two souls!"

The neighbours pressed her about the symptoms of Baorun's loss of his soul, but she was uncomfortable, and wanted to save face, so she prevaricated, saying:

"He doesn't want to go to school, he wants to be like Lei Feng" (a Mao-era model of comradely devotion to the Communist Party and the country).

"But that's a good thing", the neighbours said. "What's that got to do with losing his soul?"

She stood up, dusting down her trousers, and said:

"Of course it's connected. When other people emulate Lei Feng, they do good works. When he does it, he ties people up!"

THIRTEEN
THE RABBIT CAGE

BAORUN WAS a real blue-eyed boy at the Jingting Hospital.

Hospital Director Qiao recognised the value of his bondage skills. That Spring, the hospital, closely following current trends, had initiated a programme of more humane treatment, with the slogan: the Jingting Hospital - a Haven of Happiness. In order to create this haven of happiness, the first thing was to take every possible measure to relieve the suffering of the patients, especially those in the acute wards, where the nurses were accustomed to using leather straps and iron fetters for restraint. They worked fast and rough, which often resulted in cuts and bruises on the patients. From morning until night, the resulting howls could be heard coming from the Category 1 patients in the grey building, and the Category 2 patients in the yellow building. Passers-by on the main road outside the hospital could hear these howls quite clearly, and this was having a very negative effect on the reputation of the hospital. After careful analysis by the hospital administration, the acute wards were earmarked for the reforms' pilot scheme, to take the lead in implementing a humane programme of painless restraint. This was why Baorun was invited, in his capacity as an outside expert, to give a practical demonstration to 30 or more male and female care workers in the grey building.

He was quite nervous in the morning but, thanks to his skill and proficiency, the nurses became, one by one, fascinated by his handiwork. He demonstrated the nine different types of knot he had created, his dexterous movements clear and fluent; most of the nurses, who were generally aware of the fundamentals of tying people up, were able during the class to master the most difficult of them all, the 'pineapple knot'. Director Qiao, who was most concerned with the feelings of the patients, asked them whether the 'pineapple knot' was painful. They were unanimous in saying that, although it did hurt a little, it was much more comfortable than the methods that had been used previously.

Baorun toiled away the whole morning and the demonstration session in the grey building was a great success. Director Qiao invited him to the small dining room for some lunch and a beer. Grandfather was fortunate enough to be asked along too. Director Qiao complimented him, praising him for his contribution as the human guinea pig for Baorun's perfection of his art. Grandfather replied modestly that it was no more than he ought to do in the service of the people.

In the afternoon, the class moved to the yellow building and the Category 2 patients. Baorun felt much more at ease and more relaxed, so was not on his guard for the unexpected. Fairy Princess was delivering milk and had somehow managed to mingle with the audience to see the fun. Baorun heard the milk bottles in her basket knock against each other, and when he turned and saw Fairy Princess, he was completely put off his stride. When their eyes met across the audience, it was like two enemies meeting on a narrow road. Her expression went from surprised to questioning, and from questioning to contemptuous, all in the space of a second. She laughed abruptly and everyone turned to look at her. Tactfully, she covered her mouth with her hand but she continued to laugh until her shoulders shook. Director Qiao went over to throw her out:

"This is a demonstration workshop. What are you laughing at? If you want to laugh, you can laugh outside and not disturb us here."

Suppressing her smile, Fairy Princess agreed:

"I won't laugh any more. If I do, it will probably prove fatal for someone."

She picked up her basket and made her way out of the crowd, then out of the ward. She stuck her head back round the door and gave vent to her feelings in a loud voice:

"Him, an expert?! And you've all come to learn from him?" She made a face at the audience of care workers, and went on: "Could you lot stoop any lower?"

Baorun stood rooted to the spot as he watched her disappear and heard the rattle of her milk bottles as she went downstairs. She was so arrogant, and her arrogance seemed to confirm his own spinelessness. He followed her out and shouted at her retreating form:

"You need to watch out for me! You just wait and see!"

But beyond this, he had no idea how else to deal with her.

After this incident, Baorun found himself in an inner turmoil, which also expressed itself in his hands. The knots he was tying on the patients lost all logic and direction. He rushed slap-dash through the rest of the demonstration and threw the rope at Director Qiao, saying:

"My hands are tired, I'm not doing any more. Today's demonstration is over."

His audience was completely taken aback as they watched Baorun stomp out of the ward. They guessed that the old gardener's daughter had spoilt his fun, but they didn't know what kind of relationship existed between the two youngsters. Director Qiao felt that he had lost a great deal of face, and shouted critically after Baorun:

"You've been very poorly brought up, young man. You're worse than Liu A-dou (a classical reference to a weak and inept figure in imperial times)!"

He turned to the others:

"Do any of you know what's going on between those two? Are they a couple?"

One of the women care workers said:

"How could they be a couple? Fairy Princess despises Baorun. Do you know what she calls him behind his back?" She giggled. "She calls him a world-class stupid cunt!"

. . .

That Spring, Baorun often used to find himself in the vicinity of the old gardener's galvanised iron shack, trying to work out the best route to bring him into contact with Fairy Princess. Sometimes he would be quite open about it, leading Grandfather along with him, at others, he would hang around, furtively, by himself.

His activity was confined to within a fifty-metre radius of the iron shack, and its main purpose was to pass apparently random messages, sometimes in chalk, sometimes in brick or coal dust, on either side of the paths that led to the shack. Grandfather thought he was writing slogans and asked him if there was some political campaign going on on the outside, and who it was directed at.

"They're not slogans, they're notifications," he replied.

"Notifications should go on a big blackboard and be hung up at the main gates. Who's going to see them if you write them in those out-of-the-way places?" Grandfather asked.

"I'm not trying to notify everyone," Baorun replied rather evasively. "Just one person."

Grandfather persisted:

"But notifications are for everyone, not just one person. Who are you trying to notify? What's it about?"

"There's no point telling you, you don't know them."

Grandfather looked in the direction of the galvanised iron shack and looked back at Baorun. His eyes suddenly lit up.

"I know who it is! What do you mean I don't know her? Your mother's been making false accusations at me; I'm not the one who has infected you. The loss of your soul isn't down to me. I can see now, it's the old gardener's granddaughter who's made off with it."

Baorun had rewritten the words of a famous poem about a revolutionary martyr on a prefabricated cement slab:

"Life is cheap and so is love; both can be discarded for money."

He was sure that this great ode would attract Fairy Princess's attention, and he was not wrong. He saw her annotation and comment.

"Idiot! It depends how much!"

He was not impressed with her frivolous answer, so he added another line in coal dust:

"It's eighty yuan, payable within three days!"

His peremptory tone provoked another ribald response:

"Too little! Urination and defecation are prohibited here!"

Given her crudeness, he responded in kind. There was no room left on the concrete slab, so he found a big old plane tree and wrote Fairy Princess's name all around the trunk, accompanied by a number of derogatory annotations, which gave him a chance to vent his resentment:

"Devil! Cheat! Slut! Hooligan! Ugly bitch!"

When he went back to see what Fairy Princess had written in reply, he discovered that his own words had been erased, and a card had been hung on one of the branches of the plane tree, on which, in a rage, she had scrawled:

"Security area; dogs and Baorun keep out!"

As their conversation arrived at this crossroads, any hint of good humour began to disappear, and it descended into more and more vitriolic personal abuse. Baorun decided it was time to go for broke and play his final card. He went to the little store in the hospital and bought a sign-writer's brush and a bottle of ink with the intention of writing his slogans directly onto the walls of the iron shack so everyone could know what she was really like.

This time he chanced actually to see Fairy Princess. She was sitting at her window and the faint sound of music was drifting out of her room. She could have been sitting, or she could have been lying down; her head and the upper half of her body were hidden behind the curtain, and all he could see was a leg resting on the table by the window, swaying to the rhythm of the music. The sun was shining on her leg, which was clothed in a fashionable pair of black leggings, slender and mysterious. Her foot was bare, and the contrast with the black of the leggings made it look even more pale and delicate. As her foot danced on the table, it seemed to be chatting with the wind, and playing with the sunbeams; her toenails were freshly painted with scarlet nail varnish, and her toes were spread, restlessly waiting for it to dry. They looked like five rose petals waving in the wind, dazzling in their brightness. Those five toes seemed to be both greeting Baorun and unnerving him. They threw him into confusion and he forgot, in an instant, why he had come there. Without thinking, he crouched down.

He didn't know why he had crouched down. Voyeurism is harmful and guilt-inducing and he felt like a wound-up alarm clock which is just about to go off when its spring snaps. Beside him was the discarded, overturned water butt, with an irregular oval hole in its base. Not sure of what to do next, he put his eye to the hole and looked inside the butt. It was dark and he couldn't see anything. He spat into the hole but there was no answering echo. There was no movement inside it, except for a large mosquito which he disturbed, and which came flying out and bit him viciously on the face. He always remembered that he didn't get cramp in his legs as he waited beside the water butt for those ten or so minutes, but that his face really hurt.

At first only the old gardener was to be seen in the small garden. In his left hand he held a bunch of garlic chives and in his right, a bunch of cabbage seedlings, and he was studying them. He shouted into the shack:

"The garlic chives are old and the cabbage seedlings are weedy. The soil here's no good; there's no nourishment in it, so the vegetables don't grow properly."

Fairy Princess's grandma drew aside the tatty calico door curtain and came out, holding a rattan clothes beater. She seemed to have heard something unusual, and she stood in the doorway, looking all round her with a gaze like an eagle. When she didn't see anything out of the ordinary at ground level, she looked up to the heavens. She gave the sun the benefit of her personal opinion:

"The soil's no good here; the people are no good here; even the sun's no good!" she said to the old gardener. "See, this sun has lost its soul; it's sickly all day, with no energy. You can't dry anything in it."

A cotton quilt was drying in the sickly sunshine; it was white with green stripes and had a bloodstain on the front, a pale red stain that was still clearly visible even though the quilt had been washed. Baorun watched the old woman walk between two clothes lines. She raised her clothes beater and began to beat the quilt, and then started to criticise her granddaughter:

"I've never seen such a lazy girl; she won't even beat a quilt. If she's this lazy at home, who's ever going to marry her? She spends all day listening to that music box of hers; it's sucked the soul right out of her body and swallowed it!"

Thud! Thud! Thud! The old woman beat a familiar scent of cape jasmine out of the quilt, mixed with the smell of cold cream and Seagull brand hair cream. He could smell it. It told him immediately that that was Fairy Princess's quilt. It was her scent.

Her scent floated tantalisingly through the air. She was just on the other side of the window, her foot so close to him. Those five toenails just on the other side of the window, so close to him. Five red petals poked out of the window, opening up towards Baorun. The two of them so close, but worlds apart. He was there, but she might as well have been on the other side of the world. It was not at all as he had anticipated: he had come for revenge, but had ended up crouching foolishly beside a water butt with a sore face. He felt a little dizzy, and his shadow seemed to cringe on the ground, thin and puny, like a miserable patch of damp. He looked up at the sky and the sun was indeed weak and sickly. He felt weak and sickly himself. And contemptible; yes, why not admit it? Contemptible! He had come seeking revenge and now here he was, staring at her window, and longing for her.

The old gardener and his wife went back into the shack, and the banging of plates and bowls could be heard coming from the kitchen. Clearly the three residents were having lunch. Baorun noticed that on his way back to the shack, the old gardener had stuffed some cabbage leaves into the rabbit cage, which was left outside. It was standing under a thicket of castor-oil plants. Its mesh was painted sky blue, and there was a heart-shaped pink plastic tag newly pinned to it. Two rabbits, one grey, one white, were soaking up the Spring sunshine. Her rabbits, her pets, her friends, and so close to him! Suddenly his head cleared; just as he was teetering on the edge of despair, a new direction opened up to him. He was going to seek justice through these two rabbits, that was his inspiration. It was the easiest of choices. He left the water butt, crept stealthily over, and made off with the rabbit cage.

The rabbits did not cry out. Unlike their sharp and unruly owner, they put up no resistance. They were meek and docile, and when their agate-coloured eyes gazed at the thief, there was no fear in them, just a trace of curiosity. As the two of them jolted along in Baorun's hands, one looked up at the sky, and one clutched a cabbage leaf to its breast, as peaceful as a pair of lovers. The cage was much cleaner than he expected; the cardboard on its bottom had just been swept clean, and the grass and cabbage leaves were fresh and plump. He sniffed the cage, and the cleanliness of the rabbits themselves also exceeded his expectations; there was no trace of the smell of droppings you normally get from small animal cages. It was only now that he took a closer look at the heart-shaped plastic tag on top of the cage. It must have been cut off a cuddly toy, and on it were printed, in flowery script, the three words: I love you.

As he scurried across the hospital gardens carrying the cage, the little plastic tag kept knocking against his knee. In the name of things plastic, it addressed the unfamiliar joint, sharing its blind and abstract sentiment: I love you! I love you! I love you!

The sky-blue rabbit cage was too conspicuous, and it seemed as though everyone in the hospital grounds recognised it as Fairy Princess's. So, in order to avoid unnecessary bother, he took off his jacket and draped it over the cage. Since he considered the rabbits to be his hostages, he needed to treat them carefully, so he set about looking for a safe place for them. He headed over into the more secluded parts of the grounds, and slipped into a small wooded grove in the northwest corner. Everyone knows that rabbits' natural habitat is woodland and grassland, but these two specimens were rather unusual since, other than eating grass, they seemed to have some other mission in life. He tried hanging the cage in the fork of a date tree and, as they hung there in mid-air, it was impossible to tell from their agate-coloured eyes whether they were happy or scared. It was Baorun himself who was uncomfortable with the arrangement, feeling that a rabbit cage wasn't the same as a bird cage, and didn't belong in the branch of a tree. He looked carefully around him, and remembered an old gingko tree, beneath which there was a disused well. He had tripped over it several times when out taking Grandfather for a walk, but it would undoubtedly prove an ideal shelter for the rabbit cage. He located the gingko tree but, to his surprise, the disused well underneath it had disappeared. As he was looking all around for it, he heard someone else's footsteps in the grove. He made as if to hide but, to his astonishment, the footsteps followed him.

"Police! Stand still!" a voice said with exaggerated authority.

Baorun started in alarm but then, thinking there was something odd about the voice, he turned round to look. It was Liu Sheng, who had followed him, spectre-like, into the grove.

"Where are you going with her rabbits? Not bad! Not bad at all!" Liu Sheng said. "Just a few days after your date, and already you're looking after her rabbits for her."

Baorun relaxed. Believing Liu Sheng was responsible for the whole affair, a stream of obscenities spurted out of his mouth, cursing Liu Sheng roundly.

Liu Sheng blinked in surprise:

"What's got into you? I played Cupid for you, and all you can do is swear at me?"

"Some shit Cupid, you were. Why don't you just fuck off!"

"I'll fuck off when you start making some sense. What did she do to piss you off? If you don't tell me, how can I sort it out for you?"

Still all fired up, Baorun turned and yelled at him:

"Don't bullshit me! What can you sort out? Go and sort out your own cock!"

With surprising self-restraint, Liu Sheng just laughed, and said:

"Sorting out my cock's no small task; it'd keep me busy most of the day!"

Baorun was too embarrassed to keep on cursing Liu Sheng. He lifted up the rabbit cage furiously, and glared at the two rabbits inside:

"You might as well know that if she hangs onto my eighty yuan, I'm going to keep her two rabbits as hostages, and she doesn't even have anything to say about it."

The whole story was too complicated to tell, and also too shaming, so the best plan was to lie. Unfortunately, Baorun was not good at lying, and couldn't get past Liu Sheng's intensive interrogation. He ended up telling the whole sorry tale of what happened at the Workers' Cultural Palace. But one person's truth often raises another's suspicions. Liu Sheng smirked as he gave Baorun a knowing look:

"I don't understand. What roller skates? What eighty yuan? Are you different from everyone else? Did you jump her? If you did, then there's nothing to be done."

Baorun knew exactly what Liu Sheng meant by 'jump'; every boy on Red Toon Street knew what jumping a girl was. He blushed furiously as he denied the charge:

"What would I be doing, jumping her? She's no great looker, so why would I bother? I didn't even hold her hand."

More disbelief. Liu Sheng looked closely at Baorun, eyes sparkling mischievously:

"You didn't even hold hands? Then why is she keeping your eighty yuan?"

Baorun had no way of proving his innocence and purity, and all he could do was swear solemnly on the lives of his entire family. In the light of this, Liu Sheng had no alternative but to believe him:

"Very well, if she's made you lose face, then I lose face too. If she's pissing around with you, then she's pissing around with me. I'll look after this affair now, and I'll take responsibility for her and for the money."

Even if Liu Sheng was rather exaggerating his capabilities, at least his attitude to Baorun became more forthright and open, and Baorun took some comfort from this. The only thing that still concerned him was Liu Sheng's relationship with the girl, so he probed Liu Sheng on this:

"So how did you come to be her boss? Do you two go out together often?"

"We've only been out a couple of times; that girl is really headstrong. Sometimes she puts on all kinds of airs and graces, and there's no doing anything with her, and sometimes she's up your arse like a bum beetle, pestering you about where you're going to take her tomorrow. She's a real pain."

"So where do you take her? Roller skating? The cinema?"

"Nah! I'm not interested in taking her anywhere like that. I take her dancing at the East Gate dance hall. We dance the 'xiaola'"

"What's that?"

The xiaola? It's the xiaola. How do you expect to pick up girls if you don't know the xiaola?"

When he saw the look of incomprehension on Baorun's face, he demonstrated a few steps:

"Have you heard of the 'sailor dance'? What about the jitterbug? The xiaola has got a bit of both in it. It's all the rage out there at the moment."

Baorun tried a few steps in imitation, but he was still doubtful:

"I don't know about all this sailor's dance, jitterbug, xiaola nonsense. You're not dancing cheek-to-cheek, are you?"

"Slow dances are slow dances, and the xiaola is the xiaola. You have to do this in the right order. First the xiaola, then the cheek-to-cheek stuff. Understand?"

Baorun considered this for a while, and began to get the idea. He asked:

"I've heard that they allow slow dances at the East Gate dance hall. Have you had a go with her there?"

Liu Sheng noticed how embarrassed Baorun looked, and chuckled. He gestured dismissively:

"I know what you really want to ask, but you need to clean up that dirty mind of yours; she's still a minor. I haven't jumped her, I swear, and you haven't either. In fact, I haven't done much better than you. She likes dancing the xiaola with me, but apart from her hand, I haven't touched her anywhere else."

Thus it seemed that some kind of understanding was established between the two of them, and with it, a bond of friendship blossomed as they looked into each other's eyes. Baorun picked up the rabbit cage and followed Liu Sheng over to the water tower.

Baorun was pleased with this perfect location Liu Sheng had chosen to keep the rabbits. The water tower, which stood on the edge of the grove, was a windowless red brick building, covered in dark green creepers. The cylindrical pump atop it looked like a giant official's hat and emitted a constant low drone of flowing water, in a practical demonstration of the profound hydraulic mystery of the siphon. Their footsteps disturbed some long-tailed creature which came darting out of the tower and disappeared swiftly into the surrounding undergrowth. Baorun thought it was a weasel but Liu Sheng insisted it was a fox.

"Do foxes eat rabbits?" Baorun asked.

"Who doesn't like rabbit?" Liu Sheng replied. "If people like it, foxes surely do. But don't worry, I know a really safe place. Just leave it to me, and it'll be fine."

The hospital had had a wrought-iron gate made for the water tower but for one reason or another it had not been installed yet, and it was just leaning in position against the door frame. It presented no barrier to access. Carrying the rabbit cage, Baorun followed Liu Sheng up the tall iron staircase all the way to the pump room at the top of the tower. The pump room was a world of its own, and far exceeded Baorun's expectations. A passageway circled the giant cistern, half of it lit, and half in darkness; there were two cigarette butts on the floor, and a tatty rolled-up straw mat was leant upright against the cistern.

"What's the straw mat doing? Who comes here to sleep?"

Liu Sheng laughed derisively:

"You really are a world-class stupid cunt! No one comes here to sleep. The only reason they slog all the way up here is to do it. You know what I mean? Do it."

Baorun looked carefully all around him, and put the rabbit cage down in the window recess, which he reckoned was the best-lit place in the pump room. The two rabbits, one grey, one white, were curled up peacefully asleep, their ears twitching slightly. Rabbits are supposed to have very acute hearing, and they were clearly picking up the drone of the pump, and also the rustling of the wind in the branches outside the tower. Baorun's hearing was also very acute, and he could just make out the sound of the two rabbits' hearts beating.

As far as the rabbits were concerned, this was perhaps the most desolate spot in the world: there was no grass, there were no people, and the only noise was that of flowing water. As Liu Sheng went down the iron stairs, Baorun picked up the few cabbage leaves scattered on the floor and put them back in the cage. He went over to the top of the stairs and turned to look back. His heart suddenly became a giant void and his head started to spin. The pink plastic tag on the rabbit cage had suddenly somehow sprung open, and a ray of soft red light pierced the darkness of the pump room, saying to him the words he longed to hear:

I love you! I love you! I love you!

I love you!

FOURTEEN

MEETING

THEY AGREED to meet at the water tower.

Baorun got there ahead of time, but someone had been there before him. There were bicycle tracks on the muddy ground and a fresh cigarette butt. He knew it must be Liu Sheng but, looking all around, he could see no sign of him. He called up to the top of the tower but, apart from the answering echo, there was no reply. Everything had been arranged by Liu Sheng but he wasn't there and Baorun's heart sank. He decided to go up and see how the rabbits were. He had taken just two steps towards the iron staircase when he heard a clang behind him. Someone had knocked over the iron gate at the entrance to the tower.

Fairy Princess had arrived.

As soon as she stepped over the iron gate, that scent of cape jasmine came drifting across. Baorun jumped involuntarily as the shaft of light flashed in from the doorway, and he instinctively hid behind a barrel of diesel. He'd never been so nervous before in his life. This moment would always stick in his mind as he watched her from the shadows. She had come, and all his worries of that whole Spring disappeared. She had come, and all the waiting of that whole Spring came to fruition. Liu Sheng had blown the bugle for the attack, and the decisive battle had begun. A cold shiver ran through his burning hot body.

She was seemingly on the alert, like an explorer. She had a flashlight in one hand, and had found a wooden stick from somewhere, which she grasped firmly in the other. She tested the situation in the water tower with the stick – tap, tap, tapping as she went - until she reached the barrel of diesel. When she saw the shape of someone hiding there, she switched on the flashlight and raised the stick up high:

"Who is it? Who's responsible? Bastard!" Her shrill voice was like a vanguard in the attack. "My rabbits? Where are my rabbits?"

Baorun's face was caught in the torchlight, dazzling him. He took a couple of steps back into the shadows, lifting his hand to protect his eyes:

"Watch where you shine that thing! Keep it out of my eyes!"

When she realised it was Baorun, her self-assurance returned:

"Is the thief afraid of the light? I'm going to shine it at you until it blinds you!" She pointed the flashlight at Baorun, following his eyes, and laughing contemptuously. "I know you did it. What kind of a man are you to do such a pointless thing? Hurry up and give me my rabbits back!"

Baorun huddled in a corner, his mind in a whirl as he strove to avoid the light from the torch.

"Give them back? Do you think you can just order me to give them back and that's it? It's not that easy!" he exclaimed. "I may not be a man, but what about you? Are you a woman? I don't think so!"

She was on a search and rescue mission for the rabbits and wasn't interested in getting into an argument with Baorun. She moved the beam from the flashlight off Baorun's face and swept it around the ground floor of the water tower a few times. She called out:

"Cinderella! Snow White! Where are you? Don't be afraid, I'm here!"

As the darkness was lifted slightly by the light of the torch, a few pieces of abandoned medical equipment were revealed, along with a pile of soil-encrusted loose concrete, but there was nothing else to be seen on the ground floor of the tower. She searched under the iron staircase and then looked upwards. She saw Baorun's two sturdy legs blocking the way on the staircase. They were like two tree trunks being used as a road block. She could read his mind, and she shouted up the staircase:

"Cinderella! Snow White! Are you up there?"

Blocking her line of sight, Baorun said:

"What Cinderella? Which Snow White? They've belong in the movies. They're not here."

She shoved him fiercely but couldn't shift him. She hit him on the knee with the flashlight:

"You've got five seconds to give me back my rabbits!"

Baorun didn't know what Liu Sheng had done to get her to come, and in his absence, the rules of the game were unclear. Baorun felt helpless, not knowing what to do to pacify her. All he had to rely on was his own simple logic: get back the money, give back the cage. Taking advantage of a moment of distraction on the part of Fairy Princess, he snatched away the flashlight with one hand, and held out the other towards her:

"What about the eighty yuan? The deposit on the roller skates. Give me back the deposit first!"

In fact, Fairy Princess had something of a guilty conscience, but she slapped Baorun's hand away, and turned away herself:

"What deposit? I don't know what you're talking about."

She ran over to the door of the water tower and stood in the sunlight, blinking her eyes. Out of habit, she put her index finger to her mouth and began biting her nail, obviously pondering what to do next. She spat out a piece of nail.

"That's not a deposit, that's your fine. Just get that clear, OK?"

"What fine?" Baorun exclaimed angrily, not understanding. "What are you fining me for?"

"On the way there, you left me on the roadside, and going home you left me at the roller-skating rink. Have you forgotten? When you were about to go, you threw a Coke bottle at me, embarrassing me in front of everyone. You hurt my feelings, and ruined my reputation, and you think I'd just forget about it?"

She glared at Baorun threateningly, and raised an eyebrow.

"An eighty yuan fine is letting you off lightly, so what money do you think I still owe you?"

She had a real way of twisting things to her own purpose, as Baorun had long since found out, and he was no match for her in bandying words. Anger built up inside him, and he made his move. Suddenly he seized her by her ponytail and yanked it fiercely, shouting:

"Do you want your rabbits back or not? If you do, you have to give me the money first. Give me eighty yuan first!"

Fairy Princess shrieked. She hadn't been prepared for Baorun's sudden violence. His grip was much too strong for her and she was forced to look up at him. At close range she could feel the full force of his anger. Fear began to show in her eyes but bravado kept the smile playing at the corners of her mouth:

"I've already spent the money. How about that!" Her tone veering between open and provocative, she continued: "I needed eighty yuan to buy a tape recorder and I bought one. So there!"

Baorun couldn't believe his ears until he suddenly remembered the music he heard coming out of the galvanised iron shack that day; it was a pop song:

"Where did you come from, my friend? Just like a butterfly floating in through my window."

He stared at her in amazement; she wasn't lying, it was the truth. She had bought a tape recorder. She treated him like dogshit, and then she used his money to buy a tape recorder.

"So you think I'm a world-class stupid cunt, do you?" Baorun yelled, and dragged her over to the door of the tower, like an eagle swooping on a chick. "Do you think you can just shit on me like this? I'm not going to let you off today. Go on, I'll go back with you to get my money. If you've got it, give it to me. If you haven't got it, I'll take the tape recorder. Or you'll pay with your life!"

"Who do you think you are? You're going to kill me just for the sake of eighty yuan? Eighty yuan's not worth a fart, and that's just what you're worth too!"

Even as she struggled, she managed to maintain her dignity and to keep a clear head in her calculations. She spat at him, then said, self-righteously:

"The tape recorder cost one hundred and fifty yuan, and you think you can have it for your eighty? Are you some kind of street thief? You want to rob me?"

Baorun wiped her spit off his face and listened, dumbly, as she put a proposition to him on the spot; a proposition that seemed both intelligent and reasonable.

"I'll let you listen to it twice or, if that's not good enough for you, five times." She sounded tentative and assertive at the same time. "Alright, alright, suppose we say ten times; that's eight yuan a go, and you'll get famous singers such as Mao Amin, Cheng Lin, Zhu Mingying, even Deng Lijun. You'll be getting a real bargain!"

Baorun was distracted as he accidentally brushed against her small firm breasts. It was like an electric shock, a hypersensitivity that ran from his hand straight to his groin with a numbing heat. He let go of her immediately. As soon as she was free, Fairy Princess went on the offensive. She brandished the wooden stick she had picked up, at Baorun:

"The man who can bully me hasn't been born yet. If you try that again, I'll beat you to death with this stick."

Clearing her way with the stick, she hurried over to the staircase, and looking up towards the top, shouted:

"Cinderella! Snow White! Don't be afraid! I'm coming!"

Fleet and graceful as a young deer, in an instant she had leapt onto the narrow staircase. Baorun's reflexes were too slow, and when he tried to grab her, his fingertips only brushed the end of her ponytail. The chase led them higher and higher, and the sound of their footsteps on the iron stairs was amplified by the circular passageway. The inside of the tower sounded as though an endless barrage of thunderbolts was ricocheting round it, making an ear-splitting din. One after the other they reached the pump room at the top of the tower, and the booming echoes began to die away, until finally there was silence. Fairy Princess bent double, trying to catch her breath. She turned her head this way and that, carefully inspecting the whole area. Stimulated by these new experiences, she alternately gasped for breath and muttered to herself:

"Shit, but this is a tall tower! And listen to that wind. Shit, I'm exhausted!"

But there was no sign of any rabbits.

Overnight, a terrible thing had happened. The circular passageway of the pump room was still half in shadow, half in light. The wire-mesh cage that had been put under the window yesterday was in darkness today. The cage was still there but someone had opened the door and the two rabbits were nowhere to be seen. Baorun stood rooted to the spot in surprise. He remembered quite clearly that he had specifically checked the door of the cage the day before, and it was securely closed. He had even used a branch from a tree as an extra bolt. Was it a weasel or a fox? He had heard that foxes and weasels were very intelligent beasts, so perhaps they could open rabbit cages. He had a vague feeling that Liu Sheng might be responsible for this strange turn of events, so he hurried over to the staircase, and shouted down:

"How have the rabbits escaped? Where are you, Liu Sheng? Liu Sheng! Come up here, quick!"

Liu Sheng wasn't at the bottom of the tower. No one knew where he had gone. According to Liu Sheng's account, the affair would definitely be settled, and then they would have some fun. The three of them would hold a dance party at the top of the tower; they would dance the xiaola. The xiaola. For the xiaola he needed Fairy Princess, and to dance he needed music. For music, he needed a tape recorder. Baorun thought he knew where Liu Sheng had gone; could it be that he had gone to borrow the tape recorder? Suddenly he felt the breeze of someone moving behind him, and Fairy Princess charged up carrying the empty cage.

"What about my rabbits?"

Her face was streaked with tears, as she swung the cage at his head:

"Where are my rabbits? If you've killed my rabbits, I'll kill you!"

The decisive battle between them entered into a phase of hand-to-hand combat, and Fairy Princess seemed already to be hysterical. It was only with considerable exertion that Baorun grabbed hold of the empty cage. Some rotten cabbage leaves and black, pellet-shaped droppings fell out onto him, and the pink plastic heart-shaped tag, on which there was a fresh red bloodstain, flashed past him: I love you. I love you. He felt a sharp pain in his right index finger and, when he looked, he saw that the wire of the cage had ripped a gash in it, and it had started to bleed.

He threw the cage to the floor, and put a foot on it:

"I didn't do it! I swear on my life." He calmly sucked the beads of blood off his finger to stop the bleeding. "It might have been a fox or a weasel that snatched them. But it's only two rabbits after all. Let's say I take responsibility; how much do you want?"

She dried her tears, and looked nervously at his bleeding finger. She took a folded paper tissue out of her pocket, fiddled with it for a few seconds, then put it back in her pocket. Perhaps she thought that giving him the tissue would be seen as a sign of reconciliation, and that would be sacrificing her dignity too easily. In an instant, her expression turned to one of delight in his discomfort, and then returned slowly to its former severity. She began biting her fingernail, her gaze shifting restlessly round the room. When it settled on Baorun, she spat out a piece of nail with a *pffft*, as a new plan of action took shape. She said:

"I don't owe you anything; you've lost Cinderella, and she's worth forty yuan; Snow White is a white rabbit and she's more expensive, she's worth fifty. So get this straight, you now owe me money. You owe me ten yuan."

Baorun stared at her, wide-eyed, and laughed coldly. He wanted to make some really biting retort, but he lacked the eloquence, and ended up just stamping his foot and saying:

"What kind of bullshit is that? Everyone's seen your rabbits; you can buy ones like that for one yuan in the market at the North Gate. They'd have to be born from pandas if you think yours are worth what you say!"

Serenely, Fairy Princess picked up the cage:

"If it's too expensive for you, then find my rabbits and give them back to me; if not, then you have to pay. Rabbits reared by me are more valuable than pandas!"

She carried the cage over to the staircase and waved it at Baorun:

"Look! You've even broken the cage. Cages cost money. That's another five yuan. Now you owe me a total of fifteen yuan!"

Her revenge was founded on mathematics and fuelled by malice; it was simple and ran deep. She turned her back on him, and he heard her mutter:

"World-class stupid cunt!"

He was not at all happy with this epithet, which was more like a curse, and although she had kept her voice low, he felt a shame and a despair he had never felt before. He needed a coil of rope. A coil of rope. He automatically looked around, but there was nothing there except the rolled-up straw mat beside the cistern. It wasn't Grandfather's ward, and there was no rope. With a sudden great stride, he reached the top of the stairs, and spread both arms out to block Fairy Princess's exit.

"You can't go. Liu Sheng isn't here, and we have to wait for him."

She looked at him coldly:

"I've done the sums, you owe me fifteen yuan. Why do we need to wait for Liu Sheng? What are you two up to?"

He hesitated for a moment:

"Nothing! Liu Sheng said we could dance the xiaola."

A suspicious look flitted across her eyes, and then gradually, she began to laugh:

"You, dance the xiaola with me? What am I? A dance-hall girl? Are you mad? Dancing with you would be like dancing with a pig!"

She had an opportunity to escape at that moment, but she was stubbornly reluctant to abandon the empty cage in her hand. And when the cage tried to help its owner by getting its broken wire mesh entangled in Baorun's clothes, that only served to delay her. Once they started to struggle, entangled as they were, there could be no doubt about the victor. With his arms round her waist, he hustled her into the pump room.

"The xiaola! We're going to dance the xiaola!" he yelled petulantly. "You're going to dance the xiaola whether you want to or not."

He got hold of her neck in order to stop her biting him, so she was forced to look up into the roof of the tower. Her face was red and swollen, and tears began to roll down her cheeks. Even so, she still managed angrily to shout out some people's names:

"Do you know Lao San at the East Gate? What about A Kuan of Pearl Alley? You'd better not get on the wrong side of me; you'll be sorry if you do. I know lots of important people. Lao San and A Kuan are my friends, and if you provoke me, you'll regret it!"

No matter how specific and convincing her threats, it was already too late, and Baorun just said through gritted teeth:

"I've done nothing to provoke you, it's you who've provoked me, and

I'm not afraid of any Lao San or A Kuan! I just want to settle matters with you today. I just want to dance the xiaola with you today."

Baorun didn't know how to start; he had never even danced before, let alone danced the xiaola. Liu Sheng had given him a vague idea about the dance steps, but he hadn't had a partner to try them out with, so how could he be expected to remember them? He dragged her hither and yon across the pump room floor, knocking over the rolled-up straw mat on the way. The mat unrolled. He had a vague image, ill-defined, of two bodies, one male, one female, naked and snowy-white, blossoming like two flowers, obscene but still somehow enchanting. Xiaola! Xiaola! The inopportune vision flustered him, and he stumbled over the mat, as he felt Fairy Princess struggling in his embrace.

"If you dare touch just one of my fingers", she shrieked, "I'll have Lao San cut off all ten of yours. If you try and take advantage of me, I'll get A Kuan to skin you alive!"

He had no desire to argue with her. He heard the wind getting up outside, and something hard clanking against the wall of the tower. He looked up and saw a chain hanging from the window latch, and dangling down the outside of the tower. A silvery light glinted off its links. He remembered that, last year, the security guards at the hospital had kept a wolf-dog tied up in the water tower, and this must be the chain that they used and then forgot about. He reached out a hand to pull up the chain, which responded as though it was a tamed beast, and came rushing up, link after clinking link, until, in the blink of an eye, it lay coiled up under the window, awaiting its new master's pleasure. He gave it an experimental shake. It was very long. He felt the links. They were damp with condensation, but supple and flexible. He gave a sigh of pleasure:

"Good! Now you'll see how I settle matters with you!"

It was only as the chain settled round her shoulders, and the ice-cold links touched her skin in their first loop, that her pride crumbled, and she began to plead with him:

"Alright, alright! Let me go! I don't want your money! Let's agree I owe you eighty yuan, OK?"

Baorun laughed coldly:

"It's too late for that. We're going to settle our account today, so nobody owes anyone anything."

Her attempts at bargaining soon became cries for help to her grandfather, to her grandmother, to Director Qiao, to Head of Security Uncle Li... but she quickly realised these cries were futile. Then she thought of Liu Sheng, and her eyes filled with tears as she stamped her feet in desperation:

"It's all your fault, you bastard Liu Sheng! Come quick! Where have you fucked off to? Come and save me!"

But Liu Sheng didn't come and save her. Liu Sheng had slunk away, and was nowhere to be found. Baorun took his cycling gloves out of his pocket, and stuffed them into her mouth.

"Don't worry, they're clean; they've just been washed." He looked her closely in the eye. "So you know what it is to be afraid, do you? Well, don't be, I'm not going to dance the xiaola with you, even if you beg me!"

He pretended to aim a slap at her face:

"Are you afraid now? It's wrong to hit a girl, so don't worry, I'm not going to hit you, I'm going to tie you up." As he spoke the words "tie you up", a look of something like pride came over his face. "If I'm not the fastest in the world at tying people up, I'm certainly the fastest in China. You just see; by the time you count to twelve, I guarantee I'll have you tied up tight."

He knew that Fairy Princess wouldn't count, so he counted himself. He wasn't making empty boasts when he said one, two; he had tried it on Grandfather: one, two, three - cross-over - four, five, six - wind about - seven, eight, nine - turn around - ten, eleven, twelve - tie the knot. This was Baorun's art in action. He had never used a dog chain before, nor had he ever tied up a fit and healthy young girl. Both the material and the subject were novel and strange, so he debated with himself which knot to use, and finally decided the 'lotus knot' was the most suitable. The 'lotus knot' was a little complicated, but he was at the height of his powers and the twelve-count would present no problem. The chain was a little heavy and a little slippery, but her blue denim jacket provided just the right amount of purchase to make things easy; it was only as his heart pounded when the chain crossed between Fairy Princess's breasts that he had some trouble. He tied the first part of the 'lotus knot' there between her breasts, and as he did so, a burning hot sensation spread from his lower abdomen, increasing as it dropped, prompting an extreme physiological reaction. This flustered him. A whole Spring's worth of longing came flooding back; a whole Spring's worth of desire, rising from darkness and returning to darkness, which he had only extricated himself from with the greatest difficulty; once again he found unexpected expression in this bondage.

Tie!

Tie her!

Tie her up!

He was taken by surprise by Fairy Princess's passivity and vulnerability. Because of her helplessness and because of the extreme constriction of her breathing, her chest was heaving violently, and this storm seemed to engulf the twin peaks of her breasts, as soft as steamed bread. A scalding white heat radiated from those peaks, burning into Baorun's eyes. One, two, three... just get to twelve. The whole mysterious world of a young girl's body was being compressed until, like a rending of heaven and earth, it culminated in a great shattering sound, piercing her skin, piercing her whole body, and reverberating around the water tower. Four, five, six... just get to twelve. The lotus flowers blossomed on her body. He could feel the cold of the chain in his hands, and also the warmth of her skin. Seven, eight, nine... just get to twelve, just get to twelve. The flowers of the 'lotus knot' opened into full bloom.

The lotus flowers blossomed in the darkness of the water tower, flashing with a distinctive silvery light. Smoothly, he tied Fairy Princess to the iron staircase and said, with an airy wave of the hand:

"You only have to wait for Liu Sheng to come and rescue you. You don't owe me any money any more; we're quits."

He heard her muffled groans and saw the fury in her eyes gradually extinguished, turning them into glowing red embers. Tears started from those embers, streaking the deathly pale of her cheeks. This was the first time Baorun had seen shame, fear and even despair in those eyes. With difficulty, she lowered her head and hit the chain round her shoulders with her chin. Her silver necklace broke, and the dark red, fake agate

beads glinted as they fell smoothly into the rabbit cage. The cage itself was already broken, and only the pink plastic tag remained undamaged, flashing out its blind and frivolous message: **I love you,**
   I love you.

Baorun ran out of the water tower, where the sunlight dazzled him. The wind was cold, but it was a gentle cold. He was exhausted, and he crouched for a moment, hands on knees, on the threshold. He was sweating profusely, and the sweat drenched his clothes, sending shivers down his back. The peach blossoms were beginning to wither in the grove opposite him, but the pear trees were in full bloom. It was still Spring. Other people's Spring was full of flowers and birdsong, but his Spring was already on the wane. The vast sky pierced his heart. He smelled his hands: usually they retained the smell of his evil actions but this time, to his surprise, they smelled good. The fresh smell of cape jasmine came from Fairy Princess, and he recognised it as the last fragrance of Spring.

He heard the sound of a bicycle bell coming from the grove of trees. Liu Sheng finally put in an appearance. He noticed that the bike was very heavily-laden, with several bulging plastic bags hanging on either side of the handlebars, which made its progress a little unsteady.

"Did you settle things with her?" Liu Sheng asked.

Baorun shook his head at first, but then nodded and stammered:

"Yes, yes, I settled things."

"How? Did you jump her?"

"Not jumped, tied", Baorun said. "I tied her up."

Liu Sheng looked towards the water tower, and there was something furtive about him as he did so. Baorun spotted some strands of white fur on his trousers, and when he went over to inspect them more closely, he saw that it was a tuft of rabbit fur. Baorun sucked in his breath and cried out in alarm:

"So it was you! What have you done with her rabbits, you bastard?"

Unconcerned, Liu Sheng smiled to himself.

"What are you yelling for? Don't shout about it! I looked up Xiao Cui over in the canteen. It takes a little while to make red-cooked rabbit."

Liu Sheng opened one of the plastic bags and took out a food container. He opened the lid.

"Look, there's two rabbits-worth in here, ready cooked." He handed the container to Baorun. "Try it! They're braised in soy sauce with fennel and Sichuan pepper. Delicious!"

Baorun felt the rich, warm scent invade his nostrils. He gave a great shiver, his head swam, and his hand gave a convulsive twitch. The food container fell to the ground, splashing sauce everywhere, and a lump of rabbit meat landed on Liu Sheng's foot.

"Watch what you're doing, you clumsy bastard!" Liu Sheng yelled. "Red-cooked rabbit's delicious! I can't believe you don't like it!"

Ashen-faced, Baorun ran pell-mell out of the grove, as though he had a demon on his heels. Liu Sheng bent down and picked up the container, shouting:

"OK, if you don't want to eat rabbit, we won't, but we've still got the dance party. Where are you going? The xiaola! I'm going to teach you the xiaola. Don't you want to learn it?"

Still running, Baorun turned his head back and spat out:

"Fuck the xiaola! What kind of a man are you, wanting to eat her rabbits? Go and eat shit!"

Scarcely drawing breath, Baorun ran out of the grove, pursued by some stones that came flying out of the trees, catching the tips of the branches and falling harmlessly at his feet. In the distance he heard Liu Sheng yelling resentfully:

"Baorun, you world-class stupid cunt, I did all this for you. What was I thinking of, trying to be your friend? From now on it's over between us!"

Baorun stood looking at the water tower in the distance. A few clouds floated insubstantially over the red tower; it showed no trace of any crime, and there was no hint of her voice. Only the sound of the wind; the wind that blew the clouds over the roof of the tower like a flock of freed rabbits. White clouds, black clouds. White rabbits, black rabbits. The flock of rabbits in the sky were nibbling grass, arranged in some mysterious formation. He felt stupid. The Spring sky was full of riddles, riddles he didn't understand. The Spring water tower was full of riddles too, riddles which he didn't understand. Then there was himself; his spirit posed many riddles which his body didn't understand. His body posed many riddles which his spirit didn't understand.

He didn't understand anything at all.

FIFTEEN
THE WHITE JEEP

According to the residents of Red Toon Street, it was ages since the white jeep was last seen. Some with good memories remembered the special letters of its registration plate: ZNZF, but didn't know what they stood for. Others, better informed, however, were able to clear up the mystery: ZNZF were the initial letters of the *pinyin* 'Zhuo Na Zui Fan' – 'Arrest of Criminals'.

With the country prospering and the people at peace, the white jeep had disappeared from Red Toon Street, which was certainly a cause for celebration. But the children of the street were of a different opinion, and when they saw the white jeep crossing the bridge, they greeted it with cries of "Here comes one! Here comes one!". They ran alongside it down the street, shouting out the name of whichever criminal first came to mind: "San Ba! Arrest San Ba!" Indeed, their cries were not without some foundation, as San Ba was not only smuggling foreign cigarettes, he was also the leader of a gang of ticket-scalpers around the railway station. All this was an open secret on Red Toon Street but the jeep drove past San Ba's cigarette shop and San Ba himself, who was standing at the counter, gnawing on a chicken leg, waved unconcernedly at it. The children were disappointed but continued to follow the jeep, and took up a new cry:

"It's Li Laosi! They're going to arrest Li Laosi!"

This time, they seemed to be right. Li Laosi was in the habit of roaming the railway yards and the abandoned factory district, armed with a hacksaw and a large pair of scissors, collecting electrical wiring and power cables. Stealing military-grade optical cable was punishable by imprisonment, but the white jeep went on past Li Laosi's doorway. His mother was sitting in the doorway washing clothes, and she asked the children:

"Whose son are they going to arrest? It's been a long time since the white jeep came by."

The children finally tired of following the jeep, and sat down together for a rest. Not knowing who was going to be arrested, they began to lay bets on who the new target might be. Each had their own favourite, and the names of many innocent residents of Red Toon Street fell from their lips. Amongst those names were Wang Deji, father and son, Pig's Head, Black Balls, Little Wuhan, even an old cadre of impeccable credentials, Lao Nian, and an example to all, Teacher Feng from the Middle School. But not one of the children mentioned Baorun. Why should they think of Baorun? Baorun was a nobody on the street at the time, and many of the children didn't even know what he looked like.

We are told that, at the time the jeep entered Red Toon Street, Baorun was watching the comings and goings outside Master Ma's fashion boutique.

A man from a decorating company was using a spray gun to paint the words 'Paris Fashion' in flowery red characters on the display window. Baorun was scrutinising the words with narrowed eyes:

"So they sell Paris fashion here? What about New York?"

And there indeed, after the words 'Paris Fashion', came 'New York Fashion', this time in blue. He applauded himself and then went and leafed through the decorator's rough sketches.

"So, 'Tokyo Fashion' next? And then Hong Kong?"

The decorator deigned to nod his assent, and asked Baorun how he had worked it out.

"I guessed," Baorun said complacently. "Anyone could do it. It's just name-dropping; international name-dropping."

Master Ma's wife Madam Ma and her daughter-in-law were sitting either side of a cardboard box, one with a skirt on her knees, the other clutching a blouse, and each holding a pair of scissors. Tchak, tchak, tchak, they were trimming the loose threads on the clothes. The daughter-in-law was expressing her displeasure at Baorun's disrespectful attitude towards the boutique:

"What does he mean 'international name-dropping'? Our shop only sells quality lines, none of the rubbish you see on the street stalls. It's all imported from Paris and New York, so why shouldn't we say 'Paris Fashion' and 'New York Fashion'?"

Madam Ma rolled her eyes at her daughter-in-law and tapped her temple, as much as to say:

"He's a few cards short of a full pack; it's not worth arguing with him."

She turned and smiled at Baorun.

"Haven't you something better to do, Baorun? Didn't your mother say you're starting work at the Municipal Committee?"

Baorun shook his head, and said, truthfully:

"No, its not the Municipal Committee; I'm going to cook at the Municipal Committee guest house."

Madam Ma said with a smile:

"It's just as good as the Municipal Committee. You'll still be cooking for the bigwigs of the committee, and that can't be bad. It's certainly going to be good for your prospects."

He didn't know how to respond to Madam Ma's well-intentioned words, and he just mumbled, gesturing at his own home:

"I don't know who I'll be cooking for. They're the ones who fixed it all up."

Madam Ma agreed:

"That's right. In your family, you look after your grandpa, and your parents look after you. How is your grandpa anyway?"

Baorun gestured dismissively:

"Same as always. He'll live a few more years; he may even go on forever."

"And what about you? How's it going over there? I've heard you've got a girlfriend over at the Jingting Hospital," she enquired eagerly.

She picked up the skirt from her knees and shook it out.

"I bet she's got a great figure. If I give you a good price, you could buy this for her."

Baorun blushed, looked hesitantly at the skirt, and said, in a rush:

"That's just a rumour someone put about. My girlfriend has flown off to the heavens."

As he stepped down from the boutique's threshold, he heard the sound of the white jeep braking sharply, and coming to a halt almost opposite the doorway to Old Sun's house. The doors opened, and three men in the uniform of the Ministry of Public Security jumped out. They ran over towards the door of the boutique, their eyes fixed on Baorun's face, at first glance seemingly benign, but ominous on closer inspection. One of them was holding a pair of handcuffs. Baorun suddenly felt uneasy; were they coming to arrest him? He gave a cry of alarm and took to his heels eastwards along the street. His headlong flight performed an elegant S-curve for about fifty metres until, unluckily, he ran slap-bang into Bao Sanda's delivery trike. Bao Sanda was not going to miss an opportunity like this.

"Where do you think you're going, criminal?" he shouted, twisting his handlebars so the trike blocked the street, and Baorun ended up on top of a pile of frozen ribbonfish. One of the Public Security men seized the opportunity to grab hold of him from behind. Enveloped in a fug of ribbonfish, Baorun heard Bao Sanda say, with evident self-satisfaction:

"I always knew this kid would come to no good. Other people kept insisting he was on the level, but just take a look now and see. He's being handcuffed and taken away!"

So, one Spring afternoon, Baorun passed by his house in handcuffs.

This was the first time in his life that, instead of doing the binding, he was the one in manacles. It was clearly an unusual experience for him; one shoulder was higher than the other and his body was twisted. He was staring at the handcuffs on his wrists, as though trying to figure out a way to escape. From time to time, two of the Public Security men shoved him in the back, and he concentrated on keeping on his feet. There were silvery ribbonfish scales on his cheeks and at the corners of his mouth, making him look both comical and pitiful at the same time.

His mother, Su Baozhen, was standing in the doorway, ashen-faced, with a bar of soap in her hand and her sleeves flecked with suds. Madam Ma and her daughter-in-law were standing behind her; Madam Ma had the air of someone who wanted to help but whose hands were tied, and the daughter-in-law looked as though everything had suddenly become clear to her. Su Baozhen didn't dare intervene with the Public Security men, and just shrilly called out Baorun's name:

"Baorun, Baorun! What have you done?"

"I haven't done anything. I just tied someone up because she'd stolen eighty yuan from me."

Su Baozhen hurled away the bar of soap and stamped her feet:

"What's all this nonsense? Explain yourself! Who exactly did you tie up? Who owed you eighty yuan?"

Baorun cleared his throat, fidgeting nervously, and said:

"It's too complicated. I can't explain."

Even if he could have found the words, Baorun didn't have time to explain to his mother. Two of the Public Security men each stretched out a hand or, more accurately speaking, stretched out a white-gloved hand, one of them covering Baorun's mouth, the other twisting his ear. The latter then clapped him twice on the shoulder. That officer must have been a Northerner, because he had a perfect Mandarin accent:

"I can see this is your first arrest, and you don't know the rules, so I'll tell you. Keep your mouth shut and only speak when you're told to. Do you understand?"

Baorun nodded his head. He looked more bashful than terrified. He didn't try to distinguish properly between the two officers' faces, but he did notice the different smells of the two pairs of gloves. One had the antiseptic smell of hand balm, and the other had the more familiar, thick smell of tobacco. They quickly covered the fifty metres of his flight, and Baorun saw the white jeep waiting for him at the side of the street. It was a far from reassuring sight, and he was quite clear about its destination.

Its destination was what the residents of Red Toon Street called 'inside'. Inside! He had never imagined that the white jeep might one day come for him, and that he was going 'inside'.

He was unceremoniously bundled into the jeep by the two officers. There was someone else already inside, sitting mute like a piece of baggage already loaded onto the jeep, and occupying much of the limited space. The broad back of this figure, and the greasy hair on the back of its head reminded him rather of Liu Sheng. When the figure turned its head, Baorun gave a shout of surprise and alarm. Liu Sheng! It really was Liu Sheng! He didn't know why Liu Sheng had been arrested before him. He wasn't clear about how serious a crime he had committed, tying someone up with a dog chain, nor did he understand why Liu Sheng was being taken 'inside'. As far as he knew, all Liu Sheng had done was to stew Fairy Princess's two rabbits in soy sauce.

Liu Sheng's hands were shackled to a stainless-steel bar and he had one knee on the floor. He was wearing a white butcher's apron, which was giving off a strong smell of fresh pork. So Liu Sheng was coming with him; the two of them were back together again. He didn't know whether to be scared or relieved. Forbidden to speak, all he could do was look enquiringly at Liu Sheng. He looked directly at him, several times, but Liu Sheng kept avoiding his gaze, looking very shifty. He noticed that Liu Sheng had been injured at some point, and had a rather ridiculous-looking piece of gauze on one ear.

They were now shackled to the same steel bar, like two close friends off to share the mysteries of life 'inside' together. As the jeep jolted along, their shoulders occasionally touched, and Baorun tried to use the contact to question Liu Sheng. But Liu Sheng's shoulder did its best to avoid contact, and the man himself seemed terrified. Liu Sheng's terror made Baorun feel he himself should try to stay optimistic. Since his shoulder had proved ineffective in communicating, he carefully stretched out a foot, and deliberately trod on Liu Sheng's toes, then lifted his foot and did it again. To his astonishment, the normally self-possessed Liu Sheng had turned pathetic in the jeep. All Baorun had done was tread on his toes twice, and he started telling tales. This was the first time he had heard Liu Sheng trying to get his tongue around Mandarin, and not very well at that. He told the Public Security officers:

"This one is a bad lot. He's stamping on my feet."

SIXTEEN

THE DETENTION CENTRE

LOTS of different places could be called 'inside', and the one Baorun was headed for was the Detention Centre in the north of the city.

It was situated behind the main building of the tannery and had once born the rather poetic name: 'The Garden of Inadvertence'. But now, all the locals had forgotten this recondite name, and just referred to it as 'behind the tannery'. As can be imagined, 'behind the tannery' had a much longer history than the tannery itself. The original owner of the garden had been an important silk merchant. He had spent eight years building this private garden, but the Liberation had come before it was finished, and he fled to Taiwan, leaving the higgledy-piggledy half-finished garden behind. It was then seized by the Department of Legal Affairs as being enemy property. From a layman's point of view, the garden was pretty enough, with linked covered walkways, and courtyards leading into one another. There was a pond in the shape of a lotus leaf, with an artificial hill of Taihu rock (rocks naturally eroded into fantastic shapes by the waters of Lake Taihu in Jiangsu Province were the most sought-after ornaments for classical Chinese gardens) beside it, and the reds and greens of plants and vegetation all around. When the wind blew, it swayed the branches of the cassia trees and bamboos of the old order, and the leaves of the plants and vegetables of the new order, in concert. Together they could be seen as moving to the rhythm of history. This beautiful scenery behind the tannery was locked away from view; this little patch of the kind of beauty usually found only in poetry and paintings was now used for the incarceration of criminals. The authorities that now owned it felt that this was a shameful waste and had hopes of developing it commercially; but the tannery in front was in the way, and any development would require its demolition. The problem there was that the tannery was a major contributor to local taxes, much more so than the detention centre, and so could not really be demolished. As a result, the two establishments, front and rear, remained as they were.

Baorun had often passed in front of the tannery but he had never thought that he would one day find himself going behind it. It was though he had taken a wrong turning in a dream and, when he woke up, he was already 'inside'. Such an abbreviated and bizarre journey was far beyond any of his thoughts and imaginings.

A step across the threshold and he was 'inside'. The weird, foetid smell of the 'inside' seemed familiar. It was the standard smell of a tannery: sweet with the taint of fish, tinged with a spicy, acrid note. It was the smell of all the animal skins mourning their lost flesh. It was the smell of a kind of grief. Since April, Baorun had had a series of recurring dreams, all of which were pervaded by this smell. Nor was it just the air; everything about the North City Detention Centre seemed familiar. When he was little, he had visited the old garden with Grandfather, so now, when he crossed through the first wide iron gateway of the Garden of Inadvertence, he guessed that they would turn to the right, and would see an old-fashioned moon gate, above which should be carved the inscription: 'A Different World'. And so it happened; his guards did indeed turn right, and he did indeed see a moon gate. Diverging, however, from his anticipation, a single-leaf square iron gate had been added to the moon gate, looking like an overelaborate picture frame. As he went through the gate he wondered about the 'different world': why wasn't the inscription there? Was it, perhaps, carved on the other side? He stole a look backwards, and almost cried out: 'A Different World'! To his amazement, there, on the other side of the moon gate, arranged in a circular frame, was the inscription he remembered. His expectation was miraculously confirmed! The Different World of the Garden of Inadvertence was there on the other side of the gate.

Now he was 'inside', he seemed suddenly to have acquired the gift of foresight; of course, it might have been coincidence, but it was enough to lift his gloom. Next came the body search. Stick out your tongue. Drop your trousers. Spread your buttocks. Unconcernedly he dropped his trousers, and when he spread his buttocks for the cavity search, he did so without the least shame or embarrassment. He was amazed at his own sense of ease with the guards. He had never been behind the tannery before; no one had told him about the complexities of the admission process, so how had he acquired this self-possession? Just for a moment, he hoped for a word of praise. He was happy with the way he was carrying himself. Outside was outside, and inside was inside, and now he was inside, he didn't feel stupid at all.

The guards led him along a long covered walkway. A ribbon of sunlight, reflected off the grey-green brick floor, shimmered in front of his feet, all the way along, like the mysterious apparition of a long-lost relative, drawing him into the depths of the detention centre. Looking to left and right, he plucked up the courage to ask one of the guards:

"Is the inscription over the next gate 'Winding Path to the Secret Garden'?"

The guard looked at him in surprise, and asked:

"Is this your second time inside? Have you been here before?"

Baorun shook his head:

"No, I'm a first-offender. It's my first time in here. I just guessed."

"I wouldn't have thought you had the brains!" the guard said, sarcastically. "Now can you guess what the inside of the Zhongnanhai in Beijing looks like too? Go on, have a go!"

Baorun didn't dare reply, and clammed up. The next gate was in the shape of a shield, and sheltered by several clumps of bamboo, but through their swaying branches, he could clearly see the inscription: Winding Path to the Secret Garden. Winding Path to the Secret Garden! His wisdom had been proved again, but his self-satisfaction was tempered somewhat when he saw two Japanese lilies in pots beside the gate. He was annoyed with himself. Why hadn't he divined their presence along with the clumps of bamboo?

A prisoner holding a broom was standing next to the gate. He looked to be in his forties, tall and thin with a hatchet face and a gold tooth. As soon as he saw Baorun, he greeted him with a familiar smile:

"Ah, you've come!"

The greeting was one of an acquaintance, and Baorun looked all round him, but couldn't see anyone else. This made him rather nervous, and he said to the guard in a loud voice:

"I don't know that man."

This time it was the guard's turn to explain:

"This is the Winding Path to the Secret Garden, isn't it? You may not know him, but he knows you. That is exactly how the winding path leads to the secret garden, and everyone like you ends up here sooner or later."

The Winding Path to the Secret Garden.

Here he was, surrounded by a load of people he didn't know.

He was assigned to the Tingfeng Pavilion, the Pavilion for Listening to the Wind. This pavilion had originally been the owner's study but had been converted into a particularly large cell; the wood lattice windows had been blocked up with concrete, and the wind could no longer be heard from inside. Instead there was only the reek of long unwashed bodies permeating the air. A fluorescent light shed a crepuscular yellow light on a sea of unfamiliar faces. The faces were all pressed against the walls so they looked like a giant relief sculpture of indeterminate theme. He looked for Liu Sheng amongst the faces; he examined each one in turn, but could find no trace of him.

"Have any of you seen Liu Sheng?" he asked. "Liu Sheng from Red Toon Street."

The existing occupants of the cell tended to be rather brusque and aggressive, and one of them taunted Baorun:

"Where's Red Toon Street when it's at home? Who's Liu Sheng anyway? What's he done that's so special? Why should we know him?"

Another, less vindictive inmate asked Baorun more kindly:

"Are you looking for someone you know? Friends are no fucking use inside. Who's going to help you inside? Dying dogs don't help dying cats. If you're looking for connections, you'd best look outside!"

He didn't know why there were so many men in the Tingfeng Pavilion. Everything was peaceful and prosperous outside, so why were there so many criminals? A little questioning uncovered the information that most of the prisoners came from Broom Alley in the south of the city, and that they were neighbours there. Not long ago, they had all come together to search for a jar full of gold, and their excavations had caused the collapse of the empty house of an absentee overseas Chinese. Someone amongst the group of neighbours had informed the police, and that's why they were there. When Baorun heard the whole story, the image of Grandfather immediately appeared in his mind's eye. He felt a sudden twinge of guilt and, embarrassed to disclose his identity, said:

"How could you be so stupid? You should have known it's just part of the same rumour from Red Toon Street where I come from. No one there has done any digging for ages, so why are you still at it?"

The men from Broom Alley were not very impressed by this.

"Your Red Toon Street is a poor place; how can you compare it to Broom Alley? Weren't you lot looking for a flashlight? How much gold can you get in a flashlight? We were looking for a jar! A whole jarful of gold buried in the ground! We used to have some really rich people living on Broom Alley: a KMT general, a capitalist textile mill owner and even a brothel owner. Any of them would have had a stash of gold! Forget the little jar we were after, there used to be a whole pickle jar; a great big pickle jar full of gold. It was buried under the cesspit of the public lavatories, but someone got there first and dug it up and made off with it!"

The curiosity of the men from Broom Alley was aroused, and they asked Baorun why he was inside. He explained:

"It was an itch; an itch I had to scratch."

"Weren't you digging too? What did you dig up?"

He shook his head:

"I wasn't digging, I was tying people up. I tied someone up."

This roused the others' interest:

"What were you doing tying someone up? What were you after? Money or sex? Was it a boss you tied up, or a pretty girl?"

Baorun didn't want to tell the whole story, so he prevaricated, saying:

"It wasn't either. I don't even know myself what I was doing tying them up."

When the others looked at him in bemusement, he gave a short laugh and said, as he picked his nose:

"If I knew, I wouldn't be here!"

Liu Sheng was never brought to the Tingfeng Pavilion. Baorun didn't know why not, and still waited anxiously for his companion. One of the men from Broom Alley saw him always standing at the door, his head pressed against the bars, looking out, and teased him:

"Is it your girlfriend? Are you panting for your girlfriend?"

"It's not my girlfriend; it's Liu Sheng I'm waiting for. I don't understand it: we were brought in in the same jeep, but I haven't seen him since, not even at exercise time. Where have they got him locked up?"

The man from Broom Alley said:

"He's probably being held in the Yellow Oriole Tower, at the back. They use the Tingfeng Pavilion here for petty offences, but the Yellow Oriole Tower for more serious cases. It doesn't look good for your friend!"

Some of the others picked up the questioning, asking Baorun:

"So, what did this Liu Sheng actually do? And why are you so worried for him? Were you in it together? Were you accomplices?"

Baorun considered this for quite a while before saying, carefully:

"No, no, it wasn't like that. I don't know what Liu Sheng did. All I did was tie someone up; I didn't do anything else."

It was about a week later that the men from Broom Alley heard a rumour that they were going to be released from the Tingfeng Pavilion. It seemed that this was the first case in judicial history anywhere in the world of the excavation of a jar of gold, and there was no statute that could be applied to it. It was proving difficult to decide what crime to charge these seventeen locals with, who were only dreaming of getting rich. Since it was tricky to bring a case against them, but equally against natural justice just to release them, the authorities fell back on the old solution of imposing a fine. News had come that the owner of the building that had collapsed was living abroad and suffering from Alzheimer's disease, and was in no position to pursue his neighbours back in his old home town. His misfortune was a blessing from heaven for the residents of Broom Alley. The main reason the case had been dragging on so long was that the different departments involved were arguing over the level of fine that should be imposed. Some said that the severity of the fine should depend on the amount an individual had dug; the more digging, the heavier the fine. The determination of the fine was to be made according to the number of tools discovered in each household, with the amount set at five hundred yuan per shovel or pick. This was clearly a meticulous and painstaking method, but it was also very labour-intensive, and it was dismissed as an option. Others advocated a simpler system, based on acknowledgement of guilt: those who feigned madness or mental incompetence, and those who tacked on fake smiles and denied any responsibility, were to be penalised harder; those who named names of others, or gave helpful information, were to be treated more leniently, and allowed to go home without penalty. On the face of it, this seemed quite fair, but it was too open to manipulation, and informers could go about digging up other people's houses with impunity. It really was not very scientific. In the end, in order to avoid any such repercussions, all the relevant departments agreed that, in the interests of egalitarianism, and treating everyone fairly, each man was fined five hundred yuan, and allowed to go free once he had paid.

Even though it smacked of going to buy wool and coming back shorn, freedom asserted its importance, and the relatives of the men from Broom Alley, swallowing any feelings of injustice, joyfully went to the bank to withdraw their savings. These they then took round to the back of the tannery and paid the authorities. Most of the seventeen men were freed immediately, and the activity in the Tingfeng Pavilion declined substantially. One of their number, a foundry worker called Xiao Wu, who had got on reasonably well with Baorun, came back to pick up some of his possessions, and went over to him. He touched the flies of Baorun's trousers, saying:

"You're quite something, aren't you! To look at you, you wouldn't know you had such an itchy cock! You say your Grandfather lost his soul, but you've certainly lost yours – through your pants!"

Baorun was baffled by this. He put his hands to his crotch, and was about to curse Xiao Wu, when his heart lurched, and he asked:

"What's going on? What have you heard?"

Xiao Wu looked at him through narrowed eyes, and backed away from Baorun, jabbing his finger at him:

"Don't play dumb with me! My cousin is second-in-command at the suburban district police station, so I know what I'm talking about. He told me you raped an underage girl. You're a rapist, and you're never getting out of here."

Baorun slowly squatted down. Xiao Wu had brought a breath of outside air into the Tingfeng Pavilion; the stench of the tannery assailed his nostrils and threaded down into his larynx, his oesophagus, his stomach, his heart and his lungs. In an instant the stench had invaded his whole body, and every breath he took was filled with it.

Then he vomited.

SEVENTEEN
THE LOTUS FRAGRANCE PAVILION

THEY CAME and took Baorun to the interrogation room.

The interrogation room was in the Lotus Fragrance Pavilion on top of the artificial hill. Previously, when he was exercising in the courtyard, he had admired the particular elegance of that hill, little thinking that he would find himself climbing its stone steps and entering that elegant scene. The Lotus Fragrance Pavilion was surrounded on all sides by strangely-shaped stalagmites and Taihu rocks, and clothed in flowers and bamboo. The bamboo filtered the sunlight into regular stripes that fell across the winding steps, as if fate had laid underfoot upright bamboo needles used to torture people in days gone by. As he climbed the steps, a pain spread from the soles of his feet all the way up to his head. Those shimmering bamboo needles of sunlight, so sharp and incisive, hinting at justice and symbolising truth, were what brought him this pain, as they guided his footsteps up towards the top of the ornamental hill.

His entire future was now at the top of that hill.

It was cold and gloomy inside the pavilion. Two interrogators, one male, one female, were sitting in front of a lattice window. The man had a face the colour of tobacco, with purple lips; in one hand he held a glass jar that had once contained pickled vegetables, which he was using as a teacup. It currently held a tawny-coloured infusion. The woman was fiddling with a ballpoint pen. Her face and her hairstyle, even her expression, were all very much like Baorun's mother, Su Baozhen. Baorun sat down and, for the first time in his life, paid attention to his manners.

"Good day, Aunty; good day, Uncle."

They ignored him. A spotlight burst onto his face, blinding him. He sat up straight. His torso remained still and upright, but he kept shifting his buttocks, first to the left and then to the right.

"Are there tin tacks on your chair?" the male officer asked sternly. "Don't you know how to sit properly?"

Baorun hesitated. He felt the seat of the chair. There weren't any tin tacks. But it was wet.

They ordered Baorun to stand up and went over to inspect the chair. It was indeed damp. The male officer considered the large wet stain, and said:

"It's not water, it's urine. Prisoner No. 8, before you, was so scared by the weight of the law, he pissed his pants."

Baorun moved behind the chair, and said humbly:

"I don't need to sit down. You sit, and I'll stand."

The male officer gave him a shove:

"Who gave you permission to stand? You'll have plenty of time to stand later, but for now it's not permitted. Hurry up and sit down."

Baorun looked at the wet patch on the chair and asked the female officer:

"Do you have a cloth, Aunty?"

Frowning slightly, the female officer replied:

"We don't provide cloths here. You'll just have to tense up your buttocks. What does it matter anyway? You can wash dirty trousers but you can't wash a dirty mind. Do you understand what I mean?"

To begin with he did what he was told, and perched on his clenched buttocks, but gradually he forgot about Prisoner No. 8's piss, and settled into the chair. Xiao Wu had been right, he certainly was in a worse spot than he could possibly have imagined.

Fairy Princess – Jingting Hospital – the water tower – Tuesday afternoon – what did you do to Fairy Princess? Their questioning was very thorough, and he had to be careful. *Rabbits – rabbit cage – stewed rabbit – I didn't eat any – it was all Liu Sheng's doing.* Their expressions were very stern, cutting into him like knives.

"If you didn't do anything, why are you here? Have we arrested the wrong person?"

He couldn't meet their gaze, and lowered his head, saying:

"All I did was tie her up. I tied her up and left."

They didn't let him lower his head and ordered him to look up. When he did so, his eyes rested on the pink collar of a sweater that was poking out from under the female officer's uniform. Once again it reminded him of his mother. She had a pink sweater just like that. The female officer said:

"Let me give you a word of advice: just tell us the truth."

She spread out a sheet of paper and read out loud. He didn't understand the medical terminology, and all he heard were the shattering words – *hymen – ruptured*. The male officer then read from another sheet of paper, which appeared to be Fairy Princess's statement. He noticed that the statement used the terminology 'violated', not 'raped', and certainly not 'jumped'. According to his understanding, 'jump' was one thing, 'rape' was another, and 'violate' yet another.

"Violate. That's not the same as rape, is it?" he asked quietly.

The male officer thought he was just playing dumb, and slammed his fist on the table.

"Don't pretend you don't know! Haven't you been to school? Violate means rape, and rape means the same as violate."

He was giddy with fear. Even though he could hardly form his words, he tried his best to make matters clear to his interrogators:

"It's all a mistake. I didn't do anything except tie her up. I'll say it in front of her," he urged them. "If she really was violated, it must have been Liu Sheng who did it. Why don't you let me confront Liu Sheng too?"

"That's not necessary", the female officer told him definitively. "The victim has already withdrawn her accusation against Liu Sheng. She's only accusing you now. You are the sole suspect in this crime."

Baorun sat rooted to his chair in shock; he gritted his teeth, and tried to contain his anger:

"What about Liu Sheng then? If I'm the suspect, then what is he?"

The male officer told him again to correct his attitude, and stop his idle chatter:

"You need proof to lay an accusation against someone else. If everyone did the same as you, and tried to find a scapegoat when they're facing the death penalty, what would happen to our interrogations? We need to eat and sleep too, you know! So if you must know, Liu Sheng was released yesterday, and he's gone home."

The news came like a bolt from the blue. He leapt from his chair but then deflated suddenly as his anger left him, and he crouched down on the floor. This was so obviously the most disastrous news he had heard in his short life. He knelt there, his hands to his ears, muttering:

"It's not fair; she's not fair; you're not fair!"

After a while, he calmed down a bit, and stared at the chair, his head in his hands. The pool of urine had dried out. Some thin sunlight pierced the lattice window of the Lotus Fragrance Pavilion, and wove a fantastical net on the seat of the chair. The male officer said:

"What are you looking at the chair for? It won't save you. Get up off the floor and sit down."

Baorun returned unwillingly to his former spot. His gaze flitted despairingly across the tobacco-coloured face of the male officer, and rested on the rose-pink sweater poking out at the woman's collar. It was such a warm and familiar colour, it suddenly broke down his resistance, and he opened his mouth and began to sob. He sounded like an aggrieved child. After sobbing for a while, he put his hand over his eyes, and made a request:

"Please, Aunty, can you call my mother here; her name is Su Baozhen."

"Why not call your father?" the woman asked. "Where is he?"

Baorun choked as he replied:

"My father's too busy, and he'd be no use anyway; he's no good with words."

After a moment, embarrassed, he stopped sobbing, pulled himself together, dried his eyes, and said, abruptly:

"History will prove me right: I didn't rape her, I just tied her up."

EIGHTEEN
RESCUE ATTEMPT

EVERYONE KNEW something had happened to Baorun.

Su Baozhen went to find Master Ma and his wife in the boutique. She hummed and hawed for a bit before asking for six months' rent in advance. Madam Ma stopped her husband from giving an immediate reply, and asked what the money might be for. Su Baozhen just managed to say "My son" before her tears choked her, and she buried her face in her hands. Madam Ma guessed that she wanted to go and get her son out of gaol, and that took money, and could turn into a bottomless pit. Madam Ma was a shrewd but warm-hearted character, and she came to an intelligent decision that both protected her own interests and, at the same time, demonstrated her humanity. She started by saying that they hadn't chosen well with the site for the boutique, business wasn't good, and they might not still be there in six months' time. In these circumstances, she couldn't justify paying rent in advance, but she could give it as a loan, as an emergency measure. Su Baozhen nodded her agreement through her tears:

"I don't care whether it's payment in advance or a loan. I've never asked anyone for money before in my life, but we are in dire straits, and only money can save Baorun now."

A few days later, Baorun's father came back to the Ma's and gave back the envelope of money untouched, saying that it was no use for the moment, and that having responsibility for someone else's money was stopping himself and his wife from sleeping. Master Ma was puzzled:

"Aren't you going to rescue Baorun?"

Baorun's father hung his head in shame:

"How could I not want to rescue my own flesh and blood? But it's too late; no matter how much money we have, it's too late."

"Are you saying that the girl's family won't take the money?" Master Ma asked.

"It's not that they don't like the idea of money, they just don't want our money."

Master Ma was even more puzzled:

"How odd! Don't you use *renminbi* like the rest of us?"

Baorun's father could hardly bring himself to tell the truth but shamefacedly he mumbled it to Master Ma:

"It's because I'm useless, and don't have the connections. Liu Sheng's family got in there first, and they've already settled things. The girl's family have rolled up their bedding and gone, leaving no trace."

Baorun's parents complained persistently about the injustice to their son but, in the end, it was just one family's voice, and there was no reason for anyone else to take their side. Their neighbours on either side certainly had their reservations. Some didn't have a good opinion at all of Baorun, and gave no credence to the idea that there might have been a miscarriage of justice. They said, in private, that his poor parents would complain of unfairness even if their son was a highwayman or a murderer. The people from the cookery school paid a visit to discuss Baorun's future at the school, but found no one there. His parents had left early that morning, locking up their front door with three iron padlocks. Even in the depths of their woes, these honest people still followed the rules, and they had remembered that it was the time when both the water company and the electricity company required meter readings. So, before they left, Su Baozhen had chalked two neat rows of numbers on the front door, recording the two readings: Electricity: 1797, Water: 0285. Some ill-educated and unruly child, just to cause mischief, had snuck in and written the word 'rape' in front of the electricity reading, so that it now read:

This month: Rapes: 1797. All the passers-by noticed the writing on the door and most of them just shook their heads but all the children guffawed. Fortunately, Madam Ma quickly noticed what was going on, and performed a good deed by rubbing out the offending word with a cloth.

When the neighbours all crowded into the Ma family's boutique, it was not to look at the latest fashions but to find out about Baorun's case. Madam Ma rebuked them:

"We haven't been able to drag you in here before but now here you all are, not because we've been able to drum up a bit of enthusiasm for the shop, but because you want to wallow in Baorun's notoriety."

Fortunately, a fire burns out without fuel; Su Baozhen didn't reveal any more details about developments in the case, and Madam Ma had no new clues to work with. All she could say was:

"It won't be long; the truth will come out in the end."

The neighbours all developed their own theories, enthusiastically analysing Baorun's prospects, but since each followed their own opinion, no one managed to sway anyone else. Finally, someone brought up the subject of Grandfather:

"Aiya! What's going to happen to the old fool? If there's no one to look after him, isn't he going to start excavating again?"

The neighbours temporarily forgot about Baorun, and turned their attention to Grandfather.

Grandma Shaoxing said that, the year before, she had done Grandfather a favour, and hidden an iron shovel behind her back door. It had only been there for three days, but this year there was always a strange noise coming from behind her door - *kerchunk, kerchunk* - particularly in the small hours, and it was keeping her awake. She pointed to the pupils of her eyes, and said:

"Just look at the circles under my eyes! Blacker than a crow! I haven't been able to shut my eyes for three nights! How could I? As soon as I go to sleep, I see Baorun's Grandfather in a dream, reaching out a hand, asking for his shovel: 'My shovel, who's taken my shovel?' I think he's haunting my dreams, and only dead people come to you in dreams. Do you think Baorun's grandfather has passed away? Now there's no one from his family to look after him, how do we know he hasn't become a wandering spirit?"

No one dared lightly dismiss the possibility of Grandfather's death, but they all certainly felt that, whether he himself was dead or alive, his lost soul was certainly wandering the precincts of Red Toon Street. As to what form this lost soul had taken, whether it was hiding in the shovel or somewhere else, everyone had their own opinion. The textile factory worker, Aunty Sun, said that every day, as she was coming back from her night shift, as soon as her bicycle got close to her home, a white cat was sure to jump from the roof of Baorun's house onto the eaves of her own, yowling as it went. By the time she took out her key, the cat would be sitting beside her front door. Aunty Sun said:

"How scary is that? That cat is all skin and bone, with miserable eyes, just like Baorun's grandfather's eyes! I try and shoo it away, but it just sits there and won't budge. But when I say to it: 'Get back to the Jingting Hospital, Baorun's Grandfather, and stop fooling around here, your room is gone!' Aiya! You won't believe me when I tell you, that cat gave a great 'miaow' and ran off."

Her audience was not sure whether or not Aunty Sun was deliberately embellishing her story, but they all looked at her wide-eyed, and gave varying volumes of gasps of amazement. Grandma Shaoxing said, in summary, that cats have nine lives, and that to give one of them to Grandfather was an act of great compassion. The heated discussion continued until someone suddenly noticed the embarrassment that the subject of Grandfather was causing Madam Ma; glances were exchanged, and everyone fell silent whilst continuing to look surreptitiously at her. Madam Ma said:

"There's no point in you lot looking at me like that; I know what you're all thinking. You think the *fengshui* for my business here is no good, don't you?"

She adopted a haughty attitude and said with an unruffled, knowing smile:

"I'm telling you, you lot don't understand what a serious subject *fengshui* is. If your own energy is in good order, then the *fengshui* will be with you, and bad *fengshui* can be changed to good. But if your energy is out of kilter, you just have to go with it, and even then your good *fengshui* can turn bad. Do you think I don't know that the old fool's room has bad energy? So why did I dare to open my business here? I consulted Fortune teller Xu, so I know exactly how things stand, and good will always triumph over evil.

Her female neighbours still only half-understood what she was saying, and Aunty Sun gave voice to their main suspicion:

"Madam Ma, how do you know that your energy is in good order? How do you know that good will always triumph over evil?"

Madam Ma hesitated for a moment, then loosened her collar to reveal a shiny gold chain:

"You have to spend some money, and buy some gold if you want to get your energy in good order." She showed off the length and thickness of the chain to her neighbours. "I listened to what Fortune teller Xu Banxian told me, and I bought this chain to wear. It weighs 2.3 *taels*. Fortune teller Xu said that if the gold weighs more than 2 *taels*, it will disperse evil energy. It really works too. You lot are all seeing ghosts, but I'm completely untroubled by them. I haven't seen any ghosts, but business is not so good, and that's what's worrying me."

The neighbours all gathered round to admire the chain, wondering at its quality and involuntarily giving in to envy.

Only that damned Madam Ma could afford such a thick chain, they thought. We'd never be so lucky.

Granny Shaoxing wanted to touch the chain but, somehow or other, found Madam Ma's arm in the way, and she pulled her hand back when she found it grasping empty air. She turned and stomped out of the boutique, muttering:

"They always say you can do anything if you've got money, but who actually believes a gold chain can scare away ghosts? There are good ghosts and evil ghosts, and Baorun's grandfather's ghost would be a kind one, even if he has departed to the underworld. If you ever do bump into a bad ghost, you'll find out that you can forget about any gold chain; even if you're wearing gold from top to toe, it won't do any good.

Anyway, you're only a woman, how could you possibly see off an evil ghost?"

On the eve of Labour Day on May 1st, the grey of the street was leavened by a little more colour and a little more liveliness than usual. Along the street, a scattering of flowers had opened just in time. There were canna flowers and cockscomb flowers decorating the corners, and although most of the roses were stuck in cracked basins or old cooking pots, they still struggled valiantly to put forth their pink and yellow blooms. The sky was sparkling blue, as though freshly painted. The wind was soft on the face, a gentle spring zephyr, as children are taught to say in their essays. The hustle and bustle on the ground was mirrored by the activity in the sky. Schools, shops, factories and even the recycling centre all had banners with slogans celebrating the festival. A great hill of rubbish at the loading dock was being cleared away, and nearby there was the thud of heavy objects falling to the ground, as though the celebratory cannon salute had been set off early. On the south side of the street, the electrician from the chemical factory was perched up a ladder, adjusting the multi-coloured lights over the factory portico. Below him, a crowd of children had gathered round, shouting shrilly:

"They're lit! They're all lit!"

A festival is a festival, after all, and Red Toon Street pulsated with the rhythms of celebration. But there was one middle-aged woman whose face was full of sorrow, and her extreme sorrow marked her apart on the street, as though she were in her own private desert. She was clutching a sodden handkerchief in her hand and trembled as she walked. She neither saw the traffic or the passers-by, nor heard the horns of the cars or the bells of the bicycles. From time to time, a cyclist would berate her, or even stick out a hand and shove her out of the way, shouting:

"Hey old lady, has no one taught you how to walk along a street?"

And when they looked back, what they saw was a tear-streaked face with bags under its eyes the size of walnuts. She would look up to the sky, and ask:

"What's the time, Comrade?"

And the cyclist would immediately make allowances for this poor old lady; in such a state, how could she be expected to follow the rules of the road?

Ever since her son met with his misfortune, Su Baozhen was seldom seen on the street in daylight. Even though little more than half a month had passed, her previously pretty and delicate features had aged, and there were strands of grey in her hair, as though the dust of her troubles had well and truly settled on her. Her tears were only faint sobs and weren't intended to attract sympathy from any one. Most of the inhabitants of Red Toon Street knew who she was and wanted to comfort her but Su Baozhen was unreceptive and allowed no one to encroach on her sorrow. Even as she sobbed, she asked:

"Is someone crying? Am I crying? What is there to cry about?"

As she passed the loading dock one day, she came to a sudden halt. She had seen an enemy. Her swollen and red-rimmed eyes seemed to give off an intense radiance, and she stopped crying. On the open space of the dock was gathered a group of enthusiastic amateur performers, mostly women from all walks of life from Red Toon Street. Ordinary women, neither fat nor thin, tall nor short, dressed the same and of similar physique. Each held a large rose-red fan, and they were performing a group rehearsal under the direction of Aunty Dai from the neighbourhood committee. One *haha*, two *haha*, three *haha*. A dozen or so red fans wave in unison, as their ranks change formation like a well-ordered wave. No one expected Su Baozhen to rush into the dance and seize the megaphone in Aunty Dai's hand. She blew into it, then burst out:

"Neighbours! Let me tell you about the injustice done to my son Baorun; the monstrous injustice! Baorun didn't do anything bad; he was framed and made a scapegoat!"

This threw the troupe into disarray. Su Baozhen's voice was so hoarse with anger that she choked on her emotions and was unable to say anything more. Aunty Dai tried to snatch back the megaphone, but was unceremoniously pushed away by Su Baozhen, who said:

"Calm down, Aunty Dai, and let me collect myself. I just have one thing to say, and then I'll go."

She did, indeed, calm down a little, but she found she actually had rather more to say. Looking at her expression, everyone quickly saw that she had a particular axe to grind and that her gaze was flashing like a dagger straight at Shao Lanying as she stood in the middle of the troupe.

"Liu Sheng's mother, I want to tell you about it first. My son is going to prison for twelve years at the very least, maybe for life. Are you and your family happy? Are you happy?"

Everyone gasped and turned to look at Shao Lanying. Shao Lanying was a woman of the world and wasn't panicked by this awkward situation. Unhurriedly, she closed the fan she was holding and said, evenly:

"Baorun's mother, where did you get these ideas from? I don't have any quarrel with you. I am your son's senior in age, so why should I take any pleasure in his going to gaol?"

"I really admire the way you can still play the innocent! Your own son has committed a dreadful crime but it doesn't matter because someone else's son is going to goal for him. Why shouldn't you be happy?" Su Baozhen's grief-stricken voice and heavy breathing were amplified by the megaphone until they became almost deafening. "My Baorun is just Liu Sheng's scapegoat. Other people may not know what's going on, but you do, don't you! Do you still say you're not happy about it? If you're not happy, what are you doing singing and dancing away here? Aren't you afraid you'll put your back out, twisting away like that?"

"What's it got to do with you how I dance? Don't think you represent the Party Committee just because you've got a megaphone. What's the use of you shouting out random accusations?" Shao Lanying's face was full of anger and hatred, but she kept her voice slow and reasonable. "Baorun's mother, I know you're a reasonable person, so why are you acting so unreasonably now? It's not up to you or me to say who goes to prison and who goes free; that girl is the one who suffered and it's up to her, isn't it?"

These words hit their target and the megaphone fell silent for a moment. But then Su Baozhen's strident tones burst out again:

"It doesn't matter what anyone says, it's money that talks and back-room deals. Your family's got lots of money and lots of connections. You bought that girl!"

The women of the dance troupe all covered their faces with their fans, so they could whisper to each other. Most of them knew that Baorun and Liu Sheng had been jointly accused, but none of them dared venture an opinion as to who was the real culprit and who was the victim of injustice. But as far as Su Baozhen's and Shao Lanying's maternal reactions were concerned, they felt qualified to pass judgement. They all admired Shao Lanying's attitude, and felt that Su Baozhen was going distinctly over the top. Aunty Dai went over and snatched back her megaphone, and offered Su Baozhen some advice:

"Baorun's mother, we all understand your distress, but you can't go broadcasting it through a megaphone like this. We still need to rehearse, and we don't have much time. Red Toon Street has to take part in the flower-float parade for Labour Day; it's our political responsibility and it mustn't be held up."

Su Baozhen was forced to give up the megaphone and said, somewhat shame-facedly:

"You finish your rehearsal. Of course, I know that a political responsibility can't be delayed. I just lost my temper when I saw her dancing away there. I'm sorry, everyone!"

Aunty Dai helped her to sit down on her own little wooden stool. Su Baozhen looked up at the sky and asked:

"What's the time? I don't have time to sit down. I haven't eaten anything all day, and I have to go home and make his father's dinner."

She tried to get up but couldn't stand up straight; her body stayed curled up like a prawn, and she leaned, arching her back, against a wall.

"What's the matter with your back?" Aunty Dai asked.

Su Baozhen replied:

"These last few days, I've walked as far as a normal person would in eight lifetimes trying to get justice for my son. My feet have gone numb and my back's probably in spasm. You need to get on with your rehearsal. I'll just stay curled up here and rest for a while."

A dozen rose-red fans quickly resumed their wave-like formation, and Aunty Dai's voice began to boom enthusiastically out of the megaphone again:

"One *haha*, two *haha*. Raise your left hands. Three *haha*, four *haha*. Raise your right hands."

The interrupted rehearsal picked up again. Two mothers from Red Toon Street: one of them rehearsing in the dance troupe, posture and movements just so, not a hair out of place, almost as though it was a military parade; the other resting her back against a wall, pain in her face, a faint but penetrating light in her red and swollen eyes revealing her suffering. To an outside observer, the two mothers were each taking the other's measure to the accompaniment of the dance music. Their eyes locked in combat, like swords slashing through the air, but there was no telling who was winning and who was losing.

A little while later, Madam Ma from the fashion boutique interrupted the rehearsal, pushing her way excitedly through the dancers, calling out to Su Baozhen:

"Baorun's mother, what are you doing sitting there? You must get back to Baorun's father in a hurry; he's in a bad way!"

Su Baozhen stared at her blankly for a moment:

"I'm just catching my breath here. Don't scare me like that! What's wrong with him?"

Mother Ma said:

"I'm not trying to scare you. Your front door has three padlocks, doesn't it? He opened two of them, but couldn't find the key for the third. I heard him rattling it over and over, and cursing, and then he just keeled over on the doorstep. His eyes were bulging, and he was foaming at the mouth. I'm afraid he's had another stroke."

This time the rehearsal stopped of its own accord, and all eyes turned to Su Baozhen as she hurried off. The women all agreed that her family had had a terrible year, that it never rains but it pours, that they had had one calamity after another, and it was all a dreadful shame. Standing to one side, Shao Lanying joined in with the others' sympathising, but couldn't help adding a comment of her own, saying:

"People deserving of pity also have a hateful side."

The others struggled to understand this enigmatic utterance, and couldn't see the connection between pity and hatred. Shao Lanying explained:

"I don't have any particular theory, we are all just ordinary people and our lives are very much the same. If we plant melons, we harvest melons, if we plant beans, we harvest beans. Just look at how that family educated their son, and how they treated that old man. Haven't you all seen it for yourselves? Heaven has seen it too; heaven sees everything that men do. I don't care if anyone tells her what I said; it's just how I see things. She has no reason to reproach anyone, she has got what she deserved." Shao Lanying pointed a finger towards the sky. "If anyone is to blame, it is heaven itself. This family has provoked the wrath of heaven."

This scared the women, and they looked up to the heavens, the azure heavens over Red Toon street. Perhaps the gods were hiding behind a cloud or in a ray of sunlight; but this street had so many pitiful old people, and so many unfilial sons and grandsons, if those gods were truly acting justly, there were many households that deserved celestial chastisement, so why had they only chosen Baorun's family? The women couldn't answer this. Who does deserve divine punishment? Each of the women had their own list, but they all kept their own counsel, for fear of causing ructions.

It seemed that Baorun's father had indeed had a second stroke. Those of you with a little medical knowledge will know that a first stroke causes problems with the legs, and that a second stroke is extremely dangerous, proving fatal more often than not. Some people could not understand why the house had three padlocks; they weren't that rich, after all, so why did they need three padlocks. Others tried looking at the affair logically, and said that the loss of the third key could only have been a secondary cause of the stroke, and that Baorun's father must have received some other more serious shock. Perhaps Madam Ma hadn't, in fact, completely erased the child's graffiti on the door: Rapes: 1797. Who wouldn't be enraged at the sight of that? Of course, there was much other conjecture, all entirely without proof, nor was there any point in trying to find proof.

Baorun's father lay in the emergency ward of the hospital for five days and five nights. His progress was very far from satisfactory, and the doctors told Su Baozhen to prepare for a funeral. She went out and bought two sets of burial clothes, one for her husband and one for herself, and piled them up beside her husband's pillow. She patted the clothes and said to her comatose husband:

"I know what you're plotting. You're planning to die and leave this stinking mess for me to handle alone. Well, you can forget it! If you can die, why shouldn't I? I'm telling you, you're not going to get away so lightly; I've bought two sets of burial clothes, and either no one wears them or we both wear them. If you can turn up your toes, then I can hang myself. If you die, I'll put you in your burial clothes, then I'll put mine on, and shame on me if I'm alive ten minutes longer than you. If we're going to go, we'll go together, and as for the old one and the little one, they'll just have to fend for themselves.

It seems that Su Baozhen's despair got through to her unconscious husband, and he didn't dare die. On the morning of the sixth day, he moved one of his feet, but only his left foot and very slightly at that. During the night of the same day, he moved his left hand, and it touched the pile of burial clothes. He slowly raised one finger, as though pleading with his wife: don't get all worked up; if there's a problem let's discuss it. On the seventh day, Baorun's father came round properly, and Su Baozhen's tears turned to laughter. But the doctors warned her not to get ahead of herself in her happiness; although they had just managed to save the patient's life, he was now a mere husk of a man, very weak and fragile, who could break at the slightest touch.

"From now on, you and your family will have to be on your guard at all times, and nurse him with the greatest care."

When his neighbours went to visit the patient in hospital, his speech was so garbled, no one could understand him. Only Su Baozhen could interpret what he was saying:

"Even though he is in such a pitiful state, he still wants to educate you. He said if a family wants to live in peace, firstly it must show proper respect to its elders, and secondly, control its children."

The neighbours all nodded, recognising that he was speaking from experience, and that his brain had certainly cleared. He went on babbling, his expression becoming more and more animated, but Su Baozhen was no longer willing to interpret. In fact, not only did she stop translating, she actually burst into tears. The neighbours could guess what he was babbling about and they clustered round to comfort Su Baozhen:

"Husband and wife always quarrel, especially when they are upset. Don't translate any more if you don't want to."

Su Baozhen dried her tears, gritted her teeth, and said:

"I'll tell you what he said, and then you can judge whether he has any good reason to blame me for not being filial enough towards his father, for spoiling Baorun and for being greedy for money. He doesn't blame his father for being such a pest, and he doesn't blame his son for being lazy, and he doesn't blame himself for being useless. He just dumps the whole bucket of sewage over my head."

Morning and night, when people chanced to meet Su Baozhen on the street, her face was haggard with a wild look in her eyes, as though fate had piled all possible misfortunes upon her, and she had finally admitted defeat. Many of them sympathised with her, saying she must be the most unfortunate person under heaven. Just think: she must be totally exhausted, and of the three men in her family, one is a criminal, one is sick, and one is mad, and they are all relying on her alone. No one could share Su Baozhen's misfortunes and sorrows, and all they had were words to try and comfort her. Someone saw her buying walnuts at the dried fruit stall and cautiously engaged her in conversation:

"Who are the walnuts for, Baorun's mother? For the old man or for your husband?"

She looked at her with red-rimmed eyes, sighed, and said:

"They're for me. The doctor said I should eat walnuts as a brain supplement. There is a permanent rumbling noise in my brain, and I've heard it said that it's a warning sign of mental illness. If it keeps on like this, I'll end up in the Jingting Hospital."

The other tried to soothe her, saying:

"No, no that can't be. I've often had headaches that made my head buzz, but I haven't had to go to the Jingting Hospital."

"Your headaches and my headaches are different things. Sooner or later I'm going to crack, so I treat each day as a bonus. When I do crack it will be an end to my worries, but it will also be the end of a perfectly good family, and that's quite hard to take."

Her household still showed some signs of life, but it was on the verge of collapse. One good shake and it would crumble. One day, a representative of the court arrived with a summons. When he knocked and no one replied, Madam Ma came hurrying out of her shop. She took one look at the summons and, seeing the kraft paper envelope, knew immediately that it was bad news, so refused to take it. She helped the messenger push it under the door and heard the man click his tongue in surprise:

"Tchah! Are those some amaranth greens?"

Madam Ma looked down and saw that there, indeed, sticking out from under the Bao family's front door, were the big bright green leaves of some amaranth greens. Down the leaves rolled a single, enigmatic drop of water.

NINETEEN
HOMECOMING

One morning, Madam Ma discovered an unusual situation when she went to open the shop with her daughter-in-law. There was a horrid foetid smell in the showroom, and the mannequins were all crammed into a corner, their clothes in disarray. The two women immediately saw the old man stretched out asleep on the counter, wheezing noisily. His body was covered by two woollen coats, his legs by a cashmere cloak, and he was using an embroidered cushion as a pillow. This bedding was all stock from the shop, but under the counter there was also a pair of old-fashioned cloth shoes, and beside them was an old-style enamel chamber pot, dug out from who knows where.

They realised immediately that it was Grandfather; the long-absent Grandfather had come home.

One after the other, the two women cried out in surprise. Then, when they looked closer, they saw that a large hole had been chiselled out of a previously blocked-up concealed door between the shop and the Bao family's house. If you looked through it from the boutique side, you could see the Bao's furniture and other knick-knacks. The daughter-in-law ran out of the shop in alarm, but Madam Ma's anger was aroused, and she went over to the hole and shouted:

"Come here, Baorun's mother! Come quick and have a look! What kind of a sick joke is this?"

There was no reply from the other side of the hole. Baorun's mother must have been spending the night at the hospital, and the only thing disturbed by Madam Ma's shout was a rat, and a large rat at that, which came scuttling out of the kitchen, and went and hid under the dresser.

The noise did wake Grandfather and he sat up. His hair was so long he looked like a wild man; his eyes were deep-sunken, and their corners heavily crusted. He stared stupidly at Madam Ma:

"Who are you? Aren't you Master Ma's wife? What are you doing running into my room like this?"

The two woollen coats slowly slipped off his upper body, revealing his status as an escapee: he was still wearing the blue and white striped pyjamas of the Jingting Hospital, and round his wrist was a red identity tag that read: 9-17. His body gave off a sour, acrid smell, which rippled slowly across the showroom, permeating it.

Madam Ma had calmed down a little and as she hastily gathered up the fallen clothes, she almost knocked over the chamber pot. Incensed, she pointed at the hole in the wall, and yelled at Grandfather:

"Get back in there and hurry up about it. This isn't your bedroom!"

Grandfather took no notice of Madam Ma's instructions and just sat on the counter looking slowly round the showroom:

"Where have all these clothes come from? And where's my bed? And my cupboard? Where's my photograph?"

"They're all gone. This hasn't been your room for ages."

She tried to pull him down from the counter but he wouldn't budge. There was still some strength in his puny frame, much more than she had imagined.

"Where's my bed?" Grandfather asked. "Such a big bed! Where have you put it?"

"Your bed isn't here anymore. Your bed is in the Jingting Hospital."

Grandfather looked wildly around him:

"Where are they? Baorun? My son? Baorun's mother?"

Madam Ma didn't know what to say, but still in the grip of her anger, she yelled shrilly:

"They're not here! They're not here! None of them are here!"

Immediately the room echoed her words back at her: *not here... not here... none of them here!*

Madam Ma jumped in surprise; an echo? How could there be an echo? She shot a glance at the hole in the wall. An icy draft was blowing in from Baorun's house, swirling around her feet, like an ominous, invisible flood. Suddenly, she was afraid, and she ran out of the shop, over to where her daughter-in-law was standing.

"What are you doing, standing here like an idiot? Go and get someone! Go and get your father-in-law! Go and get Lao Da and Lao Er!"

Master Ma arrived quickly, with his two sons in tow. It has to be said that men are stronger and more cool-headed in a crisis than women. The three of them supported Grandfather down from the counter, and helped him put on his shoes. Holding his nose, the eldest son said:

"The old fool's feet stink. I bet he hasn't washed them for a month!"

"It's not his feet that smell" the younger son replied. "It's his trousers. What does the back of them look like? Are there any shit stains?"

"Don't be so rude!" Master Ma scolded them. "We all grow old one day. What makes you think you'll be any less smelly when it's your turn?"

Grandfather still remembered Master Ma's childhood nickname, and poked him in the shoulder with one finger:

"Aren't you Little Number Eight from the Ma family? What are you doing running around in my house so early in the morning? Where's the rest of my family?"

Master Ma settled Grandfather down in a chair and said with a sigh:

"Let's have a little talk, Baorun's Grandfather. OK? Why didn't you stay safe in the Jingting Hospital? What do you think you're doing coming running back here? You're quite something, though. The Jingting Hospital is really well guarded; how did you manage to escape?"

A crafty look spread across Grandfather's face, and he said, holding up three fingers:

"Thirty *yuan*. I spent thirty *yuan*."

"You bribed the sentry with thirty *yuan*?"

Grandfather suddenly realised what he was saying, and pursed his lips:

"I can't tell you. If I tell you, I'll be selling out Old Wang, and it won't be so easy next time."

Master Ma's two sons began to laugh, and the elder one said:

"Who says he's lost his soul? He can't have lost it completely if he still knows how to grease the wheels. He must have some of his marbles left if he could escape like that."

The younger one felt the back of Grandfather's head, inquisitively, saying:

"Perhaps his soul has come back. The Jingting Hospital is a long way away, and it was the middle of the night. How else could he have found his way home?"

Madam Ma had already pushed the chamber pot over to where the hole was, muttering:

"Disgusting! Disgusting!"

As far as she was concerned, once the chamber pot had gone that way, the man should follow. Grandfather had come into the shop through the hole, so it was only right he should leave it the same way. Master Ma went over to examine the hole in the wall, and he couldn't help exclaiming in admiration:

"He wields a mean pick-axe, for an old fool! He's good at digging holes, and he's good at digging through walls. Just look at this hole. See how neat and accurate it is! Just big enough for his head and shoulders, not an inch more."

Purely from a technical point of view, it was quite possible to stuff Grandfather back through the hole, but Master Ma did not agree with his wife's distinctly feminine point of view. He felt that, even though the old man was clearly deranged, he was still their elder, and stuffing an elder through a hole was being both negligent in one's duty and inhumane. He talked it over with his sons and daughter-in-law, and on this occasion he decided they should shoulder some of Baorun's family's burden, and take Grandfather back to the Jingting Hospital themselves. Once Madam Ma had been convinced, she hurried out to buy a large flat bread and a fried dough stick, saying:

"We might as well do the job properly. Since he has come home anyway, we can at least send him back on his way with a full stomach."

It wasn't long before Bao Sanda pulled up on his flat-bed trike, and sat waiting outside the boutique. Grandfather had wolfed down the breakfast he'd been given all right, but he was in no mood to cooperate otherwise with the Ma family's good works. He lay down on the floor, clutching one of the plastic mannequins, like a little child throwing a tantrum.

"I'm not going anywhere. I've come home for the holiday," Grandfather said. "Don't you know tomorrow is Labour Day. It's the workers' festival, and I want to spend it here."

It's not appropriate to use excessive force when dealing with the elderly, and no one knew quite how to proceed, so they all turned rather embarrassedly to the head of the household. Not sure himself what to do, Master Ma took Grandfather by the hand and, as he did so, he accidentally touched the Jingting Hospital identity tag, 9-17. He looked down and saw the wrinkled skin of Grandfather's wrist, deeply marked with red rope burns. He had an inspiration. His eyes suddenly lit up, as he remembered Baorun and his rope.

"Find a rope! Find a rope!" He opened the counter shutters and found a coil of nylon rope. "Let's see what happens if we tie him up. I've heard that he does what he's told when he sees a rope. Let's give it a go."

The rope proved very effective. Everyone in the shop remembered clearly afterwards, that as soon as Master Ma looped the rope a couple of times around Grandfather's wrists, it was as though he had cast a magic spell: the old man shuddered, raised his head and just stood there, docilely.

"A little looser", he said. "The democratic knot. I want the democratic knot."

At first no one understood what he meant, but then it dawned on them that he was asking to be tied up with a certain type of knot called the 'democratic knot'. No one had any experience of knots, and even after a long discussion, none of them had any idea how to tie a democratic knot. Going by the name of the knot, however, they reckoned it must be a fairly loose one. Master Ma said:

"Well, Baorun's Grandfather, that isn't an unreasonable request. We'll tie you with a democratic knot; at your age we're not going to use a legal knot."

Father and sons set to work with a will, and ended up tying a decent approximation of a democratic knot; it wasn't very pretty to look at, but it had just the right degree of tightness. Flushed with success, they escorted Grandfather out of the shop, and all climbed aboard Bao Sanda's flat-bed trike.

Bao Sanda and his trike were something of a feature on Red Toon Street:

"Stinking fish coming through! Make way! Make way!"

People on the street gave way to his strident voice, but there was always someone who would call out disrespectfully:

"Have you been conscripted, Bao Sanda? Are you taking a corpse to the undertakers?"

But this day was different; no one cursed Bao Sanda as people took note of the trike's unusual passengers. Everybody recognised Master Ma and his sons but no one could make out who the bound, haggard-looking old man was. They asked:

"Where did you find that old man you've got tied up like that? What crime can such an old man have committed?"

"Don't be so simple-minded!" Bao Sanda replied glibly. "Criminals aren't always tied up, and tying someone up doesn't necessarily mean they're a criminal. Can you understand that?"

Master Ma was a decent and honourable man, and didn't want there to be any misunderstanding. Pointing at Grandfather and then at himself, he called out:

"It's Baorun's grandfather; he escaped from the Jingting Hospital, and we're taking him back."

Sitting on the trike, tied up and smiling faintly, Grandfather seemed to exude benevolence.

He sat squarely on the flat-bed of the trike, supported by Master Ma and his sons. Seen straight on, the ropes criss-crossing his body, he looked like an aged criminal, with the Ma family members as his gaolers; seen from behind, he was a model of dignity and respectability, looking more like a VIP returning home, with the Ma family as his retainers. Grandfather had patchy but detailed memories of Red Toon Street, filtered by the passage of time, and he only recognised neighbours from 30 or more years ago. Chungeng's mother was sitting, sunning herself in her doorway, and he still observed the old conventions of many years ago, calling her New Sister-in-Law:

"How are you this morning, New Sister-in-Law?"

Unfortunately the 'New Sister-in-Law' didn't recognise him. She shaded her eyes with her hand and looked at the trike, and asked:

"Who is that still calling me 'New Sister-in-Law' when I'm going to be carted off to the crematorium any time now?"

When they passed the public baths, just as they were opening, the old boilerman, Master Liao was rolling up the door curtain. Grandfather remembered to ask him about the temperature of the water:

"Is the water boiling hot today, Master Liao?"

Master Liao, who was disgruntled about something, replied in a loud voice:

"No, it's not. The powers-that-be say we've got to economise, and we're not allowed to heat the water properly. We've only got warm water, so it's up to you whether you want to wash or not."

Later, as the trike passed over the bridge at the North Gate, there was a gaggle of youths standing on the bridge who started yelling and cat-calling, for no particular reason. One of them whistled at the trike, and this suddenly reminded Grandfather of Baorun. Stirred up, he asked:

"What about Baorun? Where's Baorun gone? Where has our Baorun run off to?"

Master Ma looked meaningfully at his two sons, and said:

"Your Baorun has left and gone travelling."

From Grandfather's doubtful expression, it was clear he didn't believe this story about going travelling.

"Baorun, Baorun where the hell have you gone? You left me all alone, and one day you'll regret it!"

He began to get agitated, and started constantly looking around at each side of the street. Several times he tried to stand up, but each time he was pushed back down by the Ma's, and the trike kept shuddering incessantly, making it very difficult for Bao Sanda to steer. He reprimanded Master Ma and his sons from the front:

"You're all being too humanitarian with him. If you want him to do as he's told, what's the use of a democratic knot? You should do it properly with a legalistic knot; tie it tight, then tighten it again!"

Working together, the Ma's tightened the knot. Bao Sanda's stratagem was successful, and kind words proved no match for the language of the rope, which manifested itself in Grandfather like a chemical reaction: the tighter the bonds, the more compliant Grandfather became. Master Ma and his sons were novices in the art of bondage, and were obliged to learn through practical application. They tried making the bonds tighter by using as much of the length of the rope as possible, and looping the remainder of the nylon rope around Grandfather's knees. This experiment was immediately successful: the thrashing of his lower limbs ceased instantly, and his stiff, desiccated old body gradually softened.

"This isn't the democratic knot, it's just a mess. I want the democratic knot!"

Even if he was still protesting verbally, the rest of him quietened down. Master Ma looked at the knot he had inadvertently created, and decided that although it looked pretty odd, it was at least reliable. He turned to his sons and asked:

"What should we call this knot?"

"How should we know? You'll have to ask Baorun; he's the expert."

Bao Sanda turned round and looked them up and down:

"If you don't read the papers, you'll never learn anything. The name has to suit the situation, so you'd best call it the stabilising knot."

In the grip of this stabilising knot, Grandfather did indeed settle down.

Later, as the trike passed the flyover across the city moat, the place was thronged with people, presenting a bustling scene of construction work. A dazzling smile broke out over Grandfather's face, and the four others on the trike heard him say with satisfaction:

"The face of our country is changing day by day and month by month!"

PART TWO
LIU SHENG'S AUTUMN

ONE
A TIME OF LUCK

Liu Sheng had been skulking in a corner with his tail between his legs for quite a few years. He had been fortunate to avoid a prison sentence, and thenceforward his life had been defined by that good fortune. His parents' sanctimonious admonitions came as regular as clockwork, berating him at all hours of the night and day:

"Your happiness is hard-won; don't let it get away! Keep your head down! Your freedom is hard-won; don't let it get away! Keep your head down! Any good fortune for the rest of your life is hard-won; don't let it get away! Keep your head down!"

Nor did he let anything get away. He had been a burden to his whole family, and the guilt he felt because of this had largely stolen from him the particular joy of youth, and made him grow up before his time. Because of him, the family's debts were enormous, and the list of creditors very long. Shao Lanying had had to apportion duties to each member of the family. Master Liu had a wide social circle, so he had the responsibility of repaying the network of contacts in the courts and the Public Security Bureau. For that he followed the accepted conventions, mostly involving cigarettes, alcohol and gift vouchers for saunas, as well as a good number of restaurant meals – very much the same as in diplomatic circles. Shao Lanying herself took responsibility for consolidating what might be called their complex propaganda campaign. She was most afraid that the popular mood would change, and if Fairy Princess were to go back on the withdrawal of her testimony, there would be no escape for her son. Money was fine for winning over the older generation, but it cut no ice with Fairy Princess and she had to find something that did. Shao Lanying knew that Fairy Princess liked pretty jewellery, so she bought a multi-coloured pearl necklace, a ring and a hair clip. But Fairy Princess turned up her nose at these things as being too vulgar and low quality. Then she saw the fine jade bracelet Shao Lanying was wearing. That lady was loth to part with the family heirloom, and staying as polite as possible, insisted to Fairy Princess that the fact that she had been wearing the bracelet for so long, would make it very difficult for her to take it off. Fairy Princess replied:

"I'm sure you can get it off if you want to give it to me. I'll get you some soap and see if that does the trick."

So there was nothing for it and, with great reluctance, Shao Lanying took off the bracelet. As she watched Fairy Princess put it on her own arm, she muttered to herself:

"I don't know who this girl is going to marry but, whoever it is, is really going to be drawing the short straw."

Shao Lanying sent presents to the old gardener's family three times a year, at the Spring Festival, on Labour Day and on National Day. These dates had the virtue of being conveniently spaced, and fixed. The old gardener and his family had moved to the Twin Mountains Forestry Management Area in the suburbs, which made Shao Lanying's unified approach much more difficult to maintain. Nothing daunted, however, she continued the gifts as before, taking a heavily-laden basket on the long coach journey to the Twin Mountains reserve. This went on for a good number of years. What she really wanted was to make Fairy Princess her adoptive daughter, but Fairy Princess always refused. The girl's grandmother, however, was happy to call her sister. This went on until one day, she arrived at the forestry reserve to discover that there was a new tenant in the old gardener's quarters. This man told her that the old gardener had ceased to be able to work, and the management of the forestry reserve had retired him. Fairy Princess had gone off elsewhere to work, and the old couple had returned to their old home in the countryside to enjoy their retirement. She stood there dumbfounded, and sighed. She didn't know whether to rejoice or despair. The new resident went back into the room and brought out a pot with a white orchid in it, which he gave to her. It was a gift from her old sister, he said. The orchid was in bloom and very fragrant. She remembered that she had once said that white orchids were her favourite flower. It had just been idle chat, and she hadn't expected that that old woman would remember. She was rather touched, and left the reserve carrying the orchid in its pot. But she still had a basketful of gifts in her left hand, and the flowerpot in her right hand got heavier and heavier so, half-way home, she checked that no one was looking, hardened her heart, and left the orchid in the undergrowth beside the road.

As for Liu Sheng himself, he had his own particular assignment. Shao Lanying instructed him to take gifts of pork offal to Baorun's family. After he had done this a few times, and each time Baorun's mother had the liver and tripe thrown straight out into the street, he wasn't willing to go any more. Shao Lanying didn't insist he continue, saying:

"It didn't cost us anything, and we were just trying to do them a favour, but if they won't take it, we won't offer it. People might get the wrong idea, and think we are acting out of guilt. Our good intentions will just give them something to gossip about, and the whole thing will become pointless."

Thus, on the one hand, the outward display of good works ended, but on the other, there was evidence of a more conciliatory mood. Madam Ma from the fashion boutique was asked to undertake a mission of mediation, and went specially to the butcher's shop to have a heart to heart with Shao Lanying.

"Our hearts are all made of flesh and blood; Baorun's parents have already accepted their fate, and have no intention of pursuing Liu Sheng. They have lost their appetites, so pig offal doesn't interest them, and all they really lack in their home is manpower."

Quite soon, the conversation turned to Grandfather: for better or for worse, he was an elder of the family; for better or for worse, he was still alive; he couldn't be abandoned, yet he couldn't be controlled, and he had become a major headache for them all. By this circuitous route, Madam Ma introduced a new suggestion: Baorun took the fall in court for Liu Sheng, so perhaps Liu Sheng should shoulder some of Baorun's family obligations, and go to the Jingting Hospital to supervise the old madman. Although Shao Lanying didn't immediately acknowledge the logic of Madam Ma's idea, she was actually thinking that it was not an unreasonable suggestion.

"Madam Ma, you can tell Su Baozhen that as far as I'm concerned, our families are not enemies; we have a shared destiny. Please pass this thought on to her: the street has produced two people with a mental disorder, and they're from our two households, so clearly we must have a shared destiny. Liu Sheng can't fully take over Baorun's filial duties, but our two families surely have a duty to support each other. Liu Sheng must try to emulate Lei Feng a little more."

Shao Lanying passed on this new responsibility to Liu Sheng, who seemed inclined to refuse the honour.

"What's the use of this pretence of friendship? One moment you're playing the whore, and the next you want to build a memorial arch. If that's the way you want to go, you go, but I don't have the stomach for it. I just have to look at that old fool, and it makes me feel sick."

Shao Lanying lost her temper at this, and hit Liu Sheng with a feather duster:

"Your wounds aren't yet healed and you've already forgotten how they hurt? We tell you to keep your head down, and you go sticking it up over the parapet. This is no sham pretence of friendship, it's the right thing to do. Have you forgotten the debts you have incurred? You're young and healthy; why are you afraid of making a few trips to the Jingting Hospital? Hold your nose when you go, if you have to, but go you will. Your father and I don't own a bank; we can't bail you out all your life."

A mother always understands her son. Liu Sheng did indeed need to keep a low profile, nor were the wounds that life had inflicted upon him completely healed. Baorun still haunted him, always there, night and day. One morning he was riding his bike past the railway bridge just as a train was rumbling over it. A black shadow came flying out of the train, brushed his shoulder, and draped itself over the frame of his bike. He composed himself and looked at it: it was a loop of green nylon rope, which looked to be just about the size of his head in diameter. Wonderingly, he tried it, and the rope fitted neatly over his head, neither too large nor too small; it was a perfect fit round his neck. He gasped in surprise and broke out in a cold sweat. The train had rumbled past, but he still stood under the bridge, not sure what to do. Suddenly he was beset by doubt: could Baorun have been released from prison? Had Baorun been on that train? He hurled the loop of nylon rope from him. His fear gradually faded away to be replaced by an all-encompassing guilt. He addressed the disappearing train:

"I'm sorry, you world-class stupid cunt!"

Liu Sheng went once to the Fenglin Prison to visit Baorun.

It was a sweltering summer's day when he took the long-distance coach to Fenglin township, carrying a travel bag full of carefully-chosen presents: cigarettes, *baijiu*, a pair of sunglasses, and a special ballpoint pen. This latter was a rare treasure that had been brought back from abroad: when you pressed its top, a blonde, blue-eyed woman on the barrel of the pen began slowly to remove her bathing costume, confidently revealing her naked body. He really liked this pen, and he reckoned that Baorun would like it even more, so he put it in his jacket pocket to be ready to slip it to Baorun when the opportunity presented itself.

The weather was very hot. He saw an old woman with a cloth bundle, sitting in the cool shade under a wall by the main gate of the prison. She was alternately dozing off and weeping silently. Beside her there was a cardboard sign that read: Li Fusheng has been falsely imprisoned. He didn't know what relation Li Fusheng was to her, nor was he interested what miscarriage of justice had occurred, but the old woman's consuming misery shocked him. As the old woman dozed and wept, she was breathing heavily through her nose, sounding like a pair of bellows; tears were seeping from her eyes, and running drop by drop down her cheeks. He stared at those tears for a while, and gradually felt more and more uncomfortable in himself.

"Miscarriage of justice!" he muttered to himself. "What's so unusual about that? There are more than enough of them in the world already!"

As he found the shade of a tree to shelter from the blazing sun, he saw a strange youth walking along the perimeter wall of the prison, going round and round, wearing only a vest and shorts. He was sweating profusely, walking a little, then stopping for a while and putting his ear to the wall to listen for a while. As he listened, he cried out:

"Da Bao, Da Bao! Get the fuck out here!"

The youth's voice was shrill and angry. Liu Sheng mocked him behind his back, and asked a nearby cold drinks vendor:

"What's he shouting about? Who is Da Bao?"

"It seems he's a rapist," the vendor replied. "That young man comes here every year, and says he wants to castrate him with his own hands."

He didn't feel it appropriate to ask who Da Bao had raped, whether it was the youth's mother or older sister, or perhaps his girlfriend. He tried guessing, but became dispirited and gave up. His face was a little hot and flushed, and since he could see it was still too early for visiting time, he bought a red bean ice lolly, which he ate as he went into the nearby Fenglin township for a stroll.

Fenglin is not only famous for its prison, it is also an ancient township in its own right. Such historic settlements are nice and cool in the summer, with tall trees reaching to the sky and high, ancient buildings generously offering the comfort of their shade to passers-by. Liu Sheng was wandering about in that shade, looking at the ancient well in the middle of the stone-flagged roadway, and the mottled earth walls of the ancestral halls.

"Boring!" he said to himself. "These old things are really boring!"

He went over to stand in the doorway of a grocery store where a gaggle of the local youth was gathered, chatting and shouting at each other, as they stood around playing snooker on a brand-new snooker table.

He stood watching the fun. His own knowledge of snooker was pretty amateurish, but the locals were even worse, which gave him an opportunity to show off. Standing beside the table he chattered away incessantly, gesticulating as he did so. The objects of his scorn were not going to take it lying down, so there was nothing for it but for him to pick up a cue himself. It did not go well for him. Liu Sheng did not like losing face. He kept on losing, but couldn't accept it, so kept playing again. He played for half the day until the shop owner came out to collect the money for the use of the table. His opponents insisted that because he had lost, he had to pay. He couldn't argue with this, and looked for his travel bag, but it was nowhere to be found. He asked all the bystanders, but no one could help, and some even asked:

"Are you sure you had a bag in the first place? We never saw it."

Liu Sheng lost his temper and started shouting and cursing:

"I'm not surprised they put a prison in the middle of Fenglin! It's no problem finding people to fill it; the town is full of thieves!"

The youths took offence, surrounded him in the shop doorway. Before he was beaten up, the shop owner stood up for him, and rescued him, but there was a quid pro quo, as the man still wanted the fee for the use of the table, and wasn't willing to let Liu Sheng off. Since he had no money, Liu Sheng was in something of a tight spot. Then he remembered the special gift in his pocket. He took out the ballpoint pen, and pressed its top, saying:

"Come and see the foreign girl. She does whatever I ask her." He issued a string of commands. "Take it off! Put it on! Take it off again! Put it on!"

The shop owner and the youths crowded round jostling each other to get a better look. They all stared wide-eyed at the ball-point pen in his hand. His status was restored at a stroke, and he finished up by pressing the pen into the hand of the shop owner, saying expansively:

"It's a German import, and you couldn't buy it for three hundred *yuan*. I had a run of bad luck today, so I'm giving it to you."

By the time he got to the gates of the prison, visiting time was over. He saw that the doors of the reception room were shut, looked at his own empty hands, spread them wide and said, with a wry smile:

"Fine! It's fine like this too."

Although he had failed in his mission, and made a fool of himself in the process, perhaps that was God's will, so he was quite happy to go easy on himself...

"In any case, I haven't got any of the presents, and he probably didn't want to see me in the first place. I wouldn't have known what to say when I saw him anyway."

He took his bus ticket out of his pocket, and waved it at the prison gates:

"Well, at least I came."

Liu Sheng's family had prospered over the last few years. According to Shao Lanying, it was the good fortune that came from virtuous behaviour and good deeds. Liu Juan's obsessive mental illness had miraculously been cured, she had left the hospital, and spent the days at home embroidering mandarin ducks frolicking on the water. Her embroidery was very vivid and realistic. Some well-intentioned person offered to act as match-maker for her, and the other party suggested was a fellow who sat in his wheelchair at the old west gate mending watches. It was love at first sight, and Liu Juan was soon married. The next year, she gave birth to little Bao Bao. Bao Bao was a girl, beautiful as a goddess, and everyone who saw her exclaimed at how fortune had smiled on Liu Juan. Liu Sheng's family had severed all connections with the Jingting Hospital, and had no need to go to that unhappy place any more. But since Baorun's family had given Liu Sheng his new duty, it fenced him in, both as a promise made, and as a moral obligation. With public opinion weighing in, too, all these factors encircled him and bound him tight. There was no escape for Liu Sheng.

That was how Liu Sheng became Grandfather's supervisor.

The Jingting Hospital was a long way for him to go to look after someone else's grandfather. And Grandfather clung to his family name as tenaciously as an old pine tree clinging to a cliff face. For Liu Sheng, looking at Grandfather's withered old face and emaciated body, was like looking at the desolation of a battlefield. Liu Sheng visited him when he had to visit him, comforted him when he needed comforting, did everything that he was supposed to do, and the rest of the time was bored stiff. Such never-ending good works would have suited a saint, but they did not suit Liu Sheng, who was always half-hearted about his charitable works. As the world outside became more and more prosperous, the number of rich families on Red Toon Street also increased, and their prosperity in every field of endeavour seemed to flow from the one sentiment: time is money. This saying bewitched Liu Sheng: he was happy to waste time, but it was even better if that time turned into money. He had a friend in Lotus Alley who had made a black-market fortune by recycling and reselling medical equipment discarded by the big hospitals. Inspired by this, he decided that there must be business opportunities to be found at the Jingting Hospital. There must be all manner of opportunities presenting themselves if he only looked for them. Whether he had business there or not, he started to frequent the hospital administrative buildings, asking:

"Is there any business for me today?"

The hospital personnel all knew quite well who he was, and none of them had any business for him, although some did enthusiastically suggest marriage partners.

"I'm going to succeed in business before I think about marriage," he would reply. "If business is going well, then naturally, I'll marry well."

He was particularly assiduous around Hospital Director Qiao, running errands for him and playing Go with him (always losing, of course, but very convincingly). He became intimately acquainted with all of Director Qiao's various goings-on, so much so that the director finally came through and offered him a genuine business opportunity. He gave him responsibility for overseeing the food provisioning for the hospital. That day he went home and announced to his parents:

"I'm going to take the plunge and start a new business. I'm going to buy a taxi van."

His parents were far-sighted people, and they recognised the changing circumstances in the world outside. They knew that there was no future for Liu Sheng in messing about in the butcher's shop, so striking out on his own was not a bad idea. They gave Liu Sheng their own savings, along with a contribution from their daughter's husband, to buy his taxi van.

He drove his van between Red Toon Street and the Jingting Hospital, and each week submitted a bill to the hospital accounts department. Then, when he went to visit Grandfather on his ward, he went in a good mood, and with a smile on his face. He was even spotted slipping a red envelope into the waistband of Grandfather's trousers, and heard to say solicitously:

"If you're short of money, just ask me. If I'm not here, and you're hungry or thirsty, find someone to go and buy whatever you want."

He even joked with Grandfather:

"If you ever want a girl, that's OK too. Just say the word, and I'll send you one."

Just this year, Grandfather's flesh and muscles had really wasted away, and he was no longer strong enough to wield a pick or shovel. There was no need to tie him up any more, and he was a lot less trouble to the warders. When Liu Sheng went to keep him company, most of the time was now spent cleaning him up, doing his hair and washing him. Grandfather's skull was not like other people's. After his head had been shaved clean, you could clearly see a zigzag scar.

"Is that from when you were denounced and criticised, and Wang Deji hit you with a poker?"

Grandfather nodded his head, saying that previously, many people had hit him, and he didn't hold it against Wang Deji. It was just that the poker had hit him in a place where it shouldn't have, and if there hadn't been that hole, his soul wouldn't have escaped so easily. If he had dared to twist his head aside and dodge that poker, perhaps he would never have lost his soul at all.

Liu Sheng said:

"Ha! What's the point of talking about souls? Other old people have all got their souls, and what use are they? Don't they all still kick the bucket? You've not got a soul, and you're living to a ripe old age, so what's the problem?"

When he was washing him, Liu Sheng noticed that Grandfather's penis looked like a river snail, hiding in a sparse tuft of white hair. He asked in amazement:

"How come you're so small, Grandpa? If I ever did send you a girl, would you still be able to do anything?"

Grandfather covered his groin in embarrassment, and said, with great honesty:

"Before, I could, but now it's giving me some trouble, and it's getting more and more constrained. As time's gone by, it's pretty much given up, and now I'm afraid it's probably no use at all."

Grandfather was rather suspicious of Liu Sheng's solicitude, and said:

"My Baorun has never had such good friends, and even if he did, they'd never have gone as far as you have. Are you after a share in my family's property? If that's your game, lad, you're fifty years too late. We used to be rich; my family owned half of Red Toon Street. You know the Bank of America on the Bund in Shanghai? We used to have a safety deposit box in that bank. Shame we didn't manage to keep hold of it all. How many property deeds didn't survive a fire? How many mountains of gold and silver didn't survive the searches and confiscations. Now I'm a member of the proletariat, and the best I can do is ask someone to write you a letter of thanks, for all you're doing for me."

Liu Sheng smiled in reply:

"I'm no great friend of Baorun, and I don't want your family property. Nor do I want a letter of thanks. Have you heard of Lei Feng, Granddad? From now on, just think of me as a living Lei Feng!"

His debt to Baorun he now repaid to Grandfather. In interacting with Grandfather, he was, in fact, interacting with Baorun's shadow. This method of repayment was quite exhausting, but it did give him some peace of mind, and as time went by, he got used to living with Baorun's shadow. The shadow, now dense and now sparse, became an indispensable part of his life. Once he heard his parents discussing it secretly in the kitchen:

"Suppose Baorun comes back one day, what will he think about Liu Sheng? Will his good intentions be repaid? Supposing Baorun doesn't appreciate his kindnesses, then everything we've done will be wasted, like trying to draw water in a wicker basket!"

His parents' worries bruised Liu Sheng's self-respect, and he rushed into the kitchen. He snatched the spoon out of his mother's soup bowl and threw it to the ground. Before his parents could work out why their son was behaving so appallingly, he snatched up another spoon, and brandished it in the air.

"What are you worrying about? The world's a big enough place for the two of us, isn't it?" he reprimanded his parents.

He began to pound the second spoon on the table, but then his movements slowed down, his hand relaxed its grip, and the spoon dropped to the floor with a clatter. He raked together the pieces of broken porcelain with his foot, and said:

"You see these two spoons? That's how I feel about Baorun. If we can get along, we'll get along; if we can't then I'll take him down with me!"

TWO
SPECIAL BEDROOM NO. 2

THE DOOR WAS THROWN VIOLENTLY OPEN.

Someone came bursting into the room, bringing with them a cold draught, and an overly sweet, cloying smell of perfume.

"Why was the door closed? Are you playing Go or cards?"

A rather plump woman's face was thrust through the opened door, the shrill voice growing angry.

"So, playing Go behind closed doors is it? Do you know why our country is so backward? It's because we've raised a generation of lazy slobs like you, who just sit around doing nothing all day except playing Go!"

The two of them were, indeed, playing Go. Liu Sheng often played a game with Director Qiao, who became completely absorbed when he played, ignored his work, and had no interest in seeing anyone who came looking for him. It fell to Liu Sheng to see off any such visitors.

Liu Sheng leapt from his chair to hustle the woman out, but she pulled a sword from her satchel, and slashed it through the air, shouting:

"Get out of the way, you gangster! Get out of the way!"

It didn't take any more to know this was Madam Zheng, who was in the habit of throwing her weight around like this. She had never bothered to find out Liu Sheng's name, she just always called him a gangster. She was a woman of forty something, dressed in the height of fashion, albeit incongruous fashion. She was wearing a scarlet puffa-jacket, black tracksuit trousers and white trainers. Slung over her shoulder, she carried a brown leather scabbard, which gave her an arrogant, overbearing appearance, like a modern-day amazon. Every time Liu Sheng saw that scabbard, he couldn't repress a laugh. When she heard his smothered laugh, Madam Zheng abruptly turned to look at him, and the sword pricked his chin.

"Are you laughing at my sword, Gangster? There are too many demons around these days, and I carry a sword to cut their heads off. Do you find that funny?"

Liu Sheng carefully avoided the sword:

"But I'm not a demon, so you don't need to cut my head off!"

"You're not good enough to be a demon, you're just a gangster. Don't you know who I am, Gangster?"

"How could I not know who you are? You're Madam Zheng, the multi-millionaire from Barrel Alley!"

Who hasn't heard of Madam Zheng from Barrel Alley and her younger brother Boss Zheng. The pair of them were something of a legend. The course of their success was closely associated with the bathing habits of the local residents. The older sister ran the Yangde Pool old-style bathhouse at the end of Barrel Alley and, to start with, her younger brother rubbed down the customers' backs. In an idle moment one day, he roughed out a most excellent advertisement for: the 100-year Yangde Baths – Modern Water Culture. This advertisement cleverly tapped into the consumerist consciousness of the majority of the bathers and their appetite for 'culture'. From then on the fame of the baths grew, and clients flocked there. Starting from Barrel Alley, brother and sister progressed rapidly, and established the 'Zheng Family Water Culture' chain with, at its height, more than twenty bathing establishments under its banner. Later, the business developed even further, and changed its name to Zheng Family International Commercial Investment Company, expanding into plastic foam, clothing, steel and gasoline. They went international and bought the operating licences for two mines in Vietnam. Without any great effort, brother and sister became the first nouveaux riches in the south of the city. But position and wealth came too quickly, and too generously; the elder sister understood how to enjoy them, but the brother was unable to adapt, and unfortunately developed a paranoia in which there were always people out to kill him.

In the middle of one night, Boss Zheng took a suitcase out onto the street and ran several kilometres with it until he burst through the front door of a police station claiming that he was being chased by people intent on killing him. The duty officer observed that he was wearing only a pair of Y-fronts, but both wrists were laden with expensive Swiss watches. When asked why he was dressed like this, Boss Zheng said:

"I didn't have time! I didn't have time!"

When the suitcase was opened for inspection, apart from a number of packets of condoms, it was packed with bundles of banknotes. The officer thought at first that what he had on his hands was a sleep-walking millionaire, but on questioning him, discovered that this was not someone unfortunate caught in the middle of a nightmare, but the terrified young Boss Zheng. He was claiming that some would-be kidnappers had left a whole load of differing lengths of rope in his office, and that his assassin had disguised himself as a beautiful masseuse, who had been waiting for an opportunity to kill him this evening. The officer quickly contacted Madam Zheng, who burst into tears over the phone, wailing:

"He's the chairman of the board! How can the company go public with him in this state?"

"Is your company going public?" the officer asked. "In Shanghai or Shenzhen?"

"Neither!" Madam Zheng said, still wailing. "In the Jingting Hospital!"

So Boss Zheng became a patient of Director Qiao and Madam Zheng became his goddess. Since it is not wise to neglect a goddess, Director Qiao looked meaningfully at Liu Sheng:

"Hurry up and get Madam Zheng a cup of tea."

He himself went over to the medicine cabinet.

"Where's the enema? Where's the enema?" he kept muttering to himself. "Is Boss Zheng still constipated? Too long a period of constipation affects the digestive system. I'm monitoring the situation closely and I ordered them to send over several extra enema bottles yesterday. I expect Nurse Li forgot again."

"Constipation, constipation!" Madam Zheng sneered. "All you can talk about is constipation! Didn't I tell you that my brother opened his bowels normally yesterday? It's not a problem of constipation now, it's a problem of location. We've given the hospital a great deal of money, but you've allocated him special bedroom no. 2, which faces west. What's that all about? My brother needs to be in special bedroom no. 1, facing south!"

"The special bedrooms are for patients with provincial government rank and above; even giving your brother bedroom no. 2 is giving him special treatment," Director Qiao explained patiently.

His eyes suddenly lit up, and he went on:

"Special bedroom no. 1 is Commander Kang's; he's a veteran commander of the Red Army and the Revolution! Have you seen him? How do you get on with him?"

"We don't have anything to do with him; he looks down on us, and we don't take any notice of him." The subject seemed to be a sore point with Madam Zheng, and she burst out angrily. "Don't try and pull rank with me; we're in a market economy now, and money is rank. I've met high-level cadres like him before; I don't need to shake hands with any more secretaries of municipal committees, I've shaken hands with provincial governors! So you can stop trying to use Commander Kang against us; he's not paying the hospital anything, and we're giving you buckets of money. Why should he have special bedroom no. 1, when my brother has to make do with no. 2?"

Director Qiao didn't know what to do with himself, and gestured to Liu Sheng to tidy away the Go board on the side table, and himself took a jar of essential balm out of his pocket. He dabbed his finger into it, then rubbed the balm into his forehead, thinking to himself:

"My head hurts! There's the Commander on the one hand, and the big boss on the other, and I can't afford to offend either."

He smiled wryly at Liu Sheng, and tried a little joke:

"The life of a hospital director is hard, Liu Sheng. He doesn't earn any money, and spends all day offending people. I might as well hand over to you!"

"How much?" Madam Zheng asked suddenly.

It took director Qiao a moment to reply:

"What do you mean, how much?"

"To buy your position as hospitel director. How much?" Madam Zheng's sword slashed through the air. "I might as well buy the whole hospital and be done with it. My brother will have whatever room he wants, so how much? Name your price!"

The atmosphere in the room suddenly froze over and an expression of shock came over the Director's face. He stared at Madam Zheng, and kept repeating:

"Preposterous, preposterous! You're being preposterous, Madam Zheng!"

"You're the one being preposterous. We're in a market economy and everything's for sale. Haven't you heard that the Japanese have bought the Empire State Building in New York? I have a friend who got a deputy governorship for a small limousine. What do you think of that?"

Standing to one side, Liu Sheng laughed:

"Ten million! Sell her the hospital, patients and all, for 10 million. It's cheap at the price, just a thousand *yuan* per patient."

Director Qiao shut Liu Sheng up with a look and thought for a while, before deciding on a softly-softly approach:

"I know you have money, Madam Zheng, but you'd do better spending it elsewhere. Your money can't buy the Jingting Hospital, it belongs to the state. I can't discuss prices with you. Besides, when you drink water, you should always remember who dug the well. Who do you have to thank for your current prosperity? Surely it's the Communist Party, isn't it? It's people like Commander Kang who fought to establish the nation and gave outstanding service to the revolution. Tell me, Madam Zheng, how can we steal his room from him?"

Madam Zheng didn't want to agree, but didn't dare disagree either. For a moment she almost felt obliged to apologise, but the look soon disappeared from her eyes, and she grew angry again:

"What day is it today, Director Qiao?"

Liu Sheng pursed his lips towards the office desk:

"See for yourself on the calendar. It's Thursday."

"Shut up, Gangster! I wasn't talking to you." Madam Zheng's sword pointed at Liu Sheng, furiously describing a circle, then dipping down to strike the floor. "Today is Thursday. Have you got the office I asked for ready or not?"

Either Director Qiao had forgotten, or he was momentarily dumbfounded, and he looked at Madam Zheng in confusion:

"What office? Are you moving your office into the Jingting Hospital, Madam Zheng?"

"Not me; Miss Bai! Do you think the PR woman my brother has hired doesn't need an office?" Madam Zheng yelled. "Don't you listen to a word I say? I told you last week, Miss Bai was reporting here today. We want to rent the empty room on the east side of the third floor as her office."

It came back to Director Qiao:

"Ah! That girl!" His expression became complex and profound, as he scratched his head and went on: "We're not entirely clear exactly what this PR girl is going to do. Having her coming and going as she pleases, in and out of a first-class hospital, might not give the right impression.

Liu Sheng couldn't help sticking his oar in too, when he heard this:

"There are three types of PR girl: jobsworths, tarts and the dishonest ones who'll say anything to steal a march. I bet she's a tart. This is a mental institution, and there'll be chaos if you bring a tart in here. How are you going to keep the patients quiet, so they can be treated?"

"Flap your lips again, you lousy gangster, and I'll stab you with my sword!" Madam Zheng flourished her sword angrily at Liu Sheng, making a stabbing motion, and then shouted out of the door: "What are you doing still standing out there, Miss Bai? Come in and let them have a look at you. Then they can see if you're a jobsworth or a tart. Let them see whether you're a whore or not!"

Miss Bai stayed out in the corridor.

A shadow moved behind the door, and only then did they realise that all along in the background they had been hearing the tap-tapping of high heels. She came in like a black rain cloud, and Liu Sheng always remembered quite clearly that, when she did so, the light in the room seemed to darken. As he greeted this young lady, it was like greeting the dark, mournful night.

She was carrying a Filofax and a mobile phone with a golden flower ornament attached to it. She brought with her a faint fragrance of cape jasmine, and her head and half her face were covered by a black head scarf. Liu Sheng could only see her eyes, which were black, and very beautiful, but deeply clouded with melancholy. She was wearing a dark brown fur coat, thick and heavy as a curtain, that hung down below her knees, showing two fine calves and a pair of purple high-heeled shoes, studded with crystals.

It was undoubtedly fate that had arranged this reunion. Their eyes met for no longer than the flash of a lightning bolt out of a mysterious tempest; somehow the black scarf fell from her head, revealing her familiar, pale face to his gaze; a face that was at first defiant, then terrified. They recognised each other. After a matter of only a few seconds, Liu Sheng saw her turn away and say to Director Qiao:

"Do you have a fax machine here?"

It was Fairy Princess. Fairy Princess had returned. His memories shattered and fell in pieces to the ground; they lay there glinting, bright and terrifying. Her fur coat dragged behind it ten years of memories. He saw two rabbits. He saw the water tower. He saw Baorun. Scarcely knowing what he was doing, he partly covered his face with his hands, and slowly edged towards the door of the office. Director Qiao noticed the unusual movement:

"Where are you going, Liu Sheng? I have a lot to do here, and I need your help."

Liu Sheng panicked for a moment, then said:

"Just a moment, I have to go to the toilet."

He ran out into the corridor, then suddenly remembered he'd forgotten something. He turned back and shouted into the office:

"She's a jobsworth; definitely a jobsworth."

THREE
THE VOICE OF A GHOST

SHE HAD RETURNED. He had imagined what the future would be like many years ahead; he had imagined a hundred different encounters with Baorun; but the one thing he hadn't imagined was meeting Fairy Princess again. He remembered vividly Fairy Princess swearing in person to his mother:

"I will never come back to this hateful city. I never want to see you or your family's filthy faces again. If I die and am burned to ashes, even my ashes won't come floating back here."

It had never occurred to him that going back on one's word was a failing of young girls. It was her failing, but also her right, and now that young girl had come back.

He was afraid. With her return, his criminal youth had come back to him too, bringing with it a chaotic jumble of memories. Over the next few days, as he drove his taxi van through the Jingting Hospital grounds, he felt that his load of meat and vegetables was trembling frenetically, that there was the faint sound of running water coming from the disused water tower, that a previously turned page of history had been blown back to its original position for him to recognise. He was afraid. He had no choice but to recognise it. A deep voice summoned him from the top of the water tower: climb up here, Liu

Sheng. Climb up here. He couldn't tell whether it was Baorun's voice, or the voice of a ghost.

Two crows were roosting at the top of the water tower. Even so many years later there were still two crows roosting at the top of the water tower. Time and place were broken by the branches of the trees, and shattered into little pieces. Dizziness gave way to terror in Liu Sheng, as he realised that his life was full of the mere semblance of happiness, whereas the reality was an unbroken thread of shadows, like a ridge of mountains, cloaked by cloud and mist, changing unpredictably in form, and ranged in the semblance of disaster. Even after so many years, he was still in the embrace of disaster.

It was perhaps three days later that he saw her standing in the main gate of the Jingting Hospital, clutching a loose-leaf binder to her chest. She appeared to be waiting for a taxi. Her outfit was, as always, fashionably arresting: a high-collared, loose-cut pastel pink sweater and black lambskin trousers. The curves of her body had a relaxed elegance that emphasised her youth and beauty. The nine o'clock morning sunshine reflected soft rays of light in her black, almond-shaped eyes, beautiful as Spring flowerbeds, and blooming with an inner beauty; in the pale golden light, her expression was both haughty and enchanting. Her deep red lips, which were moist and glistening, threw his heart into turmoil. Were those the lips he had once kissed? Then there was her bust, looking so full and ripe under the sweater, so sexy that he didn't even dare look. Were those the breasts he had once fondled? The months and years had washed away the tactile memories, but her current beauty and sexuality now rewrote his past transgressions. His guilt was secretly transformed in his imagination, ascending and reforming as some kind of glory, and even intertwining with a vein of happiness. He recalled the words of a popular song: I had her once; I had her once. He started to panic and, as he drove his van past her, with an involuntary spasm, he sounded his horn.

"Hello!"

His greeting was hesitant, but the horn was loud and clear. She turned to look, her eyes lit up, and she held out a hand to stop the van.

"Can you help me out, Driver, and take me to the city centre?" she said, peremptorily.

She opened the van door, and sat down beside him, adding: "I'll pay the standard taxi fare."

Their eyes met, and after a couple of seconds of confusion, she quickly regained her cool:

"My driver's sick, and you can wait half a day for a taxi in this godforsaken place, and still not see one." Breathing through her nose, she looked into the back of the van. "What have you got in this van? It stinks like a public lavatory."

He didn't reply, and heard her drumming on the van window with her fingers:

"Drive! I'm in a hurry. I'll just have to put up with it."

His eye was caught by a flash of green at her wrist. It was a fine jade bracelet, perhaps the very bracelet his mother had given her all those years ago. His mother had talked about it incessantly, saying that the jade was clear as crystal, that it was a family heirloom, and with the way jade prices were going up, who knew how much it was worth now? He didn't dare look at the bracelet too closely, and just said:

"Can I ask your name, Miss?"

She turned to look at him, and the corners of her mouth twitched in a mocking smile:

"We've already met, haven't we? Call me Miss Bai." Her eyes pierced him like spearpoints. "And you? What's your name?"

He didn't dare reply immediately. He had to be very careful. The unspoken understanding between them was as fragile as a sheet of rice paper, and the slightest mistake would rip it asunder. Their past was like a cup of rancid tea brewed in a shared cup. They had to pay particular attention to the lid. Once it was lifted, the secret of the rancid tea would be revealed. They mustn't lift it. They mustn't acknowledge each other. They mustn't speak… He drove on in silence, smelling the bright freshness of her perfume. Reality was mirroring his dreams; she had come back, and his dreams had come back too. She sat beside him and it was as though night had fallen, bringing with it a heavy dew and a secret grief.

As the car went through the city gates, he heard her laugh, sneeringly:

"Stop play-acting, it's killing me!" She looked at herself in the mirror of her make-up case, and brushed her eyelashes with an eyelash brush. "So, tell me: how is that world-class stupid cunt?"

So, she was the first to lift the lid off the cup. He hadn't expected her to be so impatient. Turning to look at her, he saw her expression was stiff and rigid, but her voice was quite calm. Clearly she was asking what had happened to Baorun. The cup of rancid tea was revealed, and there reflected in its surface was the fuzzy image of Baorun's face. He said, in a low voice:

"He's just the same. Still inside; he hasn't finished his sentence yet."

She looked down, took a tissue out of her purse and blew her nose.

"I've got a cold. I get one every autumn."

She took out her powder compact and touched up her make-up in the mirror.

"I just thought I'd ask. OK then, just remember one thing, I'm not called Fairy Princess any more, my name is Bai Zhen. From now on you call me Miss Bai. If you call me Fairy Princess again, you'd better watch out. It won't be pretty."

He understood her. There was no more Fairy Princess; the person called Fairy Princess was gone never to return. That was another tacit understanding between them, which he was happy to maintain.

"Miss Bai, if there's anything I can help you with in future, if you need my van, you just have to ask."

She snorted.

"You, help me? Only as a last resort. My reputation would be ruined if I was seen always getting in and out of this old heap."

She made no secret of her scorn, and he was embarrassed. He blurted out the first question that came into his head:

"You're so young and beautiful, Miss Bai, why are you working as a PR girl for a mental patient?"

She snapped her powder compact shut, and looked sideways at him:

"It doesn't take much to surprise you, does it? He wants to pay me good money, and I want to earn it. Why would you need to ask. Everyone's got to set out on their own some time. You've done it yourself, haven't you?"

FOUR

THE EMPTY HOUSE

He always drove his van straight up and down the short length of Red Toon Street, and he had lost count of the number of times he passed Baorun's house. He always put his foot down during the day, hurrying through the gaze of the crowd gathered at the fashion boutique; at night, by contrast, he slowed right down, taking advantage of the rare peace and quiet to look the house over carefully. Only to look, however, never to look around; nor was he nostalgic for any person, rather it was a tree that fascinated him. The neon lights of the boutique illuminated the long-neglected roof of its building, and every time he went past, he noticed the mulberry tree: a mulberry tree growing right out of the roof of Baorun's house. Some passing bird must have dropped a mulberry fruit, which somehow found a patch of fertile soil on the roof, and now the tree had grown to about a metre in height with lush foliage to boot.

Once, some children climbed up to the tree on the roof of Baorun's house to gather mulberry leaves, but Mother Ma from the boutique shouted at them to get down. She used to say that if it weren't for her being on the lookout, the tree would be stripped bare to feed silkworms. And it wasn't just unruly children; she couldn't be sure that there weren't a few unneighbourly residents of the street who climbed up to strip tiles from the roof. Anyone could get up there on to the roof because the rooms below were uninhabited.

Baorun's father had gone to heaven. He died from his third seizure. It seemed that just before he died, he had gone to get his slippers, but had only managed to put one on before he pegged out. He had no chance to pass on his last wishes, and he was not ready to die. His body, when it was laid out, was a fearful sight: his hair was standing on end, as though in anger; his eyes were starting out of their sockets and couldn't be closed; and his mouth was gaping open as though frozen in the act of shouting. Su Baozhen was afraid it would scare people off, so she attached a strap to the veil over her dead husband's face, and tied it at the back of his head like a surgical mask. No one dared try and lift the mask, so none of the neighbours knew what he really looked like in death.

It was the quietest funeral in the history of Red Toon Street; there was no wailing at the side of the coffin, and the bier was set down in a dark, out-of-the-way place. If the fashion boutique hadn't closed its doors for the occasion, then no one might have noticed the white paper notice on the door of Baorun's family's house that read: no condolences please. Of course, all the locals knew that a refusal was one thing, and condolences another, and those who felt they should go, still went. Shao Lanying represented Liu Sheng's family and went to offer their condolences carrying a wreath of flowers. She stopped in the doorway to see which way the wind was blowing, and when Su Baozhen didn't turn her away, she went in. Once inside, she was shocked to see the state Su Baozhen was in: her expression was dull and listless, she had ointment smeared on the pressure points on both temples, and she was sitting beside the corpse, head down, cracking melon seeds. It was a most unseemly spectacle and Shao Lanying, Madam Ma and some others put their heads together whispering their disapproval. Su Baozhen heard them at it and said:

"There's no call for you to look at me like that. I can't cry any more; my tears are dried up and there's not a single one left." She held up one of the melon seeds. "I'm shelling these for the snack food factory, not for myself. The doctor said my blood pressure was dangerously high and I should do some manual labour: one, it will help prevent a stroke, and two, it will earn me some money. If I have a stroke now, who'll take care of the funeral?"

Baorun did not come home. Everyone understood; being released to attend a funeral required certain conditions, which Baorun did not meet. But there was another family member: Grandfather. Did Grandfather have any conditions to meet? This was a question worthy of consideration. In general, the neighbours felt that, no matter what the relationship had been between father and son, when it came to the end, they should see each other one last time, and that Su Baozhen should go and bring Grandfather home. The others encouraged Madam Ma to go and speak to her on their behalf, but Madam Ma demurred. Whether this was out of empathy with Su Baozhen, or because she was afraid Grandfather would prove an encumbrance, was unclear. She said:

"There's no question of going to get the old fool; I'll decide for her. Don't kick up a fuss; do you think I don't know how things must be done? When it comes down to it, we can only work with what we've got. This family only has four members: a madman, a prisoner, a dead man and Su Baozhen. The rites are not so strict that her health doesn't come first."

After the funeral, Su Baozhen went to live in the provincial capital with her younger sister. After more than twenty years living on Red Toon Street as a wife and mother, in the end she had to rely on her original family where she was received into their warm embrace. As she was about to leave, she extended the lease on the boutique, at a lower rent, on the condition that the Ma family took responsibility for overseeing the whole building. She told Madam Ma:

"Since I married into the Yang family, I haven't had one day's good fortune, but I never expected, after a lifetime of sorrow there, I would end up having to rely on my baby sister. She's been the lucky one of the family; she married well, and her husband's official career kept prospering. So I'll live with her from now on, and see what happens to my luck."

Mother Ma couldn't tell whether the woman was broken-hearted or just hard-hearted, and tried her out, asking:

"Your sister may be a fine person, but she's not the same as your son, is she? Your son will come home, sooner or later and, like it or not, this is your home. Can you abandon it just like that?"

Su Baozhen sighed, slapped her knee, and said:

"What son? He's a disgrace! And this place isn't a home, it's a tomb. Do you know why I'm more dead than alive? It's because I'm hemmed in by ghosts. Night or day, I can't sleep. That house is just one great mass of the ghosts of our ancestors. They pop up here, jump out there, surrounding me and pestering me for their people. Generations of ghosts keep coming after me demanding their kinfolk, as though they think I mean their sons and grandsons harm."

This scared Madam Ma, and she looked nervously all around her.

"Do you think if you go, your ancestors would come and bother me for their people?"

Su Baozhen thought about this for a moment and did her best to comfort her:

"Ghosts are quite reasonable; you're a tenant, not their daughter-in-law, so why should they come and bother you?"

After this, Madam Ma asked her about Baorun's situation. She said that San Ba, from the east side of the street, had been released early from prison, and was back scalping tickets at the station, and that Piggy from the Mulberry Park Alley had also had his sentence reduced and returned home. He was now repairing bicycles on the bridge.

"Does your Baorun have any chance of early release?"

Su Baozhen lowered her head sadly:

"I've been over there so many times but there's not much hope. They say it's no use the parents trying, it all depends on the impression the prisoner makes inside. I know my own son; how can Baorun have made any kind of good impression? He's nobody compared to San Ba or Piggy. He's never made friends anywhere he's gone. We can count ourselves lucky if no one actually increases his sentence."

Su Baozhen handed the keys of the house over to Madam Ma, saying that heaven's plans always override the plans of man, and she didn't know whether she'd even be alive when Baorun came home.

"So, can I trouble you to take care of these keys?"

These parting words almost brought tears to Mother Ma's eyes. She saw that all three bunches of keys were identical, but Baorun's and Grandfather's bunches were filthy and reeked of bad luck. She extracted them and tried to give them back to Su Baozhen, but she waved them away, saying:

"Take them all, Madam Ma, I don't want to keep any of them. I'm not going to hide anything from you, once I go, I'm not coming back. It's not that I'm hard-hearted, it's just that other people are out there having a good time, and I want my share too."

So it was that Baorun's home was turned over to Madam Ma to look after. All of the Ma household were shrewd business people and, since the market for high-quality fashion on Red Toon Street was proving sluggish, they had, for some time, been considering a change of direction. Although the residents of Red Toon Street were all warm and well fed, over the last few years they had developed a morbid fear of death; prolonging life and maintaining health had become their favourite topics of conversation. The sale of medicines and health foods was, therefore, a business much better suited to their demands. Thus, the Ma family had already entered into a partnership agreement with a well-known chain of pharmacies, so the shop needed altering and enlarging. That the works had not yet commenced was down to concern for the health of their landlord family, which they had no desire to compromise. Once Su Baozhen left, however, the time was right; they shifted into gear and commenced their large-scale construction work.

Chain stores are chain stores, and the décor is in the hands of others; even the size of the shop door has to conform, and can't be a centimetre too big or too small. The original door of the boutique was 10 centimetres or less than the company template, so the wooden-plank door to Baorun's family home was called into service again, and sawn into two again. The renovators had already taken down the door and dismantled the frame when Master Ma began to feel uneasy.

"Do you think this is going to cause problems later on?" he asked. "Shouldn't we try and find Su Baozhen to discuss it with her before we cut down the door?"

Mother Ma thought he was worrying too much, and made him try out the door himself.

"You're fatter than Baorun", she said. "If you can get through, he'll certainly be able to too."

Master Ma fitted easily through the frame.

"See!" Madam Ma exclaimed. "You went through fine. What's the problem? And in the end, we have to be practical about this; our shop front is expensive enough as it is, and if you leave such a large door just for Baorun, and he never uses it, won't that be a stupid waste of money?"

Liu Sheng very seldom went past Baorun's house on foot, and certainly never stopped there. But there was one exception to this, when his mother sent him to the new pharmacy to buy stomach medicine for his father. When he got to the shop, he was immediately distracted by a brand-new advertising billboard, in the form of a movable screen covering the doorway to Baorun's house. It showed a smiling Caucasian man, black chest hair spilling out of the top of his shirt, and a blonde woman whose fair skin glowed, moist and sensual under her bikini. They were sitting embracing each other on a beach at the seaside. They weren't actually doing anything, but looked as though they just had. Most of the wording of the advertisement was in English, which he didn't understand, but there were some red Chinese characters, which were particularly eye-catching: Good News for Men! Imported Viagra! Sole Distributors!

Liu Sheng was taking a good look at the advertisement when Master Ma's oldest son noticed him. He served him with the stomach medicine he'd been sent to buy, but was in no hurry to take the money. With a glance all around him, he bent down and took a box of something from under the counter:

"This is good stuff. Try it out. It's the original imported stuff. Some people think it's expensive, but you can afford it."

He was unable to resist the other's enthusiastic blandishments, or his own curiosity, and found himself handing over the money to buy a box. Liu Sheng remembered very clearly that he had kept the stomach medicine in his hand, and put the Viagra in his pocket when he heard the mournful whistling of a gust of wind coming from Baorun's house next door. He peered round the advertising billboard; the normally tight-shut door to the house was half-open, and a gust of wind blew out of the main room, along the corridor, and out of the door, strong enough to set the Caucasian man and the blonde woman flapping in its draught. There was an old-fashioned Everlasting-brand bicycle propped in a corner, and the steel rims of its wheels flickered like icy haloes. He remembered that it was the bicycle Baorun used to ride and there, hanging neatly from the rear of its frame, was a loop of rope.

Liu Sheng stood rooted to the spot. He thought he could see a shadow moving beside the bicycle. It was the 18-year-old Baorun hiding in the shadows behind the door, blending in as another deep shadow himself. Sheltered by time, he was waiting for time itself to pass. Who was he waiting for? He seemed to see the 18-year-old Baorun, beard and moustache just sprouting, muscles developing, eyes like daggers. He saw the 18-year-old Baorun wearing a yellow jacket fashionable in former times, and swinging a length of rope in his hand.

"Come in, Liu Sheng, come in. We have a lot to talk about."

He didn't dare go in. Then he saw another human form coming out of the door. It was Madam Ma. She was wearing a hat and a veil; in one hand she carried a bucket of water, and in the other a feather duster.

"The furniture is all rotten", she said. "The mattresses and bedding are all mouldy, and the walls cracking. How am I going to be able to sort it out for her?"

He wanted to make his escape, but Madam Ma rapped him on the back with the feather duster.

"Don't go, Liu Sheng. I've got some of Baorun's letters here. You can take them to his grandfather in the Jingting Hospital."

"Why not just return them to sender. You can do that, you know. In any case, Grandfather's not going to be reading any letters from his family."

"How can I return them? His grandfather may be an old lunatic, but he's still a relative, and relatives should always get their letters."

She took a bundle of letters from her breast, and pointed at the envelopes, sighing:

"It's such a shame; his father has been dead all this time, and his son still doesn't know. Look, they're all still addressed to his father."

Liu Sheng took the letters away with him. On the way back, curiosity got the better of him, and he secretly opened them to have a look. They were all just one sheet of paper, and the characters written there were all different in appearance: some were comparatively correct, others were slovenly and ill-written. The content was all pretty much the same, as though copied from a single specimen. They all began "Dear Grandpa, Father, Mother, hello" and the rest read almost without exception "Everything is fine here, please don't worry". The endings were even more identical. Without exception they read: "I hope you are taking care of your health. Respectfully Yours".

He folded up the letters and stuffed them back in his pocket. "Respectfully Yours", "Respectfully Yours". The characters felt like a row of small, sharp teeth constantly gnawing at his thigh. Once again, across many years, and through a handful of pages of returned letters, an almost mystical connection was established between him and Baorun. Baorun's writings had retained their own body heat, which pierced the thick cloth of Liu Sheng's jeans, and gradually warmed the skin of his thigh. Baorun's life, summarised in these few empty words, weighed heavily in Liu Sheng's trouser pocket. He felt an ache in his thigh, and a slight burning sensation, and a strange scorched smell slowly spread from the depths of his pocket. Since the autumn, Liu Sheng had often smelled this strange odour, but he wasn't sure whether it came from the dryness of the season, or from the desiccation of his own memories. "Respectfully Yours". Through Baorun's letters home, he dimly saw his own future, a future from which rose a mysterious column of blue-green smoke.

A few days later, he went to visit Grandfather in Ward No. 9, taking Baorun's letters with him. It's hard to say whether it was just an impulse, or the result of a carefully considered strategy, but Liu Sheng asked Grandfather:

"Do you remember what Baorun looks like?"

"I don't know what he looks like now, just when he was little."

"He's your only grandson; do you want to go and see him?"

"There's no point; I can't even leave the male section of the hospital, so how could I visit him in prison?"

Liu Sheng digested Grandfather's words, and didn't pursue the matter. He took his hair-dressing tools out of his bag, and began to comb Grandfather's hair and shave his beard. Then he helped Grandfather put on a cheap western-style suit. He looked him over carefully, and said:

"You look different enough now. You can go and see your grandson. I'll go with you, so don't argue; I'm taking you to see Baorun."

Ignoring the rules of the Jingting Hospital, he secretly loaded Grandfather into the back of his van. Hidden in a basket of vegetables, Grandfather passed, without a hitch, through the three gates of the Jingting Hospital. Once on the public highway, Liu Sheng moved him into the front passenger seat, and said:

"Are you alright? Am I looking after you well enough?"

Grandfather looked around him out of the windows and saw a scene completely new to him. He gave a sigh of pleasure:

"My country is changing day by day; it really is changing day by day!"

The van drove on to the township of Fenglin, more than fifty kilometres away. Over many years, the whole world had changed its aspect completely, but the Fenglin prison was still the same: a high grey cement wall disappearing into the distance, surmounted by an equally endless forest of electrified wire netting. To the east there was a supplementary iron watch-tower, inside which a human form was visible. There was a loudspeaker hanging beneath the look-out window, glinting in the sunlight, and on it were perched a handful of audacious sparrows. An eye-catching propaganda banner hung from the roof of the tower, which read:

"Warm congratulations to the Fenglin Prison for its entry into the list of top ten civilised prisons."

Liu Sheng parked the van in the visitors' car park, picked up his briefcase and counted the money inside it. Grandfather watched and counted with him. The amount made him dizzy:

So much money! Too much to count! Who is it for?"

"It's a present for Baorun."

"Why are you giving him so much money? Prisoners don't have any chance to spend money. If you want to stop the cadres getting their hands on it, you'd be better off giving it to me to look after for him."

Liu Sheng pushed away the out-stretched hand, saying with a laugh:

"He can't spend money if he has it, and it's no use to you either. Best if I take care of it myself."

He underestimated Grandfather's intelligence, but overestimated his state of health. He had to support him over to the main gate of the hospital, where they arrived just as the sentries were changing over. This involved a short ceremony. The guards coming off duty marched towards them with exaggerated steps, whilst the new sentries came at them from the other direction, carrying their gleaming automatic rifles, so it looked as though they were aiming at them. This appearance of firing terrified Grandfather, who cried out in fright:

"A firing squad!"

He shook free of Liu Sheng's grip, lifted his trouser legs and ran back towards the van. Liu Sheng had no idea he could run that fast, and as he ran a murky liquid, that Liu Sheng guessed must be urine, sprayed out of his trouser legs, and spattered on the ground. Terrified by the sight of four automatic rifles, Grandfather had pissed his pants.

This was an accident that couldn't have been foreseen. Grandfather did not want to get out of the van, and nothing Liu Sheng could say would persuade him.

"Grandfather", he said, "I've come all this way with you, and if you don't go and see Baorun, we'll have had a wasted journey. Fifty kilometres! The petrol alone cost a small fortune."

Calming down, Grandfather replied:

"I don't care. I'm the grandfather and he's my grandson. He should come to the van to see me."

"You're just being stupid now, Grandpa. This is a prison; we can only go and see him, he can't come and see us."

"Then you go and ask him for me when he is going to get out. And tell him from me, I'm waiting for him to get out to look after my corpse.

I'm going to die as soon as he gets out. I've got nothing keeping me in this world and I don't want to cause anyone any more trouble."

Liu Sheng considered this for a while and finally locked Grandfather in the van. He went over to the reception room himself, where he found there were already a lot of other visitors. He pushed his way through the crowd to sign the registration form, his emotions all over the place. He hesitated as he was about to sign; at first, he was going to sign his own name but then, he wasn't sure why, he lost his nerve, and he wrote the old man's name, Yang Baoxuan, but made sure he gave the right relationship: Grandfather.

Then there was the wait. He sat on a long bench in the waiting room looking round at the other people there. He tried to figure out the crimes of the people they were visiting from their ages and faces: who was in prison for bribery and corruption; who for violence; and who had offended public morals. There was a middle-aged couple standing in a corner, the man was smoking, and the woman drying her tears, her sorrowful eyes filled with the pain of injured maternal love, and of hatred. He suddenly remembered that old woman he had chanced upon that summer; he even remembered her relative's name: Li Fusheng. "Li Fusheng has been falsely imprisoned". He looked closely at the woman, watching how the tears seeped from the corners of her eyes, and how she dried them with a tissue. The middle-aged man saw him watching her and said:

"Stop crying. People are all looking at you."

Liu Sheng smiled and nodded to them, but they misinterpreted his good intentions, and the man came over, and walked around him, crowding him.

"Have you come to see our Zhang Liang?" he asked suddenly.

Before Liu Sheng could reply, the woman came over too, and reached out a cold hand to lay hold of Liu Sheng:

"Are you a friend of Zhang Liang? Are you Xiao Huang? Or are you Xiao Ding? Why don't you back Zhang Liang up and tell them he's been falsely accused?"

Liu Sheng gave a start, and snatched his hand away:

"I don't know Zhang Liang. I'm not Xiao Huang or Xiao Ding."

He retreated to hide in a corner, keeping his head down, looking at his own knees, and muttering:

"Is there anyone who hasn't been falsely accused? I've got friends inside who are just the same."

Finally it was his turn. He heard a prison guard call out:

"Yang Baoxuan! Is Yang Baoxuan here?"

He stood up hurriedly and followed the guard along the corridor. The guard was a young man, dressed in a beautifully-cut new-style grey uniform that elegantly defined his lower back and buttocks; the trouser legs were cut thin so they emphasised the solid muscles of his legs. For some reason, his shape reminded Liu Sheng of Baorun. His memory of Baorun came into sharp focus: he had been well-built and sturdy as an 18-year-old, but what was he like now? The corridor was very long, and the slogans written on it were rather dated: Change and renew – become a new person. At the end of it, an iron door with a large mirror mounted on it, was visible. He saw himself in the reflection, following the guard, slowing down and speeding up, getting more and more agitated. It filled him with a nameless dread, and he began to cling to the walls as he walked, so his reflection was no longer seen in the mirror. The prison guard noticed this unusual means of locomotion, and turned to ask him:

"What's up with you? What are you hiding from? Do you want to go in or not?"

Liu Sheng stood beside the wall and didn't move, looking deeply apologetic:

"I'm not hiding. What have I got to hide from? I'm sorry, I misheard. I'm not Yang Baoxuan."

He made his way back to the car park, a feeling of immense emptiness in his heart. Grandfather was asleep in the van, his head to one side and saliva dribbling from one side of his mouth. He sat in the driver's seat and lit a cigarette. The smell of it woke Grandfather up, and he asked:

"How's our Baorun?"

Liu sheng thought for a moment, then blurted out:

"He's alright. A bit older, a bit thinner."

"When's he getting out?"

"Soon. Don't worry, Granddad, he'll get out when he gets out, but there will always be someone to take care of your corpse. If it's not him, I'll do it for you."

He started the van, comparing his two failed visits to the Fenglin Prison. Which one was the more laughable? He was too full of regret to think about it. He rolled down the window to look around. Over to the west, Fenglin township looked like a mirage. The simple old township had sprouted a forest of tall buildings that gave it something of an international look. An orange inflatable plastic archway stood beside the Fenglin Bridge, on which was written, in large, eye-catching characters: Welcome to the home of mutton soup! He hadn't known that Fenglin was 'the home of mutton soup', and when he remembered that time when his travel bag was stolen, he exclaimed angrily:

"When did the home of petty thieves suddenly become the home of mutton soup?"

There was a wedding going on somewhere in Fenglin, or perhaps the opening of a mutton soup restaurant, because there was the continuous noise of fire-crackers going off, and the air shook with celebration; the debris of a firework, that had arced like a bird several hundred metres in the air, fell first on the roof of the van and then tumbled to the ground. He got out to have a look, and discovered the remains of a hexagonal firework, on which he could still read the characters "Congratulations and Prosperity".

"It's congratulating me on my prosperity! That's a good omen!" he thought to himself.

He took the firework back into the van and put it on the dashboard. He turned to Grandfather and asked:

"Granddad, is Fenglin mutton soup really so famous?"

"Of course it is. When I was little, my grandpa used to take me to eat it. We went by car."

Liu Sheng developed a sudden interest in Fenglin mutton soup, and asked:

"Do you want to go into the township and have some mutton soup?"

Grandfather nodded eagerly:

"Of course I do. I was just dreaming about it. Let's go and have a bowl of mutton soup."

The old streets of Fenglin had been demolished, and there were no tall trees to be seen any more. The old flagstoned streets had expanded into wide asphalt roads, lined with European-style black metal lamp posts. As you drove down the main street in the centre, every hundred metres you passed through a cement imitation ceremonial arch. There was a large square in the middle of the township, half of it covered in green artificial turf, and the other half in a red synthetic carpet. A tall building was under construction on the west side of the square, which was already blocking out half the sky. Looked at head-on, it looked a bit like the White House in the US capital, Washington, but from the side, it looked like the framework of a temple. Liu Sheng studied it for a long time, but couldn't decide which it was supposed to be.

They had happened to arrive in the best season for mutton soup, and the air of the township was redolent with its aroma. The specialist restaurants crowding the streets all claimed to have been established for a hundred years, and all had certificates and medals engraved on their doors and name boards making exaggerated claims: some were national prize-winners, some were All-Asia medallists, and there was even one that claimed to be the designated restaurant of the International Society of Mutton Soup. Liu Sheng had no way of knowing which claims were true and which were false, so he fell back on practical experience, and led Grandfather into the establishment with the most customers.

Grandfather's appetite proved to be quite startling, and he swallowed three big bowls of mutton soup without batting an eyelid. At first Liu Sheng encouraged him to eat his fill, but then he began to be afraid he might go too far and cause himself harm, so he told the restaurant owner to take away his bowl. He opened his briefcase to pay, and suddenly came across the box of Viagra. His head still half in his briefcase, he looked at it for a while in embarrassment. He had been so busy recently, he had almost forgotten about this expensive new plaything, and he had not yet tried its mysteries or tested its efficacy. He looked coolly around him.

Apart from mutton soup restaurants, he saw that Fenglin was full of hair-dressing salons, foot massage shops and sauna centres. He had a sharp eye for the possibilities of pleasure, and knew that small townships such as Fenglin were often hotbeds of sex for sale. The steaming hot mutton soup seemed to have generated a different kind of warmth inside him, and he looked at Grandfather opposite him, shaking his head.

"Why are you shaking your head at me?" Grandfather asked. "Extra mutton costs money, but extra soup is free, so why shouldn't I have some more?"

He was not party to Liu Sheng's secret thoughts: how much he wanted to take some Viagra, and experience for himself its legendary magical effect; a plan he was unfortunately prevented from putting into action because of the grandfather sitting beside him.

"Ah well," he told himself, "the medicine won't go out of date, and there's always next time."

A hair-dressing salon opposite the restaurant had lit its red lights early, and there was a girl sitting in the doorway, one leg crossed over the other, expertly sewing some cross-stitch. She was wearing a purple sweater with a plunging neckline and black leather trousers. The rest of her body wasn't that attractive, but the deep cleavage was pretty dazzling. As Liu Sheng and Grandfather came out of the restaurant, the girl's feet suddenly circled towards Liu Sheng, attracting his attention. Looking sidelong at the feet, he was sure they were talking to him. One of them was wearing a silk stocking, and the other was nude. He was convinced that the bare, varnished toes were whispering sweet nothings to him.

He stopped dead in the street as he struggled with himself, but the temptation was still there, and he dragged Grandfather over to the wall of a building to consult him:

"You know I cut your hair today, Granddad? Well, there was a lot of crud in it, so shall we go into that shop there and get your hair washed?"

Grandfather looked over at the shop, and said:

"They charge for that, don't they? You're much better off washing your own hair; why pay someone else to do it?"

Liu Sheng winked at him:

"It feels much better having someone else do it. If you don't try it, you'll never know."

"Do you think I'm some kind of savage? I've had my hair washed before; Master Bai in Red Toon Street has been doing it for me for the past five decades."

Liu Sheng laughed knowingly:

"You call that a hair wash? It feels a lot better than Master Bai when the girls here do it. Go in and find out for yourself."

He almost manhandled Grandfather over to the door of the salon, where he put a hand on the shoulder of the girl sitting there, squeezed it, then patted it:

"Stop sewing, you've got customers."

The girl looked up and just glanced at them. Then she took proper notice, lowered her head and said:

"You'll have to talk to Madam first."

The mama-san was already getting up from the sofa inside, and she looked consideringly at the two men, one old, one young, in the doorway:

"I've never met such a dutiful grandson. Are you bringing your granddad for a hair wash? What kind of a wash do you two want?"

Liu Sheng bundled Grandfather into the body of the shop, and inspected it upstairs and down. When he was satisfied, he sat Grandfather down in a swivel chair, and said:

"It's quite simple. We'll have our hair washed separately." He beckoned to the mama-san. "You come and do my granddad, and wash his hair downstairs. When that's done, give him a massage. The girl doing the embroidery can look after me. I want a bit of peace and quiet, so I'll have my hair wash upstairs."

The girl outside threw down her cross-stitch, and came in. She crossed her arms and gave Liu Sheng a tired "come-on" smile:

"Hello Boss Zhang, how's business?"

Liu Sheng guessed she must have mistaken him for somebody else, and didn't know what to reply. She turned and climbed the stairs, swaying enticingly:

"The usual then?" she asked.

Liu Sheng thought about it, then said with a laugh:

"That's a bit boring, isn't it? How about something different?"

He followed her, and just as they reached the turn in the staircase, Grandfather called out from below:

"Come back, Liu Sheng! Where are you going? I want us to have our hair washed together. Why are you leaving me?"

"Stop yelling, Granddad; I'll just be upstairs. Elder sister will look after you. Just ask her for whatever you want, and I'll pay the bill. What's wrong with that?"

"If you're going upstairs, I'm going too. Why do you want to leave me down here? What are you up to?"

Liu Sheng didn't want to explain to Grandfather, so he turned on the mama-san:

"What's the matter with you? Hurry up and look after him! Go on, wash his hair!"

The mama-san hastily set about Grandfather's hair, tipping shampoo onto his head. Grandfather yelped in alarm, and jerked his head away:

"What are you doing? What have you put on my head?"

The mama-san also cried out in alarm:

"Dammit! I'm covered in shampoo! You've got it in my eyes! What planet is this old fool from? What do you expect me to do with him?"

"He's from the same planet as you and me; it's just that he's never been in a place like this before. He doesn't know what dry shampooing is. Give him a massage, and if you're any good, he'll soon settle down."

The mama-san followed Liu Sheng's instructions, and hurriedly started massaging the back of Grandfather's neck. But after only a few strokes, Grandfather leapt up.

"You wretched woman! What are you trying to do to me?"

With a terrified expression on his face, and his hair full of shampoo suds, he ran over to the door shouting to Liu Sheng:

"Liu Sheng! Liu Sheng! Come down here quick! This is a filthy place! It's against the law!"

Liu Sheng hurled himself after the old man, and caught hold of him:

"Stop talking nonsense, Granddad. This place is clean and healthy, that's why it's here. They're all my friends. I just want to discuss a bit of business with the young lady, and you can have your hair washed while I'm doing it. When I'm finished, and your hair's clean, we can go."

Grandfather wouldn't give up, though, and kept obstinately wrenching at the stainless steel door. Some spittle flew from his mouth and landed on Liu Sheng's face:

"It's filthy, I tell you. Listen to me, Liu Sheng. If we stay here we'll be breaking the law. Let me go, you've got to get out of here!"

Liu Sheng finally lost his temper and, eyes blazing, gestured to the mama-san:

"A rope, get me a rope."

The mama-san didn't understand what he meant to do, but obediently found him a coil of rope. Liu Sheng pushed Grandfather back into the chair, picked up the rope and passed it once round Grandfather's back. That one turn of rope hit Grandfather like a bolt of lightning, and his body immediately stiffened:

"I want a democratic knot!" he cried out, just once, then fell silent.

Liu Sheng hurriedly finished winding the rope around him, and knotting it off so that Grandfather was secured tightly to the chair. As the mama-san looked at the two of them wide-eyed from beside the chair, watching the passivity of the one, and the expertise of the other, she couldn't help exclaiming:

"Where are you from, Boss? I've been in this business a long time, and I've seen my fill of weird people, but I've never seen anyone like your granddad. He must be mentally ill!"

Liu Sheng glared at her fiercely:

"What do you mean, mentally ill? He understands everything that's going on. He just needs tying up, then he's quite normal."

He inspected his knots and brushed some dust off Grandfather's back.

"Turn on the TV, and see if you can find some cartoons. If he wants a hair wash, give him a hair wash, and if he wants a massage, give him a massage. If he doesn't want either, just let him watch cartoons."

The girl was still standing on the staircase, watching the scene unfold below, half-scared, half-amused:

"Oh, oh, oh! How terrible! Oh, oh, oh! How funny!"

Her cries of alarm could perhaps be understood as concern for Grandfather, but Liu Sheng was her client, and it was clear her sympathies lay with him. She waited patiently, watching as the rope settled Grandfather down, then asked:

"Everything OK, Boss?"

Liu Sheng dusted off his hands and replied:

"Everything's fine. Now he's tied up, he's fine."

Upstairs was completely empty. There was a strong smell of mould in the stagnant air, mixing with the smell of the seasoning powder of Master Kang-brand instant noodles. A boy of seventeen or eighteen was sitting on a cardboard box, his head buried in a computer game. When he saw Liu Sheng, he gave him a wide, girlish smile:

"Welcome, Boss!"

Liu Sheng stopped in his tracks.

"Who's this?"

Seeing Liu Sheng's startled expression, the girl reassured him:

"Don't worry, it's nothing to be alarmed at. He's my younger brother."

She pulled Liu Sheng over to a mirror mounted on the wall, where she adjusted her make-up. There was nothing else in the room, and Liu Sheng was puzzled, until the girl pushed at the mirror, saying "Open Sesame!" At her push, the mirror creaked open, revealing a secret room shrouded in darkness. The girl turned on a light, saying:

"Come in; it's quite safe."

His legs wanted to move but his body wouldn't play ball. He looked behind him, where the young lad was still sitting on his cardboard box, absorbed in his computer game. The light from his games machine lit up his childish face. Liu Sheng reminded the girl:

"Your little brother is still outside."

"I know he is; he hasn't got anywhere else to go."

"Are you really his sister?"

She nodded:

"Yes, I am, but what does it matter."

He couldn't tell whether she was just acting naïve, or whether she was really up to something. He pushed the door open, and asked suspiciously:

"You let him sit out there playing computer games while you're working in here? Don't the two of you feel at all awkward?"

She understood what he meant, and said with a curl of her lip:

"What job that earns money isn't a little awkward? If you want the money, you don't worry about that."

She stood beside Liu Sheng and whispered confidentially in his ear:

"My brother came up from the country last year. He was in the same business, servicing men. How can a man service other men? It's too shameful. I got him out of that bathhouse and now he works for me as my security."

Liu Sheng fell silent. The mirror shut behind him. The girl draped a piece of muslin over the table lamp, so the darkness in the room took on a violet tinge. He leaned in close to her, and saw that her looks were only average; her eyes were dead, and her face heavily caked with powder. Her sex appeal, and her candidness were all filtered through a world-weary façade. He smelled a familiar, indescribable odour: it was the smell of bed linen and human bodies, a smell left behind by previous clients mixed with his own. There was a large wardrobe against the wall. He opened it cautiously, and poked and prodded, examining it closely. The girl said:

"Don't worry, there's nothing there. This place has only just opened, and they haven't learned any of the tricks of the trade yet."

He still didn't relax, and felt about under a pile of bedding. He found a magazine, and pulled it out. It was called Sixteen Ways To Get Rich Quick.

"Ha! Only another fifteen to learn. You already know the best one, don't you!"

He was a habitué of salons like this. The procedures at this establishment were the same as at any other one, and he was quite familiar with them. The procedures may have been the same, but the girl's hands, her lips, her whole body were fresh and new, and he was infatuated with the fresh and the new. He lay down on the damp, wrinkled bed, and saw that there was a bottle of mineral water on the bedside cabinet. He remembered the box of Viagra in his briefcase, and groped for it.

"What's your name?" he asked.

"Number three."

"I didn't ask your number, I asked your name."

The girl grinned:

"Now you ask my name, Boss? I'm called Fairy Princess. Fairy Princess, OK?"

Liu Sheng jumped.

"What do you mean?" He sat up, staring at her face. "What do you mean by that? What kind of Fairy Princess are you? Where are you from?"

"What are you going on about, Boss? I'm Fairy Princess!" the girl said, rather aggrieved. "Everyone in Fenglin calls me Fairy Princess; everyone else in the trade calls me Fairy Princess. Fairy Princess. It's a bit more polite than just always calling us 'whore', isn't it?"

He didn't know what to say. He felt let down, and sighed deeply, lying back down on the bed.

"Of course it's not right to call you 'whore', but you can't just randomly call yourself Fairy Princess. I am not afraid of whores, but I am afraid of fairy princesses." He pointed down at his pants, and added half-jokingly, half seriously, "Look, he's afraid of fairy princesses too. If you say you're Fairy Princess, I'm afraid he's going to cause you grief and only fly at half-mast."

The bottle of mineral water was open, and the little pill was in his hand, but he felt uneasy. He didn't know whether he was uneasy at the pill, at Fairy Princess, or even at himself. He stuffed the pill back in his briefcase. The girl noticed the movement, and asked:

"What's that medicine you're taking, Boss?"

He made light of it:

"It's a quick-acting heart pill. My heart can't take the shock of meeting a fairy princess like you!"

Just then, there was a noise in the darkness outside the room. There was someone thumping their way up the staircase. Liu Sheng gave a great start.

"Who is it? Is it the police?"

The girl listened in the doorway, indicating to him to relax.

"It's not the police, it's your granddad. You obviously didn't tie him up tight enough. He's found the stairs and is coming up."

Liu Sheng went over to the door to listen. He heard Grandfather shouting out his name. He frowned.

"I tied him up really carefully. How could he have got out of knots that tight?"

The mama-san's shrill voice made itself heard from the other side of the mirror:

"The chair! Watch out for the chair! I really have met an evil spirit today! Stop running about everywhere, old man, it'll be my responsibility if you hurt yourself. Tell me the truth, old man; where are you really from? Have you escaped from a mental hospital?"

The young lad was having a great time, and replied for Grandfather:

"With skills like that, he must have come from the circus. Look at the old fool go! He can even climb the stairs when he's tied to a chair!"

Liu Sheng lost interest in anything else. He petted the girl briefly, put on his clothes, and left the secret room. Outside, Grandfather appeared, his head bathed in sweat; the chair was still tied to his back, but somehow or other it had got turned around, so he and the chair were now back to back, and it looked like a pair of conjoined twins coming up the stairs. Liu Sheng seized the chair roughly, in a fit of anger, and carried it back downstairs, shouting at Grandfather:

"I suppose you think you're really clever, climbing the stairs tied to a chair. One day I'll tie you to the van, and see whether you can lift that up on your back and run away. I thought I was doing you a favour, but if I ever take you out again, it's me who'll be the world-class stupid cunt."

It was dusk already outside, and the lamps were giving off a pink light that made the passers-by nervous. He pulled Grandfather along, looking back into the salon. The girl was standing on the staircase, cracking melon seeds, an apathetic look on her face. It was the young lad who came running out, and thrust a pink card into Liu Sheng's hand.

"You're welcome back next time, Boss", the lad said, smiling. "If it's not convenient for you to come here, you can make a booking on the phone, and we'll bring the service to you."

FIVE
THE PUBLIC RELATIONS GIRL

Liu Sheng had a large collection of business cards from places of entertainment, most of them given to him by girls; they were gaudy and drenched in perfume, and he kept them in a special metal box which he hid in a locker in his van. But he put Miss Bai's card straight into his wallet. He had acquired it somewhat differently as he had sneaked it from under the plate glass on the desk in Director Qiao's office. He really needed that card, so he told himself that taking a card wasn't actually stealing. It smelled of French perfume, and the cream-coloured card was embossed with gold and silver print, the writing in both English and Chinese: Zheng Family International Commercial Investment Company – Director of Public Relations. In the top right corner of the card was the silhouette of a woman's head with long eyelashes, a high-bridged nose and her hair in a bob. It was an artistic impression of Miss Bai. The slightly blurred beauty and understated sex appeal perfectly captured, on the card, the real person's mysterious fascination.

He had tested his courage by calling her cell phone, but had cut the call just as he reached the last digit. In fact, he hadn't really thought through what he was going to say to her. Nor was he at all clear about his complex feelings for her; which of them were regrets, and which of them gratitude; which of them stemmed from curiosity, and which from desire. And, above all, which came from that secret tenderness which could never openly be expressed.

By anyone's reckoning, Miss Bai was a beautiful woman. Everywhere, from the Jingting Hospital to the rest of the big wide world, is a beautiful woman's stage. Wherever she goes, men's eyes follow her; her CV is sometimes written in her eyes, and sometimes locked away in a secret drawer, to which gossip and guesswork are the only keys. Liu Sheng heard the staff of the hospital discussing where Miss Bai had come from; some swore that she was the hula queen of the Century Nightclub, where she sang and danced, diabolically seductive, and was the act that effectively ruled the club. This version was entirely plausible as it was well known that Boss Zheng had frequented such nightspots for many years, and Miss Bai could well have benefitted from an intimate acquaintance with him to find herself chosen for bigger and better things. But what about before the nightclub? What was she doing then? Others had heard that Miss Bai had lived in Shenzhen for many years, as the mistress of a Hong Kong businessman, and was famous as the youngest mistress on the circuit. Later, when the businessman took another mistress who was even younger, Miss Bai left Shenzhen in a fit of pique. Although this version seemed less satisfactory, it was still quite believable. But what about before she became a mistress? What was she doing then? No one knew for certain, but there was certainly conjecture, which was proffered with a fair degree of certainty, that before and after were pretty much the same, for what other, more mainstream occupation was open to such a girl? Living off her looks and her body, what else could she have been but an escort or a bar girl?

The deeper he heard these people delving into Miss Bai's past in their discussions, the more fiercely Liu Sheng's heart pounded. What about before that? And before that again? Staff at the Jingting Hospital came and went, and he believed that nobody remembered what had happened at the water tower that year. Even if someone did remember, it wasn't certain that the crime would be traced back to him. Nonetheless he prudently remained silent in these discussions, lest anyone start making deductions and insinuations that would let the cat out of the bag. Staying silent was by far the best way of concealing the turmoil that raged inside him.

For her comings and goings at the hospital, she usually arrived driving a small, lemon-yellow car, and went straight to Building No. 1, so Liu Sheng seldom bumped into her. It was in both their interests to avoid each other, and it became a binding, but unwritten, rule between them. For the majority of the time, this rule brought him peace of mind, but it also left him with an indefinable feeling of loss. He discovered that, far from letting go of her, he was binding her closer to himself. His memories of her youth were like a broken bowl; a broken bowl full of his sins and his shame. A sticky, foamy liquid seeped from its shattered rim, formed of his remaining sense of honour and pride - her first time was with me; her body once belonged to me; her whole self, every bit of it, once belonged to me.

The truth was he really wanted to see her, and he often went over to Building No. 1 to spy on her. Her office had velvet curtains hanging in the windows, and a yellow-flowering potted cactus on the window ledge. He couldn't tell what she was doing behind the curtains. What was she doing? Next door to her office was Boss Zheng's Special Bedroom No. 2. Special Bedroom No. 2 had a balcony, on which there was a parasol, shading a round plastic table. On that table, there was another potted, yellow-flowering cactus. The two identical plants with their identical flowers clearly indicated the close connection between the two rooms. Right from the start he couldn't rid himself of the suspicion that the relationship between her and Boss Zheng was not just that of employer and employee, but was rather that of employer and secret mistress. What did the so-called PR girl actually have to do for her boss?

He had never seen Boss Zheng actually use the balcony; he had only seen his Mercedes pulling up outside the building. Boss Zheng's luxurious but secretive life-style was the burning topic of conversation amongst the staff of the Jingting Hospital, but it also became a topic of scientific investigation. His phobias became more and more pronounced. They started with a fear of ropes and of the night, but progressed to fear of the morning, of dogs and of strangers. No drugs had any effect, and any attempt at psychiatric therapy proved entirely useless. The treatment team comprising specialists and psychiatrists alike were at a loss what to do. They wrote a combined paper, which they submitted to an international journal on psychiatric medicine, entitled: The explosion of wealth, and the syndrome of wealth-related mental illness amongst the nouveaux riches. Boss Zheng was the primary subject of their case study, and he entered the field of worldwide scientific research under the pseudonym 'Mister Z'. As Mister Z he presented a particular pathology which was only touched on in the published paper, as it was only just unfolding at the time. He had an exaggerated dependence on beautiful women, and it was only such a woman that could temper his violent outbursts. It was also only the presence of a beautiful woman that could persuade him to accept his various treatments with equanimity.

Director Qiao had personally told Liu Sheng that Madam Zheng had already taken over complete control of her younger brother's business, leaving him only with the means to pay for his young companions. Just the sight of Boss Zheng's Mercedes parking outside Building No. 1 was enough to tell everyone there was a girl in his room. These girls always nonchalantly carried a bunch of fresh flowers, to maintain the pretence that they were simply visiting a patient. They came every few days, each time a new face, and each face more beautiful than the one before it. Director Qiao was heard to sigh:

"This Boss Zheng really is an afront to public morals, but there's not a lot I can do about it; and I don't envy Miss Bai's job either. She's the one who chooses all the girls, always under 25 and always beautiful. It's just a beauty contest, that's all it is."

This inside information made Liu Sheng feel unaccountably uncomfortable:

"What the fuck! Has she been driven mad by poverty?" he swore to himself. "She's no PR girl, she's a full-time pimp!"

On Boss Zheng's thirtieth birthday, a luxury people carrier was given permission to enter the Jingting Hospital grounds. It stopped next to Building No. 1, and from it descended a twittering knot of girls. Once out of the vehicle, they split up into a few groups. One group was heavily made-up and scantily clad, characterised by their smouldering eroticism and sensuality; another group comprised girls dressed in white tops, skirts and trainers; clearly chaste and virtuous, they looked like fashion models from different companies, readying themselves for the catwalk, and taking the measure of each other in an atmosphere that was less than friendly. Some of them began to bicker, and one girl said in Mandarin, with a strong Sichuan accent:

"You think you look Western, do you? If you hadn't had a nose-job to pad it out, I would have gobbled it up in one bite!"

The other girl, obviously from the northeast, shouted back:

"I may look like a Westerner or not, but what about you, playing the innocent virgin? If I've had a nose-job, what have you had done? Just look at your boobs! There's so much silicone, aren't you afraid you'll explode?"

Miss Bai put a stop to the squabbling:

"That's enough! Be quiet! Have you forgotten? How many times have I told you, this isn't a night club, it's a mental hospital! Anyone who kicks off again won't get paid."

She ordered the noisy gaggle of women to form an orderly line, and they filed into Building No. 1 in a cloud of pungent perfume. Master Zhang, the porter, stood at the bottom of the staircase counting carefully: thirty girls in all. Somewhat panicked by the number, he asked Miss Bai:

"I thought you were just celebrating Boss Zheng's birthday. Why are there so many girls?"

"We're throwing him a birthday party. Boss Zheng is 30 today, so there are 30 girls and each one will sing a song. So it's just the right number, not a single girl too many."

Master Zhang said:

"If there are usually three girls to an act, and there are thirty girls going up there, what kind of a racket is that going to make? This is a top-grade mental hospital, not a dance hall. The most I'll let in is ten, and the rest will have to go home."

Miss Bai slipped a red envelope into Master Zhang's hand:

"It has to be all of them, Master Zhang. It's so quiet here all the time; quiet as the grave, don't you think? I'm really not up to anything, but don't you think the occasional party would be good for everyone's spirits and for their health!"

Thirty young girls holding a birthday party in a ward in a mental hospital may not exactly have written a new chapter in the annals of psychiatric medicine but it was, at least, a glorious moment in the history of the Jingting Hospital. The celebration started out quite restrained, and the songs that could be heard issuing from the doors and windows were harmless and pleasant enough to listen to: almost certainly they were coming from the chaste and virtuous-looking group of girls. But before long, it was the turn of the smouldering, erotic girls who were indeed smouldering and erotic, and who completely out-matched their chaste and virtuous opponents. One girl in particular started singing a very lively song, the words of which weren't very clear, apart from her heavy breathing and raucous chant of COME ON, COME ON, COME ON!

Another girl took up the chant, heckling irreverently:

"COME ON, COME ON, STRIP, COME ON, GET ON WITH IT, STRIP!"

An uproarious party atmosphere quickly developed in Special Bedroom No. 2, and its wanton rhythms soon disrupted the whole Jingting Hospital. The patients stuck their heads out of their ward doors and windows, trying to make out the words of the song and the contents of the unbridled shouts and yells. It wasn't long before someone deciphered them, and began to chant enthusiastically:

"KAMANG, STRIP, KAMANG, GET ON WITH IT, STRIP!"

The peaceful suburban atmosphere was shattered by a kind of euphoria; the kind of joy the Jingting Hospital had never, ever witnessed before. It spread to all corners of the building, intensifying as it went. It was charged with waves of sensuality, part unbridled, part shame-faced, both western and more traditional in their form, and these waves suffused some of the patients already suffering from overactive sex drives. A horde of young male patients poured out of buildings No. 1 and No. 2, rampant as wild stallions, and shouting as they ran:

"KAMANG, STRIP, STRIP! KAMANG, GET ON WITH IT, STRIP!"

Red-faced and ears burning, they hurled themselves like eager invitees towards the party room in Building No. 1.

The security guards outside the main building had no chance of halting this flood of humanity, and all they could do was shout out to the porter inside the building:

"The patients are rioting! Quick! Lock the doors! Lock the doors!"

Master Zhang came running out of the janitor's office in a panic, and saw one of the male patients, dressed only in underpants, running up the stairs, brandishing his vest, and yelling:

"Strip! Upstairs and let's all strip!"

Master Zhang hurled himself upstairs, and was just wrestling with the patient, when the riotous music was interrupted by a loud, sharp bang, followed by the sound of breaking glass. There was quiet for a few seconds, followed immediately by the screams of the girls. The guards, Master Zhang and the patient on the stairs all froze. It was the patient who reacted first, clutching his head in his hands and running out of the building shouting:

"They're shooting! Don't strip! Someone's shooting!"

Commander Kang, of Special Bedroom No. 1, had opened fire.

It was the commander in Special Bedroom No. 1 who had fired the shot.

By the time Liu Sheng had run over to Building No.1, the party had already broken up, and the rioting patients had all been dragged away by the guards. All that was left behind was a single man's sandal, looking, from a distance, like a giant exclamation mark. Through the door and window of Commander Kang's room, he could see a figure moving about, but he couldn't tell whether it was Commander Kang's army orderly, a member of his family, or the man himself. He advanced a few paces, but when he got too close, the window's mauve velvet curtains were pulled tight shut.

After a while, Miss Bai led the troupe of girls downstairs and out of the building where they all scrambled to be first onto the minibus. The great waft of perfume that came off them made Liu Sheng sneeze. Most of the girls looked terrified, but there were two of them who retained their poise, and argued as they went:

"It was only a rubber bullet. He was only trying to scare us, wasn't he?"

"You wish! The man's a commander, and he's got a real gun."

Liu Sheng saw Miss Bai carrying a column speaker, an indignant look on her face, and arguing with one of the girls who was getting a little ahead of herself:

"Get in the minibus first, and then we'll talk money. You'll get paid every cent you're owed."

Thus Miss Bai's carefully-planned, grand celebration came to an ignominious end, leaving her in a vile temper. Liu Sheng didn't know where he found the courage, but he went over to her and said:

"Let me help you with the speaker."

Miss Bai glanced at him coldly:

"Who are you? I don't know you. Get out of my way."

Ignoring her rudeness and keeping his expression neutral, he replied:

"You may not recognise me, but I know you, and if there's anything I can help you with, you just have to ask."

Miss Bai made her way over to the door of the minibus, carrying the speaker, but suddenly stopped and turned to look at him:

"Come over here; there is something you can help me with."

Fawning with gratitude for this favour, he followed her onto the minibus, and heard her say, in a low voice:

"Boss Zheng wants a pistol too. Money's no object. Can you get one?"

Liu Sheng gave a start. When he realised she wasn't joking, he gestured defensively:

"This is not a matter of keeping up with the Jonses. It doesn't matter how much money you've got, there's no way of getting hold of a pistol. Commander Kang didn't buy his gun, it goes with his rank."

She blinked at this, first showing disappointment which quickly changed to disapproval:

"You're still the same, too fond of the sound of your own voice. I guess you can't teach a dog to stop eating its own shit."

She shoved him aside with the speaker, and continued angrily:

"How do you think you can help me? I know just what you're worth. Now get out of my way!"

. . .

It wasn't unreasonable for her not to trust him.

He had spent so many years keeping his head down, living with his tail between his legs, whilst she was still the same Fairy Princess, bold, headstrong and brazen. Liu Sheng was willing to put up with her rudeness, but not her contempt. He wasn't quite sure whether he was acting out of exasperation with Miss Bai or with himself, but from that day on, he kept his ears open wherever he went trying to find a way of buying a pistol.

Liu Sheng had many friends from all walks of life, and after listening to a host of advice, someone finally suggested he go and find Li Damao, an unlicensed minibus driver at the railway station, to see what he could do. He didn't know Li, but made a special trip to the station and, mingling with a group of migrant workers, boarded his minibus. The man looked familiar, but Liu Sheng couldn't immediately remember where he had seen him before. He stood beside the driver's seat and coughed a couple of times, hoping that Li would recognise him first. Li Damao's elbow dug him hard in the ribs:

"Do you want to drive the bus instead of me? Stand back a bit."

There was nothing for it but for him to introduce himself:

"I'm Liu Sheng from Red Toon Street, a friend of Lao San from the East Gate. I think we met at Lao San's house."

Li Damao didn't play ball:

"Who is Lao San? If you've got something to say, spit it out; if you're going to fart, just get on with it."

Li Damao didn't like to beat about the bush, but nor did Liu Sheng dare get straight to the point. He tried to probe him cautiously:

"I've heard you have replicas for sale."

Li Damao glanced sidelong at him, weighing him up:

"You've got the wrong man. Go to a toy shop if you want replicas, I've only got the real thing."

Liu Sheng hurriedly bent down and whispered in his ear:

"I know. Give me a price."

Li Damao suddenly looked serious as he took one hand off the steering wheel, and flashed five fingers at Liu Sheng.

"Burmese model, 30,000; American model, 50,000. If you want the Burmese, I need an 8,000 *yuan* deposit; 10,000 for an American one."

Li Damao was so cocky, Liu Sheng didn't believe him at first, and just stood there at the front of the bus, staring. The migrant workers all listened wide-eyed to this exchange, not understanding what was going on. Liu Sheng looked round at the unfamiliar, sun-darkened faces, and felt a little afraid. He straightened up and got off the bus, saying:

"The money's no problem; I just need to go back and talk to my boss."

He hesitated for two days, but couldn't stop thinking about the affair. No matter whether Li Damao was to be trusted or not, this was an opportunity to be of service to her. He telephoned her to fix a time to meet, but as soon as she heard his voice, without a pause, she just said "wrong number" and hung up on him. There was nothing for it but for him to go and see her in person.

On the day in question, he chanced to bump into Madam Zheng as she came out of Building No.1, closely followed by two monks in yellow robes. Puzzled, he asked the porter, Master Zhang:

"Why has Madam Zheng brought these monks to see her brother?"

"She'll try anything in a crisis. She's beginning to think the doctors are useless, so she's giving prayer and incense a go."

Liu Sheng and Master Zhang were old friends, so he gave him a cigarette and made his way upstairs. When he reached the door to Miss Bai's office, he smelled the strong, sweet smell of incense billowing out of the room. He momentarily wondered if he had got the wrong room. He pushed at the half-open door, and saw that the wide room had been half opened-up to form an altar chamber. She was lying on a prayer mat, with her legs raised straight up into the air, practising her yoga. Behind her there was a rosewood altar table adorned with a gilt-bronze statue of a bodhisattva, and an incense-burner from which coiled plumes of smoke. The flickering light from red candles illuminated her face, points of light flicking on and off on her forehead and cheekbones.

"What are you up to?" he called out, familiarly.

"Do I know you?" She looked at him coldly. "Can't you see I'm in the middle of my yoga? Yoga can't be interrupted, so just get out."

Her legs were still pointing up in the air, and he examined the tips of her toes; her toenails were painted with bright red nail varnish, apparently freshly applied and still glistening.

"I know Your Excellency must be very busy, but didn't you ask me to get a gun for you? Well, I've found a way."

He had decided in advance on his own commission, and he slowly extended two fingers towards her:

"It's a 20,000 deposit, then 40,000 for a Burmese gun, and 60,000 for an American one. I don't think that's too expensive, and your Boss Zheng has certainly got the money."

She looked slyly at his two fingers:

"Is it really that easy to get a gun? All this 40,000 for a Burmese, 60,000 for an American: don't you think that's too cheap?"

He studied her expression, unsure of the implications of what she was saying. He was about to adjust his prices downwards, when he heard her snort, and begin to laugh. The sound of her laughter made him uneasy, and his expression hardened.

"Does Boss Zheng actually want to buy a gun or not? I've worked hard at this, and taken some big risks, and you're just messing me around?"

"I can't be bothered to mess you around; you're just too stupid!"

She finished her yoga and stood up, massaging her lower back.

"I was just venting my anger when I said that, but you took it to heart. Do you know why he wanted a gun? To take revenge on Commander Kang. That's a madman talking, and you took it seriously? You're the one who's wrong in the head", she said jeeringly, extending one hand with the fingers in orchid-form, pointing at the statue of the bodhisattva. "Do you know what that is? It's a bodhisattva from the Great Dragon Temple. Boss Zheng has converted to Buddhism. He spends all day now burning incense and reading sutras. Do you think he still wants to buy a gun?"

Liu Sheng stared at the glittering golden statue sitting in its shrine, and wanted to swear, but didn't dare. He looked like a lovelorn clown getting only whistles and catcalls after putting his all into his performance. He felt a little angry and humiliated. Then her cell phone rang, and she went over to her desk to pick it up, gesturing him away as she did so.

"You'd better get out; I've got to take this."

He hurried angrily over to the door, muttering:

"What's the use of burning incense and praying to the Buddha? You need to watch out for me."

From behind him, she said:

"Who are you telling to watch out? Let me tell you, Liu Sheng, you can't clear the debt you owe me in this lifetime. I just despise you too much to be bothered to claim it from you."

SIX
THE INCENSE HALL

LIU SHENG and Director Qiao's weekly Go games had come to an end. Director Qiao said he had too much on his plate and no inclination to play. Liu Sheng was not happy about this, and went straight to the director's office and knocked on the door. Director Qiao came out and shoved him brusquely back into the corridor.

"Can't you see I've got important visitors? How could I have time to play Go? Commander Kang's wife's here." Liu Sheng craned his neck to look into the director's office, and saw several figures milling around, and a white-haired old woman sitting on the sofa with an indignant expression on her face. She was wearing a khaki wool overcoat and leaning on a black lacquer cane with a carved dragon-head handle. She turned to cast an icy glance at Liu Sheng, redolent with indifferent natural authority, and Liu Sheng slipped self-consciously to one side, and closed the door on the company.

He understood the fix Director Qiao was in. Of the two patients in the two special rooms, one had money, and the other had a gun, and it so happened that they were mortal and implacable enemies. Each side was barely containing its anger, and Director Qiao was caught in the middle, like a punch-bag. Of the two, he found the pressure coming from Boss Zheng easier to deal with, and it was Commander Kang's gun that gave him the biggest headache. The commander had once crashed into the director's office, pointing his gun at Director Qiao's head and accusing him of only caring about profit, of abandoning the Party line, of pandering to nouveaux-riche capitalists by introducing corruption and depravity into the private rooms, and of supporting ancient feudalistic superstitions. Director Qiao had been scared out of his wits. Afterwards he showed Commander Kang's family the mark from the muzzle of the gun on his forehead, and suggested to them that, whatever the commander's reputation as a man of honour and virtue, he was, after all, still a mental patient. He was afraid that, if the commander were to keep his gun, there was the risk of a fatal accident.

"The hospital doesn't have the authority to confiscate the commander's weapon, but you all need to be careful, because you can't let him go running around everywhere with a gun, venting his anger."

The family were happy to endorse this viewpoint, but they also pointed out to Director Qiao how annoying the parvenu next door was, and hadn't he made his money by rubbing people's backs in bathhouses?

"With him spreading that kind of dirty money around, he's brought a nasty atmosphere into the special patients' rooms. We understand that you and your hospital are hostages to economics, but as director, you must also stick to your principles. If all you think of is money, then perhaps you won't be able to hang onto your position that long."

Although Director Qiao might say that that was all the same to him, Liu Sheng knew that any official was far more concerned about keeping his post than losing it. Besides, that post was also Liu Sheng's protection. He was very concerned to find a way out of these difficulties for Director Qiao, and bitterly regretted that he couldn't see how to do so. After racking his brains, he went down to the town's flea market and bought an old bronze coin to give to the director, as a comforting talisman. The coin carried the inscription 官运亨通 (*guanyun hengtong*) – an auspicious official career.

He took the coin in its little brocade box on a special visit to Director Qiao's office. The director was very touched by this unusual and considerate gift. Weighing the coin in his hand, he said:

"Come on in. As to how auspicious my career is going to be, I can't say, but let's see how good my luck is with a game of Go."

There was a lingering scent of perfume in Director Qiao's office; it gave the chaos of the room a somewhat ambiguous atmosphere. She had been there. Wherever she went, she couldn't help leaving some trace of herself; if it wasn't the smell of perfume and make-up, then it was the scent of money. He noticed that the drawer of Director Qiao's desk was half-open, revealing a kraft paper envelope and a finely decorated silver-coloured square box.

"You shouldn't leave your drawer open like that, director. You should shut it immediately." He closed the drawer then turned to wink at the director. "Has Miss Bai been here? How did it go?"

Director Qiao took exception to his frivolous expression:

"What do you think you mean by winking at me like that? She didn't come here to seduce me or to bribe me. Something has happened in the special patients' rooms. Commander Kang has smashed up Boss Zheng's altar room!"

Without knowing quite why, Liu Sheng snorted with laughter, but when he saw the ugly look on Director Qiao's face, he hurriedly put on an appropriately serious expression, and said:

"What upset the commander so much?"

Director Qiao took out the Go board and put it on the tea table. He sighed continuously, apparently still not in the mood for the game. Liu Sheng followed his serious gaze, and saw a mound of something, covered in a red cloth, on the desk. Intrigued, he went over and was about to lift the cloth when Director Qiao stopped him.

"Don't touch it. Try and guess what it is first."

Liu Sheng tried cigarettes first, then suggested Maotai or Wuliangye (both types of Chinese wine). Director Qiao looked at him disdainfully, rubbed his hands together in a self-satisfied manner, and lifted the cloth. There was a great flash of gold, that almost blinded Liu Sheng.

"You see? The bodhisattva from the Great Dragon Temple has ended up here with me!"

Momentarily stunned, Liu Sheng recognised the gilt-bronze

bodhisattva from Miss Bai's office, which he hadn't seen for a few days. It now had a number of crude scars on its head.

What had happened was that Madam Zheng had brought nine Buddhist monks to Building No.1 to chant sutras and exorcise demons for her brother; the incense burned more brightly, and activity increased. The pall of fragrant smoke increased, and the sound of the monks' voices grew louder; precisely the two things that most enraged Commander Kang. His army orderly went to protest, but Madam Zheng ignored him, so the commander took matters into his own hands. He scooped up the statue under his only good arm, and threw it out of the second-floor window. Madam Zheng and the nine monks couldn't believe their eyes, until they heard the loud thud of the bodhisattva landing on the lawn outside. Only then did they cry out:

"You're a commander! How can you treat a bodhisattva like this? A bodhisattva won't have any respect for your rank, so you'd better beware of retribution."

Later, the damaged statue was brought to Director Qiao's office by the nine monks. Following behind them, Madam Zheng's sorrow was already supplanting her anger. Director Qiao observed:

"Madam Zheng is such a forceful woman but she met her match in Commander Kang. It was the first time I've seen her with tears in her eyes."

Director Qiao took possession of the statue with all due sorrow and apology, but a working office was in no way a suitable, long-term resting place for such a sacred object. As soon as Madam Zheng recovered herself, they discussed the best place for the bodhisattva. They had not been able to come to any agreement, when Miss Bai brought in the big kraft paper envelope.

"It wasn't a bribe", Director Qiao said. "It was building money. Madam Zheng wants the Jingting Hospital to find a suitably peaceful spot to build an incense hall for the exclusive use of Boss Zheng."

Liu Sheng was silent for a moment, thoroughly taken by surprise, then clicked his tongue and sighed:

"Building your own temple, that's real money! That's something else!

The bloody rich really aren't like the rest of us. A gun is useful enough, but if you think about it, it's not nearly as good as having money!"

"It may not be a problem for them, but it is for me!" Director Qiao spread his arms towards Liu Sheng, with a rueful expression on his face. "Tell me, where am I going to find a vacant spot to build an incense hall? For better or worse, the Jingting Hospital has a certain reputation, and is held up as a model establishment; it has been for many years. Who could dare spoil the environment of the hospital grounds? If there's an inspection, or the media get hold of the story, it's me who will get it in the neck!"

Liu Sheng glanced at the drawer, thinking to himself:

"If you don't want to build the hall, Director Qiao, why did you take her money?"

But he kept these words to himself. It doesn't matter how grand people are, duplicity is never far away, and who wouldn't be tempted by such a fat envelope once it was in their hands? He blinked and considered Director Qiao's problem, whilst making his move on the Go board. He had just placed his first stone when the light suddenly dawned on him.

"I've got it!" he exclaimed.

Director Qiao looked at him doubtfully, and Liu Sheng continued:

"I've got just the place! Just the place for Boss Zheng to burn his incense. You don't have to find any empty plot to build on; isn't the water tower just made for the job? You just have to find someone to make a few alterations, and you can let Boss Zheng go there and burn his incense without bothering anyone. How good is that?!"

Liu Sheng had long thought he was cleverer than other people, and this was a perfect illustration. He listened to Director Qiao's unstinting praise. First he praised his intelligence, and then his business acumen, and when the praise was finished they got down to brass tacks: remodelling, redecoration, accommodating the bodhisattva and its shrine, purchasing an incense burner and some candlesticks. Naturally, all this was to be handled by Liu Sheng. He was particularly interested in the opportunities for major profit such a half-private, half-public affair offered, but it was not completely straightforward. If he was to make his profit, he had to bring workers into the water tower, and the thought of such prolonged association with the place gave him goose bumps. So he stammered out:

"There's no need for any nonsense between us, Director Qiao. Let's have our game of Go, and then talk about the works. There's no need to rush."

As far as Director Qiao was concerned there was nothing to discuss with Liu Sheng, as all the negotiation needed to be done with Madam Zheng. He spent three hours talking her round. Madam Zheng was convinced the bodhisattva was her brother's last hope. Bodhisattvas are nourished by incense, and she believed in her bodhisattva so fervently she could not possibly deprive it of its nourishment. So, in the end, she reluctantly acquiesced to the alteration of the water tower into an incense hall. She insisted that the work begin at once and that it be completed within ten days, so that Boss Zheng could start burning incense as soon as possible.

Director Qiao called Liu Sheng into his office and gave him a sum of money on the spot. Liu Sheng stared at the money then took it, but after taking it, he took fright, and said, experimentally:

"I've never built and consecrated a temple so could I put out a contract and get a specialist in for you?"

Director Qiao looked at him distrustfully:

"What do you need a specialist for? You're not building some grand temple. It's just some nouveaux riches and their superstitions; all you have to do is find a suitable spot, and glitz it up a bit. This is the first time I've seen you turn down a business opportunity. If you bring someone else in, won't you lose a lot of your money?"

Liu Sheng hesitated, then said:

"It's not a question of money but I have been thinking. My parents are Buddhists and if we put the bodhisattva in the water tower it might hold me responsible!"

Director Qiao replied:

"I'm a believer too, and I know the bodhisattva is ubiquitous and all-forgiving. It's not as small-minded as you. People build temples and burn incense in the wildest places, so why should you worry about a water tower? That tower was built in the 1950s and it's not made out of bean curd. The bodhisattva will be quite safe there, so what blame could it attach to you?"

These works surpassed any other business he could possibly have imagined. It had never occurred to him that, ten years on, he would return to the water tower and use that abandoned edifice to earn money. Taking these works in hand was like banishing a nightmare, like packaging it up. It wasn't difficult to do, but it needed strength of character. The project bothered him, but the combination of his obligations and the prospective profit, overcame his misgivings, and he ended up by buckling down to the task.

The water tower had been a no-go area for him, and he hadn't been there for many years.

Having made his way through the bushes, there was the tower, its roof still a home for the crows. It was covered in moss, which in turn was covered in dust: after the passage of so many years, no trace of the old crime scene remained. Everything should now be forgotten. The tower maintained its silence, but disturbing it still were the two crows on its roof. Liu Sheng had always thought there was something weird about their cawing, which echoed through the empty air, shrill and disturbing, enumerating the vicissitudes of his life. He was afraid of their cries. He remembered with terrible clarity that, as he fled into the dusk that time, everywhere was silent except for those two crows, shrilly cawing out their eye-witness testimony.

He brought in three workmen to work for one week, and the alterations and redecorations were complete. It was, in fact, quite a simple operation, dividing the tower neatly in two, with the incense hall at the bottom. He had the workmen block up the iron staircase that led to the upper level, intending that spot for the bodhisattva's shrine. Once the rusty staircase disappeared under a layer of reinforced concrete, his nightmare was buried, and the world of the water tower was changed completely. As he watched the workmen covering the wall with a coat of emulsion paint, his heart suddenly filled with unspeakable joy. In building that wall, it was as though he had undergone a rebirth. Because of this, against his normal inclinations, he congratulated the workmen effusively:

"Good work! Your concreting and painting are both excellent."

Once the workmen had finished, he telephoned Miss Bai, and invited her, in a very business-like tone, to come and inspect the works. At the other end, Miss Bai was silent for a moment, then suddenly swore violently. He had been expecting this, and responded swiftly:

"You have to let go of the past, and the things that happened then."

She hung up on him. He imagined her feelings at the other end of the line, and decided that her oath was the product of only a mild hatred, and that the past had indeed already been let go. He went outside, and looked up at the darkened window of the pump room where, purely by chance, a sparrow came flying out of the trees, and in through the window. From then on, only birds could access that forbidden zone. He felt a sense of gratification. With his own hands, he had blocked out a dark memory; with his own hands, he had shut off the road to his past sins. He had entrusted the bodhisattva with his secret, and from then on the compassionate deity would keep it safe.

Madam Zheng chose an auspicious day to visit the new bodhisattva, which came from the even more famous Temple of Sublime Light. But however auspicious a day is, it has no control over the weather. The day was dark and gloomy, and the water tower certainly did not look as though it had made any special preparations to welcome the bodhisattva. The Japanese creeper that wound around the tower in summer had already succumbed to the late autumn weather, and its withered branches and tendrils danced in the bitter wind; the tower looked like a giant with tousselled hair and a sinister expression on its face. Liu Sheng stood on the threshold directing two porters who were carrying the enthroned bodhisattva in from a van. The porters were novices at the job, tripping over their own feet. One careless moment, a screeching sound, and a piece of gold lacquer chipped off one of the statue's feet. He couldn't hold back a warning shout:

"Watch the feet! Watch the hands! Watch the bodhisattva's head!"

With great difficulty, the statue was manoeuvred into the water tower and placed on a marble tabletop. Its previously shrouded figure now displayed its solemn grandeur, and the water tower began to light up with its radiance. Liu Sheng looked at the statue's golden hands, one of which was raised, pointing to the southwest, a rich golden radiance emanating from its fingertips. As he understood it, the bodhisattva's gesture did not represent forgiveness, but forgetfulness. He felt at peace, his faith in that golden light complete. He remembered his mother's words:

"Whoever lights the first stick of incense for a newly dedicated bodhisattva will enjoy its protection for their whole life."

He didn't actually dare light the first stick, afraid lest a member of the Zheng family might notice the ash. But, taking advantage of the fact that the family were still on their way, he knelt down and made the first obeisance, praying:

"Bodhisattva protect me! I have renewed myself and I am no longer a bad boy."

SEVEN
SHAME

IN HIS CIRCLE OF FRIENDS, Liu Sheng was held in quite high esteem. By the standards of Red Toon Street, his lifestyle was approaching that of a celebrity. He knew how to earn money and how to spend it. Whenever he met with success, he rewarded himself with a new suit or the latest cell phone; if he'd made a real killing, he'd first brag about it to his friends, and then take them all out for a meal, or to the sauna, or to a KTV bar, so they could share in his good fortune. When the water tower works were finished, as usual he invited Chungeng and Ah Liu to the health spa. This time, as luck would have it, just as the Thai massage girl was walking on Liu Sheng's back, his cell phone rang. Just as he was saying he would reject the call, he saw that it was from Director Qiao. He picked up the phone and explained to his friends:

"I have to take Director Qiao's calls; they always mean there's a chance of making some money."

In fact, it wasn't a money-making opportunity, rather it was a heap of trouble. Director Qiao told him that someone had forced open the doors to the incense hall and he wanted Liu Sheng to install a stronger security door. Liu Sheng hadn't expected an incense hall in a converted water tower at the Jingting Hospital to attract this kind of attention; although Boss Zheng had provided the funds to build the shrine, it had not been his good fortune to burn the first stick of incense there. The people of the area all held the temple of Sublime Light in great reverence, and with the golden bodhisattva from there now in the water tower, they couldn't suppress their burning desire to kneel down before it. Very early in the morning, someone broke in and usurped Boss Zheng in burning the first incense stick. They left ash all over the place, and everything dirty and in disarray. Director Qiao said Boss Zheng was very angry that he hadn't got to burn the first incense, and he didn't want to go to the water tower to burn any incense at all. Director Qiao also said that he was very angry too:

"That was no small sum of money I gave you, Liu Sheng. Why did you try to cheat them by just using any old wooden door? You have to be honest and conscientious when you're being paid, so why didn't you install a security door from the start?"

Liu Sheng's heart sank. He put down his phone and said grumpily to Chungeng and Ah Liu:

"It's not easy making an honest buck. As soon as I've finished building the place, I have to go back for repairs. What a pain!"

He didn't dare ignore Director Qiao, so he left the spa immediately and drove his van straight to the hardware market where he bought a sturdy security door and hired a craftsman to install it. As he drove into the hospital grounds, he saw in the distance the figure of a woman dressed in black outside the water tower. It looked very much like Miss Bai, but by the time he had parked the van and helped the craftsman unload the security door, there was no sign of her, and all there was to be seen was the pair of crows standing guard on the rooftop, cawing away.

The door to the water tower had been well and truly forced. While the craftsman busied himself with the replacement, Liu Sheng took the opportunity to examine the incense hall and discovered that the interior was indeed in a terrible state. The four prayer mats were nowhere to be seen and there was a jumble of footprints all over the newly-laid cream-coloured tiles. The fresh white emulsion paint on the walls already had a smoky tinge from the lavish burning of incense. The incense sticks and candles were extinguished now, but in front of the shrine could be seen all manner of improvised incense burners: some were fashioned from cut-down Coca-Cola bottles, others from disposable paper cups, and others still from bits of broken crockery. He saw a scroll with congratulatory couplets resting in the golden arms of the Bodhisattva: **Wishing a swift return to health for all the patients of the Jingting Hospital.** There were also a lot of red and yellow coloured paper slips on the bodhisattva's lotus throne. He opened some out and read them; mostly they were wishes from the devotees for the curing of some illness or other, some of them clearly from medical personnel at the hospital. There was a prayer to the bodhisattva that a middle-school student called Pangpang should pass the examination for senior high school, another prayed that Wang Caixia should get her accountancy certificate. The last thing he expected was to see a malicious piece of white paper in amongst the devotees' good wishes: a piece of white paper with black characters, that stood out from all the others: **Liu Sheng is a rapist.** He broke out into a cold sweat, completely at a loss why anyone should want to inform on him to the bodhisattva like this. His first thought was that it must be Miss Bai, but when he looked closely at the characters and thought about it, he began to suspect Grandfather. He hadn't attended to him for ages; could that old idiot have taken this secret revenge on him. But he was well aware of Grandfather's physical capabilities, and knew that he was so enfeebled that it was a long time since he'd even been able to hold a brush. He sniffed the paper, as though he might be able to smell the author, but of course he couldn't.

"Shit!" he exclaimed, grinding his teeth, as he tore the strip of paper into little pieces.

Director Qiao instructed him to take the new keys over to Miss Bai, so he made his way over to Building No. 1. He pushed at her door, but it wouldn't open. He couldn't hear anything going on inside, but for some reason he didn't understand, he didn't dare knock. He paced around at the top of the stairs for a bit, and ended up by going back down to the porter's lodge, where he asked Master Zhang, the porter, to give the keys to Miss Bai for him.

"I'm sorry to bother you, but could you tell Miss Bai that from tomorrow, Boss Zheng can go and burn his first incense. With the door

I've installed now, those devout patients won't even be able to get in with a bazooka."

Master Zhang hung the keys on a hook on the wall, and looked straight at Liu Sheng. With a guffaw of laughter, he said:

"Even if they used your bazooka, Liu Sheng? I've heard you've got a really big one!"

Liu Sheng felt this joke was going too far:

"What do you mean, old man. You're not a girl, so what's the size of my bazooka to you?"

"Nothing to me, but what about Miss Bai? I've heard tell that in the past you and your, er, you know, you and Miss Bai...."

Liu Sheng gave a start, and his face went white:

"Did what? What do you mean?"

Master Zhang looked embarrassed, not daring to utter the word 'rape', and instead just made a rude gesture with his hands:

"Is what I heard true, then?"

Liu Sheng looked at him blankly for a couple of seconds, then pulled open the window of the porter's lodge, and shouted:

"Is someone else saying I gave your mother a seeing-to, eh? Is that it?"

He stormed out of Building No. 1. At first he didn't fully understand the damage Master Zhang's words had done; he just felt his chest tightening, his head spinning, and his legs turning to rubber. When he reached the canteen, and opened the door of his van, two cooks standing in the door of the building looked him up and down in astonishment.

"What's up with you, Liu Sheng? You don't look right at all."

He felt his face:

"What's wrong with how I look?" he asked. Then he massaged his stomach. "I've got a stomach ache, a really bad stomach ache."

Then, his stomach really did begin to hurt. He looked in the rear-view mirror of the van, and saw his ashen face, and beads of sweat the size of beans trickling down his forehead and along his cheek. A stomach ache. A really bad stomach ache. And not just his stomach; a stabbing pain pierced his whole abdomen. He felt really ill. He couldn't get Master Zhang's rude gesture out of his head: it was like a sharp knife, dripping with poison, cutting into his old wound. He thought that wound had healed years ago, but all that time it had been festering, and opened up again at a touch. All this time he had been making his way in life, he couldn't understand why he had become more and more sensitive. He had been ignoring his own self-esteem, and underestimated his fragility. As well as shame and pain, he was also feeling self-pity.

EIGHT
STORM IN A WATER TOWER

Liu Sheng went to hospital to have his stomach looked at.

The doctor gave him a gastroscopy but couldn't find anything wrong. He asked Liu Sheng what he did for a living, and Liu Sheng replied that he had his own building materials company. The doctor's opinion was that, since he could find nothing physically wrong with his stomach, his discomfort was probably caused by the stress of his work, and suggested that he reorganise his daily schedule, and give himself some time to recuperate. He was delighted with the doctor's advice, and went home to tell his parents that he was going to slow down and go off travelling. His mother and father were sympathetic and themselves took over his daily provisions run to the Jingting Hospital; the other delivery runs became the responsibility of Liu Sheng's young cousin on his mother's side.

Liu Sheng suggested to Chungeng and Ah Liu they go travelling together, first to Hangzhou, then on to Huangshan. Whilst they were taking a boat trip on West Lake, Director Qiao called Liu Sheng's cell phone, and there was another call when they were viewing the clouds on Huangshan. To Chungeng and Ah Liu's amazement, Liu Sheng didn't answer either call:

"Aren't Director Qiao's calls always a chance to make money? Why aren't you taking them?"

Liu Sheng replied confidently:

"He's not after me for anything good this time; I can always tell whether it's money or trouble."

And he was right. A storm had blown up at the Jingting Hospital over the last few days, and he was doing well to avoid it.

Boss Zheng rode in a Mercedes limousine to go and burn incense. He wore a bullet-proof vest, covered by a black wind-cheater; with his dark glasses, face mask and baseball cap, nothing of him was visible except for his two ears. He looked untouchable. With these comprehensive security measures in place, Madam Zheng chose a retired military intelligence agent as his driver-cum-bodyguard. She also appointed an ex-bodybuilder as his personal protection officer. Accompanied by these two hulking brutes, Boss Zheng looked just like a mob boss from the movies, and made a very imposing sight.

The car journey from Building No. 1 through the trees to the water tower only took about a minute. Boss Zheng often slept late, so it was sometimes eleven o'clock or midday when he went to burn his first incense stick. This was rather too leisurely a morning programme for the other worshippers of the Jingting Hospital, and there were people waiting outside the water tower at seven o'clock. They waited patiently for Boss Zheng to burn the first incense, and only when he came out could they go in to light the next sticks. This situation was not up for discussion. Everyone knew that it was Boss Zheng who had financed the alterations to the incense hall in the water tower and that his name and that of his sister were carved as lay benefactors on the hall's name plaque. Everyone knew quite well that Buddhas were part of the market economy too, and the incense hall had its own boss, whose privileges were inalienable. Only who had the right to light the second incense stick was open to debate. Thus, when Boss Zheng went into the water tower to burn incense, there was always a milling throng outside, vying fiercely for who should burn the second stick. The rivalry for the best position was so intense, that it was inevitable that conflict ensued: as people argued, fists were raised. This kind of chaos was disturbing to the institution of the hospital, and Director Qiao had no option but to assign some of his men to the water tower, specifically to keep the worshippers in order.

Perhaps they only had themselves to blame, but the other worshippers' time sharing the incense hall with Boss Zheng did not last long, and it was only two or three days before they lost the right to pray for the indulgence of the bodhisattva from the Temple of Sublime Light. One day, as Boss Zheng left the tower, his driver gave a signal to the bodyguard on duty at the door, who immediately locked the security door. The would-be worshippers surrounded him, shouting:

"Hold on a moment! Hold on a moment! If you lock the door, how can we pray to the bodhisattva?"

"I can't hang around for you," the bodyguard replied. "My job is to look after Boss Zheng, not you lot."

"No one wants you to look after us! If you leave the door open for us, we'll take responsibility for keeping the place neat and tidy, and guarantee it will be spotless tomorrow morning, for your boss to come and burn the first incense."

The bodyguard was greatly outnumbered by the crowd, and trapped by them on the threshold of the hall. He tried his best to keep hold of the key in his pocket:

"Stop bothering me! Just you watch out or I'll pick up the lot of you and turf you out. If you've got a problem, go see Driver Li."

The worshippers ran after the Mercedes, and the bravest of them got to the front of the car and banged on the windshield, protesting that Boss Zheng was being too petty.

"What loss is it to you to let us poor folk in to offer up our incense? You're such a big boss, how can you be afraid that the incense sticks of a few poor folk like us are going to bankrupt you?"

Naturally, Boss Zheng refused to reply, and the driver, afraid lest the situation get out of hand, addressed the crowd on behalf of his boss:

"Boss Zheng doesn't concern himself with keys, and nor do I. Keys are Miss Bai's business, so you'll have to discuss access to the water tower with her. What she says, goes, as far as that's concerned."

So it was that a crowd of people stopped Miss Bai's little yellow car at the gates of the Jingting Hospital. There was a certain Mrs Yao, a member of the hospital logistics team, who had come to burn incense for her son's university entrance exam. She was very conscious of her status, and quite articulate, and stepped up to make the crowd's representations to Miss Bai. But the latter had no desire to debate the matter face-to-face with Mrs Yao, so she sat in her car, pretending to be busy with her cell phone. Mrs Yao soon grew sick of this arrogant and contemptuous attitude, and abandoned any attempt to negotiate with Miss Bai. Suddenly she exploded at her:

"What kind of public relations officer do you call yourself? You're just a pathetic sham! Do you think people don't know how things stand with you? You were no good when you were little, and now you've grown up all you do is live off men. Do you think that makes you important? Just who do you think you are? Gong Li (a famous Chinese film actress)? Mrs Thatcher?"

Miss Bai wound down her car window, but not to argue with Mrs Yao. There was a *pffft* sound, as she spat her chewing gum full in the other woman's face. The little yellow car sped off in a cloud of dust, and Mrs Yao chased after it to spit at its rear end by way of venting her anger. Nobody knew Miss Bai's background, they just knew that this public relations girl had a very arrogant and dismissive attitude, and a heart of stone. However, many injustices seem to have a just logic all their own. Most of the worshippers tacitly acknowledged that the bodhisattva from the Temple of Sublime Light did actually belong to Boss Zheng, and so it had a duty to look after Boss Zheng's interests, and no duty of care to themselves, poor as they were. But there was one relative of a patient, Teacher Wu, who had made a proper study of Buddhism, and who believed devoutly in the compassion of the bodhisattva. As an expression of his optimism, he exhorted the others:

"There's no need for you to despair; if the bodhisattva were only to watch out for the rich, how could that be considered universal compassion? Distance means nothing to the bodhisattva, so even if we can't go into the water tower, as long as we're sincere, if we burn our incense outside, the bodhisattva will surely see it."

When the others heard Teacher Wu's encouraging words, they turned and swarmed back to the water tower, surrounding it, as everyone lit the incense they had brought in offering to the bodhisattva. Because they were outdoors, the water tower stood in a particularly windy spot, and the ground was wet, whatever brand of incense they used, they all had difficulty getting it to light. Some just muttered and grumbled about having to worship the bodhisattva from outside, but others exploded with anger, giving vent to the core of their discontent, and deliberately placed their candles on the steps of the tower, right up to the security door, as much as to say:

"If I'm going to have to burn my incense outside, and block the door, that's fine because at least the outdoors doesn't belong to them."

In a fit of pique, others simply abandoned such a lowly method of worship, and left the water tower to glower angrily at Building No.1, their hearts full of all the anger of their class. Through gritted teeth, they promised:

"How can these nouveaux riches upstarts call themselves devout believers? All they do is take advantage of their position to bully people. If they don't start treating the poor as people just like themselves, sooner or later they'll reap the whirlwind of their bullying!"

An undercurrent of hostility spread through the Jingting Hospital, fermenting as it went, through rumours and gossip. A new story about the nature of Boss Zheng's condition became current, which held that not only was he mentally ill, but he also had AIDS. As far as most people were concerned, there's no smoke without fire, and given Boss Zheng's wanton and dissolute lifestyle, which everyone had heard about, and his peculiarly austere attire, none of them were the least surprised.

"And AIDS is infectious, isn't it? He's had such a prosperous life, death doesn't matter to him, but if we're infected, we'll end up being buried with him!"

Some people even stormed up to Director Qiao's office, noisily demanding that Boss Zheng be expelled from the hospital. Beset from every side, the director had no option but to publicly release Boss Zheng's blood test results, which showed that all Boss Zheng had had was a case of gonorrhoea, which had been completely cured. His HIV test was negative. But the mob were not concerned about HIV status, and a blood report had no effect in calming the storm. A popular movement demanding the expulsion of Boss Zheng gradually spread through the Jingting Hospital. All sorts of ruffians and ne'er-do-wells somehow managed to jump on the bandwagon, stirring up more trouble just for the hell of it. Quite soon, everyone was convinced that Boss Zheng's room was haunted.

Apparitions in the form of large quantities of rope manifested themselves in the Jingting Hospital. No one knew where they came from, but it was quite clear where they ended up: all the rope made its way to Boss Zheng's room in Building No.1. White nylon rope. Green nylon rope. Hemp rope. Grass rope. Steel wire rope. Rope lay along the route that Boss Zheng had to take to go and burn incense; rope hung from the roof of Boss Zheng's Mercedes limousine; rope draped itself around Boss Zheng's balcony, piled up on the wrought-iron table, and invaded the potted cactus. A length of rope was tied in a noose hung from the handle of Boss Zheng's door, and attached to it was a placard: **Fuck off out of the hospital, AIDS man!** In the end, a silver-coloured metal rope, which proved to be the very last of the ghost ropes, a rope loaded with ghastly power, slid like a snake under the door of Boss Zheng's room, slithered under the sofa, and coiled up neatly in one of the boss's slippers. Boss Zheng was watching television on the sofa, and needed to go to the lavatory. He slipped his feet under the sofa, and what his feet touched was that icy metal rope. He shouted for help a couple of times, then passed out from the shock.

After Director Qiao took a phone call from Miss Bai, he rushed over to Boss Zheng's side, where he found the young millionaire still unconscious, lying like a child in the arms of his bodyguard. He was wearing black silk pyjamas. He had three gold chains around his neck, and a glittering diamond ring on his finger, the stone of which was at least three carats. The flies of his pyjama trousers were unbuttoned, and although he was unconscious, his private parts were in an excited state, tenting the material of his pyjamas up into a distinct hillock. Director Qiao pointed at Boss Zheng's genitalia and asked the bodyguard:

"What was he doing? What are you doing?"

The bodyguard looked blankly up at the director:

"There weren't any girls in today, and the boss wasn't doing anything, just watching television."

Director Qiao turned to look at the TV screen, and saw that the DVD player was still running. A naked blue-eyed blonde had her legs spread and was masturbating with considerable dedication. Director Qiao hurriedly turned off the DVD player, and angrily began to scold the unconscious patient:

"No wonder everyone's saying you've got AIDS. I've seen degenerates before, but never one as far gone as you! What good has being rich done you? You've got all that money, and all it's done is turn you into a zombie!"

Although Director Qiao furiously stamped on the pornographic DVD, shattering it into pieces, he was under no illusions about Boss Zheng's condition; it had nothing to do with pornography, and everything to do with the ropes; they had precipitated this crisis. Of course, he could do nothing to punish the ropes, but he personally stuck a notice on Building No.1 that read: **Ropes are strictly forbidden in this area**. There were too many possible alleys of investigation and too many obstacles to be able to track down the main culprits behind the ghostly appearances of the ropes. Director Qiao knew only too well the seething discontent that had spread across the Jingting Hospital, and that Boss Zheng had become public enemy number one. He didn't have the power to protect him, and the best he could do was to reinforce to those involved, the responsibilities of the security staff and porters. He asked them to keep a constant eye on the comings and goings of the ropes, and to seize them as soon as they saw them. But all these strict precautions came too late, as Madam Zheng, stirred to fury, had already mounted a punitive expedition, which culminated in her raising her sword, and dealing Director Qiao a vicious stab.

A bit later, when Liu Sheng saw the big round bruise on Director Qiao's right shoulder, the director said, mocking himself:

"It's the best present I ever got from Boss Zheng."

Liu Sheng took the opportunity to apologise for his absence:

"It would have been much better if I hadn't gone to Huangshan. If I'd been with you, I know I could have blocked the sword for you."

Later on, when Liu Sheng was delivering vegetables to the canteen, he heard the workers in there saying that Boss Zheng's Special Room No. 2 had already been vacated. The woman who cleaned the special rooms had made a killing; a whole load of stuff had been left behind: food, clothes, utensils; all top quality, of course. There were also some more specialised items, such as a whole unopened case of famous brand condoms, multicoloured and fruit-flavoured. The cleaning lady couldn't bring herself to throw them out, but was too embarrassed to take them herself, so she gave them to the male care assistants. Most of them probably didn't use condoms, so they gave the condoms to a young patient nicknamed Little Bottle:

"Here's a whole load of balloons for you, Little Bottle. Go and blow them up, then hang them on the trees."

Thus the condoms changed function, and became a great parade of multi-coloured balloons, hanging on the branches of the burgeoning plum trees. The canteen workers pointed them out to Liu Sheng:

"Have you seen them? Little Bottle blew up every one of them; they're an expression of his warm appreciation of Boss Zheng; a parting gift for him as he leaves the hospital."

Miss Bai turned up to handle the formalities of Boss Zheng's discharge from the hospital. Liu Sheng saw her coming out of the inpatient department, carrying a cardboard box and heading for the little garden at the top of the road. Suddenly, she turned back and made her way to the gymnasium. Liu Sheng remembered the galvanised iron shack over there; the one which had been Fairy Princess's childhood home. He saw her wandering round the little garden, a purple-clad figure, now in view, now disappearing as she walked to and fro in the distance. The figure flickered in the sunlight, scattering a fleeting impression of mourning and nostalgia as it went. The sound of music drifted over from the gymnasium, where a group of patients were doing therapeutic exercise under the direction of a hospital doctor. The patients could be heard stamping enthusiastically on the floor, interspersed occasionally with hysterical laughter from one patient or another. He noticed that she had stopped beside a window for some time, gazing inside with her hand to her forehead. He couldn't tell if she was looking for someone, or just looking at her own reflection. Her window had been there once. He still remembered that window, as small as a train window. How many times had he seen Fairy Princess sitting by that window, her hair dripping wet with a red plastic comb in it? She sat at that window, reading, or just lost in thought, like a traveller sitting on a train.

He watched her train from a distance, watched her journey. He could see the train, but couldn't make out the journey. From his point of view, the girl he recognised was Fairy Princess; Miss Bai was a stranger. He didn't know what image she had of him, who he was to her. Was he just another stranger, or a sinner, wicked beyond redemption? Through her silhouette, he retraced his own youth. The sound of the patients' exercises suddenly changed to a quick, energetic beat: *ta, ta, tata*. A beat from so long ago. The *xiaola*. It was the rhythm of the *xiaola*. *Ta, ta, tata*. The body sways gently, you clasp your partner's hand, tenderly but insistently you pull her to you, once, twice, three times, forward then back, you loop your arms hand in hand, turn and change positions. His own body began to sway, but then he stopped abruptly. He remembered she had been his last dance partner. His last dance partner. In the blink of an eye, it had been ten years since he had danced the *xiaola*.

She took two potted cacti out of the cardboard box and put them on the window sill beside her. It seemed as though she was putting down all her sorrows and all her happy memories too. She made her way towards the gate of the hospital, her white silk scarf catching the wind, and her high heels clack, clack, clacking on the ground. The mysterious train was about to set off. Her journey was going to be a long one, and perhaps each of her stops was meant for another long journey. He didn't know whether to be sad, or to be grateful for his good fortune. A thin, bony stray cat was following her, miaowing as it went. She stopped and took some snacks out of her bag, and dropped them for the animal. She looked at it, and he looked at her, and Liu Sheng was suddenly reminded of her as a young girl looking at her rabbit cages; his heart filled with a vague but compelling urge. He waved at her urgently out of the window of the cab of his van, then pulled his hand back in, and pressed the van's horn. She turned in surprise and looked at the van. He instantly regretted his impetuousness. He didn't know why he had pressed the horn. Indeed, he hadn't really thought whether they needed to say their farewells at all. Panicking, he picked up a cabbage and waved it at her, shouting;

"These cabbages are really fresh. Do you want one?"

This time, at least, she laughed, loudly and without restraint.

She seemed to be in a good mood that day. She cadged a cigarette off him, inhaled a couple of times, coughed, and discarded the cigarette:

"Your cigarettes are too strong. I only smoke menthol ones."

Her glance slid across Liu Sheng's face, then flicked back, focusing on the underside of his nose. She offered her critical opinion:

"You should trim your nose hairs. You've got a handsome face, but those hairs sticking out are really horrid."

Liu Sheng was almost overwhelmed by the compliment, and hurriedly shoved a finger up his nostrils a couple of times. Then he heard a clanking noise next to his ear. She had thrown over a bunch of keys.

"If you've got the time, go to the water tower and burn a few sticks of incense for me."

She tripped lightly over towards the gate of the hospital, turning back after a few steps to say to him:

"You'd better burn some for yourself as well."

NINE
TROUBLE

BECAUSE OF THIS, from then on, Liu Sheng trimmed his nose hairs.

Whenever he looked in the mirror to perform this task, he saw two faces reflected back at him: his own, and hers, which would slip in and out of sight behind his body. He could remember her nose, as pretty and smooth as a jade scallion, but where was she really now? Where was her train now? Six months passed, and he got an unexpected phone call from her. When the caller announced herself as Miss Bai, the accent was familiar but, after saying her name, she fell silent, as though waiting for him to reply.

He couldn't believe she was contacting him. He thought it must be a cold call from some telemarketer, or perhaps a girl from one of the barbershops or health spas where, when he occasionally met a girl he really liked, he would leave his business card.

"Which Miss Bai are you?" he asked.

"How many Miss Bais do you know?" the caller asked, then lapsed back into silence.

There was something mocking about the silence, and something a little oppressive. He didn't know why, but Liu Sheng's heart began to pound. For the sake of caution, he asked:

"Well, Miss Bai, can I trouble you to answer a question? Can you please tell me what you were called when you were little?"

The caller went quiet for a moment, then exploded angrily:

"Why are you such an irritating little wimp? Alright, alright, I'm not Miss Bai, I'm Fairy Princess! OK?"

He leapt from his chair:

"Ok. I know you're Miss Bai, and I know you don't do anything without a reason. What can I do for you? Just say."

There was a lot of background noise on the line, which made Liu Sheng think she was standing on a busy street.

"This time you really can't escape." She laughed abruptly. "This time I really do need your help. Shall we fix a place to meet?"

Liu Sheng was sitting at the dining table at the time, his father beside him, his mother opposite him: two grey-haired heads, one looking to the left, the other straight ahead, both concentrating on deciphering this unusual phone conversation. His mother's antennae were always finely tuned and, as she looked at her son's expression, she asked:

"What Miss Bai? Where's she from? If she's not your girlfriend, why are you so attentive to her?"

Agitated, he explained perfunctorily:

"Whose being attentive? It's Miss Bai from Hong Kong. We're going to meet to discuss some business."

He suddenly lost his appetite. He went to his room, closed the door, and asked the ceiling:

"What does it mean?"

He didn't know what she meant. Could he really help her? It was already six months since he had last seen her, and he had no idea what her circumstances were now. For a moment, he was inclined to think the business smacked of blackmail but, as he absent-mindedly opened his dresser drawer, and flicked through his bankbook and roll of cash, he thought about it more carefully. He decided he didn't have much cause for concern, because he didn't think she was that kind of person; not that kind of woman. After a short while, he began to change his clothes. He put on his best underpants, socks and shirt. He surveyed himself in the mirror, happy with how sharp he looked. Except for his hair, which wasn't trendy enough, so he applied a substantial quantity of gel. At this point, his father knocked on the door:

"What are you sneaking about at in there, Liu Sheng? You've earned so much money over the last couple of years, you're getting a bit complacent. You know plenty of girls, but there's no sign of a girlfriend. You need to look at your lifestyle, and not forget the taint you carry. You need to keep your tail tucked in!"

Liu Sheng put on his most expensive western suit, shot his cuffs, and headed out of the door, saying:

"Don't worry, don't worry, I'm used to keeping my head down; it's the only way I know how to live."

When his mother saw how he was dressed, she grabbed him by the arm:

"Isn't that your imported suit? Take it off! Take it off! That's an expensive suit, the kind you'd wear for your wedding. It's not suitable for a business meeting!"

He shrugged off his mother's hand, and said, patronisingly:

"You're just poor folk, and you think a suit is something really special. Don't you get it? It's a materialistic society out there now. What do you know about doing business? I'm telling you, people judge you by what you wear, and it can really influence the deal."

For this first meeting, she had chosen the venue. He found the newly opened Hong Kong-style tearoom in the city centre. He took his time, walking past on the other side of the road, carefully inspecting the establishment, before crossing the road and casting an eye over the menus in the doorway. It seemed safe enough, and the prices on the menus were not exorbitant. He adjusted his jacket and walked confidently in the door.

She was there first, sitting at a corner table, with a teapot in front of her. There was an artificial palm tree behind her, and the light filtering through its leaves cast a large zigzag shadow that fell across her head and shoulders. He walked over to her, and suddenly felt a strange, icy sensation, as though the whole room was waiting only for him. Be careful! Be careful! Was this a replay of the Feast at Hongmen (a famous murder attempt in imperial times)? Was it a carefully plotted trap? A final attempt to blackmail him? Was her revenge a dish she believed best served cold? All these different thoughts slowed his step. He stopped and turned to look for the toilets. Perhaps he should go to the toilet first, to stop and think, to put up his guard and then think again. He had turned away when he suddenly heard her voice:

"Where are you off to? Didn't you recognise me?"

She stood up, formed the fingers of one hand into the shape of a gun, and made a shooting gesture:

"How awful! Have I become so ugly you don't recognise me?"

Such familiarity is only possible when old friends meet again after a long time; he was pleasantly surprised by it, and immediately relaxed. Of course she hadn't become ugly: she had highlights in her hair, a large strand of which fell across half her face, hiding it. The strand was a striking blonde colour. He sat down and tried some smooth-talking, showering her with sickeningly flowery compliments about her appearance. She rapped on the table to stop him.

"Enough! I've got to see a client soon, and I don't have time for your sweet-talking. Let's get down to business."

Which is exactly what she did, telling him that she was in difficulties, and needed his help to resolve them. She looked at him meaningfully, then suddenly snorted with laughter:

"It's just like the old saying, 'train an army for a thousand days to use it for an hour'! I always knew you were going to come in useful sometime."

He understood exactly what she meant, and the problems that beset her were nothing new to him. She had borrowed three hundred thousand yuan from Boss Zheng and, in her turn, she had lent the same sum to a circus performer so he could open his own company. The original loan was for six months at high interest, but a year had already passed, the circus man hadn't paid up, and Boss Zheng was getting angry. He had already stopped her salary, and the next step would be to fire her. He knew immediately what she wanted:

"You want me to get the debt back, don't you?"

She nodded and said, quietly:

"Do you have connections?"

"This is nothing; I can do it."

She frowned suspiciously:

"What do you think I want you to do? Kill someone? Set fire to somewhere?"

"Murder and arson, no; but debt recovery, I can do." He couldn't help smiling. "It always used to be other people chasing me for money, and now it's my turn to do the chasing."

They sat facing one another. The pot of fruit tea had already gone cold, but the pieces of pineapple and banana floating in it, still looked fresh and brightly coloured. This was the first time he had sat down together with her, sat in her shadow. Suddenly he remembered the rabbit cage of all those years ago. Now, he was the rabbit, captive in her cage. He had walked into that cage, and perhaps she already had him in her grasp. He felt disappointed and frustrated.

He wanted to say: "Now we've finished talking business, let's talk about something else. Where have you been for the last six months? What have you been up to?" But, in fact, he choked back these well-meaning but rather dumb questions, because he was pretty sure he knew what her answer would be: "Who do you think you are? What's it got to do with you what I've been doing?"

He didn't want to rush things, and just waited patiently as she picked up her cell phone and sent a text. Eventually she looked up, and said:

"Madam Zheng is giving me real problems; I'd really like to kill her."

He looked at her hands. Her fingers were tapping the keyboard deftly. The jade bracelet was nowhere to be seen and, instead, a silver bracelet set with precious stones encircled her delicate wrist. When she looked up, the strand of golden hair across her forehead briefly fell away from the rest of her black tresses, and he saw there was a bruise on her right cheekbone.

"What's the matter with your face?" he couldn't help exclaiming.

"Don't look at my face. What business is it of yours?"

He shut up. As he sat opposite her, he smelled the mingled fragrances of her perfume and of leather. He couldn't help feeling there was something grotesque about this meeting. Who exactly was it he was sitting opposite? Who was she? Was she a friend or a foe? Then again, was she an old acquaintance re-encountered? Someone trying to trap an old creditor? She finished sending her text, and looked up again.

"What are you thinking about? Are you afraid of me? Am I that frightening?"

He shook his head.

"What is there to be afraid of? I know plenty of people who happily commit murder for money, so why should I be afraid of you?"

She looked him over from head to toe, even pulling aside the tablecloth, so she could inspect his leather shoes – he was wearing a smart pair that day. Suddenly, she smiled.

"You're not looking too shabby today. Your hairstyle is good, and your shoes are beautiful. That suit fits you well too."

He felt very pleased with himself, but before he could say anything, she stood up.

"But of course a really successful businessman wouldn't wear such an old-fashioned label. All Boss Zheng's suits are Givenchy or Armani."

As she left, her parting words were:

"If you get that money back for me, I'll buy you an Armani."

TEN
THE CIRCUS

EVERYONE KNOWS the East Wind Circus on Peach Tree Street.

The circus had had a great reputation for 30 years. The horses they raised and trained loved to brave the fiercest fire, and were expert at jumping through any kind of flaming hoop. The monkeys they raised and trained loved all kinds of manual labour, and were brilliant at imitating workmen, patterned towels on their shoulders, happily pulling the heaviest handcarts. A tiger they raised and trained was known as 'the musician', and had unique artistic talents. Not only did it welcome its trainer to stand on its back, playing a reed flute, it could even hold the flute in its fangs, and play the basic tune of the patriotic song 'Follow Lei Feng's fine example'. The elephant they had raised and trained loved physical exercise, and its trainer used its bulk for bodybuilding: its long trunk served him as a horizontal bar, and he could hang from it and do a hundred pull-ups.

Liu Sheng remembered once seeing a TV programme, in which one of the East Wind Circus tigers and a female animal trainer, were each interviewed by the presenter, representing the animals and the performers respectively. He remembered quite clearly that the tiger was called Huanhuan, and the girl was called Lele. What made the deepest impression on him was Lele telling how she had met an African president and a Southeast Asian king and, in the course of the story, revealing that those two VIPs had become her super-fans. The interviewer asked her about the rumours of sex scandals that circulated about her:

"Can you tell us, Miss Lele, did that African president want to take you back to Africa with him?"

Liu Sheng remembered that his ears pricked up at this as, he believed, did those of everyone in the city. Sadly, the girl evaded the question, and gave nothing at all away; neither clarifying nor proving anything. On the other hand, the tiger's performance delighted everyone. When the interviewer asked the tiger to say something to its nationwide audience, the beast gaped amiably, and spat out a rolled-up scroll. It used its claws to open the scroll, which unrolled to display the characters 恭喜发财 (gong xi fa cai) – Wishing You a Happy and Prosperous New Year!

Liu Sheng did not know the man called Qu Ying, who owed Miss Bai the money, but Ah Liu did. Ah Liu was a great fan of the circus, and had seen him perform. He told Liu Sheng that he was the one who had trained the white horses to jump through fire; he was said to be one of the best in the whole country. On top of that he was very handsome and charming, and had really hit the big time that year. Ah Liu had seen Qu Ying after the East Wind Circus disbanded, and said he had taken his performing horses to the funfair in the western suburbs, where he was giving riding lessons. Ah Liu had gone once to ride the fire horse. The ride had only lasted about ten seconds, he hadn't gone through any fiery hoop, but Qu Ying had still charged him eighty *yuan*, which seemed like a real swindle.

There was something a bit weird about going to the circus to dun someone for money, and Liu Sheng wasn't quite sure how to go about it. At first he thought of taking seven or eight strong-arm men with him, to create the right impression, but in the end, he just took Ah Liu and Chungeng. Ah Liu wanted two cartons of cigarettes in payment, but Chungeng was a bit greedier and said:

"I don't want any of your cigarettes, but if we get the money, you're going to take me on a tour of Hong Kong."

They wasted a lot of time looking up and down Peach Tree Street for the circus. The imposing arched gate of their memory seemed to have vanished in the crowds. The red building at the east side of the original location had changed its appearance, and turned into a video-games arcade. Inside, a great crowd of children was busy playing games and creating a deafening hubbub. The western building was being used as a silk emporium. Its display window was full of silks of every colour and pattern, and inside the shop itself there was a man with an electric megaphone:

"World's cheapest silks! Don't walk past, come on in and look around!"

Liu Sheng went in and said to the man:

"What's a great strapping chap like you doing selling silks? We're not shopping for silk; we're looking for the circus. How can that big old arched gate have just disappeared?"

Reluctantly, the man put down his megaphone and pointed out onto the street:

"What big old main gate? If you're looking for the circus, go and look in the corner over there."

They went back out onto the street and there, indeed, in the corner was the door to the circus. It was a small door now; just a single-panel side-door set into the western wall of the video-games arcade. Stuck on it was a default notice from the electricity company, and a small advertising flyer for a VD clinic run by an ex-army doctor, one overlapping the other. Liu Sheng pushed the door open and saw a narrow alley-like passageway, at the very end of which he could see a large, densely-foliaged tree, on which a chequered quilt was hanging out to dry. With his sharp sense of smell, Ah Liu was the first to notice the stink of horse manure. He darted into the passageway and studied a pile of some black substance he found there.

"It's horseshit. This is the circus all right."

Automatically holding their noses, they made their way down the passageway. The smell of the circus is like no other: a little rancid, a little stinky and a little spicy, it is the smell of the animals. As he approached the big tree, Ah Liu saw immediately that it was actually a stage prop, which he said was the tiger tree. Liu Sheng asked him why it was called that and, rather embarrassed, Ah Liu explained:

"I called it that when I was little because when that tree appeared, it was time for the tiger act."

A woman of fifty or so, either the concierge or performer well past her prime, was sitting under the tree, listlessly shelling fava beans. The beans fell with a plop into a bowl, and the empty pods went into an upturned brass gong. Her gaze rested on Liu Sheng's attaché case, and she asked:

"Where are you from? What do you want to buy?"

"We're not buying anything", Liu Sheng said. "We're looking for someone."

"I know you're looking for someone. What do you want to buy from them?"

"Isn't this a circus?" Liu Sheng asked in surprise. "What does a circus have to sell?"

"Anything you want. We're selling stuff to pay the wages," the woman said. "Lions, tigers, monkeys, they're all for sale. We've even started selling off the cages."

Ah Liu interrupted the conversation:

"How much is a tiger?"

The woman looked Ah Liu up and down, and pursed her lips scornfully:

"Tigers are a precious commodity; you'd need tens of thousands. They're not for ordinary folk."

"What about a monkey?" Ah Liu asked. "Monkeys must be cheaper. How much for a monkey that can pull a handcart?"

The woman looked towards an office room:

"Xiao Zhang isn't here at the moment. You'd have to discuss the price of a monkey with him; he's in charge of the monkeys."

Liu Sheng pushed Ah Liu to one side and said to the woman:

"Just ignore him, he can't even afford a monkey. We've got some business to talk over with Qu Ying. Does he live here?"

"You're looking for Qu Ying? Do you want to buy a horse, then? He's only got a few left, and he may not want to sell them. I've heard he's thinking of opening a horse-riding fair, to earn a living. If you want to find him, just follow the horseshit. He lives in the stables."

The circus was deserted. They made their way through a large rehearsal room. The doors and windows were all closed and the floor was covered in a jumble of cardboard boxes and wooden packing cases; there were a number of old take-out meal boxes with flies swarming around them, and a discarded bright red leotard left draped over one of the packing cases. All the circus's former splendours and glories vied with each other on the walls, which were covered in red banners of all shapes and sizes, and multi-coloured posters advertising different acts from across the years. A bronze drum lay abandoned under a window, its beater above it on the windowsill. Ah Liu picked up the beater and leaned forward to hit the drum. Boom, boom, boom, the rehearsal room echoed to its noise. A rat appeared from somewhere, jumped up onto a cardboard box, and carefully inspected the three visitors outside the window. Throwing down the beater, Ah Liu said:

"Sonofabitch! This place used to be amazing! What's happened to it? When I was little, I used to climb the wall to watch the rehearsals. The doorman threw me out on my ear, and said that the rehearsals of the East Wind Circus were a state secret, and not to be spied on."

They followed the trail of manure, and when it disappeared, they found themselves at the stables. It was dark and damp inside, and the mingled smells of hay and manure assaulted their nostrils. Through an iron gate, they could dimly make out three spirited fire-jumping horses, tethered to a concrete pillar, all half-turned towards them, their eyes gleaming in the dark. There was an odd-looking lean-to in the corner of the stable, its roof covered in a tarpaulin, and its walls formed of iron railings reinforced with plywood. From those walls hung countless plastic bags and bits of costume, amongst which a silver ceremonial cloak, embroidered with gold, hung solemnly on a clothes hanger, radiating grandeur. It was clear that the iron-railed shack had originally been a lion or tiger cage, but it was now functioning as Qu Ying's bedroom.

There was a movement under a quilt inside the cage, and a man slowly emerged, and stumbled over to the iron door. He was in his forties, with big eyes, shaggy eyebrows, broad shoulders and slip hips. His hair was tied back in a trendy ponytail, and he was wearing a pair of red knickerbockers. His face was a bit bloated, but his eyes were very bright and penetrating, and there was an angrily dismissive air to him.

"They're not for sale! They're not for sale!" he was shouting, his breath laden with alcohol fumes. "On your way! I'm not selling my horses."

"We're not here to buy horses," Liu Sheng said. "Are you Qu Ying? We're friends of Miss Bai, and we've got something to discuss with you. I'm sure you can guess what it is."

"No, I can't." Qu Ying looked Liu Sheng up and down. "What kind of friends of hers are you? The gangster kind, I reckon."

"It doesn't matter whether we're gangsters or charity workers, all we're concerned with is getting Miss Bai's money back." Liu Sheng considered for a moment, and took a business card out of his attaché case, saying: "Mine isn't a big company, but its professional services are wide-ranging, and this is one of them. Three hundred thousand, and we're not leaving today if we don't get it."

Qu Ying didn't take Liu Sheng's card. He looked at the three men on the other side of the iron door, and his disdainful expression turned to one of anger. He took a cell phone out of his pocket, and flashed its screen at Liu Sheng:

"Go on, take a look. Take a look and you'll understand what my relationship is with Miss Bai. I left my family for her, and I've got no home to go to because of her. So when you come here trying to collect that damn debt, you tell me first just who owes what to who! Just get out of here and stop meddling in my affairs. I'll settle things with her myself."

Liu Sheng looked at the screen, which was displaying a standard lovers' photograph. Miss Bai and Qu Ying were mounted on the same horse, and Qu Ying was holding her round the waist from behind. She had her head turned back to kiss Qu Ying. In the instant the photo was taken, she was obviously very happy; her eyes were sparkling and her blood-red lips spoke of intense desire.

"Very romantic, I'm sure!" Liu Sheng snorted, as he pushed the phone away. "Anyway, that's an old photo, isn't it? It's no use showing me that, and even if you had a pile of photos of you in bed together, it wouldn't do any good. We're not concerned with your lovers' tiffs, just with getting back the money you owe." He took a paper bag out of his case, and stuffed it through the grille in the metal door. "I'm going to show you something that we did, and then you'll understand what kind of people we are."

The paper bag slowly burst open, and a gleaming white pig's trotter, streaked with blood stains, fell to the floor at Qu Ying's feet.

"Do you like that kind of thing? Take it and braise it with soy sauce, or stew it, either would be good." Liu Sheng made a chopping motion with his hand. "So, you see, that's the kind of work I do."

Qu Ying laughed sarcastically:

"So is it pigs' trotters you chop off, or people's hands? I'm not quite clear about that. Could you be more explicit?"

"I'm an expert at pig's trotters, but I'm still working on people's hands. You don't get many opportunities with hands, so let's see if you're going to give me a chance to practise."

"Here you go! Here's your chance to practise!" Without blinking an eye, Qu Ying stuck his hand through the grill, and waggled it up and down at Liu Sheng. "Come on, cut it off if you want to show you're a real man. Haven't you brought a knife? You've come here to chop my hand off, and I've got to give you the knife?"

Ah Liu hurried over and pushed Qu Ying's hand back through the grille, trying to calm him down:

"We didn't bring a knife. To tell the truth, we just want to settle this matter. Why are you getting in such a state? We're not."

Qu Ying pushed his hand back out, and held it in front of Ah Liu's face.

"Hurry up! If he hasn't got the guts, you do it. If you chop it off, won't that settle the matter? Chop it off then fuck off! Fuck off back to Red Toon Street!"

Liu Sheng was completely at a loss for a moment, and glanced at Chungeng. Chungeng hurriedly came over and took hold of Qu Ying's hand. He tapped its palm.

"Don't be in such a rush. First I'll read your palm, and then we'll see whether we're going to chop it off or not." He narrowed his eyes, inspected the lines on Qu Ying's palm carefully, then went on, contemptuously: "This is the crappiest palm I've ever seen, a hundred times worse than mine. I'm not surprised you're in such a mess. A hand like that really needs to be chopped off! Your career line is too short, your love line is interrupted and so is your wealth line. Everything that should be continuous is broken off. What was an unlucky fucker like you doing borrowing three hundred thousand *yuan*? Or having an affair with Miss Bai, for that matter?"

Amazingly, this bit of palmistry seemed to act like a sedative on Qu Ying, and his anger gradually subsided. He seemed to be coming to terms with his own bad luck. He wiped his hand on his knickerbockers, and then studied it himself in the light coming in from outside the door. He asked Chungeng:

"Which is my career line? Which is my love line? Which is my wealth line? Dammit, I can never remember."

Liu Sheng said to Chungeng:

"Don't tell him. We'll get the three hundred thousand first, then tell him."

Qu Ying gave up the inspection of his palm and stuck his hand into the waistband of his trousers. Eyes glinting, he looked at Liu Sheng, and belched boozily.

"Don't try and scare me with your three hundred thousand; that three hundred thousand is just a fart in the wind. My luck's been right out, and I ran into a swindler; otherwise, I'd have a million by now."

So saying, he fumbled around in the dark for a while then, suddenly, with a sweep of his foot, he kicked out a tin of luncheon meat; with another kick, he produced a grain spirit bottle.

"There's eight hundred in the luncheon meat tin and a thousand in the bottle. It's all I've got at the moment; you can take it or not, it's up to you. I had a lot to drink at lunchtime, and I'm going to have a sleep. You do what you like."

The luncheon meat tin rolled to a stop at Ah Liu's feet, but the bottle was a bit bigger, and didn't fit under the iron door. It stopped just beside it. Ah Liu looked inside the tin, counted the roll of banknotes and said:

"He's right, there's eight hundred here."

Chungeng crouched down and scrabbled for the spirit bottle through the gap under the door. But Liu Sheng slapped him, saying:

"Leave it. We're not beggars, and I'm not even going to bend down for such a stupid amount."

"Little sums build up into big ones; if you can't be bothered with it, I'll take it. OK?"

They tried to push open the iron door, but failed. Everything in the stable appeared to be set against them, except for the owner himself. Qu Ying seemed still to be drunk. He thrust several handfuls of straw into the manger, walked unsteadily over to the corner of the stable, and pissed copiously into some receptacle or other. Then he returned to the comfort of his quilt inside the cage. There was some rustling and muffled thudding for a moment then, all of a sudden, a strange noise began to issue from the cage. The three men realised it was the sound of a man trying to hold back his tears. Qu Ying was crying. Qu Ying was huddled in the corner of the cage, crying. His wailing became more and more abandoned as he shook the bars of the cage with his hands, making them clang and clatter. Qu Ying's wails were mingled with indistinct mutterings, and at first they couldn't make out what he was moaning about. After a while, they made out the word 'regret':

"Regret, regret, regret, regret, regret will kill me."

Outside the room, the three men looked at each other. Regrets? Who didn't have them? Their own lives were full of regrets, so they listened quietly, without any trace of mockery. The three horses in the stable, however, took fright. Three white horse's heads craned round to listen to their master. They had never heard him cry before, and it sounded nothing like the orders they were used to. Their discipline began to falter. With considerable effort, the first horse managed to remain calm, the second one became fretful, lifting its left front hoof tentatively and swishing its tail as it waited for some clearer command from its master. The third horse seemed to misunderstand what was going on with its master, and thought it was time to enter the arena. It suddenly lifted its head, reared up on its hind legs, and gave a sharp whinny.

The horses' restlessness caused Qu Ying's wailing to stop abruptly, and he came stumbling out of the cage to calm them down, one after the other. He gently stroked the mane of the first, saying:

"Be sensible, Victory!"

He stroked the back of the second one:

"Be good, Dawn!"

The third horse was a little different, and he pinched its testicles, saying:

"Don't make a fuss, Hero! I've got worries of my own, and if you keep this up, I'll send you to the knacker's yard."

The pale afternoon light, full of compassion, came tumbling down from the roof and filtered through the iron bars of the stable, where it strove to define the outlines of Qu Ying and the three horses in its pallid light. Liu Sheng and the others watched the light dancing on Qu Ying's thin cheeks, and saw the glistening tears in the corners of his eyes. Ah Liu whispered to Liu Sheng:

"He's crying; look, he's crying."

"Maybe, maybe not", Liu Sheng replied coolly. "He might just be trying to fool us. These arty folk are all good actors."

Chungeng had lost interest in the affair and pulled Liu Sheng to one side. He picked up the spirit bottle and looked at it.

"This kind of spirit is three *yuan* a bottle. It goes straight to your head; I don't drink the stuff myself. He does drink it, and you're trying to get three hundred thousand out of him? Where's he going to get that kind of money?"

Liu Sheng wasn't willing to give up that easily, and did his best to raise his friends' morale:

"Don't give up! Perseverance is the key to victory! It's Qu Ying we're dealing with here. We'll soon cook his goose, and when he's been simmering for a while, even if we don't get the whole three hundred thousand, we may at least get a few tens of thousands to give Miss Bai."

The stable door opened from the inside.

Qu Ying came out, leading a white horse. He looked quite serene. He had thrown the silver ceremonial cloak over the horse's back, like a fine ornamental saddle.

"Put this robe on," he said to Liu Sheng. "The horse will listen to you if you're wearing it. Just take the horse."

Liu Sheng saw what Qu Ying was trying to do, and exclaimed:

"Who wants your horse? We came here for money, not a horse."

"I don't have any money, only horses. Victory here is the best of them. Take him!"

Qu Ying shoved the horse's reins into Liu Sheng's hands.

"I'm not trying to cheat you. This horse is worth more than three hundred thousand. Please tell Miss Bai I give up. She's won."

ELEVEN
THE WHITE HORSE

THERE WERE no horses in the city, and Liu Sheng had never ridden one.

He put on the horse-trainer's cloak and led the horse halfway across the city. He felt as though he was in a dream: the bustling streets were his stage, which seemed to be saying to him: "The stage is too long, too big, and there are too many people in the audience."

He felt half proud, half afraid. Victory was a tall and handsome horse, its eyes glistening and alert. When he chanced to look it in the eye, he thought he could see tears there, so he forced himself to be gentle. But other than stroking the horse's mane, he had no idea how else to pacify this horse he had taken in lieu of the debt.

Ah Liu was very jealous of Liu Sheng assuming the prerogative over charge of the horse. Despite numerous requests to ride the horse, and for Liu Sheng to let him wear the trainer's cloak, Liu Sheng refused them all.

"Don't make a fuss about it, Ah Liu. If something happens, and the horse bolts, we'll be three hundred thousand out of pocket and we'll have been through all this for nothing."

He was very afraid of the horse taking fright, and kept a firm grip on the halter, as they made their way through the quiet streets and alleyways. The sound of the horse's hooves brought a festive air to them. There's a horse! There's a horse! People came running out of the houses in droves to see the horse. One lad with a big head, who must have been a fan, followed them all the way, shouting:

"Victory! Where are you going, Victory?"

The white horse didn't recognise the lad, but he kept on following, running after Liu Sheng:

"Uncle! Uncle! Where are you taking Victory?"

Liu Sheng didn't have time to pay him any notice, but he heard Chungeng behind him saying to the lad:

"Do you like Victory, then? If you do, then go home and ask your father for three hundred thousand *yuan*. Give me the money and you can have Victory."

Qu Ying had been telling the truth; the silver cloak worked like a charm, and the horse was even more obedient than might be expected. Liu Sheng led it across the bridge at the North Gate, all the way to Red Toon Street. Once they had it back on home ground, the three men relaxed. But Red Toon Street was abuzz; Chungeng's children came out, as did Ah Liu's niece and nephew, and all the neighbours. The children followed the horse shouting and screaming, begging for a ride, but Liu Sheng was unmoved.

"Get back! Get back! Don't blame me if you get kicked."

Chungeng lied to his daughter, saying:

"We don't dare ride this horse. Tomorrow, we'll go to the funfair and ride the horses on the merry-go-round. This is a special horse; it's worth three hundred thousand *yuan*. If you spoil it by riding it, Daddy won't have the money to pay for it, and I'll have to sell you to the child traffickers."

Ah Liu tried to put his nephew on its back to take a souvenir photo, but Liu Sheng stopped him brusquely.

"Don't you know that horses are afraid of flashes?"

The whole neighbourhood seemed to be in their doorways, watching the first horse ever to come to Red Toon street, and gasping in amazement.

"Where did you get the horse, Liu Sheng? Did you buy it, or find it? Maybe you stole it!"

Some of them admired Liu Sheng's silver cloak:

"Hey, Liu Sheng, where did you get the cloak? It really suits you! You look like an international film star!"

He didn't feel like explaining to so many people, and fobbed them off with just a few words:

"I got it to cover a debt; someone else's debt."

As they reached the door to Liu Sheng's house, the horse happened to unloose a pile of black manure. His father looked at the steaming horseshit, and stopped dead in his tracks.

"What kind of business are you involved in now? Are you horse-trading?"

Shao Lanying came out when she heard the commotion, and stamped her feet in fury:

"It's too much! Too much! What do you think you are doing bringing a horse home? You're almost thirty! When are you going to learn?"

She fetched a broom from behind the door and hit Liu Sheng with it. Liu Sheng took cover, and she went on to hit the horse. The horse whinnied in alarm, and reared high onto its hind legs, as if it was about to leap over her head. Shao Lanying fell to her knees in fright. Liu Sheng hauled on the reins of the frightened horse with all his might, and yelled at his mother:

"Drop the broom! This horse is worth three hundred thousand, so don't hit it."

Shao Lanying dropped the broom and scurried back inside, slamming the door shut with a bang. From behind the door, she shrieked:

"What do you mean, three hundred thousand? I don't care how much it's worth, you can't bring it back here! You good-for-nothing child! Fuck off out of here, and take your horse with you!"

Liu Sheng was very familiar with his mother's temper and he knew he could argue till he was blue in the face, but she would never let a horse in the house. He suggested to Ah Liu they could take it to his house, and keep it in the courtyard there for a couple of days. But Ah Liu was still angry with him, and said shortly:

"Our courtyard is too small, and my mother uses it for drying bacon and pickling vegetables. You took the sales commission, and if your mother doesn't want to look after it, why should my mother?"

Liu Sheng tried Chungeng next:

"It's such a big horse, who's going to take it? You should take it to the stone quay."

Liu Sheng took this advice, and when he got to the quay, he telephoned Miss Bai, hoping to give her the good news. But he couldn't get through.

Her cell phone was turned off. Puzzled, he sent her a text: **Didn't get the money, only a horse. Get over here quick and collect it**. But there was still no reply. Liu Sheng didn't know what was going on with her, but he couldn't help being a little worried. He tried to imagine what she might be doing, but nothing he thought of was very helpful; it either made him jealous, or disappointed, or frightened, so he decided he was better off not trying. She was a mystery, and one that became deeper as time went by. He couldn't work her out. As for the real value of the white horse, that was a mystery too, but one that should prove easier to solve. He had friends in all walks of life, and one of them, nicknamed Throwaway, who worked in the pet market, told him that an ordinary horse wasn't worth anything, but a fire-jumping horse from the East Wind Circus was certainly worth more than three hundred thousand. It wouldn't be easy to sell, though, and he'd have to find the right buyer to get rid of it. He also told Liu Sheng that if this was all too much trouble, he could find him a go-between, and if Liu Sheng didn't trust this go-between, he would buy the horse himself for fifty thousand. Liu Sheng knew that Throwaway never did anything that didn't make him a profit, and replied immediately by telephone that although fifty thousand was a decent amount of money, sadly, the horse wasn't his, but belonged to someone else.

That first night, he tethered the horse to the base of a crane, pried open the rusty lock on the control cabin door, wrapped himself up in a padded cotton coat, leaned against the window to watch the horse, and spent the night like that. The cement factory had closed down some time ago, and the quay was deserted. The stray cats and dogs of Red Toon Street liked to pass the night there, and when they saw the horse, the cats angrily just sloped away; the dogs clustered round to inspect it, and when they saw it wasn't dangerous, they gave a few barks just to maintain their credentials, and left. Never before in his life had Liu Sheng spent a night outdoors, and the secret tranquillity of the quay had its effect on him. The star-laden sky spread itself softly overhead; the river flowed, burbling gently, towards the city as the occasional night boat slipped by, the faint yellow light from the lamps on their masts sliding through the darkness of the river, lighting it briefly, then disappearing letting the darkness reassert itself. The night weighed heavy on his thoughts, and he hardly slept. From tomorrow he was going to have to look after a horse. It was her horse. It was Miss Bai's horse. Somehow or other, this responsibility had fallen on his shoulders; it felt like a challenge, but there was also something strangely poetic about it. He had been watching the horse attentively during the night, and saw that it was even more serene than he felt. It slept extraordinarily peacefully, its breathing strong and even. Its mane gleamed like satin in the moonlight, and that sight drew him out of the control cabin. There was a pile of all sorts of vegetables next to the horse, and Liu Sheng explained apologetically:

"I'm sorry there's no grass, you'll have to make do with vegetables."

He stroked the horse's mane gently, and gave a heartfelt sigh:

"You really are very beautiful, Victory; more beautiful than any girl."

Keeping the horse at the stone quay was only a temporary measure and the following day he began the search for some spacious and comfortable stabling. He knew every empty plot on Red Toon Street, and knew that if he could fence one in, it would serve as a simple stable. He did not, however, have much faith in the ways of the inhabitants of Red Toon Street, and felt that this solution would not be entirely safe. A house was what he really had in mind. From his point of view the most obvious place was Baorun's house. It was empty and had a courtyard, so it was perfect for keeping a horse. He took the horse and went looking for Master Ma's son, Xiao Ma. Xiao Ma liked horses, and although he knew this business was not entirely above board, he couldn't resist Liu Sheng's blandishments. He hunted out the keys to Baorun's house and handed them over.

A thick, mouldy smell flooded out when Liu Sheng opened the door to the house and a cold draught blew down the narrow corridor. A strip of morning light slid through a crack in the door at the other end, slanting across the floor like a sword blade. He shivered involuntarily, then heard Xiao Ma asking:

"Why are you just standing there like an idiot? My mother will be here soon. Hurry up and get the horse inside; don't let her see what's going on."

Liu Sheng went inside, his arms outspread to measure the width of the corridor, which proved just wide enough for the horse to pass through. He led the beast carefully inside. First they passed through the dust-covered living room, where Baorun's father's funeral portrait still hung on the wall. The dead man's eyes followed Liu Sheng and his horse across the room, their expression full of bewilderment. Horse and man headed over to the attic staircase, where a black parasol still hung, covered in white mould. Liu Sheng knew that upstairs was Baorun's garret room, which he had never seen. He couldn't suppress his curiosity, so he let go of the horse and tiptoed up the stairs.

It was just about the most desolate garret in the world. All the owner's belongings had been stuffed into two woven plastic bags and thrown in a corner; there was a camp bed covered in old newspapers, with a padded quilt and a pillow in one corner. The pillow was so covered in dust, it was impossible to tell what colour it was. Liu Sheng picked it up to inspect it, and when the dust was brushed off, it proved to be tangerine. He noticed that there was a hair stuck to the pillowcase. It was thick and black, stiff to the touch, and undoubtedly one of Baorun's. The hair of an eighteen-year-old. He pinched the hair between two fingers.

"Hello, Baorun!"

The hair didn't reply, but just twitched between his fingers. He blew gently and let go of the hair, which whirled off to land somewhere or other on the floor of the room.

"I'm sorry, Baorun," he said, "but I'm borrowing your house to keep my horse. Please accept my apologies as a brother's."

He made preparations to keep the horse in the courtyard. As he opened the doors, the first thing he saw was Baorun's bicycle, leaning abandoned against the yard wall. A plastic rain cape covered the handlebars, and there was a coil of hemp rope on the rear carrier rack. Baorun's stone weights and dumbbells still lay on the ground. The dumbbells were rusty, and there was grass growing through the holes in the stone weights. He was about to lead the horse in, when there was a loud noise at the front door, followed by a shout from Xiao Ma:

"Watch out, Liu Sheng! My mother's here!"

Madam Ma had indeed arrived, and she let fly a string of curses.

"You've already trampled over him and shat on his head, and now you want to bring a horse in here so it can shit on him too? Your mother always says that heaven is watching our actions, so you just go and ask her. Do you think heaven won't be watching her own son? Go on, go and ask her. Heaven strikes down sinners with a lightning bolt, so what makes you think it won't strike down her own son when he sins?"

Liu Sheng had known Madam Ma was going to be a problem, so he had given the matter some thought in advance.

"You need to think about this, Madam Ma. This is a horse we're talking about. What's it got to do with my mother? Please don't kick off like this, or the neighbours will think there's an earthquake. Don't worry, Madam Ma, I'm not taking advantage of anyone. This house standing empty is just a waste of money, so I'm going to rent it, OK? I'm going to make some money for Baorun's family, OK?"

While he was busy with Madam Ma, he took his eye off the horse for a moment. Victory had stayed in the living room, and was silently staring at the funeral portrait of Baorun's father. Proud and intelligent as it was, perhaps the horse could sense the dead man's hostility. Its head suddenly swept round, and Baorun's father fell to the floor with a clatter as the glass broke. Madam Ma jumped in surprise, her face went white, and she clutched her hands to her stomach.

"This is terrible! See for yourself, Liu Sheng. Su Baozhen left that portrait behind to protect the house. Don't you see? Even the dead are against you! Aren't you afraid, Liu Sheng? If you won't take that horse away, I'll go and get your mother, and she can do it."

There was nothing for it. If he persisted, nothing good would come of it for him or for the horse so, shamefacedly, he led it out of Baorun's house.

He went to find Xiao Guai. This was his Plan B. Xiao Guai was a salvager at the recycling station, the rear yard of which was the biggest open space on Red Toon Street. He was interested in horses, and had a sharp eye for profit; all of which was good news for the horse. Liu Sheng slipped him two packs of cigarettes, but he also demanded a wind-proof lighter.

"Can this horse be ridden?" Hopalong asked.

"You don't ride this horse, it rides you!" Liu Sheng replied. "You've only got one good leg, so for god's sake be careful! I won't take any responsibility if you fuck up your good leg too."

Xiao Guai handed over the key to the rear yard and went with Liu Sheng to settle the horse in. In fact, other than Baorun's house, the rear yard at the recycling centre was the biggest and most suitable stabling for a horse on Red Toon Street. The huge platform scale could serve as a tethering post, and a big cracked iron cooking pot made a serviceable feeding trough. Liu Sheng sighed as he stroked the horse's mane:

"I'm sorry again, Victory. It's not the best, but you'll just have to make do."

Fodder was not such a big problem. Liu Sheng couldn't get hold of grass, but there were vegetables of all kinds and every day Liu Sheng brought a basket of rotting vegetables for the horse to eat. He had been looking after the horse for four days now, and the beast seemed to recognise him. He deliberately didn't wear the silver cloak when he tried to mount it for the first time, and it remained quiet, just swishing its tail, once. He was very gratified by this, and he praised the horse, and made it a promise:

"You've been really good, and if you keep it up, tomorrow I'll let you jump through a burning hoop."

It was in the early morning of the next day that Liu Sheng was woken from his dreams by the buzzing of his cell phone. He had a presentiment which proved correct when he looked at the screen: it was a text with the sender showing as Bai Zhen. It read: **Take the horse immediately to Boss Zheng's residence at the New York Gardens.**

The number was unfamiliar. He called back and a man answered in a voice with a strong Taiwanese accent. He sounded as though he was in some kind of nightclub, and there was a lot of background noise.

"Who is this?" the man asked brusquely.

"Give Miss Bai the phone," Liu Sheng replied. "I'm a friend of hers."

"We're all her friends. What kind of friend are you?"

Keeping his temper, Liu Sheng said:

"A business friend. Give the phone to Miss Bai, we've got urgent business. We need to discuss the matter of the horse."

The man burst out laughing:

"The matter of the horse, eh? You'll be better off talking about that with me. Come over here and we can discuss it over a drink."

This just annoyed Liu Sheng and he yelled into the phone:

"Miss Bai! Miss Bai! Come and talk to me!"

"She can't come", the man said. "She's in the washroom throwing up. She can't hold her liquor and the only thing she's talking to is a toilet bowl. If you really are a friend of hers, come here and do her drinking for her."

Someone snatched the phone away from the man at the other end and Liu Sheng thought it must be Miss Bai. In fact, it was another man, from Northeast China by the sound of it. This man was even drunker than the first. He laughed crazily, then invited Liu Sheng over:

"Get over here quick, my friend. Come and fuck her. It's my treat tonight."

Liu Sheng exploded with anger:

"Fuck you and your mother too!"

And with that heart-felt curse, he hung up.

He was very angry. He looked at the time and saw it was three o'clock in the morning. Clearly, Miss Bai was in a nightclub, pursuing her old profession. What else could she be doing with those men at such an hour. His mind always automatically leapt to the worst possible interpretation of events, usually a sexual interpretation. Pretty girls are all different, and the men who frequent the pleasure palaces all have their own particular intentions, but their depravity is always the same: a dark, narrow tunnel that penetrates the bodies of the innocent, then leaves them behind. He remembered that evening at the water tower so many years ago. A cursed evening. A depraved evening. But because the lips that uttered the curse were now closed, and all traces of the depravity wiped away, of the two bodies involved, all he could remember was his own. He tried to remember the young girl's body, but the memories were vague and indistinct. All he could see was the evening light amongst the trees falling on her thin shoulder blades, delineating the delicate depression between them, shallow and tinged with gold. His desire was a golden ripple, singing joyously in that shallow depression. He remembered his own golden desire, he remembered that shallow depression, but other than that, he remembered nothing else.

It was the morning of the fourth day and the sky was heavily overcast. When Liu Sheng went to collect his horse from the recycling station, he discovered that the big iron gates of the rear yard were unlatched and there was a heap of fresh horse manure outside them. He gave a shout of alarm, and pushed open the gates to look. His alarm was justified. The big platform scale stood in solitary splendour at the centre of the yard, and yesterday's lettuce and cabbage were still in the giant iron cooking pot. But of the horse, there was no sign. He broke out in a cold sweat. Picking up a length of metal piping, he rushed into the station office, shouting:

"My horse! My horse! Where is my horse?"

Xiao Guai had just arrived at work, and was kneeling down bundling up cardboard boxes. He looked in alarm at the metal piping in Liu Sheng's hand, and strenuously asserted his innocence:

"Don't look at me! I thought you'd taken it away. Who are you threatening with that piping? It's not my fault if the gates weren't shut; you're the one who closed up yesterday."

"I know I shut the gates yesterday!" Liu Sheng shouted furiously. "What I want to know is who opened it. Horses don't have hands, so how could it open the gate and escape all by itself?"

Xiao Guai wrenched the piping out of Liu Sheng's hand and threw it onto a pile of scrap metal.

"How could I have opened the gates for your horse. It must have been someone who climbed in over the wall at night, so you can just stop all this bullshit you're spouting. You keep saying the horse is worth three hundred thousand; isn't that an open invitation to any petty thief?" Xiao Guai protested. "What are you still looking at me for? If you don't believe me, go and report it to the police."

Liu Sheng went back into the rear yard and carefully examined the scene of the crime. But he searched in vain. There was part of a length of rope on the platform scale, and hoof prints in the muddy ground. Those prints led to the gates of the rear yard, but there they were swallowed up by the tar and cement of the main road, and there was nothing more to be seen.

The white horse had been seen.

It had galloped down Red Toon Street in the early morning, causing consternation in the vegetable market. Several people tried to grab it by the halter or the reins, but to no avail. It had thundered through the market as if there was no one there. Young Scabies, the fried-breadstick seller, told Liu Sheng that the horse clearly liked fire because it had stopped for at least five minutes in front of his stove. He had no idea what the horse was thinking. He had thrown it an old breadstick, but the horse had ignored it and galloped off. A woman pea-shoot seller said the horse had stopped at her stall for an instant, and stuck its head into her vegetable basket. Pea shoots are very expensive, and the woman didn't want the horse eating her merchandise. She had jerked the basket away, and the horse had run off. She said admiringly to Liu Sheng:

"That's a very thoughtful horse you've got there, better than most people. There's plenty of my human customers who'll buy half a *jin* of pea shoots and help themselves to another handful on their way out."

Liu Sheng kept up the search for his horse all morning. In principle, a runaway horse should be much more noticeable than a runaway person. The horse had headed for the city centre, and Liu Sheng walked the streets there, calling out its name: "Victory! Victory!" He sounded like a one-man demonstration, but no one took the mickey. Everyone had heard that Liu Sheng had lost a horse, and that that horse was worth three hundred thousand. On her way back from her night shift at the maternity hospital, Aunty Pang gave him the latest news, that the horse had been seen at the intersection of People's Street and Revolution Road.

It was queuing beside the ornamental flowerbed; someone had decorated its bridle with a red silk kerchief. Aunty Pang went on to say that the horse had been getting on very well with everyone, and all the passers-by had waved their silk kerchiefs and scarves at it: pink ones, red ones, patterned ones, it didn't mind. It raised its front hooves and saluted each and every one. Old Xu, the bus driver, said that the white horse had trotted in front of his No. 11 bus and he had hooted his horn at it. It seemed to have taken afront at the uncivilised noise of the horn, and had deliberately not given way to the bus. It had continued on its even-paced, leisurely way, and the driver and passengers just had to be patient as they continued at a snail's pace until they reached the end of the No. 11 route at the bus stop on Spring Wind Street. Only then did bus and horse part company. Old Xu's news revived Liu Sheng. Spring Wind Street was very close to Red Toon Street, and Liu Sheng clasped his hand to his forehead.

"How could I be so stupid? Victory knows these streets; of course, I know where he's going!"

Liu Sheng had wasted a whole morning and, by the time he started looking on Peach Tree Street, it was already noon. From a distance, he saw a white ambulance halted outside the gates of the circus building. A crowd had gathered beside it with people of all shapes and sizes all looking down the narrow alleyway. He ran over, only to hear they were not talking about any horse, but disputing causes of death. Two young lads came out of the circus, arguing at the tops of their voices:

"It was sleeping pills! Three bottles of them!" one said.

"What sleeping pills?" the other exclaimed. "He cut his wrists; slit the veins! I saw the blood!"

The manager of a small silk shop, who was also in the crowd, butted in:

"Stop arguing, you two; neither of you has got it completely right. He took sleeping pills and slit his wrists. You two should remember this if you ever tire of life. If you're going to kill yourself, like him, do it properly."

Liu Sheng had no time to find out any more, before the dark entrance to the circus was suddenly illuminated, and echoed to the sound of voices. Several men in white tunics emerged, carrying a stretcher. He saw Qu Ying's half-covered ashen face, like a pallid white moon. His ponytail was loose and a strand of hair fell across his forehead, trembling slightly with the jolting of the stretcher. A strong smell of alcohol came off Qu Ying's body, a mixture of sweet and acrid. Liu Sheng saw that there were drops of blood falling from the stretcher like raindrops and turning black as they hit the ground. He shivered, and muttered involuntarily:

"What's going on?"

Someone standing next to him said:

"What's going on? He couldn't go on, and he killed himself."

Liu Sheng made his way out of the crowd, and took some deep, gasping breaths.

"Fuck it!" he said to himself. "Clinging on to life is better than any death. How could he not know that?"

The ambulance turned on its siren and sped out of Peach Tree Street. The crowd around the circus entrance gradually dispersed. The lads rushed back to the video-game arcade but the manager of the silk shop remained standing in his shop doorway, picking his teeth with a matchstick. He addressed Liu Sheng:

"Friend Qu Ying was a famous horse trainer, a real talent, and he used to be really popular. Girls went crazy for him; they used to wait for his autograph at the stage door."

"So what?" Liu Sheng said. "So what if he was famous and the girls loved him? Who was there to look after him when he was in trouble?"

"It wasn't just girls; there were lots of important officials from central government and the province, and foreign guests, who had their photograph taken with him."

"What good's a fucking photograph? They're forgotten as soon as they're taken."

"He used to be flush with cash; never asked the price. Last month he was in my shop buying a heap of presents; he spent thousands."

"You say he had money? Did he have as much as Li Ka-shing (a famous Hong Kong tycoon)? As much as Bill Gates? What use is a few thousand? Last month he had a few thousand, and this month he was homeless and broke, wasn't he!"

The manager decided Liu Sheng was alright, and nodding continuously, went on:

"I know, I know, you're a man of the world, and you're right. No one knows what tomorrow will bring. If you've got wine today, get drunk today! I'm going to shut up shop and go to the California Beach for a hot tub. Then I'm going to have a body massage and a foot massage, go for the luxury package. Do you want to come with me? If we go together, we get one free entry."

But Liu Sheng's thoughts were on his horse, and after murmuring a few platitudes, he turned to asking about any sign there might have been of Victory. The shop manager knew the horse, and said that when he opened his shop that morning, he had seen Victory standing at the entrance to the circus. The horse was covered from head to hoof in dust, and was pushing non-stop at the doors with its muzzle. This alarmed Aunty Gong, the caretaker, who came out and led the horse off to find Qu Ying, but he was already unarousable. The manager sighed:

"Victory is a special horse; it hasn't come back before, so why did it come back today? It came to pay its last respects to Qu Ying! Qu Ying has had lots of girlfriends but did any of them come? No, they all scarpered. Only the horse came. That horse is worth more than any human!"

The side door of the circus was still open, so Victory must have been inside. Liu Sheng put one foot over the threshold, but for some unknown reason, the other one wouldn't follow, and stayed outside the door. There was the scene of a death inside, and it felt as though it was also the scene of several other people's crimes. He was a little afraid, but he didn't know what he was afraid of. As he leaned on the door frame, at a loss what to do next, he heard the familiar sound of horses' hooves from inside. His eyes lit up. It was Victory. He could see his horse. Aunty Gong led it out. She was carrying a big cloth bundle slung across her back, and her eyes were full of tears which fell with every step. Liu Sheng went over to her and said:

"Where are you taking Victory, Aunty?"

Aunty Gong wiped the tears from her eyes with her sleeve.

"I'm taking it to Secretary Xiao. Yesterday, Qu Ying took Dawn there, and the day before, he took Hero. Today, Qu Ying is dead, so it's up to me to take Victory."

"Why take them to Secretary Xiao?" Liu Sheng asked.

"Secretary Xiao's orders. The horses are state property, not Qu Ying's personal property. If anyone wants to buy Victory, they'll have to negotiate the price with Secretary Xiao. If he gets a good price, then we'll get all our wages."

Liu Sheng snatched the reins away from her, saying:

"Victory has already been taken in repayment of a debt. The horse ran back here of its own accord. You seem to be forgetting, Aunty: Victory is my horse."

Aunty Gong looked Liu Sheng up and down, then landed a heavy slap on his arm.

"You gangster! You caused Qu Ying's death. Isn't a life enough for you? Now you want to take our horse too?"

Liu Sheng kept a tight grip on the reins:

"Stop talking nonsense, Aunty. I'm no gangster. But I am recovering a debt for a friend. If I don't have this horse, I can't give it to my friend."

"Your friend is no concern of mine, and I don't care whether you're a gangster or recovering a debt. Just tell me, are you a man or not? I said, are you a man or not?"

Liu Sheng was taken aback by the question:

"Of course I'm a man. Can't you see?"

Aunty Gong bristled:

"Real men have good hearts. Do you have a good heart? If you do, then don't take this horse away from me. Look at it. Take a good look. Its body is covered in blood. That's Qu Ying's blood."

As they struggled over possession of the horse, the reins got dropped, and Victory trotted down the dark alleyway, ducking its head just as a man would, when it went through the door frame. Despite its great size, it passed easily through the narrow doorway. Now it was standing in the sunlight, head up, and body half-turned towards them. Its white coat was filthy in the extreme, but its eyes were bright and lustrous, shining like two precious stones. Liu Sheng saw it properly for the first time. Its back and flanks were streaked and speckled with red. Blood! But it was a white horse, not a zebra. He knew it was Qu Ying's blood. He had never previously been afraid of blood, but this time was different. He had a sudden, violent attack of dizziness, and he felt sick. He didn't know why the blood was making him nauseous. He walked a few steps, supporting himself on the wall, until he reached a corner, where he crouched down with his back to Aunty Gong and the horse, and dry retched a few times. Then he renounced his claim:

"Alright, I give up. It's not my horse, after all." He gestured dismissively. "I give up. It's nothing to do with me. Go on, take the horse away."

TWELVE
REGRETS

MANY DAYS PASSED without sight nor sound of Miss Bai. Liu Sheng had no idea whether or not she had heard the sad news of Qu Ying's death. Her attitude to the horse trainer was her own business, but Liu Sheng felt he had a duty towards the horse. He thought she might come to claim the beast as repayment of her debt, but he had no idea whether she actually remembered either the horse or the debt. Perhaps she was mulling over some new scheme. He tried calling her cell phone, but her number came up as outside the service area. He wasn't sure whether he was happy about this, or worried, and he imagined all sorts of unfortunate possibilities. Perhaps something had happened to her.

One day, he was driving across the Shanren Bridge, and he saw a crowd gathered on the steps of the bridge. It turned out that a fishing boat had just passed by, and the crew had fished the body of an unknown woman out of the water below the bridge. He asked the crowd of rubberneckers how old she was. Was she around 25 or 26? They all said they had just been passing by, and hadn't paid any attention to the body's age or appearance. He stood in a daze, looking at the filthy, stagnant water under the bridge. He was worrying over whether she was dead or alive, but his concern for himself asserted itself when he saw two policemen on the steps of the bridge. He believed he was an intelligent man but, against all reason, since he had met her again, he felt his IQ had suddenly dropped. Because of his carelessness, he found himself in murky waters again, and who was to say the police wouldn't be paying him another visit?

She had invaded his life, silent as a ghost. And that ghost was out there, hiding in the darkness, mysterious yet flirtatious, and redolent of disaster. She was either guarding him or summoning him. The white horse had gone, but she was still there. Her phantom presence was like a glittering sword hanging over his head. He missed that white horse, and he worried about Miss Bai. But his worries about her took strange and monstrous forms. They became more and more negative, and more and more of a moral burden.

Director Qiao always seemed to have the inside track on whatever was going on. One day, when he and Liu Sheng were playing Go, he divulged to Liu Sheng that Madam Zheng was searching everywhere for Miss Bai, and letting it be known that she was going to put the fear of God into her. She was saying that Miss Bai had cheated Boss Zheng out of three hundred thousand *yuan*, and not paid it back. She had felt hard-done-by when she was fired, so had helped herself to one of Boss Zheng's diamond rings, leaving behind a note informing her boss that she was taking the ring as her severance pay. Director Qiao further said that Madam Zheng was furious for allowing herself to be persuaded by her brother to hire Miss Bai as their PR girl. Her brother couldn't recognise a gold-digger when he saw one, but she herself should have. She personally vowed to Director Qiao:

"I will never forgive that girl. I am going to get even with her sooner or later. If she's got the money, she'll pay it back; if she doesn't have it, she has two choices: either have her good looks spoiled, or go to gaol. Girls like that shouldn't be free in society to prey on vulnerable men, and I am going to deal with her, as a service to the people."

This talk alarmed Liu Sheng, and he felt cold shivers run down his spine. He cut Director Qiao short:

"It's none of our business. Let's get on with our game."

But the state of play on the Go board was no more encouraging. When he considered it, he could see that there was no hope for his black stones, and Director Qiao was about to hunt down his Grand Dragon. The black stones were like an ornamental, but totally useless, defensive wall, about to collapse at the launch of a single arrow. He looked at the board, and laughed wryly:

"I've lost. No question, I've lost."

Director Qiao looked at him, his eyes bright:

"Yes, you've lost. But losing to me is a small matter; it's just a game of Go. But you don't want to lose to her, because that's a matter of life and death, and there's no coming back from that loss."

Liu Sheng knew there was a deeper meaning to the director's words:

"Which 'she'? Who might I lose to? What do you mean, Director Qiao?"

"You're an intelligent fellow, so go with what your heart tells you! My information is right up to date, and I'm telling you to help you."

His mother Shao Lanying's information was also hot off the press. Someone on the street had told her that he, Liu Sheng, and that Fairy Princess girl had been having an affair; that he had gone to recover a debt for her; and that he had hounded one of the circus performers to death. She was both alarmed and afraid, and had come home to give her son a piece of her mind. He insisted that it was just tittle-tattle:

"Those are all just rumours, Mum! What are you doing listening to rumours?"

"Do people normally just make up rumours about you for no reason?"

"Of course there's a reason. They're jealous! They see us doing well, and they can't bear it. You must have noticed."

A mother understands her son better than anyone. The more Liu Sheng denied things, the more suspicious Shao Lanying became. From her point of view, Liu Sheng being unmarried at a marriageable age was the biggest threat to his safety. She thought of this as an openwork bamboo fence which the wild beasts outside could easily slip in through, and through which the domestic cats and dogs could easily escape. To avoid disaster, the fence had to be closed up tight. A son like Liu Sheng always needed to be restrained, and no matter how much care his parents took, something was bound to be overlooked. If only their son could make the perfect marriage, that would be the way to be sure the fence was properly closed. Shao Lanying and her husband discussed the matter that very night, and quickly came up with a shortlist of perfect daughters-in-law. She went to visit the families concerned and, after due consideration, it turned out that Granny Shaoxing's grand-niece, Xiao Jin, was the one who best met her criteria. Shao Lanying was accustomed to playing the autocrat and, without consulting her son at all, went ahead and arranged a date. She had not anticipated that Liu Sheng would not only disobey his mother's instructions, but would also launch a personal attack on the innocent Xiao Jin.

"Who'd want a date with her?" Liu Sheng asked. "Her face is bigger than a washbasin, she's got an arse like a sack of flour and no waist at all. I'm a good-looking guy and it would be an outrage to make me go on a date with her."

Shao Lanying recognised that Liu Sheng's criticism of Xiao Jin's appearance stemmed partly from his letting his emotions cloud his judgement, and partly from his immature thinking, so she strenuously defended Xiao Jin's appearance:

"What does she need a waist for after she's married? She has big eyes and double-fold eyelids; so what if her face is a little broad? A big face brings good luck; surely you know that! And what's wrong with a big backside? Girls need big backsides, it means they're more likely to have sons."

"Your ideas of beauty are way out of date! Don't you know that the Japanese or Korean look is what's fashionable now. I don't need you to worry about my girlfriend. I'll hold an audition and have the candidates I picked go through a final, where the finalists PK each other. Then I'll bring the winner to show you. OK?" (PK is computer gaming terminology that stands for 'Player Killing', the destruction of a player's character or avatar in the course of a computer game).

Shao Lanying didn't know what PK meant, or what the Japanese or Korean look was. She really wanted to know if any of the girls on Red Toon Street had that look. And what kind of look did Fairy Princess have now? But she was in no mood for research. She stormed into Liu Sheng's room, took out his imported suit, and ordered her son to put it on:

"Put this on for me and go meet her. It's a matter of trust. The date's been made and you're going to go, like it or not."

Liu Sheng put on the suit and told his mother:

"I'm playing mahjong with Chungeng and the others today and I'm wearing this suit for luck. I'm not going to see that ugly cow, it would put me off my game. You made the date, so you go on it!"

Shao Lanying's threats and pleas had no effect, and when she picked up a broom and hit her son with it, Liu Sheng just straightened his suit, and said:

"This suit is worth three thousand *yuan*; if you want to beat it to rags, then go ahead."

Infuriated, Shao Lanying dropped the broom and stamped her feet. Her eye fell on a set of Buddhist prayer beads on the table. She snatched them up and began shuffling them through her fingers.

"These beads were blessed at the Ciyun Temple and they are very powerful. I will ask the bodhisattva of the Ciyun temple whether you can still be saved or not, my son."

She counted the beads furiously, muttering sutras. On every sandalwood bead she could see the face of Fairy Princess, sometimes indistinct, sometimes sharp and clear; sometimes as a young teenager and sometimes as a grown-up; but always the bewitching temptress. The memories into which she was plunged made Shao Lanying's face go ashen, as she lamented continuously:

"It's no good! It's no good! The bodhisattva of the Ciyun Temple has told me that a demon has entered your body. Fairy Princess is no beautiful young woman, she is the demon that's come to destroy your life. I'm telling you, Liu Sheng, if you don't untangle yourself from that girl, she will bring disaster to our family again."

Liu Sheng had to admit that even if his mother's beads were no good at predicting good fortune, they excelled at disaster. The troubles which they predicted all arrived. Whilst he was sitting at the mahjong table at Chungeng's house, he took a phone call from someone he didn't know. The man said he worked for Boss Zheng, and urged him to hand over Miss Bai's horse. Liu Sheng's heart lurched, and he professed total ignorance:

"Who is Miss Bai? I'm not a horse breeder, I'm just playing mahjong. If you want to buy a horse, go to Mongolia, that's where the horses are."

The man seemed to have anticipated what he was going to say, and gave a great guffaw of sympathetic laughter. When he finished laughing, he went on in the same comradely manner:

"How's your luck? I hope you draw the winning tiles!"

But after these friendly words, his tone changed:

"We know Red Toon Street, Liu Sheng, and we know where your family lives. Please get some good tea ready, we'll want some when we come visiting."

It wasn't long before the tea drinkers turned up.

The next day, he was hurrying back in his van from the Jingting Hospital, when he got a call from his mother. Her voice sounded very strange as she told him that there were three men standing outside the door, demanding she produce a horse. He knew immediately what was going on; the tea drinkers had arrived. Still on the phone, his mother said:

"If you've got the horse, get back here quick and give it to them; if you don't, just get on with your business. We're here at home."

When it really mattered, his mother always knew how to control her temper and keep her cool. He knew what she was really saying to him: "Whatever you do, don't come home!"

When it really mattered, he always listened to his mother. Decisively, he turned off at the crossroads, and headed in the direction of the suburbs.

He headed west, and drove for about twenty kilometres before turning off. Up ahead there was a cemetery, and he was superstitious about such places, so he stopped the van and sat down in a cornfield beside the road for a while. Who were those three men? Did he know them? He scrolled through some faces in his head, but ended up rejecting them all. Lao San from the East Gate and Ah Kuan on West Street were already past their prime, and had turned over a new leaf; he really wasn't too sure who was operating in this field now. He imagined the three men drinking tea in his house, and found he was really not very frightened; he was just thirsty. Dusk was deepening in the countryside, and the glowing red clouds changed in an instant to boundless blackness. Night came so quickly in the countryside. He began to grow nervous; there was not much charge left on his cell phone, and he could hardly call home to ask what was going on anyway, so he called Chungeng, asking him to go over and check that his parents were alright. Chungeng went immediately, and soon called back to tell him that his mother and father were fine; they were sitting at home, feeding the three men wine and crab. Liu Sheng heaved a sigh of relief. He knew his mother was mounting a full-scale diplomatic offensive, and everything should be fine at home for the time being. Chungeng asked:

"Where are you? Do you want me to come out to keep you company? If you're not coming home today, we could go to a sauna, and find a decent place to spend the night."

"Stop trying to take advantage of my situation! Do you really think I'm in the mood for a sauna? I'm going to find somewhere quiet to have a think."

"You? Have a think?" Chungeng scoffed. "What are you going to think about? What can you actually think about?"

Not knowing how to reply immediately, Liu Sheng put on the voice of a soap actor:

"What am I going to think about? I'm going to think about the road my life is taking, OK?"

For the moment, the road his life was taking appeared to be limited to the public highway. He drove on to a small roadside hotel, where he stopped and took a room for the night. When the manager asked for his ID card, he replied:

"A fleapit like this should feel honoured to get any guests at all, and you still ask for ID?"

The manager didn't take offence but explained honestly:

"The Public Security are really strict with hotels like ours. I'm sure I don't have to tell you, we get a lot of dodgy guests; more crooks than honest folk."

"Well, which do you think I am?"

The manager looked him over, and said, forthrightly:

"I wouldn't like to say. How can I tell? Dodgy folk don't have the word 'crook' written on their foreheads."

Liu Sheng searched inside his attaché case for quite a while, but couldn't find his ID card. What he did find was a key he didn't immediately recognise. He held it up to examine it more closely, and realised it was the key to the water tower, gleaming with a silvery radiance in his hand. He had a brainwave. He remembered that Boss Zheng had had a double sofa bed specially installed in the incense hall. That sofa bed would probably be both a safer and a more comfortable place to spend the night than the hotel. He left the hotel lobby, turning to the manager as he went:

"You don't worry about me, and I won't worry about you. In any case, I'm going to spend the night in my country residence."

He'd have to watch what he did that night. He remembered the gangster movies he'd seen, where the fugitive always tried to cover his tracks as much as possible. The van was clearly a liability, and for safety's sake, he should ditch it. He left it in a parking space at a filling station, and set off along the road to the Jingting Hospital on foot. Night was all around, and the sky and the roadway were both pitch black. The wind was blowing hard, it was cold, and the surrounding countryside seemed to be full of ghosts. He broke into a trot, and after he had been going for quite some time, he saw the warm welcoming lights of the hospital. He bent over to catch his breath and, unaccountably, his eyes filled with tears. He didn't know what was happening to him.

The security guards at the Jingting Hospital all knew him and he had no trouble getting a pass. He also borrowed a flashlight. The hospital grounds were eerily quiet in the night-time as he threaded his way through the dark woods. When he reached the water tower, the only things he disturbed were the two crows on the roof, that set up a hoarse cawing, as though protesting at this night-time invader. The iron door to Boss Zheng's deserted incense hall was still locked up tight, but in the light of the flashlight, Liu Sheng could see the incense offerings of the devotees aggrievedly arranged on the steps of the tower. He picked his way through innumerable plastic bowls and tinfoil containers that had been fashioned into incense burners; there were also a large number of candlesticks fashioned out of soap. When he unlocked the slightly rusted padlock and pushed open the door, he saw a circle of lights in front of the shrine, and the bodhisattva from the Temple of Sublime Light sitting on its lotus throne in the darkness, dispensing freedom from suffering for all living creatures. Its fingers pointed at him, emitting five petals of golden light. He walked over and gently touched the bodhisattva's golden hand.

"Have you been well, bodhisattva?"

He didn't know whether or not the bodhisattva could hear his enquiry, nor whether it minded him coming there in the middle of the night looking for a place to sleep. But everyone said that the bodhisattva dispensed freedom from suffering to all living creatures, so surely that included him, Liu Sheng. If the bodhisattva could bless and protect other people, then it could bless and protect Liu Sheng too.

He knelt on a prayer mat, looking up at the bodhisattva. A bodhisattva is a bodhisattva after all, and this bodhisattva seemed to want to shelter him. Its golden face was as compassionate as ever, without offence, and he felt at peace. The incense hall was equipped with electric lights, but he didn't dare turn them on. In the darkness, he kowtowed to the bodhisattva, but felt that just kowtowing did not show enough respect, and that he also ought to burn some incense. At the outset, Boss Zheng had bought a load of incense, which was all stored in a cardboard box. He found the box and lit the first incense for himself. The smoke ascended arrow-straight in the shrine, as though in some kind of hurry. The air began to fill with the scent of sandalwood and artemisia. Unable to bear the memory of past events in the water tower, he forcibly buried his memories. Then, suddenly, he remembered Miss Bai's request the other day, and solemnly offered up another stick of incense. He addressed the bodhisattva:

"This stick of incense is Miss Bai's. Please accept her good intentions."

The wind was moaning outside, keeping him awake. Although the bodhisattva was allowing him to sleep in the water tower, there was some mysterious ghost preventing him. Every time he began to doze off, the water tower immediately began to reverberate with a strange noise, which issued from the blocked-up staircase, as though there was someone slowly climbing the iron stairs, climbing up to the pump room at the top of the tower. The sound became clearer and sharper, clang, clang, and from the sealed-up pump room there came the faint sound of a drumbeat. Fear banished any thought of sleep, as he looked up and shouted:

"Who's there?"

Suddenly he remembered Baorun, and saw his eighteen-year-old face. He switched on the flashlight, and went over to stand beside the shrine. He held his breath and listened carefully for any movement. He grasped the golden hand of the bodhisattva from the Temple of Sublime Light, taking courage from it, and shouted upwards:

"Baorun? Is that you? Baorun, are you up there?"

The ghost remained silent, just as a ghost should. He didn't dare go to sleep, and all he could do was make a pile of prayer mats, and sit beneath the shrine, smoking, resigned to staying there until daybreak. He turned on the lights and looked at the two sticks of incense: his and hers. The two columns of smoke looked absolutely even in the electric light, one the mate to the other. His and hers. He sat on the prayer mats, wearily reviewing the course of his life. This kind of activity was not one of his strengths, nor had his life been a straightforward one, and he soon began to yawn continuously. Half awake, half asleep, he heard a voice coming from the pump room above him, that seemed to be someone protesting hopelessly, grumbling aggrievedly:

"It's not fair, it's not fair!"

He started, fully awake. What wasn't fair? He glanced at the burning incense sticks and realised that the voice coming from the pump room was actually a command. He had forgotten something. There should be at least three sticks of incense: his, hers and also Baorun's. He leapt to his feet, and lit the third stick. Once again he addressed the bodhisattva:

"Bodhisattva, please protect Baorun too!"

THIRTEEN

GOING HOME

LATER, Liu Sheng came to believe that the bodhisattva from the Temple of Sublime Light was biased, and that the promised freedom from suffering for all living creatures was only something devotees could hope for. In fact, the bodhisattva had its own views on who should be protected and who shouldn't. He also came to believe that, of the three sticks of incense he had lit that night, two were wasted, and that the bodhisattva, in its partiality, had only accepted the one lit for Baorun. It had not protected him, nor had it protected her; the bodhisattva had only protected Baorun.

One morning, he went to the stone quarry to pick up his van, and discovered that there was more rubbish than usual accumulated under the vehicle. He thought it must be the work of the stray cats and dogs, and paid it no more attention. He had just opened the driver's-side door, when he heard someone breathing noisily in the back of the van. He turned to look, and saw a man with his head pushed into one of the vegetable baskets, his body curled up like a dried shrimp. He was asleep. Liu Sheng yelled at him:

"Who are you? What do you think you are doing?"

The wheezing stopped abruptly, and a man's face slowly emerged from the vegetable basket. The face was pale-skinned and bloated, with red-rimmed eyes, and looked totally exhausted. A sense of foreboding suddenly filled the back of the van. Liu Sheng recognised him immediately: it was Baorun. He was wearing a loose, ill-fitting western suit, and a crumpled white baseball cap with the words 'Hong Kong Travel' in gold characters around its edge. Baorun's haggard appearance made him look middle-aged, and only the eyes under the peak of the cap retained the trace of a youthful sparkle.

"Are you Liu Sheng?" Baorun was inspecting him closely, from head to toe. "I've been waiting for you. You seem to have done alright for yourself! Is this really your van?"

A cold shiver ran down Liu Sheng's spine. His automatic reaction was to abandon the van and run away, and he already had one leg out of the cab when Baorun reached over and grabbed him by the lapels.

"Don't run away! What are you running from? Are you afraid of me?"

Liu Sheng's other leg stayed inside the van, as he struggled to keep his composure.

"I'm not afraid of you. I am afraid of ghosts, and I thought that was what was making the noise in the back of the van," he said, stubbornly maintaining his cool. "Why didn't you let me know you were coming back? As you can see, I've got a van now, and I could have collected you."

Baorun wiped his hands on his trousers, then abruptly thrust one out to shake Liu Sheng by the hand. It was rather too solemn and ceremonial a gesture, and as Liu Sheng felt the strength of Baorun's grip, so as not to seem weak himself, he increased the force of his own. The two of them matched each other in silence, eyes locked, until Baorun said:

"What are you so agitated about? Why is your hand trembling?"

Liu Sheng pulled his hand away, shook it and said:

"It was your hand that was trembling. My hand never does."

Baorun laughed:

"Ha! Alright, it was my hand trembling then. Just so long as it wasn't yours, because that would affect your driving when you take me to the Jingting Hospital to visit my Granddad."

Liu Sheng let out a long breath, and asked:

"Aren't you going to go home first? Madam Ma's got the keys. I'll take you over to get them."

Baorun shook his head:

"There's no rush to get the keys. First I'll visit Granddad, and I'll look after everything else in due course."

Without being asked, Liu Sheng gave Baorun a rundown of Grandfather's current circumstances:

"The old man is fine, although he's getting more and more confused. He's as strong as an ox, though, and eats two bowls of rice every meal." Then he went on to ask: "When you were inside, did you get to hear that I've been sending him three hundred *yuan* every month, and bought him nourishment supplements?"

Baorun just grunted: "Ah! OK, good!" by way of thanks. After a while, he asked:

"Is three hundred *yuan* today worth as much as thirty *yuan*?"

Liu Sheng wasn't sure exactly what he was getting at, and replied cautiously:

"You mean inflation? Prices are going up every day, and everything's getting more expensive, even condoms. But don't worry, the rent on your family house has gone up too. I hear that Madam Ma is collecting a thousand a month for you, and as long as you're careful, that's enough."

"Why should I be worrying? With you as my Big Boss, what can go wrong for me? Isn't that right?"

"Yes, of course!" Liu Sheng said with a mocking laugh.

Baorun clapped him on the shoulder, and asked:

"Well, Boss, how much do you earn a month?"

Liu Sheng's natural instincts for self-preservation, led him to reply cautiously:

"I'm no big boss. I just about scrape by on what I earn every day from the meat and vegetable business, but I can't even afford to buy any property. Chungeng and Ah Liu have both got kids, but I'm the same as you, still single."

Behind him, Baorun fell silent, then burst out:

"It's not my fault if I'm still single, but you've got no excuse."

Liu Sheng turned to look at him.

"What do you mean, Brother?"

Baorun laughed mockingly:

"What about Fairy Princess? She's been so good to you, why haven't you married her yet?"

That one sentence was enough to light the flame of memory; a network of dark fire burst into life in the van, and a subtle heat flowed between the two men. Liu Sheng felt it rising to his face. He wanted to discuss Fairy Princess, but after considering the repercussions, he ended up just sighing:

"Just leave it. They were unhappy times, so let's not talk about Fairy Princess."

Baorun's face was reflected in the rearview mirror, flickering in the uneven morning light, his expression now dull and sluggardly, now plunged in gloom. There was a strange sheen of moisture on Baorun's forehead as he sat stiff and upright on an upturned vegetable basket, holding a carrot in each hand. He was beating the two carrots together, producing a dull, thudding sound. When one carrot broke, he took another one out of the basket. Liu Sheng had no idea why Baorun was beating the carrots together: thud, thud, thud. This was Baorun after the passage of many years, not the callow youth of all that time ago. He was a dangerous stranger, and one who exuded that particular aura of having been **inside**. Liu Sheng was very much on his guard, the sound of a distant tempest ringing in his ears. He kept looking in the rearview mirror, and his eye fell dully on a ball of white packing twine rolling around on the floor of the van. One end of the ball was accommodatingly snug in the middle of the ball, but the other end was snaking mischievously round the van, teasing and tantalising that hand so expert at bondage. Baorun picked up the ball of twine, and began to unroll it a bit at a time, winding it round his wrist. Liu Sheng heard Baorun suddenly ask, in a hoarse voice:

"Why does she hate me? Do you know?"

A fatal question, and there was no getting round it, one that had to be asked, sooner or later, and one that demanded an answer, no matter how hard it was to find one. Liu Sheng turned over all sorts of answers in his head but all that popped out when he opened his mouth were commonplace platitudes:

"Leave it. Let the past look after the past, so we can look to the future." Then he added more honestly: "She's to be pitied herself now. She's in a whole heap of trouble. I don't know where she's run off to, but I've heard it's Japan."

It went quiet in the back of the van. Then Baorun gave a wry laugh, picked up a carrot, and bit into it. When Liu Sheng heard Baorun crunching on the carrot, he thought twice about saying anything more, and his heart began to beat faster. He rather thought the talk was going to turn to him. The framing, the betrayal, the passing the buck, for all these things, he would sooner or later have to come up with a reasonable explanation, but he had no idea how he was going to make these offences sound reasonable. He looked out of the window at the passing streets, hoping he might see a hitchhiker. Another person in the van would make him that much safer. The strange thing was that normally, as his van passed down Red Toon Street, there was always some acquaintance or other looking for a lift somewhere, but that morning he saw hardly anyone he knew, and none of them wanted a lift. As the van passed Baorun's front door, Liu Sheng deliberately slowed down. Madam Ma and her family could not have heard the news of Baorun's return; Xiao Ma's red motorbike was parked across the door, and the door itself was covered in all sorts of handbills and small posters. No one had taken responsibility for doing anything about them, so the door now looked more like a bulletin board.

"We've arrived at your home." Liu Sheng turned to Baorun and asked: "Do you want to stop and drop off your luggage?"

"Don't stop. I don't have any luggage. You just concentrate on driving, and drive on!"

Their route took them to Chungeng's house. A dark-skinned woman wearing cotton long johns was hanging out washing on a clothes rack in front of the door. She was muttering continuously, either complaining about the weather, or cursing some person unknown. Behind her came a little girl, carrying a bed cover that was bigger than she was. Liu Sheng had a sudden inspiration, and shouted to the girl:

"Hey, Tinkerbell, tell your father to come out, and see who's come home."

The girl ignored him and the woman turned to look blankly at the van.

"I don't care who has come home," she said huffily. "And Chungeng can't come out. He's still in bed and dead to the world. He was playing mahjong all night last night."

Liu Sheng was disappointed, but persevered with some introductions to Baorun:

"That's Chungeng's wife; very fierce, a real shrew. His daughter's an odd one too; hates school and only likes doing housework. You used to get on alright with Chungeng; shall we go and wake him up?"

"I didn't know Chungeng. I didn't have any friends on the street." Baorun hesitated, then laughed: "If we're going to talk about the past, you and I got on all right, didn't we?"

Liu Sheng could hear the meaning behind those words, and his heart constricted. He hastily changed the subject:

"When you come out from being **inside**, you have to go and register in the district, don't you? Shall I take you to the district office? It's on our way."

"Registration can wait. No one knows or cares if I'm in the district," Baorun said. "I know you and your stinginess, but forget it. Today's my first day out: it's a happy day, when everything should be peaceful and calm."

Everything was indeed peaceful and calm all the way. The van drove through the square in front of the Workers' Cultural Palace, where there had been an accident of some kind, and the traffic was backed up. They came to a halt beside a huge cosmetics advertisement. Liu Sheng could see in the rearview mirror, that it had attracted Baorun's attention. The girl in the poster was a typical advertising model, her enticing lips were bright scarlet, her wet, tousled hair was the colour of gold, and her bare shoulders were sharp and sexy. An empty-eyed western girl who nonetheless radiated a wanton sex appeal, that Baorun seemed to focus on. Liu Sheng found this secretly amusing, and he turned to wink at him:

"How about it? You've had to hold it in for so long, do you want to do something about it today? Just say if you do, and I'll take you. My treat."

Baorun's gaze immediately flicked off the poster.

"Do what about it? It's so shrivelled up from lack of use down there, there's no point even in thinking about doing anything."

He sat up straight on the vegetable basket, with his head to one side, thinking hard. After a while, he pointed at the gates of the Workers' Cultural Palace, and asked:

"Is the roller-skating rink still there?"

"You want to go roller skating?" Liu Sheng asked in surprise. "You don't want to fuck? You'd rather go roller skating?"

"No, I don't want to do anything. I was just asking."

"The rink went ages ago. You see the McDonald's over there? And the KFC over there? Half the rink was sold to McDonald's and half to KFC."

FOURTEEN
FAMILY PHOTO

GRANDFATHER DIDN'T RECOGNISE BAORUN.

Grandfather asked Liu Sheng:

"Who's Baorun?"

"Baorun is Baorun. Don't you recognise Baorun? He's your grandson. Your son's son is your grandson. You've only got one, don't you remember?"

"I'm a lonely old widower without family, how could a lonely old widower have a grandson?"

"You're not a lonely old widower and you do have a grandson. Do you remember Dekang? Dekang is his father and your son. Baorun is Dekang's son. Think about it. Have a good think, and then you'll remember."

Grandfather kept repeating Dekang and Baorun's names but, after a while, he shook his head decisively:

"What Dekang? What Baorun? The names don't mean anything to me." Grandfather looked pained and jittery, clutching his head in both hands. "Don't make me think about stuff. As soon as I think about stuff, my head hurts. My head's going to explode."

"There's nothing I can do", Liu Sheng said helplessly, spreading his arms wide. "Your granddad's health is fine, but he's getting more and more confused. Last year he still remembered you, but this year he's forgotten everyone, and now he only recognises me."

Baorun stood beside Grandfather's bed, his gaze darting back and forth from Liu Sheng to Grandfather, a little bit worried, and a little bit disappointed. Occasionally, a mocking smile played over his lips, as though Liu Sheng and Grandfather were performing some kind of substandard double act. He couldn't resist cheering them on with assorted random cries of encouragement: "Great!" "Outstanding!" "Fantastic!" At one point, he seemed about to give up on his befuddled old relative, and he headed out of the ward, but he only went a few steps before turning back. Liu Sheng could not have foreseen that Baorun would suddenly hurl himself at Grandfather, seize his head in both hands, and start shaking it crazily:

"Think about it: who am I? Think! Have a good think for me! Who is Dekang? Who is Baorun? Who is your grandson? Does your head hurt? I don't care if it kills you, you just think for me!"

Grandfather let out a blood-curdling shriek, and it was only with great difficulty that Liu Sheng pulled Baorun off him. Grandfather's trousers were suspiciously warm, and there was a wet patch in the bed. Grandfather had pissed himself.

"You frightened your Granddad into pissing himself. He hasn't forgotten you on purpose. He's lost his memory; can't you understand that? How can you treat him like this?"

"The old fart will be the death of me!" Baorun went over to the window and buried his face in his hands. "Lost his memory? What about me? Why haven't I lost my memory? For fuck's sake, this is really pissing me off!"

Liu Sheng took a set of hospital clothes out of the wardrobe and helped Grandfather change his trousers. It was the kind of thing he did in any case when Baorun wasn't there but, in Baorun's presence, he did it even more assiduously. Completely naked, Grandfather sat shivering on the edge of the bed, doing what he was told. His snowy-white hair had thinned over the years and now his head looked like a baby's. His body was on its last legs and all its parts were in decline: his eyelids, his eyebrows, his chest, his testicles, all in decline. And in his decline, he smelled: his hair smelled, his bottom smelled and his breath, in particular, smelled of rotting salted fish. Liu Sheng had always held his nose when seeing to Grandfather, but this time he didn't, and there was a kind of joyful liberation in the way he changed his trousers:

"Alright, I'll change them this time, but next time your grandson will do it for you. Your troubles are over, my troubles are over, everyone's troubles are over."

He glanced at Baorun, who was standing impassively by the window, showing neither gratitude nor jealousy.

"Come over here and put on his socks, Baorun. You always have to take it slow, getting back to normal with someone, and it's the same with your Grandad. Getting started is always the hardest bit, but you can start with his socks and go on from there."

Baorun took a couple of steps, then stopped. He looked at an enamel bowl on the table, in which Grandfather's false teeth were soaking. A fly came in through the window and settled in the bowl. Baorun picked up the bowl and shook it. The dentures rattled against the sides and the fly flew away.

"You put them on," Baorun said. "I'm not bothered. Let's say I've lost my memory too. What's this crap about getting back to normal? What normal? I gave up on all that ages ago."

Liu Sheng didn't know what to say to this and went over to help Grandfather with his socks, himself. He looked coldly at Baorun who was rummaging through the drawer of the bedside cabinet.

"What are you looking for?"

"A photograph. A family portrait that was taken when I was a kid. I want to see what we looked like then."

Baorun found the photograph under the paper lining of the drawer, and took it out to look at it in the light by the window. Suddenly, he laughed:

"Ha! I'm not there! I'm not fucking there!"

"Isn't it a family photo? What do you mean you're not there?"

"My face isn't there. My mum's body isn't there and my dad isn't there at all. He's alright though, he's all there."

Bewildered, Liu Sheng went over to look, and saw that the

photograph had got soaked in water at some stage, and the image had been eroded in a very peculiar way: a strangely selective way. Baorun's red neckerchief was still there, but everything above his neck was faded away; his father seemed to have completely disappeared except for one leather shoe. Only Grandfather remained in the family portrait; he had survived the soaking completely unscathed: old, wretched and gutless, he was still there. He was wearing a dark-coloured Sun Yat-sen suit, a pair of Liberation plimsolls, and his hair was neatly combed and shiny. He was hale and hearty, but his timid expression revealed a constriction of the soul. He was looking at the camera lens with an evasive expression, as though he was offering profound apologies for what was to come:

"I'm sorry, but you're all going to fade away, and only I'm going to survive intact."

FIFTEEN
BRIC-A-BRAC

It wasn't just Grandfather. Many of the residents of Red Toon Street had also forgotten Baorun's name.

Some people are destined to be forgotten by history, and Baorun was a good example. It was hard to tell the reason. Perhaps it was his family's general stand-offishness with the other residents of the street, or perhaps it was down to Baorun's dubious reputation, but Red Toon Street greeted his return with total indifference. Baorun's come home. Baorun's home. The news was of no more importance than a drop of rain on the eaves on a rainy day and, just like a raindrop, after the sound of its falling, there was nothing more to be heard.

Only Liu Sheng showed any hospitality, and he was determined to hold a welcome home celebration. He brought Chungeng and Ah Liu with him to solicit Baorun's opinion.

"What would you like to do? Do you want a meal with a bunch of friends, or would you like to go to a sauna? Or we could take a private room in a karaoke bar."

Baorun wouldn't choose.

"I don't want any of that. All I want is a suitcase with wheels. Tomorrow I'm going to the provincial capital to see my mum, and I don't know if I'll be coming back. My uncle is some kind of big official, a department chief, and I've heard he's got a lot of influence. If he can get me a decent job, then I'll stick around in the city."

Baorun took the train to the provincial capital, but after he'd been gone a few days, he came back alone.

It turned out that his aunt and her family had been very unwelcoming. He had a bad name with both his relatives and their friends, and his aunt had been very wary of welcoming her nephew. His uncle didn't deign to say a single word to him. At his first dinner in his aunt's house, halfway through the meal, one after another his aunt, uncle and cousin all found an excuse to get up and leave the table, so in the end he was left all alone. He lost his temper and smashed a half-full bowl of rice on the table. Then he got up and left the house. After his quarrel with his aunt's family, he gave up on his original plan, and all he could think of was getting his mother to come home. But his mother was no longer the mother he remembered. Su Baozhen had found an older man in the provincial capital, who treated her very well, and whose son and daughter had gradually come to accept her. One matter remained in suspense from her former life, and her son's release from prison brought that matter mercilessly into focus. When it came to the choice between her new man and her son, and between this new city and her old home, Su Baozhen abandoned her son, and abandoned Red Toon Street. His mother's decision took Baorun by surprise, and he asked her:

"What am I going to do if you don't come home?"

Su Baozhen turned the question back on him:

"You're almost thirty, and you still expect me to look after you like a kid? You actually want me to go home and take care of you?"

Baorun couldn't think of any good reason to offer to change his mother's mind, nor did he want to come out looking unfilial. He was also too ashamed to admit that he missed her. His actual answer, however, came out surprisingly aggressive, almost as a curse:

"When it comes down to it, who's going to have to look after who? Who knows? What if you get ill when you're old? Or go off your head? What if you're paralysed? What if you get cancer? Will you want me to look after you?"

Su Baozhen spat on the ground three times in her fury:

"If something happens to me, Lao Zhang will look after me. All you have to do is look after Grandfather and yourself, and I'll give thanks to heaven and earth."

Baorun still wouldn't give up, and went on:

"I think you've already got senile dementia! Have you forgotten I'm your son? Isn't a son worth more than some crappy old man? I doubt if he's going to last very long anyway, and what are you going to do when he dies? You'd want to come home, wouldn't you!"

Su Baozhen exploded with anger, and clipped Baorun round the ear.

"Curse me if you like, but Lao Zhang hasn't done anything to you, so you can leave him out of it. I'm telling you now, Baorun, I've given up on that house in Red Toon Street, and from now on, it's all yours. You can knock it down if you want, and throw out all my stuff. Even if Lao Zhang can't support me, I'll still not turn to you. I'd rather die in an old people's home than go back to Red Toon Street."

Now he could see what future was in store for him: it was a future where he was surplus to requirements, and a future in which he would no longer have a mother. With his trip home to see his family so abruptly terminated, he took advantage of the darkness to slip quietly home, close the doors and not come out. People could see a light burning upstairs in the attic, but there was no sign of Baorun. When Liu Sheng heard that Baorun had returned, he went and knocked on the door, but there was no answer, no matter how hard he knocked. Suspicious, he went next door to the pharmacy to ask Madam Ma if she had heard any movement from Baorun. Madam Ma said:

"He's like a ghost. There's some noise from the attic in the morning, but in the afternoon, there's no movement at all. Liu Sheng went to knock on the door again, and after only a couple of knocks, the door opened and Baorun appeared there, his breath reeking of alcohol. He had a length of rope in his hand.

"What are you knocking on the door for?" he asked Liu Sheng. "Has there been a death in your family?"

"No, no one's died. I came to see you; to see whether you were still alive."

"I've still got some breath in my body, and I'm not going to die any time soon."

Baorun slammed the door, then, after a few seconds, it opened again. Baorun stood blocking the doorway, the length of rope in his hand. He looked sidelong at Liu Sheng, who asked:

"Are you shutting yourself away, playing with rope? What fun is that? Let me take you out somewhere to break the boredom."

Baorun stood silent for a moment. He gave the rope a twitch, and it fell obediently on his shoulder, like a snake.

"I don't need anything to relieve the boredom, I want to do my homework. It's been a long time since I've played with rope. I've already remembered eleven of the eighteen types of knot. If you want to come in, that's fine; you can let me practise on you. I can practise the legal knot."

Liu Sheng gestured in refusal:

"Thank you for the kind offer, but I won't come in. You can practise the legal knot on yourself."

A few days later signs appeared that Baorun had come back to live, as he began a major clean-up operation. Dust had been building up for far too long in the old house; the kitchen cupboards were teeming with cockroaches; the dresser was rotting away from the humidity and its doors wouldn't shut nor its drawers pull out; the slats of the kitchen chairs were broken at the joints; and the big wooden washing-up basin leaked. One by one, he took each of these bits of kitchen furniture and put them in the doorway for sale. To start with, he set the prices very high and, naturally, no one was interested. As time went by, he gradually lowered them, but still none of the neighbours showed any interest. Finally, when the prices were at rock bottom, a junk merchant happened to pass by and, for fifty *yuan*, loaded the whole lot onto his flatbed trike. Madam Ma came out of her shop just as the final deal was being struck, and she heard Baorun say to the junk merchant:

"I've also got a big old bed; you can have it cheap if you want it."

The merchant looked at the space left on his trike, and said:

"I'll take it if it's cheap enough. Is it real wood?"

"It's my mum and dad's old bed; of course it's real wood. It's yours for fifty *yuan*. I'll break it up for you, if you want, and you can take it away now."

Madam Ma wanted to go and stop him but her son and daughter-in-law pulled her back inside the pharmacy and put her in front of the television, which was showing a soap opera. Through the glass of the shop door, she could hear the sound of Baorun's hammer next door. Bang! Bang! Bang! Baorun was breaking up his parents' bed. Bang! Bang! And bang again! As the big old bed disintegrated into pieces, Madam Ma shivered, and clutched her stomach as she exclaimed:

"An evil deed! An evil deed!"

She and her son and daughter-in-law watched the laden trike drive away; this impromptu bric-a-brac sale left them wide-eyed and open-mouthed. In the eyes of the happy and harmonious Ma family, the terrible activities next door were tantamount to parricide, and even the air itself seemed drenched in blood. Through gritted teeth, Madam Ma said censoriously:

"Poor Su Baozhen truly has had a bitter life. Rather than raising this unworthy son, she would have done better to rear a guard dog."

Her daughter-in-law expressed her feelings altogether more simply:

"That Baorun is a barbarian!"

Only her son Xiao Ma was a little more open-minded and tried to mollify the two women, saying that they shouldn't be quite so hard on Baorun; it was only some old stuff that he would have sold sooner or later. If you don't get rid of the old, there's no room for the new.

Not long after, Baorun came over. He was carrying an earthenware urn, and as he pushed open the pharmacy door, a desolate gust of cold air filled the shop floor. The Ma family stood staring at him in amazement, and then greeted him as though a murderer had come to call. Madam Ma asked him what was in the urn, and he replied:

"My father's ashes. Mum had put them under the bed."

"What are you doing bringing someone's ashes into my shop?" Madam Ma exclaimed, shrilly. "Are you trying to sell them? I'm not buying your father's ashes!"

"Do you have a set of scales? I want to borrow them to see how much my father weighs."

Madam Ma almost wept with anger:

"I don't have any scales, and if I did I wouldn't lend them to you to weigh those ashes."

Baorun looked down at the urn, weighing it in his hands:

"It's too light! I can't believe that a big man like my father could leave behind so little when he died. It's not even a kilo."

Madam Ma was superstitiously afraid of the urn, and unceremoniously drove him out of the shop, berating him as she pushed him out of the door:

"I've never seen such an unfilial son as you! The way you're mistreating him, his soul will never ascend to heaven. I can't believe your mother didn't tell you where your father's burial plot is. Go there at once and bury him properly."

As Baorun was being shoved out of the shop, he reluctantly turned and asked:

"My mother told me it's in the Guangming Public Cemetery; do you know where that is?"

Madam Ma waved her hand dismissively and replied:

"Don't ask me. Our family doesn't have anything to do with cemeteries. Go and ask Liu Sheng; he's often driven others out there to sweep their family tombs."

SIXTEEN
TOMB-SWEEPING

Liu Sheng took Baorun in the van to the Guangming Public Cemetery.

It wasn't the Tomb-Sweeping Festival, so the cemetery was deserted. The two men walked around for a while, without finding Baorun's father's plot. They went to the administration office to enquire, where they were told the plots were divided into three categories: grade 1, grade 2, and grade 3, which represented deluxe, ordinary and budget plots, with corresponding construction costs. Baorun's father's plot was a budget one. As such it couldn't be located on the south-facing, sunny slope, but could be found on the other side. When they reached the north-facing slope, they saw a very small tombstone carved with the name Yang Dekang. In fact, everything was already in place, and a black-and-white photograph was set into the stone, from which the deceased looked out across time and space, his gaze carrying all the suffering of his former life, all the resentment at failed expectations and lost opportunities, and weighing up his long-absent son. When they opened the stone drawer, it was full of rainwater, but otherwise ready to accept a funerary urn. Just to the side was the plot that had been chosen for Grandfather all those years ago, which was smaller still. Two horsetail pines had been planted there, and had already grown thick and luxuriant, thrusting up into the sky.

Baorun compared the two tombstones, and noticed that the writing on his father's tomb was black, while that on Grandfather's was traced in red lacquer paint. He had never been to a cemetery before, and didn't understand its mysteries, so he asked Liu Sheng:

"Why is one red and one black?"

Liu Sheng explained patiently that the black characters were for the dead, and the red ones for people who were still alive, and not buried yet. Baorun stroked Grandfather's tombstone, and smiled suddenly:

"Great! You can see what our family is like: the ones who should be here, won't come, and the ones who shouldn't have come yet, are already here."

Liu Sheng realised he was talking about Grandfather, and asked:

"Does it bother you that your granddad seems to be going on forever?"

Baorun thought about this for a moment, then replied:

"No, it doesn't bother me. When it comes down to it, he's family, and he's all I've got left."

An old man came over carrying a plastic bucket, and showed them how to bury the remains. Following his instructions, they put the urn into the stone drawer, then sealed all the cracks with the lime plaster paste in the plastic bucket. The old man smoothed it all over with a trowel, and said:

"All done. That's fifteen *yuan* for the plaster and five *yuan* for the labour; twenty *yuan* altogether."

Only twenty *yuan*. No digging or filling in. Baorun had not expected it to be so easy to fulfil his filial duty. Rather at a loss, he asked Liu Sheng:

"Is that it, then?"

"That's it. Did you think you were going to have to dig the tomb, then? Do you know what kind of society we're living in now? We're in a service-based society. All that matters is speed and simplicity."

Quick and simple indeed!

Liu Sheng was moderately familiar with funeral services, and he made Baorun kneel on the ground, and kowtow three times to the tombstone. When Baorun had finished his kowtows, he suddenly put his ear to the stone drawer, listening attentively to something.

"What are you listening to?" Liu Sheng asked. "Is there a cricket in there?"

"It's not a cricket. You come and listen. My father's remains are jumping about in there."

Liu Sheng went over to listen and he could, indeed, hear some faint noises coming from inside the drawer, like rice grains being stir-fried in a wok.

"It's not his remains jumping, it's your father's soul which can't escape. He's unhappy with his death, and he probably wants to tell you something."

Liu Sheng struck the drawer gently a few times, but to no effect; the remains inside were still restless. He looked at his hand.

"It's no use me hitting it, he wants to tell you something. You give it a try, and tell him you hear him."

Baorun hesitated a moment, but in the end, he stretched out his hand and began to pat the drawer, saying:

"Don't make a racket, Father; I heard you. I heard everything."

Baorun hadn't expected that he himself would have such a gift for pacifying the dead. The drawer had indeed gone quiet.

Baorun said in amazement:

"That's really it! He's gone quiet!"

Liu Sheng went over and listened for himself. He could tell that Baorun's father's spirit had indeed quietened down. He said solemnly:

"Your father is a good man and easy to pacify. Look, isn't he at peace now?"

Later, the wind got up, and they made their way against it, to the exit from the cemetery, passing the many tombstones of people unknown to them. Bits of paper money and fragments of tinfoil were blowing in the wind, floating and fluttering over their heads, following them like a swarm of golden moths. They both lit cigarettes. Liu Sheng drew in a lungful of smoke, and asked Baorun:

"What did your father say to you? Did you get it all?"

"I don't know what he said. What did you hear?"

Liu Sheng put his hand to his forehead:

"Let me guess: I'm sure he was telling you to let the past stay in the past, and to look to the future.

Baorun stubbed out his cigarette with his foot, and said, slowly:

"That's the kind of stuff you hear on the TV, or read in the papers. Leave the past behind? How can you possibly do that?"

PART THREE
MISS BAI'S SUMMER

ONE

JUNE

One day in June, she came back.

There seemed to be some kind of unequal agreement between her and our town; an agreement written by fate, by which, although the town didn't belong to her, she belonged to the town. She came back again. A fish can swim to and fro as much as it likes, but in the end it will get caught in the open net.

The nine-day tour of Europe with Mr Pang was just a distant memory: Paris, Rome, the Eiffel Tower, the Vatican, places all over Europe that she had visited, in the end, just became fragmentary recollections, drifting in her memory, there one minute, gone the next until, finally, Europe disappeared completely. All that was left behind was some of Mr Pang's seed, growing within her like poisonous grass in fertile soil. It was a one-time accident. She vaguely remembered the deep-purple-coloured room in the chateau on the Loire. Because of the beautiful river scenery outside the window; because of the roses by the bed, because of the bottle of champagne on the balcony, because of a romantic evening unlike anything she'd experienced before; because of all these things, she took pity on Mr Pang, and allowed her sentiments to find expression honest to the occasion. That night she didn't hold back from Mr Pang, and she allowed him to undress her completely. Roses and champagne are dangerous things and she allowed Mr Pang enthusiastically to explore her reluctant desire, and gradually to intensify it, until it surged up into a frenzy. She had no idea why her contraceptive measures had failed, she just felt like a fool. The price for one night's affection might be payable for a lifetime.

Her pregnancy took her badly, and she had to cut short her stage career. The revolving stage lights of the bars made her nauseous; the suggestive shape of the microphone made her nauseous; the vigorous rhythms and movements of the songs and dances made her nauseous. One day she was singing on a small dance platform in a bar, and as she reached the climax of the song, she suddenly began to throw up all over the drum kit and the drummer, who fled, head in his hands, to the great amusement of the customers. The female manager realised that she was pregnant, and felt around her belly with her hand. She pulled Miss Bai down from the platform, saying:

"You should go home. Singing is one thing, and making money is another, but we can't risk harming the next generation."

The first time it happened, she didn't panic, she just felt depressed. She had been involved with men for so many years, she thought she was really on top of this kind of thing, but now her woman's body was having to foot the bill. And it wasn't just in her body that she had lost control, a number of her fundamental attitudes to life had also suddenly been terminally challenged. Why? She wasn't in love with Mr Pang, so why should she be lumbered with carrying his flesh and blood in her belly. She discovered that she was as vulnerable as a bamboo shoot after rain: whenever rain falls, a bamboo shoot can push its way through the earth anywhere, without warning. If it grows into a bamboo, all well and good, but it may equally well be cut down and eaten.

She was depressed. Wealth, good looks, admiration, love, these were the criteria by which she chose her men friends, and for her to get pregnant by one of them, all of these criteria would have to come together in him. In her eyes, Mr Pang was a run-of-the-mill Taiwanese businessman, short, a bit overweight, not ugly, but not what she would call attractive, rich but not really wealthy; and as for love, the question had never even arisen. She had been working the bars and nightclubs for many years, and had had her fair share of big brothers and daddies to sort out problems for her. Mr Pang was different, and he fell somewhere between the two: more needy than a big brother, but easier to manage than a daddy. She had called him Mr Pang from the outset, and he was something of a conundrum as an admirer: half open, half closed-down; part of him was open and friendly, and part of him was a slave to his hormones. There was yet another part, that was vague and shadowy, and hard to pin down. When she analysed why Mr Pang treated her so well, she used to say it wasn't so much that he was in love with her, but that he was terrified of being alone, and she acted like a herbal plaster healing that wound. The way she thanked Mr Pang was very straightforward: a kiss on the cheek, a glass of wine with him, those were free; if she had to accompany him to meet clients, all the toasts and the flirtatious looks and banter all counted as work and were to be rewarded by Mr Pang buying her a designer handbag or the latest model cell phone. It was as simple as that. Their relationship proved more ephemeral than the dew.

She was depressed. She had thought that Mr Pang's invitation to the European tour was her final bonus, his way of saying thank you, and that the trip to Paris was a kind of closing ceremony. Instead, it had turned out to be a grim and fateful opening ceremony. As she left the bar, she heard the manageress talking to a travel agency about the itinerary for a European tour: Paris, Rome, Vienna, the names stirred up her emotions, and she said, impetuously, to the manageress:

"Europe is all very well, but you can't put your travels in your suitcase and bring them home; so what's the point? It's just a waste of money!"

"Haven't you just been yourself? If you can go, why shouldn't I?"

Miss Bai realised she had been rather too abrupt in her outburst, and added hastily:

"I'm just thinking of you. If you've got the money to spend, then go, but, whatever you do, stay away from the Loire! That place is cursed, and something terrible will happen if you go."

Her roommate, Miss Shen Lan, who was a year younger than her and also a bar singer, had already had two abortions, so fortunately had a gold VIP card for a gynaecology and obstetrics clinic. She was happy to accompany Miss Bai there. It was located in a new industrial district and, from the outside, looked like a health club. It had the unique and humane name of the Athena Centre for the Care of Women.

A number of women of about her own age were waiting outside the operating theatre. However different they were in looks and shape, they all had the same expression on their faces: an expression of fretful resentment. They formed an exclusive club, all concealing the terse synopsis of a human life in their wombs for the sole inspection of the doctor. A sexual misadventure. These days, many such misadventures are rectified by surgery. There was a two-seater sofa standing empty, and Miss Bai and Miss Shen Lan went over to sit down on it. When they looked, they saw that it was covered with a sheet of plastic; on lifting the plastic, they saw that the fabric underneath was covered in blood-spots. In some places they formed a dark-red network like a road map and in others they had flowed together in rivulets. The two girls shrieked in alarm. A bespectacled girl next to them explained where the blood came from. Her account was calm and concise:

"There was a girl with a Chanel handbag sitting there, head down, not looking up. I thought she was sending a text, but as I watched, she gradually stretched out on the couch. I wondered why she needed to stretch out to send a text, but I never imagined she had a razor blade in her hand, and had come here to slit her wrists."

The two girls sprang away from the sofa, and went to wait in the corridor. Miss Bai casually analysed the girl's strange behaviour:

"She was wearing Chanel and was actually waiting outside the operating theatre before she slit her wrists! She took it all too seriously!"

Miss Shen Lan turned to look back at the sofa:

"Maybe not; maybe she was making the best of it!"

The Athena Centre for the Care of Women was doing good business, and even VIPs had to wait their turn. Miss Bai sat on a bench, listening to her girlfriend chattering on about her plans to buy an apartment in Shenzhen. At first she paid attention, but she gradually became distracted by the other young men coming to wait in the corridor. They made her think of Mr Pang. She took out her cell phone to search for the photos of her and Mr Pang in the chateau on the Loire. First she looked at herself: she looked so happy, a red rose in her hair at one temple – a free spirit! How things change with the passage of time! She wondered why she had been so happy then. Then she looked at Mr Pang: he was wearing a red scarf, and had his arm around her waist. There was a happy, but slightly reserved expression in his eyes. The angle at which the photo was taken hid his physical shortcomings, and he looked younger and taller than he was. Pregnancy is a subtle thing, and not only did it change her, it changed him too. He was its beneficiary. In that instant of time, she thought Mr Pang looked revitalised. He was no longer just a lonely, sentimental businessman; in that peculiarly masculine way, he had infiltrated the most secret place of her body and, as tiny as that space was, it now enveloped part of her future. Because of it, she and Mr Pang were now intimately connected. She sighed as she admitted to herself a huge, but entirely unexpected revelation: there was now a man in her world, who she neither cared about nor loved, but who she had begun to miss.

For the first time, she showed her friend the screen of her cell phone, revealing what Mr Pang really looked like.

"What do you think of him, this Taiwanese businessman?"

Miss Shen Lan scrutinised the photo, and pursed her lips in a smile:

"He's just another Taiwanese uncle, nothing special; not a patch on that horse trainer of yours."

She knew her friend meant Qu Ying and, angrily, she snatched back her phone.

"He was a good-looking guy, but no meal ticket. I learned ages ago that you can't turn a guy's looks into cash."

Abruptly, she decided to cancel her appointment. There was a girl, who looked like a student, standing next to her, exhaustion written all over her as she dozed, leaning against the wall. Miss Bai stood up and said to the girl:

"Come and sit down. Sit down and get some sleep; we're leaving."

"Aren't you going to have the procedure?" Miss Shen Lan asked in amazement. "Where are you going?"

"I'm going to buy a plane ticket and go home. I'm going to look for Mr Pang."

"Didn't you swear you'd never go home?"

Miss Bai waved her hand dismissively, and said with a wry smile:

"You really shouldn't take my oaths seriously. I've sworn so many of them: I was going to make a pop record; I was going to start my own business and get rich; I was going to marry a knight in shining armour. Which of those has actually happened? Even I don't believe them now."

They left the hospital and went out onto the main street of the industrial district, where the traffic was heavy. The early summer sunlight was illuminating the new, southern city, which she had visited so often but which had never become home to her. She patted the trunk of a roadside palm tree, and said:

"Fuck it! I'm out of here!"

"You were going to leave, sooner or later," Miss Shen Lan said. "The question is, where should you go? Last year you said you were going to Japan; this year you said you were going to Australia; now you suddenly flip around and say, after all, you're going home."

"It's not really my family home. The rest of you all have family homes, but I don't. Wherever I go, it's just me."

Miss Shen Lan felt she was being too hasty:

"Have you got any kind guarantee from him? Have you actually talked about the future?"

"I haven't a clue how to raise all this with him. I'm just putting one foot in front of the other, and I'm walking in the dark. I'm feeling my way, and I'll go wherever I see a glimmer of light."

"And Mr Pang is that glimmer of light?"

Miss Bai considered this carefully, and replied:

"I don't know whether he is or not, so I'm going to find out."

TWO

MR PANG

AT FIRST, Mr Pang was a glimmer of light.

He drove out to the airport to meet her. They enjoyed a long, slow embrace in the arrivals' hall. The length of the embrace stemmed not from depth of emotion, but because her arrogance needed the time to make a substantial adjustment, both physical and emotional, to being in the flabby arms of this short fat businessman. She felt that the crowd of people in the arrivals' hall were all watching them embrace, like a tired bird landing on the branch of a dead tree. Partly from humiliation, partly from nervousness, and yes, partly from affection, tears sprang to her eyes. She didn't want Mr Pang to know she was crying, so she dried her eyes on his shoulder. She didn't know whether he could feel the dampness on his shirt, but she heard him greet her in the way he always did:

"You're looking very beautiful today."

The music system in the car was playing a CD she had made herself, of Taiwanese and Hong Kong pop songs she used to sing in the nightclubs. She knew he had done this specially for her, and she was moved a little by this gesture. As a reward, she leaned her head on his shoulder.

"Are we going to your villa?"

"We're better going to a hotel, the villa isn't convenient; my wife is coming back any time soon."

"How is it that your wife is never there except when I'm around?"

He shrugged his shoulders:

"I don't know. In any case, it's a very good hotel: five-star standard at a four-star price."

She slowly raised her head from his shoulder:

"How many days have you booked?"

Mr Pang looked at her and said:

"You can stay as many days as you like; your whole life, if you want. I'll foot the bill."

"Only prostitutes stay in hotels all their life."

Seeing her expression, he went on: "If you don't like staying in a hotel, we can rent a place. I'll find a nice apartment or a villa even. I'll still pay for it."

"That's not renting an apartment, that's keeping a mistress. Do you want to keep me?"

Mr Pang was a little embarrassed, and he kept glancing at her, before mustering the courage to say:

"I will if you want me to. Our company is being floated on the stock market next year."

She turned to look out of the window, and scoffed:

"Floated on the market, eh? Why do I feel as though I'm being floated on the market?"

"A prostitute can be said to have been floated on the stock market because she's in circulation. You're not in circulation so you can't be considered to have been floated on the market."

She stared at his profile in silhouette:

"So I'm not in circulation? And I'm sleeping with you only?" Suddenly, she patted his cheek and, turning more serious, said: "Do you know what I want to talk to you about?"

Mr Pang turned the music off.

"So, what is it? What has brought you all this way by plane to discuss?"

"Guess. Go on guess and see."

Mr Pang fell silent, then said, after a while:

"I don't like guessing games. Let's wait till we get to the hotel."

The hotel was in the city centre, across the street from the Paris Nights nightclub. When she left the Paris Nights club, the hotel was still under construction. Returning now to her old stamping ground, she was surprised to find herself entering this great skyscraper and confronting a page of her own history. Standing at the window of their room, she could see that the neon lights of Paris Nights were already switched on: English, French, Japanese, Chinese, the different languages served to emphasise the night club's international pretensions. Multi-coloured strip lights picked out the figure of a young girl, her profile, pert buttocks and high-heeled shoes of indeterminate nationality. These neon lights were her CV, her past, their garish but functional glare illuminating its emptiness. She drew the curtains. Mr Pang put his arms around her from behind, breathing heavily.

"I'm not in the mood", she said.

"You may not be, but I am, so how about it?"

His hands lingered on her breasts a moment, slipping under her sleeveless blouse, and then under the waistband of her culottes, slowly moving downwards and downwards. She struggled free of him, and said, sternly:

"No! Be careful, you might hurt your child."

The words were like an electric shock on his hands, and he snatched them back.

"What do you mean?"

"I said, be careful. I'm pregnant. And it's yours."

The atmosphere in the room became charged. He retreated to sit on the arm of the sofa. He looked very serious, and caution filled his reserved expression. His gaze fell on the lower half of her body, then slowly rose to her face.

"Mine? In France? That one night? How?"

"You're not happy?" She looked sidelong at him. "I'm not happy either. If it was Roberto Baggio's, or Li Ka-shing's that would be fine; even Jackie Chan or Chow Yun-Fat would do. But yours? There's no way!"

"It's not possible!" he said. "Not possible! I remember quite clearly I used a condom."

"Not possible? What do you mean, not possible?" Her voice became shrill and uncontrolled. "I'm the one who's pregnant, not you! So, tell me, what exactly do you mean by, not possible?"

"I mean it's not possible you're pregnant." He gave a dry laugh. "I wore a condom, a top-brand one, so you can't be pregnant."

Ashen-faced, anger flared in her eyes, its flames sweeping him from his head to his waist. He tugged nervously at the crotch of his suit trousers, and crossed his legs, swinging one foot backwards and forwards. She looked at his feet, and noticed that his calves were even whiter than the white socks he was wearing. She looked at the scattering of fine black hairs above the socks.

"Fuck it! I don't give a shit about the condom. Just tell me this: if it isn't yours, do you think some kind of devil got me pregnant?"

"No, not any old devil", he muttered to himself, before looking up at her. "A foreign devil! Didn't you always say how handsome and sexy they are?"

"What a good memory you've got. So tell me this, then. Which foreign devil was it?

"Let's be clear about this: you're the one who's pregnant, not me!" The smile faded from his lips, as he launched his counter-attack. "I'm the one who should be asking who it was, not you!"

"Do you think I'm just a common whore? Even a whore's only got one body! I was with you for nine days in Europe, in your company night and day. Who else could I have done it with?" she shrieked. Her blood was up, and she picked up a glass and hurled it at him. "How can I have been so blind? If I'd known you were going to be like this, I would have found a foreign devil; anybody's genes would be better than yours!"

He didn't manage to dodge; a cut opened up on his forehead, and blood began to flow. The sight of the blood startled her and stopped her in her tracks, and covering her eyes, she cried out:

"Shit! Why didn't you get out of the way?"

Mr Pang fled into the bathroom. She followed him, but found herself locked out. After a while, Mr Pang stormed out of the bathroom, clutching a towel to his forehead, muttering:

"All right, all right!"

"I've got a sticking-plaster in my suitcase."

But she had no chance to give him the plaster, as Mr Pang was already standing in the corridor. His hands were all bloody, and there was a look of loathing in his eyes. There was a decision of some kind clear on his face.

"I've seen you for who you really are today, Miss Bai", he said. "Shall I tell you what you are? You're just a whore. A low-class whore!"

Mr Pang's blood had dripped onto the cream-coloured carpet, red at first, gradually turning to black. She knelt down and rubbed at it with a tissue; the tissue turned red, but the carpet still showed a trail of black spots. Her mind had gone blank. Some of the blood had fallen on the luggage, and spread out on the nylon material like the silent explosion of an intricate firework. All her hopes had turned to dust, and as she knelt there on the floor lamenting what she had done wrong, she suddenly remembered the girl who had slit her wrists outside the operating theatre. The idea of following her example formed in her head. She opened the suitcase, took out a fruit knife, and put it to a blood vessel on her wrist: she wasn't sure whether it was a vein or an artery. She pressed the blade recklessly to the dark blue vein, but couldn't go through with it in the end. She was afraid of blood, and afraid of pain, and really didn't want to die. But, other than through death, she didn't know how to punish herself. In the end, she just concentrated on cleaning the suitcase. Through gritted teeth, she began to weep, soundlessly. Hatred consumed her grief as she suddenly remembered that Mr Pang had bought the suitcase for her in Europe. She aimed a malevolent kick at it.

"Hah! Who are you calling a whore?"

She was still asleep at noon the next day when the front desk of the hotel phoned her, asking whether she wanted to keep the room. Blearily, she replied:

"Don't ask me, ask Mr Pang."

"Mr Pang has already settled his account, and he's not paying for the room anymore."

Shocked fully awake, she stared dumbfounded at the phone for a long time, then spat out an obscenity.

"I would ask Madam not to swear at me."

"I'm not swearing at you," she yelled into the phone. "I'm swearing at Mr Pang. Are you called Pang? No! So what the fuck's it got to do with you?"

She couldn't afford such a swanky hotel herself, so her thoughts turned to another of her "daddies", a man called Section Chief Ma who worked in the Foodstuffs Bureau. He had always been most solicitous of her, and seemed to be able to put anything through his office expense account, even the shoes and perfume she bought when she went shopping with him. She tried to call him, but his mobile came up as an unknown number. When she called his office number, the woman who answered was brusque from the outset, asking what her relationship was with Section Chief Ma.

"I'm his adopted daughter"

The woman laughed coldly:

"Adopted daughter, you say? He's got a lot of those; which one are you?"

"Miss Bai, the singer," she said reluctantly.

"Oh yes, and where do you sing? Paris Nights? Palm Springs? California Sunshine? The 24K Club?"

Miss Bai could tell there was something odd going on in Section Chief Ma's office and, as she was wondering what sort of trouble he was in, she heard the rustling of paper at the other end of the phone.

"Have you got one of the Bureau's BMWs, Miss Bai?"

For a moment, she was at a loss what to say.

"I don't know what you're talking about. How could I have one of the Bureau's cars?"

The woman went silent, and went on flicking through the pages of whatever document she was consulting.

"I'm sorry; I've found it now. It isn't Miss Bai who's got the BMW, it's Miss Huang." Finally, the woman returned to the original subject of the call. "Are you looking for Section Chief Ma? You'll have to ask the Discipline Inspection Commission. Section Chief Ma has been detained for investigation, and only the Commission know where he is."

She sat stunned for a moment, then hung up the phone. She thought to herself about those nightclub girls whose predictions about Section Chief Ma had come true, that sooner or later he was going to get into trouble, and that they should milk him while he was still around. So there was going to be no help forthcoming from Section Chief Ma. She wondered whether Miss Huang was that lounge manager from the northeast at the Paris Nights; a dreamer who loved the rose-tinted novels of Chiung Yao. She was a dark horse! She herself had only got a few pairs of shoes and some perfume out of Section Chief Ma, but Miss Huang had driven off in his BMW.

The most important thing now was to find somewhere to live; there was no time for her to feel sorry for herself, nor did she feel like congratulating herself. She deleted Section Chief Ma's number from her cell phone, and the name of another of her 'daddies', Director Yang, leapt out at her. Director Yang was the director of a charitable foundation, and a habitué of Paris Nights. Whenever he arrived there, she had to accompany him singing the Taiwanese song *Stake It All on Love to Win*. The man had a face like a baboon, but he spent money like water at the club. It was a shame that he wasn't very clean, and that the price of his money was his wandering hands. She hunted out Director Yang's business card, but when she looked at it, she imagined two coarse, hairy hands; one reaching for her breasts, and the other getting ready to attack her buttocks. So, when she punched in his number, her body stiffened involuntarily, and her hand went protectively to her chest. The call connected, but Director Yang just said "Hello" and then went silent. He thought he had muted the call, but she could clearly hear him complaining about her to someone:

"This girl's a real nuisance. Nothing good ever comes out of her calls, I'm going to ignore her."

He was undoubtedly in some club or other and, separated from him by all that distance, she heard the familiar strains of *Stake it All on Love to Win*.

Infuriated, she yelled down the phone:

"Go stake yourself! Stake yourself to death, you horny old goat!"

She paced around the room, taking stock of her remaining social connections in the city. On the surface they seemed numerous and reliable, but in fact they were all as thin as a cobweb, and broke at the slightest tap. She decided to give up the hotel room for the time being, so she packed hastily, and went down to the lobby to check out. The girl on the desk seemed to know who she was, and looked her over with some disdain. Miss Bai never let anything go when her temper was up, and she pounded on the counter, saying:

"Where do you lot get off, looking down on people like this. Why are you all dressed like crows, anyway? This is a hotel, not a funeral parlour!"

Seeing the receptionists staring at her, she continued to vent her anger:

"I couldn't bear to stay here any longer. The fittings are awful, and so's the service! This place is six stars short of being a five-star hotel!"

She knew the city very well, but she felt disoriented, and couldn't decide where to go. Mr Pang's route had turned out to be a remote alleyway, a dead end. She adjusted her thinking to recognise that he had only ever been the faintest of glimmers, which she had extinguished herself by her own carelessness. This had brought her to another desperate realisation: her world was now so narrow, one impetuous move, one foreign trip, and she had already reached its limits.

There was a taxi waiting at the hotel door, and the driver stuck his head out of the window, ogling her legs.

"Where to, Miss?"

"Wait a minute; I haven't decided yet."

"The station or the airport? The traffic is always jammed to the station, so you have to leave in plenty of time."

She flared up at the driver:

"I'm not going anywhere. I'm staying here. Is this your home? Is there some reason I can't stand here?"

The driver laughed, and drew his head back into the car. As he drove off, she heard him retort:

"You stay there on the street; you tarts are all the same, you all end up on the street."

She stayed standing there, thinking about the next stage of her life. The possibilities were very limited. The thought of going back to the South barely even registered; she didn't want any part of it. She still had the child in her womb; that affair wasn't over, and she was in no mood to admit defeat. Irritated, she was in no mood to forgive, either. She was ready for battle. She wasn't prepared to let Mr Pang go, for the sake of such an uncertain future.

Opposite was the Paris Nights, and on the eleventh floor of the building there was a beauty parlour which she and the others had frequented. Some things change, some things remain the same: since she'd left, the club had become more and more fashionable. There was a man changing the poster in the glass display window: a new foreign dance troupe had arrived, and a gaggle of boys and girls in a coconut grove stood gaudily in a window looking out. She couldn't make out the face of the female lead singer, and was keen to know whether she was pretty or not, so she crossed the road and asked the lad who was changing the poster:

"Do you remember me, Xiao Bo?"

The lad looked her up and down, scratched his head, and said:

"I know the face. Are you Mary or Lucy?"

She realised he didn't recognise her, and didn't press the point. She tapped the display window, and asked:

"Where's this troupe from?"

"The Philippines."

She laughed disdainfully:

"I thought as much." She looked at the poster again, and made a withering assessment of the heavily made-up singer: "She looks like an ape-woman! She'd be better off staying in the jungle, rather than come running over here to try to make a dollar."

She walked along the sidewalk towards the Workers' Cultural Palace. After giving it some thought, she decided to find Lao Ruan. Lao Ruan was contracted to manage the guest house attached to the Workers' Cultural Palace, and although the accommodation there might be pretty grim, at least it wouldn't cost her anything. Having made the decision, she felt aggrieved. Why was fate always so unfair to her? Why did she always make the wrong choices? Life owed her, so when was it going to settle the debt? She was like an unhappy fish which, thinking it has travelled a great distance, discovers it has all been an illusion, and it has just been swimming to and fro. She still hadn't managed to escape the meshes of this city.

The towering new office blocks of the city swallowed her up, like a huge fine-meshed fishing net always ready either to free her or to enmesh her. She even seemed to smell faintly of fish herself. No, no she wasn't like a fish; fish have the whole ocean to swim in, but her ocean was already dried up.

THREE

SOMEONE ELSE

A YOUNG MAN followed her across the crossroads at the top of the road. She checked him out briefly, and he looked like the usual sort of loafer you saw on the city streets, a plastic bag in his hand and a rather grim look on his face. He had a square, sun-blackened face, a gold chain around his neck, and he was wearing a horizontal-striped short-sleeve shirt, above vertically-striped red and black beach shorts. On his feet was a pair of plastic sandals that slapped the pavement as he walked, and the overall effect was clearly of a ruffian from the lower echelons of society. She knew she was pretty, and it wasn't unusual for her to be followed on the streets by young lads like this. But the way this one was looking at her made her uneasy. There was nothing sexual about it, nor was it the look of recognition of old acquaintances, but it was as sharp and cold as a knife blade, and it chilled her. She wanted to shake him off as soon as possible. She passed a little restaurant, and caught the scent of chicken soup billowing out of the wooden basin in the doorway. She had always liked the *wontons* in chicken broth they sold there, so she pushed open the door, went in, and ordered a bowl. But she had only just sat down, when she saw the youth had followed her in and sat down at a table opposite her, not moving, just looking at her through narrowed eyes. Looking at her. He took a length of green nylon rope out of the plastic bag and put it on the table, all the time looking at her through narrowed eyes. Suddenly a name from long ago came to her: Baorun. Heart pounding, she stood up hurriedly, turning her back on him. From behind, she heard him say:

"Shall we go and dance the *xiaola*, Fairy Princess? Do you still dance the *xiaola*?"

She leapt away, and rushed out of the shop, dragging her suitcase behind her.

Silently, he followed her, carelessly stuffing the rope into the pocket of his beach shorts, leaving one green end sticking out, swaying to and fro like a snake.

"Why are you running away? If you're not going to dance the *xiaola* with me, how about buying me a bowl of wontons? Or shall I buy you some?"

She looked back, and said:

"You've got the wrong person. I don't know you."

"You may not know me, but I know you. If we're not going to dance the *xiaola* and not going to eat wontons, let's just go for a stroll, shall we?"

"Stop following me; it's making me uncomfortable. If you keep following me, I'll scream!"

"What are you going to scream? Rape! Rape!", he asked, putting on a woman's voice then beginning to laugh. "Go ahead and scream. Go on, I'm waiting. I'm quite happy."

"I'm not scared of you. There's a police station ten metres ahead to the left. If you keep following me, that's where I'm going."

"Fine, go to the police. You lead and I'll follow. If I run away, you'll know I'm not a real man."

Panicked, she scurried off, dragging her suitcase, but the sidewalk had recently been dug up, and there were potholes everywhere. The suitcase shed a wheel, and wouldn't roll any further, so she picked it up and ran on a few metres. Suddenly, it all became too much for her, and she kicked the suitcase over and sat down on it.

"So what do you really want? You're out of prison, aren't you? So you were **inside** for a few years; you weren't killed or injured, so what's the big deal?" Her manner was challenging and belligerent, but she also seemed to be trying to offer some kind of comfort. "A few years **inside** is no great loss, is it? It's not so easy outside is it? Troubles everywhere!"

"You think I was better off **inside**?" He nodded his head impassively. "I can see where you're coming from. Have you got any more lessons for me? You won't get a better chance than this, so go on, tell me!"

Her high heels were against her, too, and one of the heels suddenly came loose. Angrily she banged it back into place on the ground.

Tap! Tap! Tap! "Why am I having such bad luck?" Tap! Tap! "Fuck it! Look, my German suitcase is broken; it cost two hundred Euros at Frankfurt airport. These are good shoes too; big-name Italian make, and they're ruined too."

Seeing him unmoved, she felt embarrassed so she dropped the subject and slowly put her shoe back on. Then she returned to their original subject:

"Let's leave the past in the past! Anyway, you brought it on yourself; who told you to tie me up?"

A strange smile played over his lips, somewhere between ridicule and sorrow. He jiggled his legs and crossed and uncrossed them; it was apparent that this kind of conversation was demanding extreme patience from him, and great self-control. He fixed his eyes on her and said, suddenly:

"Tying you up was wrong, but rape is rape, and that's a crime. It's quite straightforward, but are you saying you're not sure about who tied you up and who raped you?"

"It's not my fault; I lost my soul then," she mumbled as she stood up.

She tried out the heel on her shoe, then suddenly remembered what a vulnerable position she had been in, and yelled at him:

"If you hadn't tied me up, do you think he would have done what he did to me? You're both bastards! You're both criminals!"

"You're right, we're both criminals, but what I don't understand is why you were alright with being raped, but tying you up was so wrong. Can you tell me just how much you got out of them then?"

"What do you mean, got out of them? What was there to get then? Soft words and promises!"

She looked at him frankly, hesitated a moment, then abruptly changed her tone:

"Anyway, it's all old news now. I'll tell you the truth. You were really ugly then, uglier than you are now, ugly and stingy. Liu Sheng was really good-looking, and knew how to spend money. And he was a good dancer. He was a looker, and all the girls fancied him."

Baorun nodded his head, and sniffed.

"You're right. Now I see: you liked him and hated me, so you let me take the blame for him. Is that it?"

She almost admitted it, but saw his dangerous expression, and sighed carefully instead:

"I know you hate me, and I know you feel wronged; but if you've been wronged, haven't I been too? You've come looking for revenge? Well, I want revenge too, but I don't know who I should be looking for."

"You know I feel wronged? Then tell me, how should I get my revenge?"

"How about an apology, face to face?" she asked. "I know I owe you some kind of apology, so I'm sorry. I'm sorry. Will that do?"

"Do you think 'sorry' will get rid of me? Even a total idiot wouldn't accept that!"

"Then tell me what you do want!" A cautious expression crossed her features, and there was a hint of remorse in her eyes, along with nervousness, grievance, cunning, and an extraordinary degree of courage. There were tears in the corners of her eyes, and she wiped them away. Suddenly, she cried out:

"I'll say I'm sorry a hundred times if you want: I'm sorry, I'm sorry, I'm sorry, I'm sorry, I'm sorry, I'm sorry. How's that?"

Passers-by on the other side of the road had stopped to watch. Baorun folded his arms, coldly admiring her hysterical performance. He waited for her to quiet down, then shook his head.

"Your attitude is all wrong. Saying you're sorry is useless, and screeching it is even more useless. You could screech it a million times, and it wouldn't mean anything. I was inside for ten years. Ten years! And you're going to pay me back for them."

"You want money? Why didn't you say so?" She hurriedly rifled through the money in her purse. "Don't try and take advantage of me. One thousand two hundred, one thousand three hundred, will that do? It'll be OK if I cut back a bit; I've only got one thousand five hundred, so if I give you one thousand three hundred, will that see us quits?"

"Repayment doesn't have to be in cash, and I don't want your money." Baorun put his hand on hers, and said, seriously:

"I want you to pay back what I lost. Firstly, that's time, ten years of time, and secondly it's freedom. You owe me ten years of freedom."

Stunned, she stood and stared at him:

"How do I pay back time? Or freedom? You'd better tell me just what it is you want."

"I haven't thought it through yet. We need to have a talk. Let's find somewhere to sit down. Or we could go and see a movie again. There's no rush; the one thing we have is time. We can think it over and discuss it, take our time, and work it out."

"Who do you think is going to a movie with you? Who do you think you're going to talk it over with? I'm afraid you are going to have to excuse this young lady!" Blushing furiously, she stuck her finger under Baorun's nose. "Do you think I'm afraid of you? Do your worst, I'm ready!"

She wanted to run away, but Baorun had his foot on her suitcase, stopping her. He gestured at the street with his chin:

"Go on, scream! There's lots of people about, someone's bound to come and help you. Go on! Thief! Rape! Murder! I'll join in with you."

She looked at the passers-by, but kept quiet as the tears gathered in her eyes. An old man walked past them, but thought they were just having a lover's tiff. He tried to encourage them:

"If you two have got a problem, for heaven's sake, take your time, go home and talk it through."

She wiped her eyes and retorted:

"What do you mean, take your time? Who do you think he's shacked up with? It's you, isn't it!"

The old man turned away, muttering:

"How could an old man like me be shacked up with a youngster like that? Young people today don't appreciate people who're trying to help. That will teach me to mind my own business."

Baorun took the nylon rope out of his pocket, and wound one end round his wrist and hand, so that his hand was soon covered by a five-pointed green star:

"Well, what do you think?" he asked, showing it to her. "Pretty, isn't it?"

It was his old way of flaunting his skill and making a show of force simultaneously. The rope. The dog chain. She felt her scalp crawl. She looked down at his bare feet in their sandals. They were cheap plastic shoes, and there was dirt between his toes. His toenails were grey and cracked. Shoes and feet together clearly illustrated the wretchedness of their owner's current situation. Not far away, there were some workmen laying underground piping, and there was an iron shovel leaning against a wall. Her heart lurched, and she ran over to lay hold of it. Baorun went after her, but it was like running into the muzzle of a gun. She thrust the shovel at him, like a soldier with a submachine gun.

"Do you think I'm afraid of you? Do you think I haven't learned to handle men? When do you think you're living, still trying to frighten people with your rope? Don't make me laugh!" She thrust the shovel at Baorun's sandals. "There are lots of miscarriages of justice these days; you're not the only one. Some of them even die **inside**. What time do you want me to pay back? What freedom? People like you just waste your time anyway: **inside** or out, what's the difference?"

She thrust the shovel at Baorun's feet again, and took advantage of him dodging out of the way to snatch up her suitcase and run across the road to a red taxi that was waiting there. It was broad daylight, and that held Baorun back. He chased after her for a few steps, then stopped. She heard him behind her, shouting:

"Go on, run away! Each day you run, counts as another year. I'll keep count for you. You're going to regret this."

She thrust herself and her suitcase into the taxi. The driver stuck his head out of the window to look at Baorun in amazement.

"Who is that man back there?"

"He's a rapist! Now get a move on and drive. Go round the block twice then take me to the Workers' Cultural Palace. The taxi roared off, and she could see Baorun standing on the sidewalk behind them, bending down to look at the cut on his foot. The driver turned to ask her, wonderingly:

"What's that about a rapist? Who did he rape?"

She thought she'd better correct herself, and told him:

"I was only joking. He's not a rapist, he's a madman escaped from the Jingting Hospital."

FOUR

THE FOLLOWING WIND GUEST HOUSE

As a last resort, she had to fall back on Lao Ruan.

Lao Ruan's Following Wind Guest House had formerly been the guest house attached to the Workers' Cultural Palace, but even before that, it was the celebrated Workers' Cinema. She could see that the glass double doors of the guest house had once been the main entrance to the cinema. She could still dimly remember the two pretty girls who collected the tickets there: they wore pale green uniforms and had long ponytails. One of them had her ponytail hanging full-length down her back, while the other wore hers coiled on top of her head. She remembered, too, her childhood dream of becoming one of these usherettes when she grew up, so she could wear that uniform herself, and could also watch all the movies for free. So many of the splendours of the past are inexplicably diminished, and this was the case with the Workers' Cinema. All that had been reluctantly allowed to remain was one tiny room with a screen, huddling in a corner at the side of the guest house, showing a motley assortment of horror, spy and war movies.

Rooms at the Following Wind Guest House were cheap and so, coupled with its prime location, Lao Ruan pulled in a good number of long-term residents. On the ground floor there was a private clinic specialising in the treatment of vitiligo; its door was covered in newspaper clippings, award certificates and letters of thanks, and behind the door curtain you could vaguely make out the figure of a middle-aged man in a long white medical gown. He was always to be heard loudly trying to pacify his patients, in a strong Sichuan accent:

"What's the emergency? Vitiligo isn't like catching a cold; you can't just take a pill and it's cured. Slowly does it!"

Next door to the clinic was the agency office of a Wenzhou shoe factory, where a group of chattering girls sat, not getting on with factory business, but arguing over who was the prettier movie star, Gong Li or Liu Xiaoqing, or whether Chow Yun-fat was more handsome than Leslie Cheung. On the first floor, two rooms had been knocked together and someone had set up a school for fashion models. Inside, a tall, very skinny woman was teaching a young girl the model walk for the catwalk, and another, even taller and even skinnier girl was stretched out on a sofa having a siesta; because she was wearing a blonde wig, and because of the way she was lying, she looked like an Egyptian mummy. Upstairs, there were also a number of unoccupied rooms, their doors adorned with the name plates of all sorts of different commercial and consultancy companies. The desks and chairs inside were all covered in dust. The occupiers had disappeared heaven knows where, and all that was left was the dust and the silence.

Lao Ruan was delighted that Miss Bai had come to seek shelter with him. He gave her a rent-free room, and told her that he was having a mahjong party that evening to discuss some business. He asked her to come along and sing some songs to jolly things along, and said that, at the same time, he could make some contacts for her. When she turned up, as arranged, at the games room, in the fog of cigarette smoke she could see three strangers: one silent, one uncouth and the final one, who seemed rather more open and expansive, was a big fat fellow. She had long ago lost her appetite for men like these, but she dutifully took the microphone, and catching the mood of the occasion, sang a Cantonese New Year song, *Kung Hei Fat Choi*. The fat man laughed as he listened, and asked her:

"Is it Lao Ruan you're hoping is going to prosper?"

"All of you are my elder brothers, aren't you?" she replied playing along. "I'm wishing everyone good luck."

After this, she made herself sit down next to Lao Ruan, saying she would collect his money for him. Unfortunately, Lao Ruan's luck was out that evening, and she sat there for a long time without collecting a cent. Then, when she saw that he was finally holding a full colour-set of tiles, but was discarding them one by one, she tried to warn him. When he pinched her waist under the table, she understood he was deliberately sacrificing the tiles because he was playing to lose, not to win. It was at that point that she lost interest. As she sat there, yawning, she suddenly realised the air around her was filled with a foul smell. Why, she wondered to herself, did such a high percentage of the middle-aged men she met, have bad breath? Someone stood on her foot. It was Boss Guo, who was sitting on her left. She had already privately nicknamed him 'The Boor'. The Boor was leering at her, trying to put on a flirtatious expression. She knew what he was up to, but she couldn't be bothered. She jumped to her feet, saying:

"Some fruit. Let's have some fruit."

She apportioned the fruit from the platter onto small dishes, and put one beside each of the players. Afraid that she would just have to put up with more bothersome advances if she sat down, she feigned a headache and made her excuses.

Miss Bai did not attend the first round of negotiations with Mr Pang; it was Lao Ruan who made the arrangements. In fact, Lao Ruan didn't go personally either. He was good friends with one of Mr Pang's suppliers, and it was this man who went to put Miss Bai's case to Mr Pang, using the pretext of an account meeting. The negotiations took many twists and turns, but the end result was short and sweet. Mr Pang wanted her to have the baby, and then do a DNA test. If the child was his, he guaranteed he would accept full responsibility for both mother and child. When she asked what Mr Pang meant by "full responsibility", Lao Ruan replied:

"Money, of course! When a man takes responsibility for his mistress, doesn't it always come down to money? But remember he's from Taiwan, and you can't afford to push him too hard. If you do, you'll be breaking a taboo, and that could seriously affect cross-strait relations. You understand the politics, don't you?"

"I don't care about any politics; I just want justice."

"Justice can be bought and sold; it still all comes down to money, doesn't it? So tell me the truth now: do you want his money, or do you want him?"

She was conflicted, and avoided Lao Ruan's gaze.

"Who would want a man like him?" she mumbled. "He's short and fat like a winter melon. What could I do with him? Make pork and winter melon soup?"

She felt as though she had gone as far as she could along this particular route, and she seemed to see a signpost ahead that said: no through road. Mr Pang had no nice surprise waiting for her. The fecund tenderness and sweet desires of the Loire valley had crumbled into the mud. In any case, he was married, and any mutual respect between them was gone. She was just an encumbrance to him now, and the glimmer of light he had brought into her life was already completely extinguished.

The second visit to Mr Pang could be said to be more eventful. Lao Ruan took three strong-arm boys with him and Miss Bai when they went to Mr Pang's company offices. Mr Pang responded prudently by summoning a number of security officers, who stationed themselves by the door to his office. Actually, all that gangster stuff is confined to the movies, and they all behaved in a fairly civilised manner. Lao Ruan was suited and booted western-style, looking every inch the negotiator; he asked Mr Pang for a statement of indebtedness, which the latter refused to provide.

"I don't owe Miss Bai any money, so I can't give you that statement. We're not clearing a debt here, we're arranging a business matter, and that has to be done by the rules. We'll be better off drawing up a contract."

Mr Pang rummaged through his filing cabinet for a while, and came up with a sample contract for a financial futures company. She looked at the document without understanding what it meant, then exploded:

"Shame on you! Turning my belly into a futures commodity! I'm not signing!"

Mr Pang stayed remarkably calm.

"A woman's belly is like a mine that produces people. Iron ore, copper ore, cotton, petroleum: they're all traded as futures. Why shouldn't babies be treated the same? I am a fair and trustworthy man, so you can believe me when I say that if you read through the terms of this contract and sign it, I guarantee that neither of us will lose out."

Unsure of herself, Miss Bai looked at Lao Ruan for support, but Lao Ruan clearly didn't understand the futures market either. Not wanting to sound weak, though, he waved the contract away.

"Let's not complicate things, Mr Pang. We don't trust the futures market; we're more used to spot trades."

"The child is still in her belly, so it can't be treated as a commodity. Let's just follow the rules: if I make a one-off payment, it shows that I trust you, and I'm taking the risk in making you an offer. If you trust me to pay in instalments, then it's up to you to name the amount. It's got to be one or the other."

One or the other. Given the level of trust between them, it had to be one or the other. Lao Ruan considered for a while, then whispered in Miss Bai's ear:

"So, it's a futures deal. The child is still in your belly, so what else can it be?"

She sat woodenly opposite Mr Pang, and for the first time she felt ignorant and useless. There was still a faint scar on his forehead. She studied his chubby, well-groomed face, reading what was written there: on one side there was the man of business, and on the other the man of morals, but any sign of his previous infatuation with her was completely obliterated. For such a shrewd and worldly-wise man, infatuation was a single-use commodity, used and discarded, so why should it leave any trace. She didn't doubt his trustworthiness, just her own calculations. If Mr Pang himself wasn't her future, could his flesh and blood provide her with one? She didn't have a handle on her own greed, nor did she have an accurate inventory of her love and hate. She wasn't at all sure she wanted to keep the pregnancy, or whether she actually wanted to be a mother at all, so she lowered her head, dejectedly, and said:

"I don't know. Lao Ruan, you choose for me."

She left Mr Pang's office with a contract in an envelope on which was printed, in big black characters: **Futures sales contract.** From then on, she came to think of her body as a seam of ore to be mined; from then on all she had to do was look at her gradually swelling belly to bring to her mind that crushing verdict: a mine that produces people.

She was terrified of seeing someone she knew, so when coming and going from the People's Cultural Palace, she always wore a surgical mask. Disguise was essential in this town with which she had, without quite knowing how, forged some kind of ill-fated deal that could bring down all sorts of trouble on her head. She had returned to this place of her nightmares, to stake everything on one ill-omened piece of business; a piece of business, moreover, which would have been cursed by the spirit of her departed grandmother. That old woman had predicted at a very early stage her granddaughter's descent into shame: one rainy day, many years ago, when Fairy Princess was coming home from the roller-skating rink at The Workers' Cultural Palace, her grandmother had stopped her in the doorway, and dried her hair with a towel. The old woman's expression was inexpressibly sad, and her eyes were full of reproach, as she said:

"I'm amazed you still know your way home now you've lost your soul, Fairy Princess. You've lost your soul out there. A young girl can't afford to lose her soul: lose your soul today, and tomorrow you lose your face."

Now she knew for certain that her grandmother's worldly wisdom had correctly predicted her future, and the old woman's irritating ramblings had, in fact, had some kind of divine inspiration. She accepted she had lost her soul, and she accepted that she had lost her face. But she had no intention of appeasing her grandmother's ghost, and was more forgiving of herself. Soul or face, it didn't matter, if it was lost it was lost, and she wasn't going to be shamed by it. Who was she now? She wasn't anyone; she was just a seam of ore to be mined.

One weekend, the little cinema downstairs was putting on a Hollywood horror movie. The man sitting in the ticket window had a small loud hailer and was shouting:

"Come on in! Come on in! Two for one on tickets! New Hollywood zombie movie! Free popcorn! Money back if you're not scared!"

She got some popcorn and went in. As she sat in the darkened screen room watching zombies coming out of the wall, and vampires emerging from the toilet bowl, at first she smiled condescendingly at these fake monsters, but gradually she began to feel her neck prickling, as though sharp teeth were nibbling at her. Blood and putrefaction seemed to be dripping down from the screen and silently pooling on the tiled floor. Automatically, she held her feet up off the ground, and she began to feel sick. She rushed to the washroom where she dry-retched for a bit, before fleeing the cinema completely.

Her own development had been quicker than that of the Workers' Cultural Palace. She had been to Paris now, and the palace was no longer the high point of her world, as it had been in her youth. All that remained for her of its former glory were the crowds and the hustle and bustle, and even how she felt about those, depended on her mood. When she was in an ill temper, she hated the sweat and cigarette smoke in the air; if she was in a better mood, she revelled in the noisy fairground atmosphere. She hid herself away in the Following Wind Guest House, and strolling round the Workers' Cultural palace was her only amusement. As she was walking elegantly across its granite floor, a youth whizzed past her on a skateboard, flying towards the central plaza. You didn't see any kids on roller skates anymore, and her beloved roller-skating rink was no longer there. On the southern side of its former position there was now a replica Eiffel Tower, and to the north was a newly-built white shopping centre which, because of its colour, was known locally as the White House. Beneath the Eiffel Tower, there was a food street lined with stalls selling delicacies from all over the world: fragrant, stinky, fishy and even sour. Her pregnancy had given her a taste for sour things, so she went to one of the stalls for some fish with pickled cabbage; but whether it was the fish, or just her stomach, after a couple of mouthfuls, she began to feel sick again. She put down her chopsticks and demanded a reduced price from the stallholder. Before he could even make up his mind, she threw a couple of *yuan* at him, knocked over the saucepan of fish, and stormed out. She was heading under the Eiffel

Tower towards the White House, when she bumped into a mother and daughter, obviously tourists, who asked her to take their photograph. With rather ill grace, she agreed and, not taking much care, snapped the pair with the Eiffel Tower in the background. Despite her contempt, she managed to conceal her distaste, but when the girl looked at the photo, and asked Miss Bai to take it again because it wasn't exactly what she wanted, she refused, and walked off, saying curtly:

"You're just the kind of people who like knock-offs! Whoever saw such a small Eiffel Tower? If you want a picture of the Eiffel Tower, go to Paris! What is there worth photographing here?"

She went into the White House, which was constructed in circular galleries. It made her feel like a spinning top, whipped on by her unforgiving solitude, as she made aimless circuits of the galleries. There were little shops everywhere, selling imported clothes but, look as she might, the only impression she got was that the shop owners all had very peculiar taste: the styles were very ordinary, and not at all fashionable, and it was only with some difficulty that she found a pair of white hot pants that she liked. But when she tried them on, she couldn't get into them, and she complained to the shop owner that the size tag must be wrong. The shop owner eyed her waist and said:

"The size is right, it's your body that's wrong; you're pregnant, aren't you?"

Miss Bai rolled her eyes, but there was nothing she could say to that, so she made a hasty exit. She was indeed pregnant, and she had to recognise that her body was changing shape. Hot pants were no longer appropriate.

All she could do was go back to Lao Ruan's guest house. Lao Ruan was away on business in Guangzhou, so she had a temporary reprieve from any social engagements. This relieved her greatly. She had never had any longstanding hobbies in her free time, so now she went to bed early and watched soap operas on the television. As the twists and turns and highs and lows of other people's lives unfolded on the screen, part of her watched entranced, and part of her picked apart the plot and characters as false, deceitful and laughable. Later in the night people kicked up a racket outside her window, where a group of high school students were celebrating someone's birthday in the coffee shop on the ground floor and singing 'Happy Birthday' in English. She had sung that song many times for clients and, for reasons that weren't entirely clear to her, she detested it; and now, as she lay in her cramped hotel room, it seemed particularly loathsome. Other people's birthdays seemed to mock her own miserable existence, and other people's happiness just increased her sense of isolation in the city. Suddenly filled with self-pity, and annoyed by the voices coming in through the window, she jumped up and ran into the bathroom. She filled a tooth mug with water, and flung it out of the window. In total, she threw three mugs of water, one after the other, out of the window, until she heard a girl's shrill voice shouting out in protest. Someone had received their just retribution, and that made her feel a bit better, so she used the fourth mugful to brush her teeth. She looked at herself critically in the mirror, where she saw a tired and resentful face with dark rings under its eyes, and toothpaste foam at the corners of its mouth. It was her face and she detested it, so she threw the remaining half mug of water at the mirror.

She had many enemies lying in ambush for her in the city. Someone, she did not know who, had already given the cell phone number she had just had changed, to Qu Ying's widow, who was now phoning her continuously, and sending text messages asking about Qu Ying's Omega watch:

"I don't want the man back, I just want you to return his Omega watch!"

When she heard Qu Ying's name, Miss Bai remembered him and his white horse as though it were a scene in an old movie, something that had happened a lifetime ago. When she received a call from a number she didn't already know, she always tried to remember who that set of Arabic numerals belonged to, and the faces of all her old enemies scrolled, sternly, one by one, past her eyes. It wasn't going to be good news, so why answer? She assiduously pursued those people who owed her money, but she herself had no way of paying back her own creditors. With Mr Pang's contract in her hand, all she wanted was to sever all of her myriad connections with the city.

One day, at midday, she decided to leave but, try as she might, she couldn't open the door of the room. Through the crack that did appear, she could see a length of green nylon rope attached to the door handle, and the other end tied to the stair post, so taut it trembled slightly. The rope had come. It was Baorun's shadow, and she knew that if the rope was there, so was Baorun. Baorun had arrived like a vengeful ghost. She called down to the reception desk, and let loose a storm of abuse at the girl who was manning it. The girl hurriedly went up and untied the rope, saying:

"Don't get angry with us, we didn't know what the relationship was between you two. He's downstairs waiting for you; he says he's your husband. Did you walk out on him?"

Miss Bai wagged her finger under the girl's nose:

"Are you soft in the head? You've seen what he's like! Do you think I'd be seen dead with him, let alone marry him? He's a lunatic escaped from the Jingting Hospital."

Still, there was no avoiding him, so she decided to confront him. Baorun was sitting on the sofa in the lobby, reading a newspaper. She carried her suitcase over and stood in front of him.

"So, you're my husband, are you? I've walked out on you, have I? Alright then, now I'm going to go home with you, so can you tell me, please, where do we live?"

At first her directness seemed to intimidate Baorun but, sadly, not for long. A knowing smile spread across his face:

"Alright then, come home with me. It's your idea, after all. Come with me and I'll show you my villa; then you'll see."

"You've got a villa? Well, I've got a helicopter then!" she said, mockingly. Then she looked at the two receptionists behind the desk. "What are you gawping at? Get your cell phones out and take his picture. If something happens to me, then he'll be the one who did it and you can go report him to the authorities."

The two receptionists were completely confused, but one of them, a young man, was bold enough to ask:

"Do you want us to call the police?"

Miss Bai glanced at Baorun, and said:

"There's no point yet. We need some evidence, so take his photo first, and that'll do the trick."

The young man took out his cell phone but, when he looked at Baorun, he lost his nerve. Baorun went over to him, and stood to attention.

"Get on with it, then. Take several. If I'm not scared, what have you got to be scared of? Go on, take your pictures, then when you have to report me, you'll get a cash reward."

Miss Bai glared at Baorun as he struck several poses: full-face, profile, he even let the young man take a shot of the back of his neck. When the photography was over, Baorun walked over to Miss Bai and picked up her suitcase.

"Alright, you've got your evidence; you've even got one of the back of my neck. Are you happy now? That's enough talking, we can go now. Follow me to my villa."

She snatched back the suitcase and parked herself on the sofa, refusing to move.

"There's no point in trying to talk to someone like you. I'm going to get Captain Liu from the police to have a word with you."

There was something a little menacing about the smile that played on her lips as her index fingers skipped nimbly over the keyboard of her cell phone, searching for a number. Finally, she said:

"Forget it! There's no point bothering Captain Liu with shit like this. Let's try diplomacy before declaring war. How about me taking you for something to eat. You choose the restaurant, an expensive one if you want, and I'll drink a few glasses with you."

"I wouldn't mind a drink or two," he said. "But you need to think how cost-effective it is taking me out. How many glasses can you drink in one meal? One glass will only offset one week, and I was inside for ten years. How many glasses will it take to work off ten years?"

"I'll drink whatever I can drink. When we've had our meal, we can go to the mall and get you some new clothes; the ones you're wearing now are filthy and you look like a refugee. Then I'll take you to a karaoke bar. How about that?"

He shook his head:

"You still don't get me, do you? I don't care about clothes, and a suit would only buy you one day; forget about the karaoke, I'm not interested, and it wouldn't even get you back an hour. It would be a total waste of money."

"So tell me, what would represent a worthwhile investment?" She looked at him shrewdly, and then gave a wry laugh. "What if I slept with you? What would that be worth? Is that what you want? To sleep with me? To sleep with me?"

Baorun's gaze faltered, and he looked flustered for a moment, as his eyes slowly left her face and fell on the suitcase. He saw the baggage-check labels and asked:

"Have you been to Paris? I recognise some western writing; I studied some languages when I was inside." He traced some of the letters on the label with his finger. "Why is everyone who's been to Paris so vulgar? A few drinks aren't the solution to our problem, nor is us sleeping together. If I ask you to dance the *xiaola*, would you do it? Would you dance the *xiaola*?"

She jumped as though she had been stuck with a needle. Her face went ashen, and she said, through gritted teeth:

"I won't dance. I can't dance. I'm not dancing the *xiaola*."

He seemed to have anticipated her refusal, and didn't react.

"You're still determined to humiliate me, then? The *xiaola* is the only dance I know. I can't do any others. I practiced it **inside**, but I had to dance with men. For 10 years I danced with men, and now I want to dance with a woman. I want to dance with you."

"Well, thank you for the compliment, but I can't dance the *xiaola*; I forgot how to, long ago. Times have changed. Go to any dance hall or night club, and see who's still dancing the *xiaola*. Only a few yokels and country bumpkins, that's who!"

"So I'm a country bumpkin, and this country bumpkin is asking you to dance the *xiaola* with him, OK?"

She looked sidelong at him, studying his eyes. She stayed silent for a while, then laughed derisively:

"You want to dance the *xiaola*? It's as simple as that? Please don't treat me like an idiot. Tell me what you've really got in store for me!"

"There isn't anything else; just the *xiaola*. Come with me and see. I haven't got anything else in mind, I just want justice."

He clearly meant what he was saying, and she began to take his talk of justice more seriously; but he just took out a cigarette, and didn't continue. His fingers that were holding the cigarette were trembling, and for the first time she could see the hurt in his eyes, along with the exhaustion. He rubbed his temples, and tried to say something, but couldn't get it out immediately.

"What is justice? What would count as justice?" She guessed that was what he couldn't say, or perhaps wouldn't say.

She took a cigarette from his packet, lit it for herself, and went on:

"So let's make a deal. I'll go the whole hog today, and pay back everything I owe you. If I do that, then the slate's wiped clean, and from now on we go our separate ways. OK?"

FIVE
THE WATER TOWER AND THE XIAOLA

A RICKETY old van had pulled up outside the Following Wind Guest House, and she was startled to see the figure of Liu Sheng. He was wearing a white shirt and black trousers, looking very dapper, and was polishing the windscreen of the van with a cloth. Seeing her standing and staring on the threshold of the guest house, his face burst into a broad smile, and he winked at her.

"Hello, Miss Bai. You're back from Japan then."

She hadn't expected to find Liu Sheng waiting outside. She was puzzled by the relationship between these two men from Red Toon Street, and she wasn't clear whether they were friends, enemies, or just co-conspirators. She didn't know, either, which one was the boss. The only thing she was clear about was her own position. She was the hunted, and they were the hunters. She was trapped and surrounded.

"Fuck!" she exclaimed, and turned back into the guest house, glaring furiously at Liu Sheng through the glass doors.

"What devilment are you two plotting now?"

Liu Sheng wiped his hands on his cloth, and came over to shake hands, but she brushed him aside, brusquely.

"You've got us wrong," he said. "We've just come to talk about the old days with you. Baorun asked me to drive, as his chauffeur and your bodyguard. He said he was going to ask you to dance the *xiaola*, and he was afraid you'd refuse. If I'm there, you can stop worrying, can't you?"

"You're no better than he is. What's so great about you, that I can stop worrying?" she asked fiercely.

Liu Sheng grimaced, and looked at the Following Wind Guest House's nameplate.

"So I don't reassure you? Go and ask Lao Ruan if he knows me. I used to supply him with vegetables when he was running a restaurant a while ago. Go and ask him whether Liu Sheng is OK or not."

She looked up in thought for a while, then walked boldly down the steps of the guest house.

"OK or not, this girl isn't afraid of anyone." She popped a tablet of chewing gum into her mouth, and went on, derisively: "If you behave, I'll behave, but if you try anything, I'll be much worse than you. So I'll come with you today; I want to see how you dance the *xiaola*."

She wasn't very good with directions, and it was only when the van took the road out into the suburbs, that she recognised this was the route to the Jingting Hospital, and that Baorun's so-called villa was, in fact, the hospital water tower. This venue for the dance party struck her as very ill-starred. This path to reconciliation surrounded her with a dark and sinister halo; there was a crashing of thunder in her head, and she could make out the dim outline of a snare. Her confidence of ten minutes ago, evaporated like a wisp of smoke.

"Stop the van! Stop the van! I'm not going with you! Why should I want to go dancing with you?" she yelled, grabbing Liu Sheng by the arm, making the van weave across the expressway.

Liu Sheng braked, and pulled the van up beside the road.

"Calm down, Miss Bai! You've got to calm down a bit! All we're going to do is have a chat about old times, and have a little dance. I'm here, so what can possibly happen?"

She spat in Liu Sheng's face.

"Even if you add both your IQs together, it would still be lower than mine, but you think you can treat me like an idiot. If you want to dance, you can go to a dance hall. What are we doing going to the water tower? Go on, tell me! Just what are you up to?"

Liu Sheng wiped his face, muttering aggrievedly:

"I don't know exactly, it's his idea to go to the water tower; he's the one who wants to dance the *xiaola*. He didn't get to do it ten years ago, and he wants to make up for it now."

She turned to glance at Baorun.

"Make up for it? Is that what you want to do? Make up for it? Make up for something you lost? Who's going to make up for what I lost?"

Baorun tilted his chin at Liu Sheng, in the driver's seat.

"He's the one you need to ask about making up your loss."

At this, she lost any remaining composure, and made to jump out of the van, shouting:

"You pieces of shit! You go and dance your *xiaola*, but you can do it alone. I'm not going to be your dance-hall girl."

She didn't actually manage to get out of the van, because Baorun caught hold of her from behind. She could feel his breath on the back of her neck. Then the rope appeared. Baorun's rope appeared. First it looped round her shoulders, then her arms and, within ten seconds, she was immobilised, as Baorun had her trussed up like a parcel.

"We can't have the dance party without you today, and as you won't come willingly, I've got to tie you up. You'll just have to accept my apologies," Baorun said. "This is the 'as-you-like-it' knot; do you remember it? Whether it's 'as you like it' or not, depends on how well you behave. If you're good, it'll be just as you like it, but if you're stubborn, you certainly won't like it at all and, bit by bit, you'll find that out for yourself."

The van set off again, and Baorun shoved her onto a plastic vegetable basket. He put a hand over her mouth; a hand that was large and rough, and had a slight salty tang. The 'as you like it' knot was as sinister as Baorun described it, and the more she struggled, the tighter it became. It constricted her body, and strangled her willpower so, gradually, she quietened down. A memory had returned. A nightmare had returned. A pain had returned and her shame had returned too. The water tower was up ahead, waiting for her. She didn't dare look Baorun in the eye. His eyes were angry but empty. The emptiness was the same as it had been all those years ago, but the anger was hotter and more intense. She looked hopefully at Liu Sheng, who turned to look back at her from the driver's seat. There was apology in his gaze, but even more it seemed defensive, as if he was saying:

"Don't blame me! It's not my fault. You're the one who claims to have a high IQ. Do people with high IQs put themselves in this kind of situation? You've been living the high life all these years; you've been to France and Japan. Did you think there wasn't a price attached? So please don't play the martyred wife with me, and be a bit more honest!"

She understood what he was saying to her. Don't play the martyr. Be more open. They despised her and, in their eyes, her body was a secret garden which they had tickets to visit, and which she had to open up to them. What was it that gave them this permission? What was it that so degraded her? That had so disgraced her? There were a thousand possible reasons hidden in past events, but not one of them seemed just to her. She stared hatefully at Liu Sheng's nose, that straight, high-bridged nose, that verged on perfection. There was a shiny point at its tip. A memory that she had kept sealed away, suddenly announced its clamorous arrival: she remembered Liu Sheng's young man's groin, and his penis, like a purple radish, in the light of the setting sun that flickered in the old water tower. A savage, primitive light that caught a body unawares, and robbed a young girl of her virginity, and ruined a young girl's future. She thought of the *xiaola*. The *xiaola*: the steps of a dance that she had forgotten for ten years, now came rushing back to her. *Dong da da dong*. The *xiaola* had been the start of her tortuous love life, and the beginning of her burning hatred too. *Da da dadong one, two, three, four*. The rhythm of the dance was like an incantation: you are corrupted, you are corrupted. The *xiaola*, the fucking *xiaola*! All its steps were an incantation of corruption.

Her tears fell on Baorun's hand. He looked at it, then flipped it over and wiped the tears off on the rope, which greedily swallowed them up. The rope had been tied by an expert hand, fluent and precise, demonstrating a kind of geometry, and if she kept still and calm, she wasn't too uncomfortable. She wasn't sure whether her subsequent compliance stemmed from wisdom or despair. When they reached the Jingting Hospital, she heard Liu Sheng and the gatekeeper greeting each other warmly, and the van passed, unhindered, through the three guarded hospital gates. It came to a halt in the empty ground in front of the water tower. Finally, Baorun removed his hand from her mouth, and looked at her. He wiped a tear away from the corner of her eye with a finger.

"It doesn't matter how pretty the face, crying always makes it swollen and ugly," he said. "Why are you crying, anyway? You owe me ten years of time and ten years of freedom; one dance and you wipe the slate clean, so what have you got to lose?"

They went back into the water tower.

She noticed a small wooden sign newly hung on the door to the tower, that read: Care-Workers' Dormitory. She caught the rank, sweaty smell of a male dormitory: a smell of shoes, socks and unwashed clothes. The original layout of the incense hall wasn't much changed, and the bodhisattva that Boss Zheng had brought in was still in its shrine, with an offering platter of dusty plastic fruit in front of it. There was a camp bed laid out below the shrine, with Baorun's T-shirt and tracksuit trousers dumped on the crumpled sheets, along with a few gaudy magazines. The most surprising sight was up above her, where a wire was stretched across the empty space, and from it hung a selection of hempen ropes, thick, thin, coarse and fine, which began to dance in the draft when the door was opened, as if warmly greeting the new arrivals.

She demanded that Baorun untie her, but she was met with a refusal:

"What? We're inside the water tower and you're still thinking of running away?"

Undaunted, she went on:

"Do you have any brains in that head of yours? Don't you want to dance the *xiaola*? How can I dance if you keep me tied up?"

Baorun examined her expression, trying to decide if she meant what she said or not; he glanced at Liu Sheng for his opinion. Liu Sheng said:

"Don't disrespect Miss Bai. She is a woman among women, and you can trust her word. Hurry up and untie her."

She didn't show the least gratitude to Liu Sheng, and as soon as she was free, she raised her hand to slap Baorun, but was stopped by the ferocity of his glare. She stepped back, and looked for another target. She stopped in front of Liu Sheng, and gave him a resounding smack round the ear. Liu Sheng clutched his head.

"Alright, go ahead and hit me. It doesn't matter; I take it as an honour to be hit instead of my brother."

She spat angrily:

"You both deserve to be hit. Men who tie women up aren't men, they're worms."

At that moment, her ears filled with a sound that had hurtled up from the past. The barrel-shaped space of the water tower echoed faintly with the shrill cries for help of a young girl. The tower had preserved them for ten years, floating in the atmosphere of the Jingting Hospital, with no one to hear them until today. She looked up at Baorun's array of ropes which, despite the door now being closed, and there being no draft, were still swaying gently, as though whispering to her their passions and longings of all those years. In them, she saw the strands of her soul swaying gently on that coarse iron wire. Her spirit had been scattered to the four winds, but had now been gathered together by Baorun and hung out, one by one, either to exhibit it, or maybe to expose it. This water tower was her memorial stele, and perhaps it had been waiting for her all this time; waiting for her to come and worship her own soul; to come and make an offering to her own soul. Liu Sheng offered her something to drink, but she pushed it away. She tapped her feet on the floor: *dong, da, dongda*, starting off the rhythm of the *xiaola*. Then she kicked off the sandals she was wearing, and suddenly clapped her hands:

"COME ON! Put the music on! Today, I'll go for it, and just this once I'll be your dance-hall girl."

Her sudden disinhibition seemed a little suspicious. Baorun leaned against the wall, not moving, but following the path of her sandals: two wedge-heeled, pink sandals, one of which she kicked onto the camp bed, and the other of which ended up under the bodhisattva's shrine.

"I don't have any music here," Baorun said, slowly looking up so his gaze fixed on her bare ankles. "I danced the *xiaola* when I was **inside**, and we didn't have any music there; we danced unaccompanied. Will you dance with me?"

Without any sign of indecision, she replied:

"With or without music, it's up to you, but you have to remember the rules: I'm your dancing partner today, not your whore."

Liu Sheng was reclining on the steel-mesh camp bed, and at first glance he seemed to have an amused expression on his face, but in amongst the amusement, there was a thread of tension. Suddenly he gave a mocking laugh, jumped to his feet and made his way towards the door:

"You can dance; I'm going for a piss."

Flustered, she cried out:

"Stay where you are, Liu Sheng! Where do you think you're going?"

Liu Sheng turned back to look at her:

"I'll be outside, and you've got the bodhisattva in here. What are you afraid of? He's trustworthy, and you know how to handle him, Miss Bai."

The door of the water tower thumped closed. She stood, leaning against it, and looked at the bodhisattva's shrine.

"I'll find out how trustworthy he is when we dance."

The two of them each stood in one corner of the tower, at a stalemate, with neither willing to take the first step towards the other. She stirred uncomfortably as she leaned against the iron door, and said tentatively:

"This is too weird! Let's just leave it shall we?"

Baorun shook his head, looking directly into her eyes. He beckoned to her:

"Come over here; come a bit closer."

Unwillingly, she went over to Baorun.

"This is ridiculous; it's absurd. Whoever heard of dancing the *xiaola* like this. It's laughable!"

Baorun grabbed her hands; first the left, which he grasped lazily, then the right, with rather more urgency. She could feel the cold sweat on his hands, which felt like two damp metal pincers. *Dong, da, dongda.* She called out the rhythm carefully. The *xiaola* is a dance with four distinct beats: first you pull, then you push away. You dance a little, then you turn.

"I get dizzy easily, so don't turn me too quickly", she said.

He pulled her by the hand, then looked blank and stopped completely.

"You've got the hands right," she said. "What's the matter? Have you forgotten the steps?"

He shook his head, as though in pain.

"What is it? Do you want me to lead?" she asked.

"This won't work. I can't get going."

"We haven't got any music, that's the trouble. It's very difficult to get going without music."

He put an arm around her waist, and looked up at the ropes hanging overhead. With his other hand, he reached up and pulled down a length of hemp rope.

"The music doesn't matter; what I need is a rope. I'm sorry, but I'm going to have to tie you up. I can only dance if I tie you up."

She hadn't even thought that Baorun would still be dependent on his ropes, and all her attempts to meet him halfway had come to nothing. She struggled furiously.

"Let me go! Pervert! Idiot! I should have known a dog will always eat its own shit! You're worse than a dog! At least a dog means well, but you don't! I've done everything you asked, so why do you still want to tie me up? How can I dance if you tie me up?"

"I've got to tie you up whatever, but let's not dance the *xiaola*, let's dance the cheek-to-cheek. I've never done that; you can teach me."

She couldn't tell whether he was making up this new plan on the hoof, or whether it was something he had set up in advance, but either way, she felt she had been cheated. She shouted out to Liu Sheng to come and rescue her. Liu Sheng banged on the door, shouting back:

"What's going on with you two. All you're doing is dancing the *xiaola*, so what's all the fuss?"

"We're just negotiating," Baorun shouted. "We're not going to do the *xiaola*, we're going to do the cheek-to-cheek."

Liu Sheng considered this for a moment, then said:

"Don't be in too much of a rush, Baorun. It's a big step from the *xiaola* to the cheek-to-cheek."

She was hurt by Liu Sheng's off-hand manner. She tried to struggle free from Baorun's embrace, all the while trying to work out how to escape.

"Relax a bit, Baorun. We'll dance the cheek-to-cheek if you want; there's no need to tie me up, I guarantee I'll dance with you. Why don't you show me a bit more respect?"

"I'm quite relaxed; you need to relax too. I told you, nothing's going to happen to you today."

As he was talking, he was concentrating on the rope, but it wasn't clear whether he was looking at it with melancholy or affection. The hemp rope was soon tied tightly around her upper body, with a knot in the shape of a flower blossoming across her belly.

"Don't say I'm not respecting you; this is the 'plum-blossom' knot, and you'll soon see how comfortable it is."

She screamed at him:

"I don't care what knot it is, I'm not a mule or an ox! You know you're breaking the law! You've only just got out, and when I inform on you, you'll go back inside for another ten years!"

"I don't care. You go and inform on me when we've had our dance. Why should I be afraid of going back to gaol? I've already lost the best ten years of my life, so why should I worry about another ten? Even if they cut my head off, it only leaves a wound the size of a soup bowl!"

At first, Baorun didn't put his cheek next to hers, only his body. He used it to push her forwards, not like a dance, but like a piece of childish mischief. Apart from the bite of the ropes, she could also feel his chest, hips and thighs pressed against her from top to bottom, and a random, rhythmless jerking. She was paying particular attention to the movements of his groin, but fortunately, for the moment, all was peace and quiet down there. She was familiar with all different kinds of dancing, but Baorun's furious jerking steps were something she'd never encountered. She had experienced her fair share of violence before, but this despairing abandon was hard to resist. She had been felt up in bars and nightclubs before now, and she had always adapted her response to the situation, either with a slap or with a shouted reprimand. But Baorun's encroachment on her was different, almost as though it was exacting justice: it almost seemed just and reasonable. Either through weakness or because she felt a twinge of guilt, she chose to put up with it. When his face suddenly pressed itself against her left cheek, she didn't try to avoid it, but let his stiff, rough beard scrape against the skin of her cheek. She bit her lip, mentally preparing her first line of defence: cheek to cheek was fine, but no kissing, and absolutely no tongues. But the hot, rough face didn't move; it remained glued to her left cheek for a long time, like a rock pressed up against a cliff face, or like a frightened child helplessly clinging to its mother. Then she felt moisture on her face, and the warmth and restraint of a man's tears.

She heard the choked-back sobs. She didn't dare move, she didn't dare look at him. She stood still, maintaining her posture, looking detachedly at the bodhisattva's shrine to her right, which had been turned round so the figure was leaning on a corner of the wall, with one blessed golden hand pointing downwards, about a metre away from her: pointing at her belly. She stretched out to touch the hand, just reaching it, and feeling a small, cold sensation in her index finger. Then there was a sudden burst of dizziness, which caused her to sway on her feet, and separated Baorun's face from hers. Baorun stared at her left cheek, then lowered his gaze after a few seconds, so that it fell on her shoulder blade. She felt a burning sensation run down her body. His breathing became more urgent, stinking of alcohol and tobacco, and warm on her cheek. She didn't know what provoked the reaction from her pregnancy, nor if its timing was significant, but her stomach lurched, and she began to vomit. She vomited and vomited, vomiting continuously on Baorun's shoulder.

Baorun let her vomit drip down his body, at a loss what to do, his hands dangling at his side. After a moment he took a towel, and carefully wiped the mess off his shoulder.

"Do I make you vomit? Am I that disgusting to you?"

"No, it's not you, it's the child!" she exclaimed, still alternately vomiting and shaking her head vigorously. "There's a little baby. Let me go, I'm pregnant!"

SIX
THE HIGHWAY

As the iron door of the water tower slammed shut behind her, she heard Baorun's hoarse voice:

"Take Liu Sheng with you! From today, the slate is clean between us."

The slate was clean. Crouching on the threshold, she automatically looked up at the water tower. It had aged: the dense growth of Japanese creeper had blackened, and its branches and tendrils had reached the roof of the building, spreading over it so that it gave the tower a completely superfluous hat. The window of the pump room was half boarded up, and its other half gaped blackly. One of the crows was perched on the windowsill, and the other had flown off no one knows where. The remaining bird looked down on her with its ancient gaze, surveying her peculiar destiny. She did not understand why her fate was so inextricably linked to this water tower. The tower was her memorial stele, and as she crouched underneath it and looked up, she saw a soiled banner drifting slowly down from its roof. She wasn't sure whether this banner was her shame or her misfortune.

Liu Sheng got out of his van and offered her a slice of watermelon.

"Here, it's Hainan watermelon. It will cool you down."

She spat at him and the fruit.

"Fuck off! Get away from me, you piece of shit!"

Liu Sheng wiped his face, looking unconcerned.

"You came out alright this time, didn't you? It's always better to bury the hatchet, and now the slate is wiped clean for all three of us, isn't it?"

"It's not as easy as that! Your debt with me isn't cleared yet!"

She was furious with Liu Sheng, and refused to get in his van."

"Have you forgotten where this is?" Liu Sheng asked. "If you don't get in the van, how are you going to get out of the gates?"

She ignored him and took her suitcase out of the back of the van. She ran back to the electronic gates and shouted to the gatekeeper:

"Open the gates for me, Lao Qian!"

Lao Qian stuck his head out of his booth, and looked at her and the suitcase.

"What ward are you from? Do you want to leave the hospital? Why don't you have your doctor with you? Where's your discharge certificate?"

"I'm not a patient, I'm Miss Bai! Don't you recognise me, Lao Qian?"

Lao Qian looked up at her face.

"You do look familiar. Are you a new doctor? Where's your hospital ID?"

With some difficulty, she remembered her ID number from when she was working for Boss Zheng:

"I'm number 078; I forgot my card today."

Lao Qian scrutinised her carefully again, and suddenly burst out laughing:

"Ha! There's no point trying to play games with me, Miss. I've worked the main gate for more than twenty years, and you still think I can't tell a doctor from a patient? Hurry up back to your ward!"

Lao Qian's certainty in his own judgement hurt her self-esteem, and made her both ashamed and angry. She stamped her foot, saying:

"I'm Fairy Princess! Fairy Princess from the old iron shack. My grandfather used to be the gardener here, and you used to give me sweets. When I was little, I used to do Xinjiang dances for you. You can't have forgotten!"

Lao Qian blinked at her, as though trying to summon up the past. But prudence prevailed, and he still wouldn't open the gates.

"I know you used to be a fairy princess, but fairy princesses get sick too. If you want to get better, and be a princess again, then hurry up back to your ward."

Liu Sheng's van slowed to a halt beside her, the door opened, and she heard Liu Sheng say, in a self-satisfied tone:

"Stop being so stubborn and get in the van."

There was nothing for it but for her to do as he said, and as she got in the van, kicking the door on the way in, she cursed:

"Has the whole world gone blind? What makes him think I'm a patient? Do I look like a patient?"

Liu Sheng smiled slyly:

"Just at this moment, you look very like someone who's just escaped from the women's ward."

As soon as the words were out of his mouth, he saw she was going to lose her temper, so he gave himself a gentle slap, saying:

"Don't fly off the handle, I'm joking. See I've even slapped myself for you."

It was a long way to the airport, but Liu Sheng insisted on seeing her off. She was desperate to get home, so she didn't object, but just sat back and phoned Miss Shen Lan. For whatever reason, Miss Shen Lan didn't pick up. There were some onions or garlic chives rotting away somewhere in the back of the van, and the smell was making her nauseous. Holding her nose, she complained loudly:

"What do you carry in this thing? Dead bodies? Horseshit? Why does it stink like this? I know I'm going to throw up on the way."

Liu Sheng disposed of the rotting vegetables and got back into the driving seat, stealing a glance at Miss Bai's belly.

"I hear you're pregnant."

She pretended not to hear. Liu Sheng's hand moved along the seat until it was almost touching her leg but he pulled it back at the last minute.

"Who's your boyfriend at the moment? What does he do?" he asked cautiously, afraid she would tell him off. Excusing himself, he went on: "I'm only asking because I care about you, but if you don't want to say, then don't."

She wiped the corners of her mouth with a tissue, and said coldly:

"It doesn't matter whether I want to or not, I just can't see the point in telling you. You drive a delivery van, and he drives a BMW. You're not in the same league."

With a mocking smile, he replied:

"Rich, is he? Rich is good, but they're always up to something. If he tries it on with you sometime, give me a shout, and I'll come and sort him out."

"Don't try and sweet talk me; I'm sick of the sight of your face. Just get on and drive; if I hear another word from you, I'll throw up."

The afternoon sun splashed across the highway, turning it into a river of gold. As they approached an old elm tree, Liu Sheng suddenly changed gear and the van slowed down. She heard Liu Sheng exclaim in alarm:

"That's not good! I can see Baorun's granddad; he must have escaped again."

There, indeed, standing under the elm tree was an old man, clutching a cardboard box to his chest. On his top half, he was wearing a blue patient's tunic from the Jingting Hospital but, below the waist, all he had on was a pair of tatty underpants, revealing two skinny white legs. As Miss Bai was wondering how Grandfather had escaped from the hospital, whether he was there to hitch a lift, or sell something to a passer-by, a white rabbit's ear suddenly poked out of the top of the cardboard box, twitching in the wind. Miss Bai pressed up against the windscreen to take a closer look at the cardboard box, and saw that there was another rabbit, a grey one. In a strangled voice, she exclaimed:

"Rabbits! Two rabbits!"

The van came to an abrupt halt under the elm tree. When Grandfather saw Liu Sheng's face, he dropped the cardboard box and ran off into the surrounding countryside. The rabbits seized the opportunity to jump out of the box, and the two of them, one white, one grey, set off down the highway at high speed. As if by agreement, Grandfather and the two rabbits set off in different directions, making it more difficult to stop them. Miss Bai wanted to chase down the rabbits, but Liu Sheng began turning the van to go after Grandfather, which was how it ended up temporarily across the road. Whilst they were arguing the toss, they heard the frantic hooting of a coal lorry. Liu Sheng hit his own horn, swearing at the coal lorry:

"What's the fucking rush? In a hurry to get to the morgue, are you?"

A bald man stuck his head out of the driver's-side window of the coal truck. A dark green jade ornament on a red cord swayed around his coarse neck. Lorry and van blared their horns at each other, drowning the driver's curses, but Miss Bai could see his lips moving, and his eyes shooting daggers. There were a few seconds of silence, as if driver and lorry were catching their breath then, with a clang, the coal lorry came hurtling like a great beast towards the delivery van. She remembered putting her head in her hands, and screaming:

"It's coming!"

In that instant she saw clearly how her destiny had been laid out in advance, and she cried out:

"It's coming!"

Not only that, but just before the van careered into the elm tree, she also heard the lorry driver yell furiously:

"You whore! Let's see who it is who'll be going to the morgue!"

There was a terrible rumbling noise, the world seemed to tremble slightly, and a great weight toppled onto her, crushing her chest. The sky swallowed her up and, floating in the air, the golden hand of the bodhisattva seemed to be pointing gently at her belly. The inverted world whirled round her like a carousel. Bundles of purple light pierced her head from inside and flew off like arrows; this was her soul escaping, she guessed. She watched what remained of her soul, in purple tufts, fly off too. She had no idea where it was flying off to.

SEVEN
COMING TO

LATER, the doctor told her she'd been unconscious for eighteen hours.

The first things she saw when she came to were three IV bottles hanging above her head. In the chaos of the emergency room, the white-clad figures of two young nurses were bustling to and fro. The place was packed with other beds, either side of her, and there was a sour smell in the air. One old woman was groaning loudly:

"It hurts so much! Just let me die! It's so crowded here, if I die, at least it will free up a space."

Someone next to her picked up on the theme:

"As soon as you go, another emergency will be right in there, so what space are you actually freeing up? Hanging on is better than dying, because at least you're still alive!"

She was alive. She could remember the strange scene at the side of the road: Grandfather clutching his cardboard box, the two rabbits inside the box, and the coal lorry and its furious driver. Eighteen hours later, she recognised quite clearly that she had received a beautifully wrapped present from death itself. The lorry driver's shouts were fresh in her ear:

"Off to the morgue! Off to the morgue!"

A total stranger proclaiming her fate like this, succinct and totally justified. But she wasn't in the morgue just yet, and she had come back to life. Who was it who had reversed the sentence? Yes, she was alive, but she didn't feel in the least like celebrating. Her heart was full of grievance and anger.

There was a feeding tube in her nose, IV ports in her hands, and her body was wrapped in bandages. She couldn't move. She tried her legs; her left leg was immobilised, but she could move her right leg freely, so she kicked off her cover, and shouted:

"Is everybody dead? Someone come and let me loose. Hurry up and let me loose!"

Her shouts attracted an angry nurse, who was about to reprimand her, until she saw her expression, angry and wretched at the same time. The nurse turned and walked away, saying:

"I don't have time to argue with you. I'll go and find one of your relatives."

At first she thought the nurse must have confused her with someone else. Apart from her dead grandparents, what other relatives did she have? After about ten minutes a woman came hurrying into the emergency room, carrying a bunch of bananas. She thought this woman looked familiar, but it was only when she slowly approached the bed, and leaned over to look at her, her face worried and mournful, her eyes as sharp as needles, that Miss Bai gave a gasp of recognition: it was Liu Sheng's mother, Shao Lanying.

Shao Lanying had aged greatly over the last few years; her hair was grey, and her formerly fair skin, which had succumbed to the inevitable ravages of time, was wrinkled and covered in liver spots. She stroked Miss Bai's hair, picked out a speck of coal dust, dropped it on the floor, then wiped her hand on the bedsheet.

"It's filthy in here!" she said.

Miss Bai let Shao Lanying sit beside her, but turned her face away to show her she wasn't ready to make conversation. She waited for Shao Lanying to say something, but that lady just sat there without speaking, emitting a non-stop barrage of sighs of varying lengths. In the end, she could stand it no longer, and broke the silence, protesting:

"Why are you sitting there, sighing, Aunty? What are you sighing about? Your son is alive, isn't he?"

This unfriendly attitude just made Shao Lanying sigh even more:

"Aiya, Fairy Princess! I'm not going to argue with you. You've never spoken nicely to anyone, ever since you were little. Even though you've grown into such a beautiful young woman, your lousy temper hasn't changed. Yes, he's alive and you're alive, and that's a great blessing amidst such tragedy, so why aren't you happy about it?"

"Please stop sighing next to me. I don't care about any blessing. I'm already uncomfortable, and listening to people sighing makes me nauseous."

Shao Lanying peeled a banana and tried to feed it to Fairy Princess, but when she saw her lips tight shut, she didn't force the matter, and ate it herself.

"Fairy Princess, Fairy Princess, I know you're upset. I'm upset too. Fate brought you and our family together. Recently, since Liu Sheng lost his soul, my right eyelid has had a permanent tremor and I'm always on edge. I don't care whether you want to hear it or not, but the only thing I'm afraid of is that you and Liu Sheng will get together. When you hit a patch of bad luck, there's nothing you can do, and your worst fears are realised. Liu Sheng has been driving that van for years with nothing happening, and now what happens? He picks you up, there's a terrible accident, and he almost dies."

"You don't have to tell me, Aunty; I know it all already. I'm jinxed and I can't deny it." She closed her eyes, making it clear she wanted her visitor to leave. "I've only just come to, and I don't have the energy to talk with you. Go and talk to your son instead."

"I never said you were jinxed," Shao Lanying retorted. "I know you're too tired to talk, so just lie back and listen to what I have to say. The world is a big place, and you are very beautiful. You can sing and dance, and you could go and make a career in Hong Kong or Taiwan. At the very least you could be a star in Beijing or Shanghai. Why do you want to come back to this backwater? If you do want to come back, I won't get in your way, but why set out to provoke Liu Sheng? We all have memories, and there's no need to remind you that you were predestined to be enemies. It's disastrous whenever you get together and nothing good can ever come of it."

"I can remember, but your son can't! Now be off with you; go and ask your son why he has lost his memory."

"He has earned your curses. All men are moral lightweights; they just have to see a pretty girl, and it brings out the worst in them. They lose all self-control."

Shao Lanying off-handedly criticised her own son, whilst actually continuing to direct her barbs at Fairy Princess. But when she saw the tears gathering in her eyes, she stopped, reached out and pulled the cover up for her.

"You've been very lucky, and nothing terrible has happened to you, and you can throw a tantrum when you wake up!" Shao Lanying said. "My Liu Sheng hasn't been so lucky: he's lost property and health. He's broken three ribs and a leg; he's got six stitches in his face and he's scarred for life. His van is a write-off, so how's he going to make a living now?"

The tears in Fairy Princess's eyes soon dried up. Shao Lanying put the bunch of bananas down beside her pillow, but Fairy Princess brushed them away so they fell on the floor.

"You have no idea how many troubles I have, Aunty, so do me a favour and leave now. If you don't, then I'll get up and leave myself."

Shao Lanying picked the bananas up off the floor, and when she saw that all the other patients were looking at her sympathetically, she smiled graciously and said:

"Young people today, there's no talking to them; they have no manners! It's because they've all been spoiled by their parents. When they lose their temper with you, you just have to grin and bear it."

As she consoled herself with these words, she swivelled back to the bedside:

"I know you're in a bad mood; so am I. I just have one more thing to say to you, and then I'll go." Shao Lanying's eyes shone and, for whatever reason, her nostrils flared. "Fairy Princess, I don't want to argue with you on your sickbed, so I will just ask you: after all these years, is Liu Sheng's debt to you still not repaid? Even if it wasn't repaid before, surely it must be now, after all this."

Fairy Princess looked at her in astonishment, gnawing her lip, as though considering these words. After a few seconds, her expression returned to normal: restless, penetrating and headstrong, a hard smile twitching the corners of her mouth.

"Settled? Not necessarily", she said in an exaggeratedly cute voice. "No, Aunty, not necessarily."

The baby was still in her belly, safe and sound.

The doctor told her that it was amazing that she hadn't had a miscarriage after such a serious accident, and that the baby was even luckier than her. She responded coolly to this good news, and massaged her belly thoughtfully with her fingertips.

"It doesn't matter; I really don't care."

The truth was that her maternal instincts were themselves embryonic, unformed, somewhere between the liquid and solid state, vague and indistinct, now shrunken, now expansive; she was still a long way from a true mother's love. She had never been one of those women who loved babies; she only loved little animals. Now she had lost everything except for a foetus, and she didn't know whether or not that was a cause for celebration.

She was busy for several days, making phone calls and mobilising contacts, trying to recover the suitcase she had lost on the highway; but she was ultimately unsuccessful. The coal truck that had caused the accident had disappeared (no one knew where) before the traffic police arrived on the scene. The local farmers had descended on the place and picked it clean: of her billfold wallet, cell phone, clothes and branded make-up not a piece remained, and all she collected from the police station was a pair of sandals covered in coal dust. It seemed that the locals drew the line at a dead woman's shoes, and had kicked them into the grass at the side of the road.

Lao Ruan agreed to send her some money, and after a few days one of the girls from the staff of the Following Wind Guest House arrived with two thousand *yuan*. The girl was newly arrived in town from the depths of Guizhou, and she looked and sounded very much the country bumpkin. She awkwardly passed on Lao Ruan's apologies, saying that the boss had been very busy recently, and was strapped for cash. She also said that the boss had had his fortune told by a great soothsayer who had warned him to stay away from pregnant women in order to avoid a bloody catastrophe. Fairy Princess understood Lao Ruan's message as soon as she heard it: he wanted to be rid of her. She was a massive nuisance, and he wanted to be rid of her. She was both bitterly disappointed, and reluctant to admit her own mistakes. Without waiting for her to finish, she gave the girl her marching orders:

"Be off with you! I'm a bloody catastrophe, and anyone near me had better watch out for themselves."

The girl, however, showed herself to be both straightforward and considerate:

"I've seen all kinds of catastrophe, natural calamities and man-made disasters alike, so I don't think I've got anything to be afraid of in you. Lao Ruan ordered me to take care of you."

"Do you think I want you to take care of me? You're too dim-witted to understand anything; how could you look after me?"

The girl look rather stubborn, and plonked herself down on the bed, saying, huffily:

"If I don't understand, I can always learn. If I leave, I'm the one the boss is going to shout at, not you."

Fairy Princess realised that the girl was simple and straightforward to deal with, so she picked up a crutch, and prodded her in the back with it:

"Run along, run along. If you stay here, your work at the guest house will go to pieces. Go back and tell Lao Ruan that I can look after myself. I know he has done his best by me, and from now on I won't bother him any more."

Lao Ruan's money saw to her immediate necessities but, as her discharge approached, she began to worry about what she was going to wear. She spent an age walking round the department store close to the hospital, and finally settled on a famous-label dress, which she tried for size and told the shop assistant to wrap up. Only then did she discover there was no money left in her purse. She ran back to Liu Sheng's ward to borrow some more, but bumped into Shao Lanying and Liu Juan. Shao Lanying eyed her defensively, as if finding herself next to a deadly enemy. Fairy Princess beat a hasty retreat. Liu Juan, however, seemed quite friendly, and followed her, calling out:

"Fairy Princess! Fairy Princess! I made some chicken soup for Liu Sheng; I'll leave you a bowl."

Fairy princess looked back and said:

"I don't like chicken soup."

Fearing that Liu Juan would nag her, she ran and hid in the toilets, locking herself in one of the cubicles.

She sat quietly in the cubicle, chin in hand, planning her future, and the more she thought about it, the more flustered she became. It was a future hidden by black clouds, not clear at all. All she could see was her gradually swelling belly, like a mysterious seam of ore containing an unknown life. Her body held two lives and she wasn't sure whether she was pregnant with a foetus, or the foetus was pregnant with her. So, was her future that child? And for the present, was the foetus her only asset? Her waist had thickened, her legs were a little swollen; her pregnant body made her curious: it was like a deserted farm, where all the remaining fertilizer had been given to a single tree, but the man who had planted that tree had already upped and left. She thought of Mr Pang: inevitably, she felt let down, but that feeling came and went in a flash. The foetus formed a bridge, connecting her body with Mr Pang. She suddenly realised that she had the right to abandon Mr Pang, but Mr Pang did not have the right to do the same to her; and that, compared to all the local playboys she had met, Mr Pang had a duty to treat her well or, to be more explicit, at least to treat her body well.

She recalled that according to her contract with Mr Pang, she was not to see him before the child was born, but despite this, for the sake of that beautiful dress, she picked up her phone and called him. The sound of that Taiwanese accent almost made her burst into tears. "Take me with you! I'll be your no. 2 wife." These words trembled on her lips, but the coldness of his tone held them back. Abandoning all preliminary groundwork, she asked him to help her one last time by going to a certain shop to buy two summer outfits, and bringing them to the hospital; while he was there, he could also settle what remained of her bill. When Mr Pang asked why she was in hospital, she replied:

"I tried to kill myself. I threw myself under a car on the highway, but unfortunately I survived."

Mr Pang almost certainly saw straight through this lie, and replied:

"Please stop bothering me with this nonsense. I thought we'd settled all this. We'll only get back in contact once the baby is born."

She was particularly humiliated by his use of the word 'nonsense', and fell silent for a moment. Finally, she said calmly:

"Alright, very well! I won't bother you with any more nonsense. I'll go and bother your wife. You like black or white choices, don't you? Well, here's one for you. Go ahead and choose!"

She even frightened herself with this naked threat of blackmail, and the realisation of her wickedness made her gasp for breath. But she had overplayed her hand, and underestimated Mr Pang. Over the telephone, the latter said:

"It's been a while since I've seen you; you seem to have grown up very fast! So it's blackmail now, is it?" He gave a strange little laugh. "You're committing a crime here; do you understand that? I'm recording this call. Do you want me to play it back to you? If you don't dare listen, shall I take it to the police?"

She was stunned for a moment then burst out:

"You mangy old fox! You slimy toad! Did you have a tape recorder when you were slobbering all over me in Europe? Why didn't you record those disgusting noises?"

Mr Pang gave a dry little laugh, followed by a long sigh:

"So corrupt! So degraded! I should have seen through a degenerate like you long ago. How blind I was, thinking you were so pure and innocent!"

Stunned, she went back to her ward and just sat there for a long time. Suddenly, she turned to the bed next to her to borrow a pen and two sheets of paper. Her neighbour saw how miserable she looked, and asked her what she wanted to write:

"Nothing special, just a statement of account."

She lay on the bed on her stomach and began to write. She'd only written a few characters when she began to sob spasmodically. Her unusual behaviour soon attracted the attention of the whole ward. Someone came over and asked to see what she was writing, but she thrust the paper under her pillow and got under her cover, saying:

"I'm not going to write anything with you spying on me, I'm going to go to sleep."

Later on, Liu Sheng came in, leaning on a crutch, and his face still covered in gauze.

"I hear you're writing your last will and testament, Miss Bai: your 遗书 (yishu). Can you tell me how you write the character 遗?"

He sounded almost happy, as though the tragedy that should have been there had somehow been dissipated. She didn't want to talk to him, and turned her face away so he couldn't see her crying. This gave him the opportunity to snatch the document from under the pillow, and that was how the hurried, incomplete testament was brought to the attention of everyone in the ward:

"I hate this world, and I hate all the people in this world."

Afraid that Liu Sheng would read out the whole thing, she got up and snatched it back. Angry and ashamed, she tore it into little pieces. Liu Sheng was about to laugh, but thought better of it. He shuffled the confetti under the bed with his foot, saying:

"Who doesn't hate this world? I hate it too, but not enough to write it in a testament. Don't you think it's a bit soon to be writing a testament?"

"What's it got to do with you if I want to write it now?" she said. "Now fuck off and stop bothering me."

He sat down determinedly beside her bed, turning things over in his head for some time. He picked up the ballpoint pen from the bedside cabinet, slammed it on a piece of paper, and said:

"You brought yourself back from the dead; why don't you value life a bit more? For you to throw your life away like this is not only to bring shame on the Party and the government, it leaves me with nowhere to put myself either. Is it all because you lost your suitcase?" he went on to ask out loud. "In a little while, write down what you need, and I guarantee that within three days I'll buy everything for you."

. . .

Thanks to Liu Sheng she passed the rest of her days in hospital quite satisfactorily. This untrustworthy man became her only support. This rapprochement between them was both inevitable and unavoidable. She had previously never considered the possibility that Liu Sheng's attentiveness, and even his frivolity, could become the foundation of her salvation. Over the following days, they clung to each other like a pair of disaster survivors, and like a pair of lovers, they ate together, sharing everything. As they sat together, her knees accidentally brushed against his lower leg and, because he had his trousers rolled up, she could feel the coarse black hairs on his legs; she also picked up a faint odour of testosterone, emanating impudently from his lower body. Distractedly, she thought of how he had looked as a young man ten years ago: handsome, vain, frivolous, with too much Diamond-brand pomade in his slightly wavy hair. He was her dance partner. The *xiaola*. They danced it together. The *xiaola*. *Dong, da, dadong.* She remembered the steps of the *xiaola*. She remembered the smell of the Diamond-brand pomade. She remembered her early chaotic feelings for Liu Sheng, now detesting him, now liking him. If they had, after all, danced the *xiaola* that time in the water tower; if he had only known at the start how to show affection for a girl; if she had loved him a little more at the outset; if the meeting in the water tower had happened three years later: what would their story have been then? Her heart ached at past events, there was a sour taste in her mouth, and tears sprang unbidden to her eyes. Liu Sheng noticed the change in her expression, and asked, concernedly:

"Is the food no good?"

She pulled herself together, smacked him on the thigh with a stainless-steel spoon, and said, sternly:

"Roll down your trouser legs!"

Her staying in the city until the birth was the most practical plan, and also the object of Liu Sheng's urgings. She agreed, and imagined that it might even be Liu Sheng who wheeled her into the delivery room when her time came. Mixed emotions welled up inside her at the prospect of handing over the running of her life to Liu Sheng. There was a rope even now tied round her body, and her soul. She couldn't resist fate, and her fate was circumscribed by a rope, a mysterious rope that was passed from hand to hand by various men, and ended up with Liu Sheng. She was immobilised by it. It spoke to her, saying: "Stay here." It spoke to her, saying: "You've lost your soul, so do what I say."

EIGHT
THE TENANT

THE HOUSE LIU SHENG rented for her was on Red Toon Street.

She had imagined for herself the battered and poverty-stricken atmosphere of this street in the north of the city, but the unceremonious warmth of her welcome from her neighbours as a new tenant, took her by surprise. When she got out of the taxi with Liu Sheng, into the spotlight of the gaze of the residents of Red Toon Street, she felt like a model on a catwalk, facing either the criticism or adulation of the crowd. She felt as exposed as if she was walking naked through the streets of the city. There was a general buzz of approbation in the air, and she could clearly hear the comments, most of them praising her appearance and her beauty: how fine her figure was, and how pretty her face. An undercurrent of spitefulness also reached her ears: pretty is pretty, but isn't there a hint of the tart about her? She rolled her eyes at the woman who expressed this opinion, and was just about to let loose a volley of curses, before she managed to stop herself. She didn't want to get into an argument when she'd only just arrived. Besides, Liu Sheng reminded her that there were all sorts of women on Red Toon Street, but they all had one thing in common; a god-given gift for argument.

The woman who ran the pharmacy next door was standing in her doorway, studying her face and body like a medical examiner, paying particular attention to her belly. She heard the boss's wife say to Liu Sheng:

"You're a crafty fellow, Liu Sheng! Becoming a father without any of the fuss!"

As she walked past the self-appointed wise woman, Fairy Princess felt a sly prod at her belly from a finger. She shot a look at the woman, but stayed calm and said:

"Excuse me, but could you keep your hands and feet to yourself, OK?"

With a curl of the lips, the woman replied:

"I'm not a man, so what does a little prod matter? One touch and I can tell how far along you are."

Fairy Princess lowered her gaze and went inside, grumbling:

"What business is it of yours how far along I am?"

Liu Sheng said:

"You really shouldn't talk like that. On this street, your business is everybody's business. They all mean well, but if it bothers you, just shut the door, and you'll be left in peace."

At that, she slammed the door shut. With all the inhabitants of Red Toon Street on the other side, she stood and listened for any signs of activity outside. She could hear one of the women laughing; it was hard to be sure, but the laughter sounded ribald.

"Aiyo! They've shut the door in this heat! They are impatient!"

There was a lot of laughter and someone said:

"That Liu Sheng! Last month I saw him out and about with one girl and, no time later, here he is bringing home another one, who's knocked up. If she's pregnant, why didn't he take her home?"

"How dumb are you?" another replied. "It's called getting ahead of the game. Shao Lanying isn't going to let that girl through the door, so Liu Sheng's rented this house. They're going to live together: it's what all the young people are doing nowadays. Time enough to talk about what happens next when it happens."

Infuriated, Fairy Princess yelled at the door:

"That's disgusting!" Then she turned and demanded of Liu Sheng: "You think I'm living with you? You're living with me? What have you told the landlord?"

"I haven't said anything," he replied innocently. "Don't have a go at me, it's them that are thinking it. The people of Red Toon Street are OK, they just like to gossip. Give your ears a rest and take no notice."

The house had been got ready on the fly, and although it was clean enough, the interior was gloomy, the furniture and walls gave off a musty smell, and a rat scampered down from the dining table and scurried over to a corner of the room. Looking up, the room's pitched roof was very high, its beams were blackened, and there were water stains where the walls met the roof. As she stood under the beams of the unfamiliar old house, she had the impression that there were thousands of germs, ancient and mysterious, floating through the air, and as so often before, she felt hemmed in; hemmed in this time by the ghosts of an ancient household. Those ghosts were whirling around in consternation, asking each other:

"Who is this? Who is she?"

Liu Sheng put the kettle on the stove, and came out of the kitchen. He noticed her wandering gaze, and asked her whether she had chosen her bedroom.

"What choice is there? Everywhere is gloomy and depressing in this broken-down hovel. Anywhere I choose, I'm afraid I'll be disturbing ghosts."

Liu Sheng smiled disingenuously:

"If you're afraid of disturbing ghosts, I can stay with you." He saw she was about to get annoyed, so he didn't pursue that tack, but changed course: "You don't need to be afraid of ghosts. You're pregnant, aren't you? Pregnant women have two lives in them, and it's the ghosts who will be afraid of you."

"I'm not in the mood to listen to your nonsense," she said sternly. "Are your lips capable of saying anything serious?"

Liu Sheng replied sincerely:

"I'm quite serious. All the old folk on Red Toon Street say the same thing. Pregnant women are the most important people under heaven, and even ghosts don't dare mess them around."

He looked at her face, then picked up a broom and began half-heartedly sweeping the floor.

"I know this house isn't up to your standards, but if you just grin and bear it for six months, until the baby is born, things will begin to look up for you then."

She looked over the house with loathing. First she inspected the garret in the roof; half of the stairs leading up there were concrete, and the rest were assembled from assorted bits of wood; a man's hat hung on the stair-post, bearing the logo 'Hong Kong Travel'. She asked Liu Sheng:

"What kind of man is this friend of yours? He's obviously poor, but he can afford to go to Hong Kong?"

Liu Sheng laughed and said:

"Even paupers can travel. You've been to Paris, haven't you? So why shouldn't he go to Hong Kong one time?"

"If he's the landlord, why hasn't he shown his face?"

"My friend doesn't like staying at home, and he's off on his travels. He hasn't just been to Hong Kong, you know, he's been to lots of other places too."

She was intrigued by the garret and, picking the cap up as she passed to brush the dust off the handrail, she climbed the stairs. It was stuffy up there, and a ray of sunlight fell on an old-fashioned camp bed with a new rush sleeping mat, which filled the room with a pleasant aroma of fresh straw. The bedding had not yet arrived, and there was only a greasy pillow, without a pillow-case, in one corner of the bed. There was an oval-shaped patch of light dancing furtively on the bed, and she suspected someone outside was using a mirror to spy on them. She went over to the small window that overlooked the street, and poked her head out. She saw that there was indeed still a throng of people standing around in the street, and she pulled her head hastily back in. Stamping her foot, she said:

"Shit! They're still there. What do they hope to see?"

"They don't know themselves," Liu Sheng replied. "They've all been laid off work and have nothing to do. If you don't want them to see you, hang that sheet up as a curtain."

She picked up a sheet from where it was draped over the back of a chair, looked at it, then put it back down.

"I can't put it up now; I know how these people think: if I hang a bed sheet up now, they'll be even less inclined to leave."

A familiar woman's voice made itself heard above the noise of the people on the street:

"Liu Sheng! Liu Sheng! Get over to the clinic now, you need to change your dressings!"

She hid beside the window, and peeped out to see Shao Lanying standing opposite their front door, talking to a group of other women, and occasionally looking up to throw a glance at the little window.

"Wash your ears out, Liu Sheng!" Shao Lanying shouted. "Your wounds aren't properly healed; go and get your dressings changed and hurry up about it: the clinic is closing soon."

Fairy Princess suggested to Liu Sheng that he get a move on, but he just felt his bandages, and said:

"I'm not bothered whether they get changed or not. Ignore her, I'll just help you get settled in, then go."

She blocked his way, chivvying him towards the door like a farmer chivvying a duck:

"Don't use me as an excuse, there's nothing more for you to do here. Just hand over the key, and go and get your dressings changed. Then you can go and tell your mother that I haven't seduced you, that I haven't forced you into anything and it's only because I'm in dire straits that I've come to live here on Red Toon Street."

Liu Sheng nodded, and took the key out of his pocket, but was reluctant to hand it over:

"Do you want me to have another one cut? It would make it easier for me to come and go." He saw her reaction, and went on tentatively: "Don't worry, I'm not getting ideas, but you're new around here and don't know how things work. If I have a key, it will be easier for me to help you."

She scowled and said harshly:

"That would be the same as you moving in with me, so stop trying to sweet-talk me. I may not be pure and innocent any more, but I haven't fallen so low as to want you to move in with me!"

She held out her hand, palm up:

"Hurry up! Hand over the key and run back to your mummy."

Liu Sheng grudgingly gave up the key, and had just reached the door when he thought of something, and turned back to look at her.

"I'll come back tomorrow. Chun Geng and the others want to give me a welcome-home dinner. We're going to go for seafood; you can come too."

She refused curtly:

"What seafood? Rotten crabs and mushy shrimp? I prefer shark's fin and abalone. Will your friends buy me those? Even if I did go with you, I wouldn't be going as your girlfriend."

She casually turned on the television, and a noble warrior with a long grey beard and whiskers appeared on the screen, wielding a sword in mortal pursuit of an evil demon. She smacked the television with her fist.

"How boring! Yet another of those rubbish films. How am I going to get through the days here if there's nothing decent on television?"

"If you're having trouble passing the time, how about getting some DVDs instead of the TV? Ah Liu's brother runs a DVD shop, so just ask him for anything you want."

She didn't say yes or no but, when she saw Liu Sheng still standing in the doorway, she said:

"Are you still here? If you're not going, let me just tell you one more thing. We are just friends, ordinary friends. Do you understand? You've got me prisoner here, so if you want to make a prison visit in future, phone ahead first to ask."

She was trapped under the roof of a stranger.

There was a wooden door into the courtyard, and through the window next to the door, she could see the moss-covered yard, and the junk piled up outside, along with an old-fashioned twenty-six-inch bicycle propped up against a wall. It was covered in rust spots, and had some rope coiled neatly on the back of the frame. She pushed at the door, only to discover that it was festooned with locks so there was, in fact, no way out into the yard. She went up to look out over Red Toon Street from the garret window, and the first thing she saw was a neon-lit advertising case in the pharmacy window, which read: 'Extend Your Life,

Avoid Old Age, Stay Young'. This boring street and this ancient house seemed to have been specially designed for her in her current poverty-stricken state. She was a prisoner, a prisoner of her unborn child. She was a hostage, a hostage to an unknown future. She was a mortgaged property, picked up by the hand of fate, and dumped in the garret room of a stranger.

That first day, she was exhausted, and went to sleep early. It rained during the night and a bit of a chill crept into the stuffy atmosphere. Red Toon Street was as quiet as the grave, completely undisturbed, but something inexplicably startled her and woke her up. It was as though there was a man sleeping next to her, but when she opened her eyes to look at the sleeping mat, lit by a ray of light from the moon, there was no man there; but there was the familiar scent of a man, and that was what had woken her. The smell was seeping out of the bed and scrambling up from the pillow, permeating first her face, and then her body. Whose was it? She shouted down the stairs, but there was no reply. Still very suspicious, she went over to the garret's small window, and pulled back the curtain to look out. On the window sill she saw a cigarette butt, which had been put out by the rain. There was no one in the street. The night rain had left puddles on the newly-laid asphalt, all different sizes, none the same, but all of them circular, and reflecting the moonlight like shards of broken glass. A white cat was standing on the roof of the house opposite, looking like some kind of sinister guardian. She picked up the cigarette butt and threw it down into the street. Startled by the movement, the cat disappeared in a flash.

The next morning she heard someone knocking at the front door. Thinking it would be Liu Sheng, she opened it only to find it was the manageress of the pharmacy next door. She was carrying several large plastic bags, and said:

"Liu Sheng asked me to give you these. Isn't he considerate!"

Fairy Princess took possession of the various fruits and vegetables, and was about to close the door, but the woman had already stopped her by putting one foot over the threshold. She was looking over Fairy Princess's shoulder at the room inside.

"Are you living here alone? Aren't you afraid?"

"What's there to be afraid of? Is the place haunted?"

The woman had the look of someone with secret gossip to impart and dismissed this suggestion with a wave of the hand:

"No, no, that's not it; besides, ghosts don't bother pregnant women. It's men you've got to worry about. This street has some shady customers, and you absolutely must make sure you lock your doors and windows at night."

"I know. I even keep them locked during the day."

She was making it clear she wanted her visitor to leave, but the woman showed no inclination to go. She was gazing with great interest at Fairy Princess's waistline.

"You're in your fourth month now, aren't you? Is it Liu Sheng's?"

Fairy Princess smiled haughtily, and said:

"How could that even be possible? Can you actually see me making a couple with him?"

"I don't know about that. Many pretty flowers grow out of manure."

The woman was stealthily stretching out a hand, trying to measure her waist, but Fairy Princess stepped out of reach.

"Why are you afraid to let me touch you? One press and I'll know whether it's a boy or a girl. There's no point in being stand-offish with me: you can do that with anyone else, but not me. Ask anyone on the street; they've all heard of Madam Ma. If any of my neighbours have problems, it's me they come and talk to."

"I don't have any problems. After all, I'm staying here, I eat, I drink, I shit, I piss, I sleep; what problems can I have?"

"I wouldn't be so sure. I've heard you're going to stay here until you're due. That's another six months. It's not a long time, but it's not a short time either. There are a lot of bust-ups on our street, and you need to be really careful. Don't go out too much."

"Whatever bust-ups you have on your street, they're nothing to do with me. If I don't think I can get used to living here, who says I won't move out tomorrow? Besides, I got robbed when I used to live in a hotel; there was nothing I could do about it, I just had to grin and bear it."

Seeing how stand-offish Fairy Princess was determined to be,

Mistress Ma's enthusiasm began to wane, and she slowly retreated towards the door.

"Your temperament is so expansive, it could harm the foetus. You need to look after the foetus, and I've just got in some medicine specially for that next door. Do you want me to bring you a box?"

"Thank you, but I don't care whether I protect my foetus or not. If I keep it, I keep it; if I lose it, I lose it."

NINE

THE LANDLORD

For her, catching sight of her mysterious landlord was like seeing a ghost.

The television was on, and she was cooking noodles in the kitchen when she heard movement by the staircase. She turned to see the silhouette of a man, bent over, fiddling with a cardboard box at the bottom of the stairs. At first, she thought it was Liu Sheng:

"Liu Sheng, is that you? How did you get in? Sneaking in here like a thief! Why didn't you phone first? Who gave you permission to come in?"

The man straightened up, unhurriedly. He turned to look at her, and waved a key he was holding at her.

"I'm not Liu Sheng, I'm the landlord," Baorun said. "I'm your landlord. This is my house, and I've come to collect a few things."

An involuntary cry of alarm escaped her and, thinking she must be having a nightmare, she pinched herself hard enough for it to hurt. She jumped up from where she was sitting and ran over to the kitchen door, snatching up a vegetable cleaver from the table on her way. Clutching the cleaver, she hid in the kitchen, behind the door, stamping her feet and shouting:

"Bastards! You pair of bastards! You've tricked me again! Why have you trapped me in your house? What are you going to do?"

Everything remained quiet outside, then she heard Baorun say:

"Go and ask Liu Sheng. Ask him what he's going to do. He's tricked me too. He said he was renting the house for his girlfriend. I didn't know you were his girlfriend." He paused for a couple of seconds then asked: "Are you his girlfriend?" Without waiting for her to reply, he went on, with a hollow laugh: "I see what's going on! The bastard! You two are living together, are you? Very interesting! Very interesting indeed!"

Crying with anger, she shouted through the door:

"Bullshit! You think I'm his girlfriend? Do you really think I'd shack up with anyone like you two?"

She gradually stopped crying and managed to calm down a bit. She heard Baorun rummaging around in his box, so she banged on the door with the back of the cleaver:

"Are you acting out a horror movie for me? No, it's worse than that!" she said. "The world's such a big place, how did it happen I've ended up living in your house? No wonder I've been having nightmares. Now I know it's your house, I'm moving out tomorrow."

"Up to you; move if you want to," Baorun said. "I'm renting the house to Liu Sheng, not you."

The water had been boiling on the gas cooker for a long time, and the noodles were cooked to a mush. The kitchen was full of steam, so she went over and turned off the gas. She began to cool down a little herself. Now she came to think about it, the reason the lingering male odour upstairs had seemed so familiar was because it was Baorun's particular combination of hair oil, body odour and smelly feet. Perhaps this wasn't a secret plot against her; perhaps Liu Sheng was just trying to save money, and the only thing playing tricks on her was fate. Even after so many years, there was still some demon manipulating them together, so elaborately and so wickedly, she couldn't see how to free herself. She stole a look at Baorun through a crack in the door, and rebuked him:

"What are you looking for out there? You're a big boy, and you should know the rules by now. When you rent out a house, it's not yours any more: it belongs to whoever's paying the rent. What do you think you're doing coming back here to search for stuff?"

Baorun was kneeling beside the cardboard box and finally pulled out a photo frame, and tucked it inside his jacket.

"There's no need to make a fuss, I'll be off in a minute. My Grandfather ran off from the hospital again yesterday, and I've been looking for him ever since. I've come to get his photograph, so I can put up some missing-person notices."

She believed him, but what puzzled her was that the wall around the Jingting Hospital was so high, and there were so many gates, how could Grandfather escape? She was very curious, but felt it beneath her to ask. Still looking through the crack in the door, she could see the beads of sweat on Baorun's forehead. Although he already had the photo frame, he was walking to and fro, as though still looking for something. What could it be?

"You're getting on my nerves, wandering about like that. Please go."

"There's no need to get on my case, I'll be gone in a minute. Do you want to get into the courtyard? If you're sick of being stuck in the house, you could go out into the courtyard for some air. Do you want me to unlock the door for you?"

The offer sounded quite sincere, and she was surprised by his consideration. She thought about it for a moment, then said:

"Up to you. If I can't get into the yard it won't kill me, and if I can, it won't make me live any longer."

Baorun went over to the door to the courtyard.

"My family isn't afraid of burglars and we don't take any precautions. The keys are here on top of the door frame. Just feel around and you'll find them."

He stood on tiptoe and felt around as he had described.

"There's a bicycle in the yard. You've ridden on it before. I took you to the Workers' Cultural Palace; do you remember? If you pump the tyres up, it's still rideable. If it's not too ugly for you, you can use it, if you want."

"Thank you for being so thoughtful, but I don't ride bicycles. I always take a taxi if I go out."

She heard the sound of him opening the locks. Kerchack! Kerchack! The sound of two padlocks opening, and a shaft of light pierced the gloom of the living room. Baorun's chunky legs appeared beside the door, his ankles striped by the bright sunlight. He put the keys down on the threshold.

"I'll put the keys here, so you can relax, I won't come in again. Our slate is clean; we're not friends but we do know each other. It's the baby who's important, so you just stay here until the birth."

He was outside the kitchen, and she was inside, the door between them. The two of them stood looking at each other in silence; a silence which finally got to her. She welcomed his consideration, which came at just the right time. Their reconciliation, although still partial, had come about a little quicker than she had thought it would, but she had faith in it. She looked at the photograph he was clutching to his chest, Grandfather's face hidden by his brawny arm, clinging to which there was a dust-devil, that was catching the sunlight and glinting in it. She suddenly felt that Baorun was being kind, and that she ought to reciprocate, and be a bit more polite to him.

"How did you let your grandfather escape?" She asked through the crack in the door. "Didn't you tie him up?"

"I was too busy," Baorun replied. "I'm a day-worker at the hospital now. They've got fewer and fewer male care workers now. I tie up lots of patients every day, but somehow I overlooked Grandfather." He paused, then went on: "Anyway, I don't like doing it; Grandfather's half-dead already, and it shouldn't matter if he's not tied up. I really didn't think he could run very far."

"You have to tie up the ones who need to be tied up; it's the only way you can stop worrying." The words were hardly out of her mouth before she regretted them and bit her tongue. What was she doing giving an opinion about tying people up? To hear the suggestion about tying people up emanate from her own mouth inevitably struck her as faintly ironic, even a bit contemptible. She hurriedly revised her standpoint:

"He's your grandfather; it's nothing to do with me. It must depend on the circumstances whether you tie him up or not. Now, hurry up and go, I have to go to the lavatory."

Baorun left. The cardboard box on the stairs was still open. She went over and had a quick look through its contents. The bottom of the box was covered in all kinds of rope and, on top of them, was an assortment of photo frames of all different sizes. There were quite a few formal portraits of Grandfather, all in the same type of black plastic frame: the old man was in the same pose in all of them, his distracted expression rich with interrogation, as if asking her:

"What about my soul? Do you know where my soul is?"

She picked out a different frame and saw the photo in it showed a group of people sitting in front of Tiananmen in Beijing. The figures were faded, and Tiananmen was hazy and indistinct. She wiped it with a damp cloth, and the outline of the gate became clearer. It was one of those family portraits popular in the 1970s, and the majestic Tiananmen was just a painted backdrop. The faces of four family members pushed their way through the dust: an old man and a husband and wife were sitting stiffly upright, their fixed smiles forced reluctantly out of them by the photographer. The only unsmiling figure was a young man at the back, clearly recognisable as Baorun: he was standing alone, his hair brushed up into a cockscomb; his posture was aggressive, and he had the look of someone who thought they had been tricked into doing something. She could just make out two pinpricks of fury in the pupils of his eyes.

That afternoon, she went out for once, carrying a black parasol, and went to Lao Sun's locksmith's stall, where she picked out a door lock. She asked Lao Sun to come over and change the lock for her. Lao Sun looked at her suspiciously:

"Whose new wife are you, Miss? I know everyone on the street, so why don't I recognise you?"

Reluctantly, she introduced herself:

"I'm nobody's new wife; I'm a jinx that's fallen to earth; a jinx that's fallen on Red Toon Street."

Lao Sun blenched, and asked, earnestly:

"Which household? Which household have you fallen on?"

She saw that her joke had frightened the old man and she laughed behind her hand.

"As long as it's not yours, what have you got to worry about? Funny that you're still afraid of jinxes at your age."

The sun had warmed up the asphalt of the road and, as her sandals click-clacked along, Lao Sun who was following behind her with his toolbox, decided that the view was even better from the back than from the front. Her hips swayed so vigorously when she walked, that it gave her gait an extraordinary sexiness; her miniskirt was in the fashionable red peony pattern setting off two long, slender white legs; but most alluring of all were her ankles, on one of which she wore a chain of multi-coloured beads, which tinkled and glittered as she walked.

Most of the residents were having their midday nap and, in the silence, the street was already plotting the gossip and rumours that it would spread when dusk fell. On their way back, Fairy Princess and Lao Sun chanced upon Aunty Shaoxing's cat, standing next to a concrete waste bin. Fairy Princess was fond of cats, and miaowed at it in a friendly tone. To her surprise, the cat rejected her well-meaning advances, and turned and ran home to report the situation to its mistress. Aunty Shaoxing came hurrying out onto the street and surveyed Fairy Princess, using a palm-leaf fan to shade her eyes. She gave a long, low sigh of admiration:

"Ai yoyo! So beautiful! It's really not surprising!"

Fairy Princess heard this praise with some amazement: what did she mean by 'not surprising'? Puzzled, she rolled her eyes at the old woman, and walked on past her. Frustrated in striking up a conversation with her, Aunty Shaoxing tagged on behind Lao Sun, and prodded him in the back with her fan:

"Hey, Master Sun, where are you off to with this beauty?"

"Beautiful or ugly, they're all just customers, and I'm going to change this customer's lock."

Fairy Princess noticed the furtive silence behind her, then heard Aunty Shaoxing say, knowingly:

"Locks can be changed just like that, can they? You need to watch out for yourself, Master Sun!"

She looked back and muttered at Aunty Shaoxing:

"Why don't you drop dead!"

She crossed the road and stopped to buy an ice lolly at a cold drinks stall; licking it contentedly, she turned and continued on her way, sandals click-clacking on the road, until soon she reached the front door of Baorun's house. Leaning on the door, she gestured dramatically at it to Lao Sun, as though providing the answer to a riddle:

"This is where the jinx landed."

Staring at her blankly, Lao Sun said:

"Isn't this Baorun's house?"

She opened the door and went in, saying:

"It used to be his, now it's mine. I'm the boss here, so stop rolling your eyes, Master Locksmith, there's nothing to be alarmed about. Just hurry up and change the locks."

Madam Ma came out of the pharmacy next door, carrying a lunch box. Lao Sun lifted his chin at the house, and whispered to Mistress Ma:

"Is this girl Baorun's new wife?"

Madam Ma's face took on an enigmatic expression:

"No, no! It's very complicated with this girl."

"I thought as much. But give me a clue, at least. Should I change the locks for her or not?"

Madam Ma avoided his question, eager to explain the complexities of the matter:

"Have a guess, Lao Sun. Guess who she is. You'll never believe it." Without giving Lao Sun a chance to think, she whispered urgently in his ear:

"Do you remember Liu Sheng and Baorun's trial back then? I just heard Shao Lanying say that this is the girl from the water tower. It's that Fairy Princess!" Madam Ma slapped her knees in delight. "Would you ever have thought that those three old enemies would end up together here?"

TEN
OUTSIDE

THERE WAS a confused hubbub of voices outside while she was having her siesta. At first she thought it was her neighbours squabbling and didn't want to get up to investigate. But as the clamour grew louder and louder, she realised she couldn't get away with it, so she scrambled out of bed and went to look out of the window. She saw that a crowd of people was already thronged around the doorway, blocking it. Like stars around the moon, the crowd had its attention centred on the figure of a haggard, wizened old man.

Grandfather had returned.

Most people were dying to hear about the whereabouts of the flashlight and whether Grandfather still had any hopes of getting his soul back; there were some who sang his praises, saying that over the years, so many apparently healthy old people on Red Toon Street had died, but Grandfather was still there like an ageless pine tree. And what did that signify? It signified that you can live a long time without your soul, and who was to say that losing your soul wasn't the best way to ensure a long life? So what need was there to keep searching for the flashlight, then? And what was the point of continuing to strive to get his soul back? People focused on the phenomenon of Grandfather's tenacious grip on life, each offering their own opinion, but the man himself just stood there shaking his head, a wretched expression on his face. Someone brought him a slice of watermelon and Grandfather bit greedily into it, covering his face in red juice. His clothes were filthy but the blue and white stripes were faintly visible still, along with the red crescent moon on the breast, which was the emblem of the Jingting Hospital. Fairy Princess surveyed the scene despondently, and couldn't help blaming Baorun:

"You didn't tie him up again! Your own grandfather and you didn't tie him up! How useless are you?"

Eventually, the crowd outside began to bang on the door.

"Open the door, Miss Bai, Baorun's grandfather wants to come in!"

"Think of his age and do the right thing: let him come in and sit down for a bit. He's sick in the head and unsteady on his feet; it hasn't been easy for him to find his way home!"

"Don't be so mean, Miss Bai. This isn't your home, it's his. It's his ancestral property! It's such a shame, he's lost his soul. Would it kill you to let him in to look around and rest for a bit?"

Her indifference inflamed the righteous indignation of the neighbours. Everyone was feeling sorry for Grandfather and wanted to help him; some people began to throw stones at the little window by the door, whilst others just threw themselves against the door itself, whilst issuing an ultimatum:

"Miss Bai, if you're rude, we won't treat you politely. We know you've changed the locks. If you don't open up, we'll smash the door down and we won't pay you for it either!"

She was pacing up and down at the bottom of the stairs and when she heard the cracking noises coming from the locks, she lost her temper, snatched her purse up from the table, and hurled herself at the door, shouting:

"Do you think I'm so desperate to live here? Come in! Come in, old man! And the rest of you! Come on in!" She opened the door. "I'm off. You can have this dump back!"

She pushed her way through the crowd, chest out and head held high, leaving Baorun's house with a kind of pride. Behind her, the crowd fell momentarily silent, then erupted into cries of triumph. Grandfather had come home. She had been chased out. She had been chased out by the Street. After she'd gone a little way, she turned back to look. The crowd around the door was dispersing in an orderly fashion. Some people were going in, some were coming out, and there was even somebody's big, yellow dog bounding merrily into what had once been her home. She imagined everyone looking at her kitchen, her bed, her shoes, her underwear, her CD player... She imagined them looking at all her possessions, free to ferret out all the supposed secrets of her private life. But it was already common knowledge on Red Toon Street that she was called Fairy Princess, and what else did she have to conceal? She wasn't too upset, just angry:

"Go on and look then! Look as much as you like! What do you see? A wretched life laid bare to people who are even more wretched themselves."

By the time she reached the Shanren Bridge, her legs were getting a little tired, so she sat on the railings of the bridge and phoned Liu Sheng. Liu Sheng listened patiently while she berated him, not taking it too seriously, and even encouraging her to talk:

"Given everything that you've been through, are you still afraid of one old madman? You have to stay strong, and grin and bear it. We'll go and clear the place out for you soon."

She was both angry and full of self-pity, and almost burst into tears. But with all the people passing by the Shanren Bridge, it was not really a good place to start crying. So, unable to think of any way of changing her mood, she half-hid behind her mobile phone, and looked down at the pitch-black waters flowing underneath the bridge. Those waters made her think of the pale corpses of the drowned, and that made her feel nauseous. She suddenly remembered her unfinished testament:

"I hate this world, and I hate all the people in this world."

If she was going to go on writing, what was she going to write next? Her mind went blank and she knew why it had gone blank: because she didn't want to die. But as to how to face the world, and face the people in it, other than hatred, she had no other tactic.

A young couple came down from the bridge, hand in hand. The young woman was pregnant and they were walking slowly and happily:

she would probably be going into labour soon; her belly was as round as a hillock. She stared at the young woman's belly, and the young woman studied hers in return. Their eyes met and Fairy Princess was the first to blush. She always felt embarrassed when she saw another pregnant woman, but she didn't know why. The woman was past her by now, but she turned back with a smile, and said:

"You must be around five months, aren't you? Have you had an ultrasound scan? Do it now, then you'll know whether it's a boy or a girl."

She shook her head to show she wasn't interested in discussing her baby with a stranger. The young woman didn't say anything more, but the young man next to her declared proudly:

"My wife's having a boy."

"Idiot!" she muttered to herself.

Then she looked down at her own belly and felt a moment of uncertainty. What was she carrying? A boy? A girl? Either way it was Mr Pang's. Her maternal instincts had been faintly discernible until now, sometimes full of love, sometimes full of amazement, but most of the time fuelled by a deep-seated fear. Was she capable of being a good mother? What could she rely on to make her one? She thought of her life of defeats, fuelled by every kind of misguided wager: so many mistakes, thousands of them, but perhaps none of them as stupid as this one. Apart from a few paltry cents, what did she have to gain from this monumental gamble? She looked down at her own belly, and suddenly exclaimed:

"Enough of this! I don't want you!"

This evil sentiment echoed across the Shanren Bridge, even making herself jump. Her hatred was, in fact, so far removed from the baby itself, that these brutal words caused her a moment of self-reproach. She remembered how Madam Ma had prodded her foetus, so she pointed her finger at her own belly, first on the left, then on the right, and she tried to explain her position to it as gently as possible:

"Are you a boy or a girl? Either way you're his. I don't want you. You could have had anyone as your mother, so why did you insist on lodging in my womb? You shouldn't wonder at my lack of feeling, but at your own stupidity. I'm sorry, but I'm not going to be your mother; you'll have to go and find someone else."

She came down from the Shanren Bridge, hailed a taxi, and went straight to the maternity hospital.

A maternity hospital is, of course, full of pregnant women, but she was different from all the others, as she stood amongst them, looking round furtively. A nurse assumed she had come for an antenatal appointment, and showed her where to go.

"I'm not here for an examination," she said. "I just want to have a look around."

She hung around the door to the procedure room for a while, then abruptly pulled the curtain aside. She made to go in, but the nurse stopped her."

"It's empty, isn't it? I want an induced birth."

The nurse didn't show any surprise, but just glanced at her belly, frowned, and asked:

"Have you quarrelled with your husband? There's no need to take it out on the baby. It's your child as much as his, isn't it?"

"A baby doesn't earn me any money. Anyway, my husband doesn't care; he's working abroad, in Paris."

Without really meaning to, she had managed to offend the maternal instincts of all the expectant mothers there, and their eyes turned censoriously on her from all corners of the room, hemming her in, as if she were some unconscionable demon. The nurse, who was certainly a mother too, asked:

"Babies may not have any financial value, but what really does?"

She didn't reply immediately, and the nurse's expression darkened:

"So, your husband's in Paris? Paris isn't that far if you get on a plane. Tell him to fly back. A termination can kill the mother, and we can't take that responsibility. We need a family member to sign."

Fairy Princess was rather put out by everyone's unexpected rancour, so she retreated to a corner to turn things over in her head. Then she went back over to the nurse.

"The truth is I was orphaned when I was very little, and I'm divorced now, so I haven't got anyone to sign for me. I'm my only relative, so why can't I sign for myself?"

The nurse was getting tired of this little troublemaker, and looked at her sharply.

"I have no way of knowing if you're telling the truth about being an orphan, but seeing how fashionable and pretty you are, I'm quite sure you're not short of relatives; even if you're divorced, your ex-husband or your boyfriend must count as a relative. How else could you be pregnant?"

When she heard the innuendo in the nurse's words, she lost control, and shrieked:

"Alright, so if I don't have an ex, it's no good? And if I don't have a boyfriend, it's no good either? How about I'm a whore then, will that do? I'm a whore, pregnant with a client's baby. Can I have a termination now?"

The nurse had seen it all before, and didn't overreact:

"No one said you were a whore, young lady. We only want what's best for you, you must see that! How is your mental state?"

"It's fine right now, but if anything else happens, I wouldn't like to say."

"If you're stable now, then do the right thing now. Don't degrade yourself; go home and calm down a little; have a rest; you'll feel better tomorrow."

Fairy Princess stamped her foot:

"You can stop trying to play the good guy! What home? What tomorrow? You may have a home, but I don't! You may have a tomorrow, but I don't!"

She leaned against the wall, beating her fist against it, and wailing. The other expectant mothers all looked on hostilely, and none of them went to comfort her. Her cell phone was ringing constantly, and when she'd finished weeping, she answered it. It was Liu Sheng, who told her that Grandfather had been sent back to the Jingting Hospital, everything was quiet and orderly in the house, and she could go back there. Wiping away her tears, she replied:

"That's not my home. I'm not going back. Get over here to the maternity hospital; I need you to sign for me."

When he asked her what she was up to, she replied huffily:

"Women's stuff! Why are you asking all these questions? Just get over here as quick as you can, and remember, today you're one of my relatives. And that's the biggest honour of your life!"

She waited an age for Liu Sheng to arrive, and when he finally did, she offered no explanation, but dragged him straight to the administration office.

"My signatory is here," she said triumphantly to the nurse. "My boyfriend's here; my husband's here; my relative's here; take your pick. Now you can do the job for me."

The nurse looked askance at Liu Sheng and then at her:

"He's got back from Paris very quickly! Did he take a spaceship? It's no use anyway. An induced labour isn't the same as an abortion; it can be fatal, and normal parents don't do it. Even if you're shirking your responsibilities as parents, our hospital can't do the same. First you have to make an appointment, then we have to consider the date for the procedure. Go home and wait to hear from us."

Liu Sheng very quickly caught on to what was happening, and saw that Fairy Princess still wanted to argue the case with the nurse.

"Hold it! Listen to me, her relative!" he shouted. He took her out into the corridor and, sticking his finger under her nose, went on: "Has all that time you've spent out and about in the world been wasted on you? If you get rid of the baby, all you've been through before will be in vain, and you'll have no prospects for the future. I'm beginning to wonder just how clever you are!"

She leaned, exhausted, against the wall, and said:

"I've changed my mind. I'll forgive that Mr Pang, and save myself."

Liu Sheng looked at her belly, and chuckled:

"Isn't it too late to change your mind now? And it's a bit late to save yourself too! Still, there is victory in persevering, and if you hang on for a few months, everything will work out."

"I can't hang on any more, and I'm not going to play games with him over this. I'm going to get rid of the baby, and go and sing in Shenzhen. Start all over again."

Liu Sheng shook his head:

"The more you go on, the more nonsense you talk! Start over again?

That's a line from a song! A few months more and the Taiwanese gentleman will be paying you. Six figures, isn't it? Tell me, how many songs would you have to sing to earn six figures?"

"Poor people like you spend all day thinking of money, but I don't want that cash! All his assets don't make up for me being pregnant; **he** doesn't make up for me being pregnant!"

Liu Sheng didn't dare challenge her new plan, nor her newly-found self-belief. Rubbing his hands together, he said:

"Calm down, calm down! Let's have another think." He blinked, still rubbing his hands, then his eyes lit up. "Even if you do get rid of the baby, you can't let that Taiwanese off so cheaply. What kind of contract did you sign?"

She looked down and said, regretfully:

"The contract says it's one thing or the other: if there's no baby, he gets away scot-free."

"That's not a fair deal!" he exclaimed. "He's the one with the money, so why should he get away with it? If you have the baby, he's got to pay, and if you don't, he should still have to pay: maintenance, compensation for psychological suffering and for the loss of your youth. We should go and demand the money from him. Once he's paid, then we'll see what to do next."

Red-eyed, she considered Liu Sheng's proposal, decided he was right and, embarrassed at having to backtrack, struggled with her own thoughts for a while, then mumbled:

"I don't want to see him again. You go for me, if you're not afraid you'll lose face."

"No problem as long as we go fifty-fifty if it works."

"You think you're worth fifty per cent?" she asked furiously. "Are you the one who's pregnant? Have you got a uterus?" When she saw him looking uncomfortable, she cut him a little slack: "Alright. How about sixty-forty? Sixty to me, forty to you. How's that?"

ELEVEN
LIU SHENG AND MR PANG

THINGS WERE PUT ON HOLD.

It appeared that Madam Pang had come over from Taiwan and Mr Pang had taken her first to Guilin, and then on to Lijiang. So Liu Sheng didn't find him. After a few days, news came that they were back, and Liu Sheng went to the villa Mr Pang was renting on the banks of the river. He went with his sleeves rolled up ready for battle, but he returned crestfallen. He told Fairy Princess that Madam Pang was confined to a wheelchair, and her legs were no thicker than chopsticks.

"He pushes her around and they're never parted. I didn't get a chance to talk to him alone."

Fairy Princess was astonished. She had once made Mr Pang open his wallet to show her a picture of his wife, and she remembered an ordinarily attractive Taiwanese woman, but cheerful and friendly-looking; her eyes revealed a kind-hearted and gentle temperament. All Mr Pang had said was that his wife was an accountant, and had some health problems, but about anything else, he kept quiet. So she had had no way of knowing that Mr Pang's wife was confined to a wheelchair. She stood looking blank for a long time and then asked Liu Sheng:

"Is the wife pretty or not?"

"She's old, how pretty can she be? She's a Christian. She goes about with a Bible on her knees, studying God from her wheelchair."

She herself couldn't say why, since she no longer had any feelings for Mr Pang, but she couldn't relinquish her curiosity about his wife. With a surprising fervour, she tried to imagine her, as though she was trying to imagine the end of some cinematic thriller. When Liu Sheng heard her say she wanted to see Mrs Pang, he thought she was joking.

"It's not a joke," she said. "I really want to see her." In response to Liu Sheng's astonished expression, she went on: "Why are you staring like that? I'm going to see Mrs Pang, not visiting a ghost. What are you afraid of?"

Liu Sheng gave a strangled laugh and blurted out:

"I'm not afraid; you're the one who should be afraid. What do you want to see her for? You're the other woman, aren't you?"

This once, she made herself overlook Liu Sheng's rudeness, telling herself he was just saying what most people probably thought. Her lips twisted in a smile, mocking herself:

"What's wrong with a mistress talking to the wife about feelings, about children and about god?"

She ordered him to go with her to the riverside villa, and asked that he dress respectably. He should wear a designer suit, and if he didn't have one, he should go to the market and buy a knock-off. Amused, Liu Sheng replied with a knowing smile:

"Do you want me to be your knock-off relative again too? Which is it? A knock-off boyfriend, or a knock-off husband?"

"What difference does it make? Haven't you heard your mother spreading the word on the street? I'm the local bicycle, there for anyone to ride – boyfriend, husband, any old male, it's all the same."

It all happened on a Sunday. They pretended to be employees of Mr Pang's company, and tricked their way past the compound's security guard. They followed the drive down to the riverside and soon discovered that there were no people to be seen in this lofty and refined environment, only a wide assortment of dogs, on faithful guard in their owners' gardens. These dogs barked alright, but their barking was very civilised compared to the dogs on Red Toon Street: they barked when you approached their fence, then stopped once you went past. Fairy Princess and Liu Sheng each had their own particular interest in the surroundings. She kept looking in through the windows along the drive: if the curtains were drawn, she looked at the colours and patterns of the curtains; if the curtains were open, she looked at the furniture, lighting and ornaments inside, as well as any figures that might be moving around in the living rooms and bedrooms. Liu Sheng, on the other hand, was only interested in the different types of car parked in the garages and on the roadside: Merc! Beamer! He announced the makes to her as they walked along, pronouncing each name with a sigh:

"Shit! Another big Merc! And a Land Rover! What the fuck is that? Is it a Cayenne?"

She wasn't overimpressed by this, and said disdainfully:

"You really don't get out much, do you! What's so amazing about those cars? I rode in a Lamborghini in Shenzhen. It cost millions. It wasn't very comfortable, either; really cramped, and I threw up when I got out."

Their steps became a bit more hesitant as they arrived at Mr Pang's villa. In the garden, European and Chinese roses were in full bloom, in brilliant purples and reds; there was a swing seat on the lawn on which a lightweight green blanket was thrown carelessly over a book. The iron gate was open and a gardener was weeding the lawn. He told them that Mr Pang had taken his wife to church for the Sunday service and there was no one home. Fairy Princess looked at the white blinds, then at the garden terrace, and said to Liu Sheng:

"Well then, we'll wait on the terrace."

She picked up the book from the blanket on her way past and carried it up to the terrace. It was crudely bound, as though it was a proof copy, and the title, in traditional characters, was also rather odd: *How To Redeem a Lost Soul Before God*. On the terrace there were a parasol, a table and some chairs, and on the table were a vase of fresh flowers and a purple clay tea set, some tea still in two of the teacups. She picked up one of the cups and sniffed it:

"Dongting Oolong, and still fresh."

"Shit!" Liu Sheng said. "Tea on the terrace every day, watching the world go by! That's the life!"

She turned the two teacups upside down on the table to empty them and sat down on one of the beach chairs. Then, for some reason, she sighed. When she opened the book, she saw that the first chapter heading was: *Your Devotion Makes God Hear Your Prayers*. A thought struck her and she asked Liu Sheng:

"Have you ever prayed?"

"What do you mean, pray? Is that the same as reciting sutras? The year before last I went to the Great Benevolence Temple to recite sutras, and last year, I went to the Great Compassion Temple; my mother wanted me to go. What a waste of time! But if reciting sutras made me live in a villa like this, I'd do it every day."

"Praying is praying, and reciting sutras is reciting sutras: they're two different things. You pray to God, and you recite sutras to a bodhisattva. God is more powerful than a bodhisattva, and a bodhisattva is ruled over by God. Don't you even know that?"

"God or bodhisattva, it's all the same to me. I make sure I'm in with the God of Wealth, he's the most powerful of all. If you don't believe me, go to the temple and see where the most incense is being burned. Then you know who's the most powerful!"

As they were talking, they saw the gardener stand up and look towards the drive. Mr Pang's car sounded its horn and Fairy Princess automatically covered her ears with her hands. Mr Pang had clearly noticed the uninvited guests on the terrace, and he looked at them as he opened the car door, then again as he got out of the driver's seat. It was a startled look, part frightened, part disgusted and, on closer inspection, with a hint of shame there too.

He took the wheelchair out of the trunk, its nickel-cadmium frame glinting in the sun. They saw him carry a woman from the car to the wheelchair, his movements deft and economical. The woman looked tiny in his arms, like a child, but seemed much bigger, once in the wheelchair. It was Mrs Pang. She was wearing a cream western-style two-piece suit; she had no make-up, and an old-fashioned hair-do. On her knees was a book with a dark-red cover, which must have been her

Bible. She looked much as Fairy Princess had imagined her, except that her face looked older than in the photograph, and yet her eyes were brighter and kinder.

Mr Pang recovered his composure quicker than she expected. He pushed the wheelchair over to the terrace, and introduced Fairy Princess to Mrs Pang in a clear, steady voice:

"This is the Miss Bai I told you about."

She realised that she was no longer a secret to Mrs Pang, and that the story that she had so carefully concocted in advance was unnecessary. It was her. It was her, and that's all there was to it. There was no need for play acting, there was no battle of wits to be fought, and no competition. The straightforwardness of the situation, however, didn't reassure her, but left her dismayed. It was as though she had got herself all dressed up for a splendid banquet, only to discover that it was being held in a public bath-house, and she had to sit in front of the other guests stark naked.

There was the smell of some unknown herbal medicine about Mrs Pang, not pleasant, but not exactly unpleasant either. She immediately looked at Mrs Pang's crippled lower limbs, but they were covered by long trousers; she was wearing cloth shoes that left the tops of her feet bare, like two pale arcs. Other than this, there was nothing remarkable about her.

"So, you must be Miss Bai." Mrs Pang took the initiative in greeting her. "You're a very beautiful girl; your reputation is quite deserved. Very beautiful indeed!"

"Not as beautiful as you." She spoke defensively, like a hedgehog curling into a ball. She felt clumsy and ill-mannered, but didn't know how to redeem herself. She flashed a look at Mr Pang, as much as to say: "My quarrel is with you, not your wife. My rudeness is your fault."

Mrs Pang shook her head, still smiling faintly. And because that smile was full of magnanimity, it felt warm and expansive, but somehow also inflexible. Mrs Pang reached out her hand to her:

"Let's get to know each other. I'm Mrs Pang."

She almost said: "I know who you are", but stopped herself from going too far, and said, instead:

"It's good to meet you. I'm Miss Bai."

Mrs Pang's hand was thin and bony, and there was a jade bracelet on her wrist. Fairy Princess held her hand gently, looking at the bracelet.

"What a beautiful bracelet! What grade is it? It must be worth hundreds of thousands."

Mrs Pang laughed faintly:

"It's nothing special; it's not *feicui* ('kingfisher' jade – the highest grade of jade). I bought it at a stall in Lijiang. It only cost fifty *yuan*. Anyway, I never wear expensive things; that's a sin."

Fairy Princess scoffed at this:

"Fine jade is a sin? Based on what? Who says so?"

Mrs Pang picked the Bible up from her knees, lifted it high, and said sternly:

"Jesus says so. Extravagance is a sin."

Before she could say anything in reply, beside her, Liu Sheng took exception to Mrs Pang's views:

"What does it matter what Jesus says? Jesus is only concerned with foreigners, not with us Chinese."

Mrs Pang looked at him, her eyes full of gentle reproach, then turned to ask Mr Pang:

"And who is this gentleman? You haven't introduced him."

Mr Pang spread his hands and shrugged:

"I don't know this gentleman. You must ask Miss Bai."

Fairy Princess could read in Mr Pang's guarded expression, his contempt for Liu Sheng and his disregard for her. She hesitated over how to introduce Liu Sheng; should he be her boyfriend or just her friend? Or should she introduce a little colour, and say he was an underworld acquaintance. But Liu Sheng couldn't wait, and thrust a business card at the couple, introducing himself:

"I'm no one special; I've just come along to right an injustice. Mr Pang, Mrs Pang, let me first ask you a question. If wearing jade is a sin, what about having your way with a young girl? Is that a sin? There are some men who have their way with a girl, knock her up, then pull up their trousers and walk away. What does Jesus have to say about that kind of thing?"

Pushing the wheelchair, Mr Pang warned his wife:

"He is blaspheming. You don't have to answer that kind of question. I'll push you inside."

"I can answer that," Mrs Pang said, stony-faced, her eyes boring into Liu Sheng. "It's a sin."

"Good! Yes, that's good that it's a sin," Liu Sheng said with satisfaction. "Tell me then, how should this sin be punished?"

"Every sin must be expiated. He must confess. He must repent and seek atonement from the Lord. He must ask the Lord to hear him, and forgive his sin."

"I have great admiration for your intelligence, Mrs Pang, but I have to tell you that the baby is in her belly, not the Lord's. How does it help Miss Bai, if the Lord forgives him?"

"The Lord comes to save you all." Mrs Pang thought for a moment, then continued earnestly: "Salvation, that's the benefit. How can salvation not be considered a benefit?"

"But if there's no benefit, how can it be considered salvation? The salvation is all for nothing." Liu Sheng leaned against the wall, his arms crossed, and his legs trembling slightly. "Let's be a bit more practical, shall we, Mrs Pang? We're talking about **mah-nee** here. Tomorrow, she's going to have an induced birth. There has to be a maintenance allowance, so how much **mah-nee** are you going to shell out?"

"Mah-nee?" Mrs Pang looked at Mr Pang in bewilderment. "What's this mah-nee he wants?"

"It's English; he means money," Mr Pang said awkwardly.

Mrs Pang's face took on a grey tinge, as she made the sign of the cross on her chest and covered the bible with her hands.

"Such filth!" she muttered to herself, looking at the two visitors with a bleak expression. Then she turned her head, and said furiously to Mr Pang: "You're filthy too! You have sinned as well! I don't want to talk to you. Just push me inside, and hurry up about it!"

She watched Mr Pang wheel her into the villa, and noticed Mrs Pang's faintly medicinal smell pass by her and disappear, trailing a refreshing sense of pureness and sanctity. There was a bang as the villa door closed.

"Hypocrites!" she heard Liu Sheng say. "See? One mention of money, and they're off. Total hypocrites!"

She bit her lip, unable to speak, but she could hear her heart thumping in her chest. She recognised that she was at fault too. The meeting with Mrs Pang hadn't been at all what she had been expecting. Why had she wanted to see her? She couldn't tell whether what she had received from Mrs Pang was an unreasonable humiliation or a justified criticism. Part of her wanted to cry, but the other part stopped her. She was going to leave, but then rebelled at the thought. She was at least going to see inside the villa before she went.

She walked resolutely towards the door of the villa. Looking through the door glass, she could see the wheelchair on the other side. It was empty, and the Bible had fallen onto the footrests, lying with its pages open. Within that short space of time, husband and wife appeared to have quarrelled over something, and her astonished gaze fell on Mrs Pang lying on the living room floor, half on her back, with Mr Pang striding back and forth across her body, facing first one way then the other, as if he was searching for something. She could just make out Mr Pang's angry voice:

"I'm not afraid of extortion, we signed a contract, we have an agreement!"

Mrs Pang's hand was waving in the air, his bracelet tracing a glistening, dark green arc, trying and failing to catch hold of Mr Pang. Her hand fell to the ground, and kept beating, incessantly, on the floorboards.

"Sinners! You are all sinners! Did you make your agreement with the Lord? You are all corrupt; beyond forgiveness; beyond salvation! The Lord cannot save you!"

She didn't dare go in. The scene inside the room distressed her, and Mrs Pang's shrill wailing drove her back. For a moment she felt dirty, genuinely dirty. She felt she had sinned, really sinned. She turned to leave the garden, but Liu Sheng followed her and held her back.

"Are you leaving? How can you think of leaving now?"

"I've had enough. I'm not fighting with a cripple."

"The woman's a cripple, but the man isn't. How can you let that Pang creature off?"

"I said I've had enough. It's not that money isn't important, but I forgive them."

Liu Sheng stared at her in amazement.

"So this trip has been a waste of time? Have you sold me out?"

She ignored him, pushed open the gate and went out. She looked back at him, and said:

"Pick me some roses to take back. I want yellow ones."

She had gone about fifty metres, leaving Liu Sheng behind, when she saw a group of uniformed security guards running towards the villa, looking as though they were spoiling for a fight. One of them was saying into his walkie-talkie:

"Security is on its way!"

Alarmed, she turned back and followed them. There was a hubbub around the door to Mr Pang's villa and, from a distance, she could see Mrs Pang's wheelchair overturned on the ground, and Liu Sheng and Mr Pang scrapping together, as though they were fighting over the wheelchair. She heard Mr Pang yelling:

"Gangster! Scum! Call yourself a man? Steal a cripple's wheelchair in broad daylight, would you?"

Liu Sheng was also shouting:

"If I'm a gangster, you're a fancy fraud! You're not a man, you're a lousy skinflint! I'm taking this wheelchair as a guarantee against Miss Bai's maintenance."

Liu Sheng hadn't gone to pick roses, he'd gone to take the wheelchair. She understood his logic but she still blushed in shame. Only Liu Sheng could think of something that mean: over-the-top and low-down at the same time. She considered going over to try and resolve matters, or help Liu Sheng extricate himself from the situation, but when she got back to the hedge, she looked over to see the movement of the villa door as Mrs Pang emerged through it, trying to pull herself up.

"Miss Bai, you've come back! We are sisters, you and I! I want to talk to you," Mrs Pang cried out, raising her head with tears glistening in her eyes. "You must believe in God, Miss Bai! Believe in God! If you carry on being depraved like this, you are surely going to hell!"

She lost her nerve and hid behind a large tree, surveying the scene. She decided to take off her high heels, and then consider her options. She stuffed the shoes into her bag, and swapped them for a pair of flat-soled shoes with no heels, which she shuffled onto her feet, then made a beeline for the gate of the compound. Behind her, she could hear the shouts of the security guards:

"Hit him! Grab him! Don't let him get away! Call the police!"

Amidst the hubbub, she could hear Liu Sheng appealing to her:

"Come back, Miss Bai! Come back and tell them I'm not stealing the chair, I'm taking it as a guarantee."

She stopped for a moment, hesitating as she turned her back on the precarious situation. In the end, however, she didn't have the guts. After dragging her feet for a few seconds, she continued her flight, alone.

TWELVE
A NIGHT TOGETHER

SOMEONE WAS KNOCKING on the door in the middle of the night. She guessed it was Liu Sheng.

She opened the garret window, and there indeed was Liu Sheng, huddling in the porch. He looked up at her.

"I pulled a few strings, and I've just been released from the local police station. They reckon it's a civil matter." He flashed a victory sign at her. "They released me without charge; I'm in the clear."

"That's good. I owe you an apology today." She started off contrite, but immediately switched to criticising him. "What are you thinking of, coming here and kicking up a racket in the middle of the night? Go home and come back tomorrow. We'll talk about it then."

"I can't go home," he said in a low voice. "My mother's furious with me, and won't let me in. Can I spend the night here?"

She gave a hollow laugh:

"Fuck off!"

She closed the window and turned off the light. Then she thought again, and reopened the window:

"A grown man like you, and you can't spend the night where you want? Do you think it's reasonable for you to spend the night here?

When your mother hears about it, she'll be calling me a bicycle again tomorrow!"

"It was her idea I should come here."

"Your mother hates me, and she's doing it out of spite. What's the point of her telling you to come here? I didn't say you could! Go home and ask your mother if she thinks I'm running a brothel here, where people can come and go as they like in the middle of the night?"

In the street, Liu Sheng fell silent for a moment, then muttered:

"That's not fair. Women are never fair."

He strode furiously out into the street, looking back at the garret window.

"You just get worse," he said. "I know what you're like, you never give anything back. You have no conscience, no conscience at all."

She could see his disappointed expression in the glow of the streetlights: his pale face and straggly beard, heroic and haggard at the same time, gave him a peculiar kind of sex appeal.

"My conscience was swallowed up long ago. Have you only just discovered that?"

But, even as she returned fire at him, pity suddenly got the better of her:

"Alright, alright!" she said, rapping on the windowsill. "If I'm a bicycle, I'm a bicycle. Open the door for yourself."

She wrapped the keys carefully in a cloth and threw them out of the garret window so they landed on the street with a dull thud, just where she had aimed them. As she did so, before closing the window, she looked around at the darkened windows of the neighbouring houses, dimly aware of the hidden eyes and ears.

"Gossip away as much as you like tomorrow; I lost my reputation long ago, so it's all the same to me."

She didn't want to come down from the attic, and told Liu Sheng to go into the kitchen and make himself a bowl of instant noodles, then to set himself up in the main room downstairs. He washed himself in cold water in the courtyard, then went back inside and asked:

"Do you know where Baorun's clothes are?"

"There are some men's clothes in the wardrobe in the main room. I don't know whose they are. Look for yourself."

He went into the main room and opened the doors and drawers of the ancient wardrobe. A succession of creaks and groans drifted upstairs, accompanied by Liu Sheng's grumblings:

"How can I wear these tatty old trousers? They must be his father's or his grandfather's: either a dead man's or a madman's anyway. Can I come upstairs to look for a pair of Baorun's trousers?"

"No, you're not allowed upstairs, and I don't have any of his trousers here. Stop worrying about who's dead or alive, you'll just have to make do with those."

She carefully placed a cardboard box at the top of the stairs as a symbolic barrier. Then she put out the light, Liu Sheng did the same downstairs, and all went quiet. It was a strange kind of night, with her asleep in the garret, him asleep downstairs, and them both asleep in Baorun's house. It seemed weird to her that she and Liu Sheng should end up sleeping under Baorun's roof. For no reason, she remembered that sky-blue wire rabbit cage, and the two rabbits she had cared for. Liu Sheng and her, the two of them, were like those two rabbits, one white, one grey, asleep now in Baorun's cage.

She slept fitfully, vaguely aware that the old smell of Baorun had seeped back into the building: the greasy hair, the unwashed socks, and the sour smell of overactive sweat glands, all of Baorun's odours had returned. They surrounded her, asking sly questions of her: How are you? How are you doing?

As dawn was breaking, she was startled awake by a noise on the stairs. Liu Sheng's footsteps feeling their way up the wooden staircase, cautiously at first, then suddenly more bold until, with a crash, the silhouette of a big, rough man was standing at the top of the stairs.

She sat up in bed, and shouted fiercely at Liu Sheng's black outline:

"What's this? Are you going to rape me again?"

The black figure gave a start, and stood there without moving.

"Don't say that. That's not what I'm after. Your belly's so big now, only an animal would do that."

The figure stepped over the cardboard box, and Liu Sheng said:

"I'm bored out of my mind, and I can't sleep. I just wanted to have a chat."

"Alright, I'll keep you company, but you've got to stand over there."

She turned on the light and picked up a pair of scissors.

"Go on then, what do you want to talk about?"

Liu Sheng sat on the cardboard box, scratching his head:

"There's so much to say, I don't know where to begin. Let's start with the past, I suppose. That… that… that… that business in the water tower. You must know I'm a good man at heart, a good man. After all these years, I've never understood how I could have done that to you. Everyone said I'd lost my soul, that my soul had left my body. It had happened to a lot of people on our street that year, hadn't it?"

"I know, I don't blame you for raping me, I do blame you for losing your soul. But you've got it back now, haven't you?"

"Now? Things are a bit complicated now. When you weren't here, my soul was, but now you're back, it's gone again."

"What do you mean? Do you think I'm a ghost that's stolen your soul? That's the kind of thing your mother would say. What's it doing coming out of your mouth?"

"No, no, it's not the same at all. My mother is superstitious, and she blames you, but I don't."

Liu Sheng looked all around him, until his eye finally came to rest on the electric light.

"That light is burning my eyes. It's making me uncomfortable. Can you turn it off? There are a few more things I want to say to you, then I'll go downstairs and get some sleep."

She hesitated for a moment, then turned off the light, still holding firmly onto the scissors.

"Go on then, but keep it short. Don't try and justify yourself, and no talk of love. I don't believe in anything any more, and I'm sick of all that."

"It's nothing to do with love, and I don't want to justify myself. I want to tell you what I really feel." He was desperately searching for the right words, and his voice became strangled. "It's you that I love, but it's not you. When I'm being nice to you, it's actually Fairy Princess I'm being nice to. That's what's so complicated. My family don't understand. Do you?"

She tapped the bed impatiently with the scissors, and said, severely:

"If you've got something to say, get on and say it. Stop trying to make a silk purse out of a sow's ear. Don't pretend it's more complicated than it is! If you can't get it straight, let me do it for you. Fairy Princess is me, and Miss Bai is also me. It's me who's let you get away with it all these years. You've got a guilty conscience, and you feel you owe me, and that's it. What's so hard to understand about that?"

"No, it's more complicated than that. It's not a question of guilty conscience or debt. It's not that simple." He hesitated for a moment, his eyes glinting with sincerity in the dark. "Can you admit that, in all these circumstances, I'm not really a bad fellow? Do you know why I've never married? I'll tell you the truth. Over the years, I've slept with a lot of women, a lot of beautiful women, even more beautiful than you. But I always felt that none of them were as pure as Fairy Princess, none of them were as exciting or as sexy as Fairy Princess. I don't know what demon possessed me, but I lost interest as soon as I'd slept with them. Can you help me understand why this is?"

He was talking to her about Fairy Princess as though he was not talking about her, as though he was talking about someone else. As she sat motionless in the dark, the dull ache in her heart gradually became sharper. She ground her teeth and hurled the scissors at Liu Sheng.

"I'll tell you why, you scum! Because she was tied up! Because she was a virgin! Because she was only fifteen! Because you men are all rapists. Fuck off back downstairs, rapist!"

He dodged the flying scissors and stood up dejectedly.

"Calm down, calm down. If I'd known that was how you felt, I wouldn't have come up to talk to you. Everyone always says, let bygones be bygones, so why the fuck can't I do that with this?"

He stopped at the top of the stairs, and looked back, crushed by regrets:

"It's a bore, isn't it! I think of you as my best friend, and you think of me as a criminal."

It was already light, and the milkman was passing along the street, ringing his bell. She tossed and turned restlessly upstairs, and she could hear Liu Sheng snoring down below. That one unsuccessful conversation had reawakened all her anguish, but had seemingly been good enough to settle his mind. Agitated, she banged on the floorboards with a plastic sandal.

"One minute you're spilling your heart out and the next, you're snoring away like a pig. Is that what you are? A pig?"

"A pig couldn't be more tired than I am!" A voice floated up from downstairs. "I won't snore; I'll try sleeping on my side."

Perhaps he really was that tired, because he didn't seem able to maintain his sleeping position, and promptly started snoring again. She still had the plastic sandal in her hand, but couldn't bring herself to bang on the floor again. She just had to endure it. Endurance is a kind of chemical process, which produces a very unexpected result. Gradually the sound of the snoring seemed to change into a lullaby, a kind of background music whose every note was urging her:

"Go to sleep. You can go to sleep safely now. I'm keeping you company downstairs. I'm keeping you company."

It was after daybreak when she began to feel sleepy. The kitchen tap was dripping and the sound gave her a feeling of serenity. And behind the serenity, there was an indefinable sweetness. That was it, sweetness. After the night, daytime was sweet. She began to savour the daylight. Time is a strange thing. Time conjured up the rabbit cage of her youth, creating a sky-blue cage which she was trapped inside like a rabbit. There was someone with her, trapped in the cage too. But for the moment she couldn't recognise who it was who was keeping her company. In the dawn light in the garret, she could dimly make out the figure of Baorun. He was roaming back and forth, up and down the stairs, his sad, innocent eyes surveying them, and protecting them. She dreamed intermittently. Dreams are strange things. Baorun was not in her dream, nor was Liu Sheng. But Grandfather was. She dreamed she could see Grandfather sitting on the roof, bound from head to toe, his face covered in tears. His eyes were those of a nightjar, gloomy and full of sorrow.

"I've lost my soul, and I don't know where it's gone. Have you seen a ray of light, little girl? A little girl stole my soul. Was it you? Was it you who stole my soul, little girl?"

She slept until after nine, when she made her way leisurely downstairs. She heard Liu Sheng out in the courtyard, saying:

"I've made a pot of congee. Eat it while it's hot. I'm hanging the washing out, yours and mine; everything's clean."

She glanced out into the courtyard, and asked:

"Why haven't you left yet?"

The question seemed to catch Liu Sheng off guard. He hung a purple pleated skirt of hers up on a bamboo pole, and put his head on one side to admire his work as he fixed it in place with two pegs.

"That's a pretty skirt," he said.

The stove was still alight with a low flame, and the pot of congee was giving off a fragrant odour of fresh rice. There were salted duck eggs cut up on the table, along with a dish of pickled vegetable shreds. She sat down to have some congee, and suddenly felt that this morning was particularly fine. Everything was good between her and Liu Sheng. They weren't in love, they weren't married, they weren't even going out, but there seemed to be an unspoken connection between them, like that of an old married couple. He was hanging out the washing in the yard, and she was eating congee in the kitchen. Munching on a mouthful of pickled vegetables, she said:

"It's comical, really comical."

How could it not be comical? It was the scene of family life she had imagined so often. In her mind, this was the minimum happiness a woman should expect. She had thought the horse trainer, Qu Ying, might give it to her; she had thought Mr Pang might give it to her. She had met a good number of sincere men, and she asked them all the same question:

"Will you make me congee one day?"

They all promised solemnly that they would but, when it came down to it, they all disappeared without trace. The man who ended up making her breakfast and washing her clothes was none other than Liu Sheng. How could that not be comical?

She wanted another bowl of congee and was just standing up when she suddenly felt the foetus in her womb move. It kicked her once, lightly, then moved to the other side of her womb, and kicked her again, a little harder this time. She saw her nightdress move slightly. It was like magic. She sat back down, and said:

"Well that's funny! I didn't know you could move."

Liu Sheng came into the kitchen, and saw her staring blankly at the bowl in her hand.

"What's up? Don't you like congee?" he asked.

"It's not the congee. It's the baby. It's alive. It can move."

"You can't see it; how do you know it moved?"

She put down her bowl, put her hand to her belly, and followed the line of the baby's mischievous foot.

"It's in my belly; if I don't know, who does? This is its little foot, its little foot that's kicking me."

This pleasant surprise continued for several minutes then, as the foetus calmed down, so did she. She looked very solemn as she asked Liu Sheng:

"I'm only in my fifth or sixth month, how can it kick like that? I hope it's not some kind of monster."

Liu Sheng winked at her, and said:

"That rather depends on whether the father's one, doesn't it!"

"I'm worried to death, so please be serious."

Liu Sheng immediately adopted a solemn expression:

"I'm being serious. I'm talking about genes and heredity. Do you know Dong Feng? Dong Feng's father has six fingers on his left hand, and Dong Feng has the same. Then there's Ah Liu: Ah Liu's dad has a Roman nose, and so does Ah Liu. Their two noses are identical."

"What about you, then? What are your genes and heredity like? If you have a son, will he be a rapist too?"

Liu Sheng choked with embarrassment, and didn't say any more. She looked down, and ran her fingers over her bump. Her fingers began to tremble as the baby moved again.

"I'm scared," she said. "Did you hear what that nurse said. If I go to the hospital the day after tomorrow, it won't be for an operation, it will be for a murder."

Liu Sheng clapped his hand over his mouth, to indicate he had nothing to say. But when he saw her persistent expression, he spread the fingers of his hand, and said:

"Don't look at me like that. It's not my baby. It's up to the mother and father, and if the father's a devil, but the mother's human, then it's up to her."

"I'm confused. What if I ask you to decide?"

"I wouldn't dare decide for you. Everything I do is wrong, and you don't put trust me. Whatever I decide, it would end up cursed."

She gave him a peculiar look, and went back to her congee. The television was on in the living room, showing a recording of a League A match. There was some ecstatic chanting from the crowd: Goal! Goal! A goal at long last!

"What a racket!" she said. "It's only people like you who want to watch Chinese football. Turn it off. Now it's my turn to talk to you."

Hesitantly, Liu Sheng hurried over to turn the TV off. When he came back and saw her expression, he suddenly felt very nervous.

"Do we have to be so serious when we talk? Why don't you take it a bit easier? You're eating for two now. Is the congee enough? I can go and buy you some *baozi* (steamed buns or dumplings) if you want."

He wanted to escape but she dragged him back to his chair.

"Sit down there, I want to ask your advice about something." She looked him straight in the face, her eyes glinting. "Everyone says I'm a bicycle. Do you think I am?"

"Is that what you want my advice on?" He laughed mockingly. "If you're a bicycle, then I'm a cyclist! Hahahaha!"

"A good answer!" He couldn't tell whether her expression was angry or serious. She ran a trembling finger round the rim of her bowl. "If I'm a bicycle, and you're a cyclist, then we make a good match, don't we!" Then she went on abruptly: "Now listen carefully, I want to ask you my next question. Do you want to ride my bicycle?"

Liu Sheng sat rooted to his chair, blushing furiously. He waved his hands in denial, saying:

"That was just a joke, Miss Bai. You mustn't take it seriously."

"You may not take it seriously, but I do," she said. "I'm quite resigned. There's no bright future waiting for me, and as far as I can see, I have two possible routes: one, I have the baby, and it can keep me company. But it's the other route I want to ask you about. If I get rid of the baby, will you still keep me company?"

"Keep you company? What does that mean?" He banged his head on the kitchen cupboard, making the pots and pans inside rattle. He put his hand to the top of his head and looked at her shyly. "Do you mean keep you company as a husband or a lover?"

He hesitated, licking his lips nervously, as a shy smile flitted across them:

"I'm not right for a husband, I'd rather be your lover."

The atmosphere in the kitchen froze into stillness. She felt suffocated. She found herself about to start sobbing, as tears gathered in her eyes. She put her head in her arms on the table, so Liu Sheng couldn't see her face.

"Well done, Liu Sheng! This time I think I can see everything clearly." Her head still down on the table, she began to laugh. "It's funny, really funny! Fresh flowers grow out of manure, but it's the manure that disdains the flowers. The girl wants to marry her rapist, but her rapist spurns her, saying she's unclean, saying she's a bicycle."

She kept laughing for a while, but finally calmed down. She tapped Liu Sheng on the nose with a chopstick:

"I fooled you! But I've found out your true feelings. Did you think I was serious? What makes you think you could be my lover? You're not fit to be my dog. Now fuck off!"

Liu Sheng moved over to her to try to give her some kind of minimal comfort. He made to pat her on the shoulders, and twice lifted his hands to do so, before finally, prudently, letting them drop. From the corner of her eye, she could see him slowly moving away. Standing in the kitchen door, he said:

"You shouldn't let emotion cloud your decisions; try to calm down a bit. Chungeng called me: we're going to the car market today."

She didn't look up. She picked up her bowl of congee and slurped a mouthful. Liu Sheng's footsteps stopped again at the front door.

"Chungeng's shouting for me," he said in a loud voice. "The car insurance paid out, and we're going to look at vans. If I don't have a van, I don't have a business. I'm going to buy a Jin Bei from Shenyang."

THIRTEEN
LIU SHENG'S WEDDING

She made her choice, and prepared to become a mother.

Having made this difficult decision, her restlessness and irritability settled down considerably.

She began to go out more, carrying a parasol to visit the shopping mall. She still loved shopping, and as long as she had money in her purse, she could spend the whole day there without tiring. Skirts, jewellery, nail varnish, mascara: these were the things she used to covet; but now, her former interest had waned, and when she went to the mall, her focus was more pragmatic, and centred on the maternity and baby goods. She was so heavily pregnant, there was no point in trying to doll herself up and as she had nothing else to do, combing the mall for things for the baby gave her otherwise empty time a sense of purpose.

She wanted to buy a good-quality baby buggy, but her desire for quality was constrained by her lack of money. Look as she might, either the build wasn't good enough, or the price was too high. She complained to the sales staff, and moved on to the clothes department; but wherever she looked she remained unsatisfied. Finally, on the shelves, she saw a little sun-hat decorated with multi-coloured flowers, at an affordable price. Perversely, there was another pregnant woman, head on one side, studying the same hat. She hurried over and snatched it off the shelf. She took it over to the salesgirl, and asked:

"Is this hat for a girl baby? Could a boy baby wear it?"

The salesgirl replied:

"It's fine for either. With baby clothes, all that matters is that it's pretty. Are you expecting a boy or a girl?"

She gave a start, and said:

"I don't know yet, and I don't want to know. I'll buy it anyway and see."

She was taking the hat over to the cashier, when a woman pushed across her path, and stood blocking the till, sweating profusely. She never had much time for people like that, and gave her a shove.

"In a hurry are we? Got a busy day? There are only two of us, and you still have to jump the queue?"

The woman turned to look at her, and reached out a hand:

"Give me the little hat; I'll buy it."

Fairy Princess gave a start as she recognised Liu Sheng's mother, Shao Lanying. She took a couple of stunned backwards steps, and hid the hat behind her back.

"Give me the hat, then I can give it as a present to my little grandson." There was an overly enthusiastic smile on Shao Lanying's face. "Don't look at me like that. I'm not your enemy. You're my adopted daughter, remember? It's only right that I should buy the little baby this hat, isn't it?"

"Are you following me?" She glared balefully at Shao Lanying. "What for? I've already made a clean break from your baby boy, so what reason do you have for following me?"

"What kind of talk is that? You're not an American secret agent! Who would be following you?" She pointed at the up-escalator. "I was on my way up to the fifth floor to buy some bedding, and I happened to see you. I don't usually come into fancy places like this, but there was nothing for it this time. I'm fixing up a bridal chamber: my Liu Sheng is marrying Xiao Li."

Fairy Princess stared at her in amazement, but she quickly recovered herself and said, acidly:

"What Xiao Li? Is it a girl?"

Shao Lanying rolled her eyes, as if to say she wasn't going to argue.

"You've met Xiao Li, haven't you? She's really pretty!" she said with extraordinary pride. "She's not just pretty, she knows her place, and is very dutiful. She's a civil servant."

Fairy Princess didn't know who Xiao Li was, nor had she expected Liu Sheng to get married so quickly. It was clear to her that Shao Lanying had come to the mall specially to tell her this news because there was a sparkle in her eyes that spoke of pleasure, satisfaction, happiness and relief. It was like the fireworks at a victory parade, and each glittering burst that she saw in Shao Lanying's eyes, said to her:

"The exorcism has worked. You've been driven out, you troublesome demon. My son, Liu Sheng, has been saved."

Although she felt she had been stabbed in the heart, she kept an aloof smile on her face.

"Marriage? Xiao Li? That all sounds good," she said. Then she suddenly thrust the baby hat at Shao Lanying. "If they're getting married, you'll have a grandson soon. Buy this hat for him."

She swore to herself she would never see Liu Sheng again, and Liu Sheng tactfully stayed away from her front door. As for the news of his sudden wedding, she didn't have any opportunity to check whether it was true or not. Normally, information like that coming from a mother would be reliable, but Liu Sheng's mother was Shao Lanying, and Shao Lanying was full of tricks. She couldn't help thinking this was one of them. Self-respect prevented her from trying to ferret out the truth about it, but she did take to making frequent trips to Madam Ma's pharmacy next door, to listen to what was being said. She ended up with a whole heap of medicines that she didn't need, but the money was wasted, as she never asked the one question she needed to ask. The matter stayed floating around inside her head, like a sampan adrift on the river, rocking and swaying until, one day, a brand new Jin Bei van pulled up on the other side of the street. Liu Sheng had arrived with his bride-to-be.

Liu Sheng sounded his horn, and she knew he was sounding it for her. She stood helpless for a moment, then ran upstairs to look out of the garret window. She saw Liu Sheng getting out of the van, dressed in a western suit and leather shoes, and going to stand in the doorway of the pharmacy. It was still the same old Liu Sheng, but a little different. His hair was freshly permed, and he was shimmying from foot to foot as he smoked a cigarette. He was chatting to Xiao Ma from the pharmacy, and looked flushed with pride. The new van was a silver-grey colour, and there was a young woman she didn't recognise, sitting in the passenger seat. Her skin was quite dark, and her features fine enough. Her hair was freshly permed too, and piled up in a way that made her look older than she was. She was leaning out of the van window, and Fairy Princess noticed her penetrating gaze, alight with inquisitiveness, moving upwards and upwards, hither and thither, prying and spying, towards her window.

After the van had left, she found a wedding invitation that had been slipped under her front door. Some characters had been added in Liu Sheng's untidy hand: *Can I trouble you to come and sing a few songs? There will be a red envelope.* Not knowing whether to laugh or cry, she examined the invitation for any information about the bride, but found nothing, except that her given name was Xiaoli, and her full name was Cui Xiaoli. Liu Sheng had never mentioned any Cui Xiaoli, but Fairy Princess had the distinct feeling that Cui Xiaoli knew her.

Not just on Red Toon Street, but all over the country, the eighth day of the eighth lunar month was the most popular day for getting married. Everyone loved that date.

Liu Sheng got married on the eighth day of the eighth lunar month. She had no desire to go to congratulate Liu Sheng, nor was she interested in singing any celebratory songs at the wedding party, but she kept worrying away at the date: the eighth day of the eighth lunar month. How was she going to get through the minutes and seconds of that day? How was she going to make it pass more easily? She had the romantic idea of holding a party at the Paris Nights, of asking some others to sing songs for her, to dance for her, to lay out roses and open champagne. She could pass the day in noisy celebration like that. But who would pay for this lovely idea? She knew she was embarrassingly short of money, so she had to shelve that plan, and tailor her fun to what she could actually afford. Accordingly, she wrote out a schedule for the eighth day of the eighth lunar month: have a make-over at the Lirenxing beauty parlour; go to Haägen Dazs for an ice cream; go to a jade merchant and buy a cheap trinket; go to the Western Steakhouse for a steak. Finally, she reminded herself, she must buy herself a bottle of Poison perfume. If she could go home wearing Poison as her perfume, the day would be perfect.

Quite a few families on Red Toon Street were holding weddings on the eighth day of the eighth lunar month, and there was an air of competition swirling around. In Lotus Lane on the other side of the river, a girl was leaving her home to get married, and an ear-splitting barrage of firecrackers had been rending the air since early morning. Fairy Princess was doing her make-up to the noise of the firecrackers, when she heard the sound of an explosion on her roof. Something had fallen onto the tiles and, very soon, the air was filled with the smell of burning saltpetre. She ran out into the courtyard to look, and saw that some family's firework had flown onto the roof, and was lying there, still smouldering. She was worried that a piece of bituminous felt on the roof under the tiles might catch fire, so she found the bamboo pole she used to hang out the washing, climbed on a chair, and knocked the firework down. When she began sweeping up the debris with a dustpan and brush, she discovered that, as well as the bright red remains of the firework, there was also a flashlight, quietly lying in a corner of the yard.

It was a heavy, old-fashioned metal flashlight, its tubular body already dark with rust; its glass and bulb were broken, it was coated in mud from which, miraculously, sprouted a tuft of grass. She swept it away at first, and it rolled away, rather belligerently, and soon came to rest. It was very heavy, and its tube seemed to be filled with some kind of alien matter. She was intrigued and, with considerable effort, managed to unscrew its lid. A noxious smell filled her nostrils, and she saw a lump of earth, which had congealed over time, stuffed into the narrow tube. Sticking out of the mud were two bones which were crawling with a knot of little grey insects.

She cried out in disgust, and dropped the flashlight. Her stomach turned over, and she retched a couple of times. A strange flashlight that had appeared in an even stranger fashion. She looked carefully all around to try and see where it had come from. She thought it must have fallen into the courtyard from the roof, and might have come down with the firework. But what was it doing there in the first place? Why was it filled with earth and bones? Why had its fall coincided with the fireworks that filled the sky on the eighth day of the eighth lunar month? She wasn't in the mood to linger over these questions, so she held her breath, wrapped the flashlight in a cloth, and threw it with all her strength over the wall. She heard it rolling down the abandoned stone steps, then there was a plop as that grotesque, nauseating torch, must have fallen into the water.

Full of suspicion, she washed her hands three times and went next door to the pharmacy with a sullen expression on her face. There she asked Mother Ma whether she had thrown a flashlight into her courtyard. At first, Mother Ma didn't understand what she was on about, but she gradually caught on, and her eyes lit up. She gave a cry of alarm, and exclaimed:

"And you threw it away? Baorun's grandfather has been looking for it for more than ten years! His family doesn't have its ancestral tombs anymore, and all that's left of them are those two bones. You didn't throw away a flashlight, you threw away their ancestors. You're responsible for this catastrophe, and you're the one complaining and making a foul-mouthed fuss? Go and fish it back up immediately!"

Fairy Princess had heard Grandfather's story and she was shocked but also determined not to show any sign of weakness.

"I'm not going to fish it up! It wasn't me who threw it into my yard! It was disgusting, and I had every right to throw it away!"

Just before noon on the eighth day of the eighth lunar month, Baorun came knocking on the front door.

He was dressed western style, in a suit and tie, clearly in preparation for a wedding banquet. He stood by the door asking if what Mother Ma had told him was true. He didn't dare look at her, but kept his eyes fixed on the door frame as he said:

"I hear you found my granddad's flashlight."

"I didn't find it, it fell down from the roof."

He kept looking at the door frame.

"I hear you threw it into the river."

She lost her nerve a little, and tried to regain the initiative:

"That flashlight was disgusting; there were bones and insects inside it. Where else was I going to throw it?"

He fell silent for a moment, but there was no sign of anger on his face.

"Is it alright if I come in. I want to go down to the river to have a look. Can I take a shortcut through the yard?"

She opened the door, beginning to feel the situation was more serious than she had thought, but that his attitude was also friendlier than she might have anticipated. She followed on behind him, attempting to justify herself:

"It's not my fault. How was I to know your granddad's soul was in that flashlight? How was I to know his soul was hidden in the roof?"

Baorun made his way down the narrow alley, an indifferent expression on his face.

"I don't blame you. It's just a few bones. Superstitious nonsense, made up to trick people. My granddad's soul flew away long ago; how could anyone call it back?"

She found Baorun's reasonableness rather gratifying, and she nodded in agreement.

"That's right. Your granddad's a weirdo. If they were his ancestors' bones, why didn't he bury them properly? Why did he put them up in the roof?"

Baorun seemed equally puzzled:

"I don't know either. He used to say he'd buried them under a holly tree, so how did they come to be falling down from the roof? It's spooky!" He thought for a moment, and said with great sincerity: "My granddad's not a weirdo, but he had all his courage scared out of him, and his soul was frightened away too. The ancestors probably didn't trust him any more, and went away themselves. When it comes down to it, up in the roof was probably safer than buried in the ground, don't you think?"

The courtyard backed onto the river, but the little gate that led to the riverside had long ago jammed shut. Baorun went next door to the pharmacy to borrow a ladder, and climbed over the wall onto the little stone landing stage. Leaning slightly forwards, she gingerly climbed the ladder to see how Baorun was going to fish up his grandfather's soul. Because she felt to some degree responsible, she shouted instructions to Baorun from the top of the ladder:

"That way a little, towards the rock. A bit further out."

Baorun went under the water several times, but each time came up without success. He brought up a grindstone, a small blue-and-white porcelain bowl, but mostly several handfuls of black river mud. She couldn't make up for her mistake; the river had carried the flashlight away, no one could tell where. People came down from Lotus Lane on the other side of the river, to see what all the fuss was about.

"Who's that there? What are you dredging up from the river?"

"We're fishing for a flashlight," she replied on behalf of Baorun.

"What's in the flashlight? Is it gold?"

"Do you think anyone would have thrown it in the river if there was gold? No, it's just a couple of bones. Do you want to help?"

The rubberneckers from Lotus Lane soon dispersed. Baorun climbed out of the water and sat down on the landing stage, dripping wet from head to toe, to catch his breath. She threw him a towel, and Baorun nodded to her. He seemed unable to say thank you, but there was gratitude in his eyes. He was naked from the waist up, tanned and brawny, and a wet patch on his shoulder glinted like a piece of silver jewellery. She watched the water flow slowly down his upper arms and dry out. The sunlight lit up some tattoos on his arms: one on each arm, the one on the left read 'man of honour', and the one on the right, 'vengeance'.

This was the first time she had seen Baorun naked, and she hadn't known he had such arresting tattoos on his arms. They were like dark blue flames, blazing out from his skin. **Man of honour. Vengeance.** Wasn't ten years too late for a man of honour to seek vengeance? But ten years was now, and now wasn't too late. Who did the man of honour want to take vengeance on? It was as if she had seen an arrest order, an arrest order on which she could dimly make out her name. Suddenly she had trouble breathing, and her legs went weak. Hurriedly, she climbed down from the ladder.

She wasn't afraid of men with tattoos, but Baorun's tattoos filled her with dread. **Man of honour. Vengeance.** As she recalled the characters, she heard in her ear, the whispering sound of rope crawling round her skin, and she felt a subtle but piercing pain shoot through her body from her shoulders to her waist. It was the pain of the rope tightening around her skin. She ran headlong back into the house, to find the cardboard box at the bottom of the stairs. She took all the ropes out of it, and carried them up to the garret. But taking them up there was no use: it was still his house, and there was nowhere to hide them that would be safe. Thinking fast, she found a pair of scissors and began furiously to cut up the ropes. It wasn't easy work, but she gritted her teeth, and exerted all her strength. Only when a portion of the ropes was cut up into lengths so short they couldn't be used to tie anything, did she stop, but there were still a number of lengths of nylon rope of peculiar strength that she couldn't cut no matter how hard she tried. She was getting exasperated when she heard a noise in the courtyard. Baorun had given up on the fishing and come back into the house.

No doubt he was thinking of Liu Sheng's wedding when he shouted up from downstairs:

"What time is it?"

She hurriedly stuffed the lengths of rope under the bed:

"It's late; it's after one already."

"Yes, it's late. I'm going to stop searching. At two o'clock, I've got to help Liu Sheng fetch his new wife."

"You'd better get a move on. It's not good to be late collecting a new wife."

She waited for him, holding her breath, but he obstinately stopped at the bottom of the stairs.

"Can you come down for a minute, Miss Bai?"

Her scalp crawled as she said, automatically:

"What for? What do you want me downstairs for?"

He was silent for a few seconds, then said:

"I've got a water lily, but if you don't want it, that's fine."

She looked down the stairs, and saw his sun-tanned hand holding a water lily.

"I don't know where a lily could have drifted in from. Don't you like flowers?"

"Of course I do!"

But she stayed rooted to the spot where she was, not willing to risk going down, but shooting furtive glances at his arms. His body glistened as though it had been glazed with old bronze. The towel was carefully draped over his right arm, so she could only see the '**Man of honour**' tattoo on his left. She still didn't go downstairs. He seemed a little embarrassed, and a little disappointed. He put the flower down on the table as he walked past it.

"It's just a water lily; if you like it, keep it, if you don't, throw it out."

She went downstairs with the scissors, and picked up the half-opened red water lily. For some reason, it made her think of the light of the setting sun in the water tower all those years ago. She carried the flower into the kitchen and found a large soup bowl which she filled with water. She dropped the water lily into it, so it floated, half-open, half-closed, as though it was about to say something, but had changed its mind. Through the kitchen window, she could see Baorun, his underpants in one hand, his suit in the other, making his way towards his parents' bedroom. He called out:

"I'm sorry, I've got to get changed."

She heard him open the bedroom door, then there was a creak, as he locked it from inside. She relaxed, and gently shook the lily in its soup bowl. She called out:

"Are you going to come back to search some more? To look for your granddad's soul?"

"No, it's too tricky." Inside the room, he hesitated for a moment, then went on: "I'm just not going to look any more. My granddad's soul isn't worth anything, and it's better off at the bottom of the river."

That was what she had hoped to hear, but she didn't want to say so.

"Are you sure you're quite happy leaving your granddad's soul at the bottom of the river?"

"It's for his own good." He seemed to be opening some drawers in the bedroom. "I've known for a long time why my granddad has lived so long. It's because he doesn't have a soul. He keeps on going because he doesn't have a soul, and he's at peace because he doesn't have a soul. If I insist on finding his soul, won't that just be speeding up his departure for the Western Paradise?"

She laughed, covering her mouth with her hand, and asked carefully:

"This crazy granddad of yours, who's living so long, aren't you getting tired of having to look after him?

"No. Even a crazy granddad is still a granddad. For better or worse, he's family, isn't he?"

The noise of searching came from the big bedroom, drawers being pulled out and wardrobe doors being opened. Baorun had a fit of coughing, and when it quietened down, she heard him ask abruptly:

"Where are my father's boxer shorts? The grey ones. He always kept them in the wardrobe, so why can't I find them?"

A pair of boxer shorts. A pair of dead man's boxer shorts. She remembered the details of the night Liu Sheng had stayed over, and she blurted out:

"Liu Sheng's got them; he left wearing them."

She knew immediately she had spoken too hastily, but it was too late for regrets. Everything went deathly quiet in the bedroom. Maybe five minutes passed before Baorun came out of his parents' room. He was suited and booted, and his hair was already dry, but his face was dark with a stern and severe expression. She stood despondently beside the door, hoping she could explain, and redeem her mistake. When she noticed his white tie was crooked, she saw salvation, saying:

"Why does your tie look like a fried dough twist? It doesn't look good, crooked like that."

She reached out to straighten his tie for him, but he slapped her hand away, and shouted:

"Don't touch my tie, you whore!"

It was too late for regrets. She could clearly see the tears gathering in the corners of his eyes. She watched him heading for the door. She hoped she could still explain, maybe even get him to stay for a while, but in the end, the words just wouldn't come out. In the back of her mind, she was aware that any explanation would sound just as much like her trying to make excuses. His tears frightened her. She followed him a few steps, not knowing how to say goodbye. She ended up leaning against the wall, watching him pull open the front door. She said:

"You're in a bad mood; go and have a few drinks, but don't get too drunk."

A shaft of sunlight from the street fell on Baorun's black leather shoes, making a triangle of light flash intermittently. He stood in the half-open door, looking either at his shoes or the bottoms of his trouser legs. Suddenly, he turned back to look at her, and smiled:

"You'll know tomorrow just how much I had to drink. **You just wait and see.**"

She shivered, and seemed to feel that in the street outside, with a terrible rending noise, time had begun to flow in reverse. In that instant, she heard the voice of the eighteen-year-old Baorun, and found herself looking into the eyes of the eighteen-year-old Baorun.

FOURTEEN
THE WATER IN THE COURTYARD

A STRANGE SOUND echoed around the courtyard in the middle of the night. It sounded as though someone was continuously pouring water onto the ground, splash, splash, splash, patiently following a steady rhythm. She stayed timidly upstairs for a long time, not daring to go and investigate. Instead, she shouted down into the courtyard:

"Who's there? What are you doing? I'm pregnant!"

Strangely, as soon as she shouted, the sound of splashing from the courtyard diminished, until it was just a murmur, like rainwater flowing down an overflow pipe. She didn't know whether the spirits of Red Toon Street really did leave pregnant women alone, so she switched on the light, and gripped the scissors tight, not daring to go back to sleep. But so much had happened that day, and she was so tired that, in the end, she fell into a deep sleep.

In her confused state, once again she dreamed she saw Grandfather. He was sitting on the eaves, his two stick-like legs hanging down in front of her window, the moon lighting his filthy black toes, from which water was dripping continuously. She rapped his toes with the scissors:

"What are you doing up there? Get down! Get down! If you don't, I'll cut off your toes!"

But Grandfather wasn't afraid of her scissors; he just sat there wailing:

"Give me my torch back, young girl. Why did you want to throw my soul into the river? Give me my soul back, and I'll get down."

In her dream, she remembered what Baorun had said, and she urged Grandfather:

"You don't know what's good for you: it's only because you lost your soul that you're living so long. It's better off in the river."

"I don't want to live that long; not having a soul is just suffering, and I've had a lifetime of suffering. The only hope I have is that my next life will be better. Now you've thrown my soul into the river, I'm going to come back as a fish. I've had a lifetime of suffering, and now I'm going to come back as a fish? Be a good girl, and give me my soul back!"

She was woken up by Grandfather's persistent entreaties. Emerging from her dream, she saw that the two blades of the scissors she was still holding, were glistening with water. She didn't dare close her eyes again. She remembered the story of how candidates for the imperial examinations used to stay awake to study by tying their pigtails to a roof beam, so she tied her own pony-tail to a clothes' hook on the wall, and sat bad-temperedly, waiting for daylight. All was quiet outside on Red Toon Street, and the sound of water in the courtyard had stopped; but there was a thumping noise coming from the wall that ran along the river, as though someone had failed in an attempt to climb over it, and was thumping it jerkily in vexation. Madam Ma's prediction had come true: she had caused a great catastrophe. She had disturbed the spirits. She had, indeed, disturbed the spirits in Baorun's house. Nor was the water content with its lot, as she could just make out strange noises coming form the rippling surface of the nearby river: they were clearer than the sound of the bubbles blown by the fish, and deeper than the mutterings of humans. They were mournful, depressed, poised and insistent, and, listening carefully, she was sure they were coming from the flashlight on the river bottom. She thought to herself that they were the voices of the bones of those two long-dead ancestors:

"Fish us out!

Fish us out, fish us out!

Fish us out, fish us out, fish us out!"

Only when it was light did she find the courage to go downstairs. She ran into the courtyard to look, and there was indeed a large wet area on the ground, and the top of the wall looked as though it had been underwater for several centuries. Within one night, the cracks between the bricks were full of fresh green moss. She had provoked all the generations of Baorun's family's spirits, and now they had all arrived. As she saw it, the courtyard was full of their tracks. As well as the grotesque wet patch, there was a triangular leaf stuck to the ground which, try as she might, she couldn't sweep away. When she inspected it more closely, she saw that the brown colour was actually a layer of mould. A pearl-shaped granule was stuck to one of the red bricks; she brushed it away, and the granule disappeared, but a white moth flew out from the leaves of the broom. There was also a multi-coloured pebble which stayed as wet as a sponge, no matter how she wiped it, almost sticking to her hand. She saw a miniature lizard, which she took for a replica and pushed away with her foot; it scrambled up the wall as if it was flying, and froze in position in the moss at the top. She knew the arrival of these signs was ill-omened; she had disturbed Baorun's family's ancestors, and they had come to condemn her.

She spent all morning pondering over how to expel the spirits, but she didn't have much experience in matters of this kind, and she failed to settle on any effective method. First she hung a bamboo broom on the courtyard wall, but then she began to doubt whether such a tatty old broom would be robust enough to suppress the spirits. She brought out a plaster bust of Chairman Mao from Baorun's parents' bedroom, and put it in a corner of the wall. But then she decided that was no good either: Chairman Mao had already been dead a long time, so his power must have diminished. Moreover, he might not want to help her, since a woman as degenerate as she was, certainly didn't meet his expectations for the next generation. She knew that only the bodhisattva delivered all living things from suffering, and could drive away evil spirits for certain. Unfortunately, Baorun's family didn't worship the bodhisattva and the best she could do was take off her platinum necklace, and hang that on the wall because, as luck would have it, the jade charm attached to it was in the form of a Buddha. When she had finished, she put her ear to the wall, listening carefully to the sound of the river. It seemed that none of her methods had succeeded in chasing the spirits away, as all around was still thick with the aura of the spirits, and she could hear the river constantly repeating its refrain, deep and low, but still clear: fish us out, fish us out, fish us out.

At the end of her tether, she went next door to ask advice from Mother Ma, who was not the least bit surprised by her horror story.

"I've always known it. Baorun's family's house is haunted. You threw the only two remaining bones of their ancestors into the river, without batting an eyelid. Of course they're haunting you. And, of course, you've got to fish them out of the river."

When she heard Mother Ma siding with the spirits, Fairy Princess cried out despairingly:

"Fish us out, fish us out, that's all I hear from the spirits, and now you're saying the same! Don't you have any humanity? I'm so pregnant I'm about to burst, I can't swim, and you want me to fish a flashlight out of the river. Are you trying to kill me?"

Mother Ma shot a glance at her swollen belly, and then explained on behalf of the spirits:

"The spirits were human once too. How could they be so heartless as to want a pregnant woman like you fish anything out of the river? But they're worried about your attitude. Your attitude is wrong!"

Fairy Princess reviewed her behaviour for a moment, and recognised the truth of this.

"How can I change my attitude?" she asked. "How can I make my peace with the spirits?"

Mother Ma was very experienced in this kind of thing, and she believed that relations between humans and spirits were just the same as those between neighbours: a matter of mutual respect. She told Fairy Princess that she mustn't rush into trying to get rid of them, and that the best way to get them on her side was to burn paper money.

"Ancient, modern, living and dead, everybody likes money. You must burn money, burn it every day, burn it until the spirits are satisfied. Then they'll stop bothering you."

Only half believing her, Fairy Princess said:

"But I'm just a tenant, I'm not part of the family; what chance is there the ancestors will accept my money? Supposing they hold a grudge, and take my money but still come to frighten me?"

Very sure of herself, Mother Ma replied:

"That won't happen. Don't you think the spirits adapt to changing times? Of course, I can't say for certain that today's spirits will take an outsider's money, so the only thing for you to do is to hurry up and buy some paper money. Buy a lot, burn a lot, take it step by step and see!"

She went to Lao Yan's grocery store and bought a pile of sheets of gold tinfoil.

Lao Yan suggested she buy some hell money as well:

"I've got one-hundred-thousand denomination Rmb notes, and I've also got American dollars, Japanese Yen and Euros. If the spirits get some foreign currency, they can go travelling abroad. That's bound to make them happy."

She laughed, covering her mouth with her hand, and took his advice, buying another pile of Rmb and assorted foreign currencies, and put them into a plastic bag. Unfortunately, Lao Yan's plastic bags were of very poor quality, and before she had gone very far, she heard a rending sound in her hand, as the bag split, and the gold foil and the various currencies took the opportunity to escape from the bag and scatter themselves across the ground. Without thinking she tried to kneel down, but her bump got in her way, and she found even that simple task of picking up the money, very difficult to carry out. As she was guarding the money as best she could, she asked a young lad who was passing by for help.

"Come on, do your best Lei Feng impression, and help me pick this stuff up."

The lad bent down to pick up a handful of the hell money, and his eyes widened at the huge denominations. He suddenly realised what was going on, and he threw the notes back on to the ground as if they'd scalded him.

"This is fake money! It's money for dead people! Pick it up yourself!"

She watched him disappear down the street like a puff of smoke. Annoyed, she shouted after him:

"Idiot! If it was real, do you think I would have asked you to help pick it up?"

It was a bright, cloudless day, and Red Toon Street was bathed in a clean, clear early autumn light. She didn't know whether or not the wind was that evil wind of legend, the wind that seems to rise up from the ground with a short, sharp whistling noise that belies its strength and durability. First the wind swept up the foil from the ground, and then the hell money. Futilely, she tried to catch it in mid-air, but how could she counter the strength of the wind? She watched helplessly as the gold foil notes flew away over her head, one by one. Then it was the Rmb, the US dollars and the Euros. They looked like a multi-coloured spirit army, circling in the air, before breaking off to fly away eastwards, over the roofs of the houses and disappearing from sight. All that was left was a bundle of Japanese Yen which was held together by a rubber band. Venting her anger, she gave it a kick so that it too flew away.

She was sure that the wind was just a ruse, and that the real culprits were Baorun's ancestors. The street was their ancient territory, and they knew it all by heart. They were haunting her; they were putting on a show of force. It was clear that Baorun's ancestors were vengeful ancestors, difficult to get along with. They were treacherously refusing her gifts, and that caused her bitter disappointment. Everyone was refusing her, everyone was spurning her, and even the spirits were joining in. It made her very sad.

She left empty-handed, and swiftly made her way back to her front door, where she saw a crowd of people inside the pharmacy. It was clear from their animated behaviour, that something big had happened on Red Toon Street. From inside the shop, Madam Ma saw that she had returned, her eyes lit up strangely, and Fairy Princess had a premonition that whatever that something big was, it concerned her. She didn't dare stop and listen but, equally, she didn't want to walk away, and as she hovered between the two, Madam Ma came hurrying out.

"Come over here, Miss Bai! Something really serious has happened!"

Fairy Princess turned to look at Madam Ma, but stayed in the doorway without moving.

"I know something has happened, but what and to who?"

Madam Ma came over and held her by the arm.

"Someone's dead! Yesterday evening, Baorun caused a scene in Liu Sheng's bridal chamber. He got drunk, and stabbed Liu Sheng three times. Three times!"

Fairy Princess cried out in alarm:

"But why?"

Madam Ma clicked her tongue:

"It's all very confused, and no one knows exactly why. According to Chungeng's mother, it's touch and go with Liu Sheng. His guts all spilled out, and I'm afraid he probably won't make it."

Fairy Princess stood rooted to the spot, and although her body was trembling like a leaf, she struggled to stay calm, not wanting to believe Madam Ma.

"Don't listen to their nonsense. If Baorun had wanted to stab Liu Sheng, he would have done it long ago. They're good friends now, they even share their trousers. Baorun went to the wedding banquet yesterday; he wouldn't have stabbed the groom."

"They say Baorun drank a whole bottle of *baijiu*, and his old madness came back. He got drunk and wanted to start tying people up. Sadly, his eye fell on the bride, and he chased her all over the house with his rope. People tried to persuade him to stop, but he wouldn't. Chungeng and his friends tied him up, and pushed him out into the street to sober up. But he managed to free himself, and he took a knife, and charged into the bridal chamber. Three times, I tell you, three times! They say the bridal bed was covered in blood!"

She didn't remember how she burst into sobs.

"It's not my fault, I didn't go to the wedding banquet." Still sobbing, she pushed open the door. "I didn't do anything wrong, I wasn't even there."

Mother Ma caught up with her, all concern and sorrow:

"We don't blame you. Whoever stabbed him is the criminal. Everyone understands that. But Shao Lanying has had a terrible shock, and she's not thinking straight. She's saying this was a settling of accounts, and that you incited Baorun to do it. She says that the three of you had old scores to settle, but we all knew that already. We all believe you, but the people from the other side of the street all believe Shao Lanying, and they say that you are the killer behind the curtain."

She nodded silently, the tears that she had just wiped away, flowing freely again now.

"Alright, alright, so be it!" She buried her face in her hands, and took a deep breath. "Let's say I'm the killer behind the curtain. Fuck it! I'll wait here for the police."

FIFTEEN
BREAKING THE BLOCKADE

THE WORST STORM of her life fell on her just like that, swift and violent.

First came the grievous news. That afternoon, Mother Ma came knocking on the door to tell her that Liu Sheng hadn't made it, and was gone.

Momentarily dumbfounded, she misunderstood:

"Gone? Gone where?"

Mother Ma saw that she wasn't pretending, and raised her eyes to heaven:

"Just look at that! This girl who isn't normally afraid of anything, has been scared witless!"

Fairy Princess's ears were filled with the shrill whistling of the wind, accompanied by the faint sound of something shattering, which seemed to come from her tightening chest. The storm whirled round her, then picked her up like a dead branch, and hurled her into the swirling vortex. She struggled with all her might to stay on her feet, arms spread to block the door, and fixing her eyes on Mother Ma.

"Don't talk to me about them; it has nothing to do with me."

"Why are you being so prickly? Do you think I enjoy being your messenger? It's only because you're pregnant. Anyway, it's in your interest to know what's going on with them over there."

Fairy Princess didn't give anything away to the other woman, and Mother Ma went on to ask:

"Did you know it was a shot-gun wedding? Poor Xiaoli is pregnant too; a bride one day, a widow the next."

Fairy Princess stood stunned for a moment, then turned on Madam Ma:

"What exactly are you trying to say? So she's pregnant, and now she's a widow. What's that got to do with me?"

She slammed the door shut so hard and so fast, that Madam Ma was taken unawares, and her hand got caught. She gave a yell of pain.

"You don't make it easy to like you, Miss Bai!" She gave the door a kick, and unceremoniously announced that their friendship was over: "You're the kind of girl who hurts anyone who gets close to you. No wonder everyone says you're a jinx!"

She paced to and fro behind the door. She felt as though the whirlwind out on Red Toon Street was going to come swirling in, and tear the whole house from its foundations and sweep it into a deep, dark abyss. All the decisions she had taken since her pregnancy, now revealed themselves as mistakes: this street, this house, neither had proved to be a refuge for her. She came to a decision, and ordered herself to leave this place far behind. She took herself at her word, and ran upstairs to the garret to put her things together. When she opened her suitcase, a big grey moth flew out, making her jump. She suddenly remembered the suitcase was the one Liu Sheng had bought for her, and that that moth could well have been his soul. She couldn't possibly use it. She was holding an armful of multi-coloured baby stuff, and didn't know where to put it. After a moment's confusion, she saw the folded-up baby buggy leaning against the wall in a corner of the room. Inspiration struck. She opened it up, and dumped everything in there. Substituting a baby buggy for a suitcase was a stroke of genius. As she packed her stuff in the buggy, she phoned Miss Shen Lan to tell her to get ready for her arrival. But this time, it wasn't Miss Shen Lan who picked up, but an unknown man, with a Shandong accent. She thought it must be her new boyfriend, but it turned out to be her father. He hummed and hawed, obviously unwilling to disclose her whereabouts. She introduced herself, saying:

"I'm Miss Bai. Last time you were in Shenzhen, we went to the Window on the World together, and we had a seafood barbeque. Do you remember?"

The man fell silent for a moment, then burst out angrily:

"You'll find her in rehab! What kind of friend are you? Why didn't you try to stop her taking drugs? You didn't even know she was in rehab! With friends like you, who needs enemies?"

Appalled, she said:

"I'm sorry, I didn't know. We haven't been in contact for ages. I really didn't know."

She threw down her mobile, exclaiming:

"What has happened?"

Maybe she hadn't been such a good friend to Miss Shen Lan. When did she start taking drugs? Why? She really hadn't known. She was such a nice girl. What had led her down that terrible dead-end path? She compared to herself the courses that her and Miss Shen Lan's lives had taken, and found she couldn't tell whose misfortunes had been more pitiful, the one who took white powder, or the one who had degraded herself. In the midst of her resentment she came to a conclusion that both satisfied her negativity and fed her hatred: in the end, it was degeneracy; it all fucking came down to degeneracy.

Once she had calmed down, she hurried out into the courtyard to collect the clothes that were drying there. The little jade Buddha she had used for warding off the ghosts was still hanging on the wall. She took it down as she passed, and hung it back round her neck. She patted the wall and said to the spirits hiding there:

"So I couldn't scare you, but I can get away from you! I'm off; you can have this house back to haunt as much as you like."

The old wall remained silent, as the spirits showed themselves inclined to be lenient, as if to say: "Go or stay as you please; it's all the same to us." She went back into the kitchen and had a look around, but there wasn't anything worth her while taking with her. All there was, was Baorun's water lily, still floating, in full bloom, in the soup bowl. The red flower was now half submerged, and she added some more water to the bowl, saying:

"You keep flowering, I'm off."

But she couldn't leave.

First it was a handful of pebbles thrown against the garret window, then half a brick, and finally a beer bottle came flying in with a crash, shattering the window pane. The bottle skittered across the room, rolled down the stairs, and ended up under her foot. She picked it up, and went back upstairs to stand by the window. She looked down on a shifting sea of heads of all different sizes. There was Shao Lanying, her white hair hanging loose, and her face ashen, sitting in the doorway. Someone had brought her a low wooden stool, which was only just big enough for her to sit on. Her body was gradually subsiding, as though she was about to faint, or was going to kneel down. Her daughter, Liu Juan, was supporting her. The younger woman was already wearing a white flower (a sign of mourning) in her hair.

The crowd of people surrounding Shao Lanying, including Mother Ma, all moved away when they saw her appear at the window, except for a few teenagers, who looked foolishly at her, and chanted:

"There she is! There's Miss Bai!"

She saw that Shao Lanying had her hands clasped together as though in prayer, a solemn look on her face as she muttered to herself. That wasn't a prayer, she told herself, it was surely a curse. Shao Lanying's voice was hoarse and broken, perhaps from too much crying, so Fairy Princess couldn't hear the content of the curse. But one overexcited youth took it on himself to act as a loudhailer and, hopping from foot to foot, shouted his interpretation up at the window:

"Listen up, Miss Bai! Granny Shao says that even when you were young you were a slut, and a degenerate temptress who was always seducing men!

"Listen up Miss Bai! Granny Shao says you're an evil temptress who harms the nation and brings suffering to the people, and that the bodhisattva will get rid of you for the good of the people. Granny Shao says your conscience was eaten by a dog, and that you're not fit to be human!

"Listen up, Miss Bai! Granny Shao asks why, if you're a fox demon, why don't you go and roam the mountains and forests, instead of coming to Red Toon Street and harming her son. Her only son!

"Are you listening properly, Miss Bai? Granny Shao says you're not fit to give birth, and if your child is born alive, it surely won't have an arsehole!"

There was some muffled laughter from the crowd, and she picked up the beer bottle and threw it at the lad. There was a shout of alarm down below:

"Look! Look how arrogant she is! She's even got the nerve to throw a bottle at us!"

This was followed by a hail of soft drink cans, bits of sugar cane and shards of broken glass, flying up at the window. Hands over her head, she fled the garret, and took refuge in the courtyard.

The courtyard was some way from the street, and the noisy clamour diminished somewhat. But she could still hear the anger of her neighbours drifting in through the atmosphere. It provoked the spirits in the courtyard, goading them, and making them restless. The spirits that had been so long dispersed, scrambled up from the stone pier on the river, and up the cracks in the wall. They mustered in the courtyard where, acting in the shared interests of their clan, in voices muffled by their passage down the generations, they took up their familiar war cry: fish us out, fish us out, fish us out, fish us out!

Futilely, she brandished the broom, as she saw the courtyard fill with an unearthly pale blue mist, under cover of which the spirits of Baorun's family, according to ancient military tactics, formed up in the ranks of a spectral army. Crying out their demands, they advanced upon her. It was an army come to settle accounts. She had brought death amongst men, and disturbed the spirits; now both men and spirits were coming to settle accounts. Now she understood that the roaring tempest that had been ringing in her ears for the last two days, was the mingled demands of man and spirit for their accounts to be settled.

She pushed the buggy full of her belongings over to the front door, and prepared to break her way out of the encircling crowd outside. In order to be prepared for any eventuality, she armed herself on the way with Baorun's family's fire tongs as a make-shift weapon. But she found herself unable to leave. Someone had locked and chained the door, and try as she might, she couldn't open it. Looking through the crack that did open, she saw Shao Lanying's pitiful head, a white flower now in the greying hair which hung loose around her face. Liu Juan was outside too, looking at her with red-rimmed eyes, that radiated hatred.

"Where do you think you're going? If we let you run away, then my brother will have died in vain! You are the killer behind the curtain; how can we possibly let you go? You just stay in there for me, and wait for the police to come and arrest you."

A coarse, pallid hand felt its way along the chain, and slowly infiltrated itself in through the crack in the door. She saw it climbing slowly upwards, trembling with the effort, as if it was trying to catch hold of her hair. For the moment, she wasn't sure whose hand it was, and she pinched it fiercely with the fire tongs. The hand didn't flinch in the slightest, and she immediately knew that it belonged to Shao Lanying. Unafraid, the hand grasped the fire tongs, and it was followed into view by a bloated, grey-tinged face. Twisted and decrepit behind the tongs, Shao Lanying's face was streaked with tears, which glinted with white brilliance like a salt-tinged frost.

"Fairy Princess! I'm sorry! I'm sorry! If I'd known today was coming, I would have let Liu Sheng go to prison in the first place, to pay his debt to you. Fairy Princess, Fairy Princess, I can't fight you, and I'm not going to curse you; I just want to ask you one thing. Now Liu Sheng is dead, are you satisfied?"

Fairy Princess dropped the fire tongs, tapped her foot on the ground, and said, sharply:

"I'm satisfied."

She was determined to leave. She decided that if the road was closed to her, she would take the river route. She left the baby buggy at the door, and ran over to the kitchen. She moved a table and two chairs out into the courtyard, and stacked them up beside the wall. She began to climb over the wall; she began to break the blockade. She climbed carefully to the top of the wall and looked around to find the best way past the blockade. She saw the stone landing stage, and the waters of the river. She saw the silhouettes of the people on Lotus Lane on the other side of the river, and she couldn't help feeling a little afraid. All the viable routes were to be found in the waters of the river, but she didn't know how deep the river was. Wading in water is dangerous, and she might drown. If she drowned, the baby would drown too. Her mind went blank, and she dimly heard someone on Lotus Lane shouting:

"Quick! Come and see the pregnant woman! A belly that big, and she's climbing over a wall!"

She was thrown into confusion, but she knew that if she hesitated now, she'd be putting herself on public display, so she gritted her teeth, and jumped down from the wall. She landed on her backside on the green moss of the landing stage, and the even thicker moss on the stairs cushioned her and let her slip gently down into the watery embrace of the river. It was completely unexpected, but also went without a hitch. She felt her body jolt like a train going off the rails, and heard a shrill scream from deep in her body. She didn't know whether it was the baby crying out, or whether it was her own soul.

The water was quite dirty, and there were patches of industrial oil on the surface, which glinted in the sunlight in circles of rainbow iridescence. There was no route laid out on the water, so first she headed slowly out into the middle, testing the depth. After only a few steps, the water reached her chest, so she had to abandon the route across to Lotus Lane. Instead, she retraced her steps, and followed the landing stage and the river bank. Her sandals had fallen off, she didn't know when, and mud and detritus on the river bed nibbled at her feet, a little cold, and a little sticky, but mostly very painful. She began to wonder if she was in the middle of a nightmare, and she pinched her arm. Ouch! Definitely, ouch! It wasn't a nightmare, it was reality. It was a real day in her real life, and she had to find one final road out from the river.

She passed Schoolmaster Pei's window that overlooked the river. The window was open, and Schoolmaster Pei's granddaughter was sitting beside it, doing her homework. The girl saw Fairy Princess's head moving past her and she gave a cry of surprise:

"There's a ghost! Come quickly, Grandpa, there's a water ghost in the river!"

Fairy Princess put her finger to her lips, telling the girl to keep it secret. She was making slow progress through the water, not because anyone was holding her back. What was impeding her were the bits of rubbish clinging at the base of the stone-clad river bank. A condom made her feel nauseous: it looked as though it had been freshly used, and there was a thread of something sticky at its opening. It followed her mischievously, whispering reminders of a certain mistake she had made in Europe that time: I'm very important to human lives, and if you don't treat me well, I'll make you pay a bitter price. She agitated the water to push the condom away from her, gritted her teeth, and moved on past a dozen or so more households. Finally, she saw the long-abandoned stone quay. Two fixed cranes from the 1970s still spread their long arms out over the river, watching over forgotten barges. The stone stairs of the quay were one of the escape routes she had thought of. She searched out the submerged steps, which were covered in green slime. They were too slippery to climb normally and she had to crawl up them. When she was halfway up, she heard a noise that made her jump. She looked up to see that there was a knot of people already standing on the quay.

"There she is! There's Miss Bai!"

It was a young man's voice, and Liu Juan pushed her way past the others. She was carrying a long bamboo pole of the kind used to hang out washing, but she used it to smack the surface of the water all around her:

"Back! Go back! Back into the river!" Liu Juan's normally angelic eyes, were now gleaming with fury, and focused on Fairy Princess. "Princess of death! Princess of corruption! Other people don't know you for what you are, but I do! What kind of fairy princess do you think you are? You don't know how filthy you are! Get back in the river and cleanse yourself!"

She tried to grab Liu Juan's bamboo pole, but Liu Juan pulled it away, and she couldn't get a grip on it. Liu Juan held it like the lance of a soldier in a tight defensive formation. The concrete surface of the quay was bathed in autumn sunshine as several youths standing behind Liu Juan got their first proper look at her. They saw a young woman whose body was covered in muck and green slime, a muddy moustache on her upper lip. Some of them sniggered, but others felt a sudden and unexpected compassion. One of them hurried forward to the bank of the river, and called out to her:

"Don't be so stupid, Miss Bai! Why are you trying to get out here? You could have got out at Schoolmaster Pei's place, or Tinkerbell's house. Get back in the river and find another place to break the blockade!"

She smiled at him, and was about to say something, but thought better of it. She felt as though Red Toon Street was rejecting her, as though the whole world was rejecting her. Only the water welcomed her. The river wanted her to stay with it, so she lowered her stiff arms, relaxed her knees, and the green slime on the river bed eased her gently back into the water.

She did not struggle.

She did not resist the force of the river.

Strangely, she now found herself floating on the surface of the water, following the current at the speed of a raft of rubbish, in the attitude of a dead fish. Carrying her baby inside her, and following the current. She hadn't realised that drowning was such a pleasant sensation. The sky was very blue with a few cotton wool clouds. She saw her own maroon-coloured soul, her tufty, maroon-coloured soul, drifting lazily upwards, tuft by tuft, to join those clouds. The river water was also particularly lovely: its surface was like a soft, slack conveyor belt, propelled by the wind, carrying her down with the current. The houses on the banks rolled gently past, window by window, silhouette by silhouette. On the dilapidated landing stage of the grocery shop, a neglected pot of hydrangeas, half green half red, were in full bloom; an old woman was hanging a bath mat out to dry on her windowsill, and seeing Fairy Princess in the river, took her for a swimmer:

"Don't hang around in there, the water's too old and dirty! Hurry up and get out!"

She travelled this river route smoothly and unhindered. The hand of death supported her in the guise of the water, and for its own unknown reasons, was unwilling to let go. She followed the current downstream, thinking all the time this was her last time on earth. Soon, very soon, she would sink beneath the waters, so she should seize the moment to say something to the world. There were so many things she wanted to say, but she didn't know where to start. Her ears were filled with the crazy monologue of the water, endlessly repeating Liu Juan's words: "Cleanse yourself! Cleanse yourself!" She rejected Liu Juan's malice, but accepted the water's admonishment: "Cleanse yourself! Cleanse yourself!" She calmed herself down, dipped her hands in the water, and pressed them to her belly, using the water to pacify the foetus:

"Child, let's cleanse ourselves, cleanse ourselves all over, before we die."

Her fingers felt the foetus protest, strong, crude and furious. Every inch of the taut skin of her belly transmitted the searing heat of her unborn child. Despairingly, she realised that the baby, her baby, no longer wished to stay in the belly of its disgraced mother. Gradually, the watery conveyor belt slowed down; up ahead was the Shanren Bridge, and the shape of an arch suddenly appeared. The broad path to freedom the river offered, was finally blocked. Major repairs were being carried out on the bridge, and a group of migrant workers were standing in the water, stripped to the waist, driving piles, pumping water and filling sandbags to reinforce the crumbling structure of the ancient bridge.

She dimly remembered being pulled onto the bank by some of these workers and seeing, for the first time, the broken stone tablet bearing the name 'Shanren Bridge' – the Bridge of Virtuous Men. She remembered being on the bridge, and coming down from it, and wherever she went, being followed by a wispy maroon-coloured mist. That mist was so fine and graceful and her body was so heavy and unwieldy. Her body was like a water-logged sandbag, and her unborn child wanted to burst out of that sandbag. She remembered thinking, in a moment of unusual clarity before she lost consciousness:

"I want to die. It's the baby that doesn't."

And she said to the workers:

"My baby doesn't want to die. I'm going into premature labour. Can you please send me to the maternity hospital?"

SIXTEEN
THE RED-FACED BABY

THIS CITY of ours is always short of news, so the birth of a red-faced baby made the society column of the evening paper, the entertainment channel of the TV station and even the scandal sheets sold on street stalls. Thus, many people saw the photographs of the red-faced baby, full-face and profile, one of each, in a variety of media. Fully aware of the laws regarding child protection, the editors all pixelated out the baby's features, a deed which caused their audience a predictable degree of regret, but also triggered a frenzy of research. Since autumn, it seemed as though the whole citizenship was frantic to know just how red the face of the red-faced baby was, and was it a fiery red, a purple red or a scarlet red? Then again, could it be a peachy red, or even pink? To put it in contemporary parlance: no truth without pictures. As it was, everyone used their own imagination.

It also has to be admitted that imagination is often the breeding ground of rumour, and gradually rumours spread all round the city. The most romantic held that the red-faced baby's mother had been travelling in the Amazon rainforest, and had fallen in love with a wild Indian, a so-called redskin; the baby's face was a mark of this mixed blood, and would serve as a permanent souvenir of an international love affair. The most pragmatic held that the red-faced baby's red face was just a large birthmark, the kind that other babies have on their buttocks. It was just by chance that the red-faced baby's birthmark was spread evenly over its face, and that was all there was to it. The most widespread rumour was also the shortest; in fact it was pretty much just a name: **Baby Shame**, the baby of shame. **Baby Shame.** The name was a synthesis of all the residents of Red Toon Street's bad impressions of the mother, and illustrated the inseparability of reputation of mother and child. Or perhaps it wasn't a rumour, perhaps it was just prejudice. This prejudice hit the nail squarely on the head, in holding that the baby's face was red because it was born out of the shame of its mother.

There was a nurse in the maternity hospital nursery, who was something of a star on the internet with a blog called *I've Seen Your Baby*. In order to increase the number of hits from her fans, she uploaded a large number of photographs of the red-faced baby. In a different take from the mainstream media, the young nurse concentrated on the redness of the baby's face, correcting all the errors and omissions on the subject. We can see that at seven o'clock in the morning, the red-faced baby's face is bright red, like roses in full bloom. We can see that at half past twelve in the afternoon, the red-faced baby's face is a fiery red, fiercer than flame. We can see that in the evening, the red-faced baby's face has become scarlet red, matching the sunset outside the window. We can even see that, at night, the red-faced baby's face is like a little charcoal brazier burning in the dark and giving off rays of a transparent orange light. We can see that it has thick curly hair and large well-formed ears. We can see its normal butter-coloured body, and even its adorable belly-button, but there still remains one regret. We cannot see its eyes because, day or night, in every photograph the red-faced baby is wailing. Wailing, not just sobbing, but wailing with grief. It is not the sickly crying of a premature baby, it is the grief-stricken wailing of an old man. The red-faced baby clenches its fists and wails with grief, it raises its hands and wails, it looks up and wails, it turns on its side and wails. Always it wails with its eyes screwed tight shut as though it is not just furious, but also despairing.

It was not just young mothers, and the residents of Red Toon Street who avidly followed **I've Seen Your Baby**; many intellectuals were also fans. One famous lyric poet illustrated his impressions of the red-faced baby by posting the name he had invented for it using his poetic skills. He called it the Raging Baby. **Baby Rage.** Very quickly, all the netizens who had seen the photographs of the red-faced baby seemed to have been moved by this new name, and Baby Rage replaced Baby Shame as the most popular nickname for the red-faced baby.

It seems that Miss Bai suffered from severe post-natal depression, losing her own appetite, and refusing to feed her baby. When she was discharged from the hospital, many people came on the pretext of seeing her off, but they all knew they were, in fact, there for the chance to see the red-faced baby with their own eyes. But this simple ambition proved difficult to realise. Miss Bai covered the baby's face tightly with a red silk cloth, and that was all that could be seen, dancing in the wind like a flickering flame, as mother and baby were escorted into a waiting car. Other than hearing the furious wailing of the baby, the crowd of well-wishers gleaned no other information. Someone noticed that the Volkswagen Santana that collected Miss Bai carried the insignia of the Jingting Hospital, and asked:

"Why isn't she going back to her family home? Isn't she suffering from post-natal depression? Why is she going to the Jingting Hospital?"

Someone else who knew a little about Miss Bai replied:

"She grew up at the Jingting Hospital. She doesn't have any relatives, so you could say the Jingting Hospital is her family home."

For her, returning to the Jingting Hospital really was like going back to the ancestral home. Director Qiao could be considered an elder and, at a stretch, the Jingting Hospital could be seen as her maternal home. Director Qiao and his colleagues were happy to extend an olive branch to her, but they were nervous of the consequences of the fame of the red-faced baby. They were afraid that if the move didn't work out for mother and baby, it would cause unnecessary problems. Many of the hospital's patients read newspapers and watched television, and were addicted to following celebrities. The women's section of the hospital was clearly not suitable accommodation for this unusual mother and child, and the hospital authorities were at a loss where to put them. Fairy Princess had her own suggestion for Director Qiao, that she might live in the hospital's gymnasium for rehab. Of course, he remembered the old gardener's galvanised steel shack, and that the site of the gymnasium was where she had spent her youth. Rather put out, he replied that although the gymnasium did indeed have a small bedroom, taking a child to live there, when the patients used the gymnasium every day for their exercise, could have an adverse effect on both sides. She immediately replied:

"I'm not afraid of any bad influence from them. I lived here from when I was very little, and I've seen any kind of patient you care to name."

Director Qiao laughed, and said, candidly:

"You may not be concerned about their influence on you, but the patients' self-control is not all it should be. They might be influenced by you!"

Director Qiao thought it over again, then sounded her out on how she felt about living in the water tower. Perhaps that spot was too special, too sensitive. Suspecting that the director had an axe to grind when he said that, she blushed, saying:

"What do you mean, Director Qiao?"

With great sincerity, he enumerated the many advantages of the water tower. She considered the idea for a bit, and finally agreed, saying that since she had ended up in such a plight, she couldn't really be too picky, and the water tower was at least a quiet spot. She agreed to move herself and the red-faced baby into the water tower.

Thus, Miss Bai set up home in the water tower.

And thus, the former Fairy Princess returned to the water tower.

It wasn't long since the water tower had been Baorun's dormitory. In his sudden departure, he had left behind for her a large number of packets of instant noodles, a lot of dirty laundry and a room in urgent need of cleaning. She spent two days making sure the water tower was spotless. She washed Baorun's shirts and trousers too, and hung them out to dry on the branches of a pine tree. On another, shorter pine tree, she hung out her own clothes and the baby's nappies.

Now she was a mother.

Although her maternal love for Baby Rage was not ostentatious, it was unquestionable. Director Qiao often saw her sitting listening to music and breastfeeding the baby in the doorway of the water tower. He wasn't sure whether she wanted to listen to the music, or whether she was playing it for the baby. The water tower echoed to the sound of tragic pop songs with bland rhythms, sometimes by Na Ying, sometimes by Tian Zhen, and sometimes even by Hong Kong's Wang Fei. Because she was a patient suffering from clinical depression, and because she was a mother, she went to the hospital office to take her medication, and to the canteen to eat, but she always had her extraordinary baby cuddled in her arms. Even in the Jingting Hospital, no one saw Baby Rage's red face. She seemed to pay particular attention to preserving the baby's privacy, and Baby Rage's face was always covered by a little home-made surgical mask, on which were embroidered two rabbits, one on the right, and one on the left. But many people did see Baby Rage's eyes. Those eyes were, by all accounts, the deepest of blues. In the shade, they were the colour of the sea, in the light they were the colour of the sky.

Later, the leaves of the trees around the water tower began to fall, as autumn deepened.

On the day of one of Miss Bai's doctor's appointments, the temperature suddenly dropped. Director Qiao and the doctors gave up waiting for her, and went off in a group to look for her at the water tower. They found Grandfather sitting in the doorway of the tower, cuddling Baby Rage. There was a square bench in the doorway, on which was a pile of folded clean clothes which, on a second look, proved to be Baorun's, including a set of brand-new worker's overalls, which Baorun had apparently never worn. Dumped behind the bench was a large woven plastic bag, filled as tight as a drum, from which was emanating a vegetal odour. Director Qiao opened it to take a look, and shut it up again very quickly. He said to his colleagues:

"I guessed it was his ropes. And, sure enough, ropes it was; all of Baorun's ropes."

Grandfather said Miss Bai had gone to buy milk powder for the baby. She had handed over to him Baorun's clothes and the woven plastic bag, and she had also handed over her baby. He grumbled to them that she had only asked him to look after it for a while but that he had ended up holding it all morning. And why hadn't she come back yet? Director Qiao and the others guessed that she had left, and it was unlikely she was coming back. It could be that her depression had worsened, or it could be that she was cured. They stood in the doorway, discussing where she might have gone. Some of them were optimistic, and some of them were pessimistic, and there were some who were only interested in the baby. This was the red-faced baby they were talking about, this was Baby Rage, this was a wonder in the annals of local childbearing history. Now the mother was gone, this was an opportunity to examine that wonder. One young doctor made to remove the surgical mask, wanting to see the mysterious red face, but Grandfather pulled the mask tight, just in time, saying:

"Miss Bai told me that while she isn't here, the baby's mask isn't to be removed. You can see the baby's face when she comes back."

But Miss Bai had disappeared; the red-faced baby's mother had disappeared, and no one knew whether she was coming back or not. Nor did anyone know when they would be able to see the red-faced baby's face. Director Qiao and the others noticed that, contrary to the story that was being told, when Baby Rage was nestled in Grandfather's arms it was quiet and settled.

ABOUT THE AUTHOR

Su Tong, pen name of Tong Zhonggui, was born in Suzhou, East China in 1963. He rose to international acclaim after his book *Wives and Concubines* was made into a blockbuster film *Raise the Red Lantern* by director Zhang Yimou, featuring actress Gong Li. The film won a BAFTA award in 1993 for best non-english language film. He was the joint winner of the prestigious Mao Dun Literature Prize for *Shadow of the Hunter* in 2015. His earlier novel *The Boat to Redemption* was awarded the Man Asia Literature Prize in 2009.

Su Tong is a prolific and unconventional writer whose work explores the darker side of human nature. Having grown up in the Cultural Revolution, Su Tong's novels and short stories depict everyday life in 20th century China with a dark twist. In addition to his many striking novels, he has also written hundreds of short stories, many of which have been translated into French and English. He currently lives in Nanjing.

ABOUT THE TRANSLATOR

James Trapp has published China-related books on language, astrology, science and technology. His translation works include new versions of *The Art of War* and *The Daodejing*. Much of his work revolves around integrating the study of Chinese language and culture, and breaking down barriers of cultural misunderstanding that still persist.

About **Sino**ist Books

We hope Su Tong's saga of social dysfunction in 1980s China moved you.

SinoIST BOOKS brings the best of Chinese fiction to English-speaking readers. We aim to create a greater understanding of Chinese culture and society, and provide an outlet for the ideas and creativity of the country's most talented authors.

To let us know what you thought of this book, or to learn more about the diverse range of exciting Chinese fiction in translation we publish, find us online. If you're as passionate about Chinese literature as we are, then we'd love to hear your thoughts!

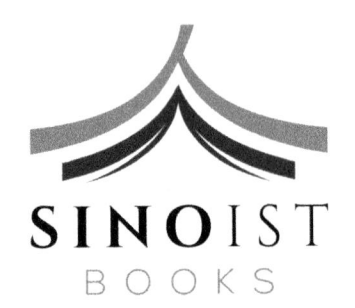

SINOIST

BOOKS

sinoistbooks.com
@sinoistbooks